Ealdræd of the Pæga

Warriors of the Iron Blade
Volume One

JP Tate

Other publications by JP Tate

http://jptate.jimdo.com

Contents

Maps: There are several colour maps online at http://jptate.jimdo.com/maps showing the geography of Ealdræd's journey which may enhance the reader's enjoyment of this novel.

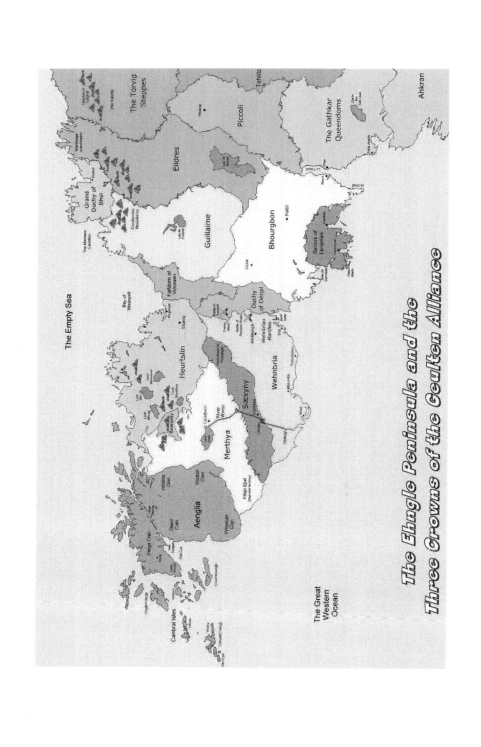

The Ehngle Peninsula and the
Three Crowns of the Geulten Alliance

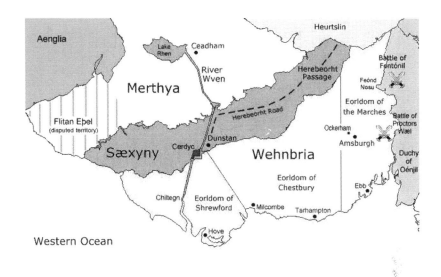

Sæxyny and Wehnbria

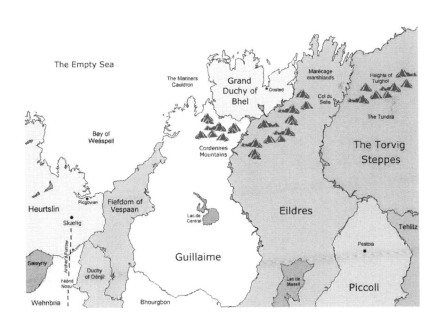

The Archer's Furrow to the Torvig Steppes

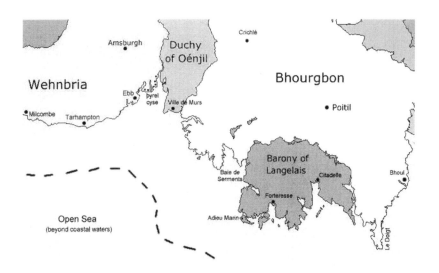

The Barony of Langelais

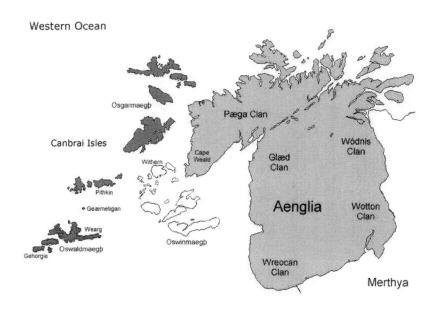

Aenglia and the Canbrai Isles

Chapter 1

Written in Salt

The heavily tattooed face of the Heurtslin marauder creased in disbelief as he was overwhelmed by an awareness of his own precipitate death. In the end there was only a confusion of pain and surprise in a panic of entrails. Sudden mortality left no time for regret or denial. Yet every day of his twenty-four years the Lord Wihvir might have claimed him for the void of Hálsian, from his boyhood on the shores of Loch Mòrethne to this day of bloodletting in the forest west of the mountains that separated his own land from that of Merthya. He had come with his brothers to raid the Merthyans but it had not been a man of that nation who had killed him and slain his siblings. He could not see his brothers from where he lay impaled by a spear in the damp grass but he knew that they were dead.

On foot and armed only with their *kelpie-corc*, the cleaver-knives that were the all-purpose tool of the fishermen of the lochs, the three Heurtslin had hunted westward to steal sheep, cattle, or anything else that might pass within reach of their hands. Raised in hunger and privation from the time they first sucked the watery milk of their mother's malnourished tit, and forced by the circumstance of their birth into a serfdom of unrelenting labour, they had abandoned their fishing coracles and their pregnant sister to follow a more predatory road. They had resolved to take what life would not give. Barefoot they had tramped over the mountains to live fat off the farmers in the valleys of Merthya.

Brice, the eldest of the brothers, had promised full bellies to Niall and Donal, who had required little convincing. They had even deceived themselves with talk of returning home with purses of coin before their sister's baby was born. But for two months they had nearly starved. The farmers went armed when they shepherded their livestock, often stood guard in pairs, and never strayed far from their villages. The three Heurtslin fishermen had found marauding a far less rewarding occupation than they had imagined.

In fact, they had all but decided to trudge back to Loch Mòrethne for the spring run of the salmon. But then a final chance of a prize presented itself. Donal had been sitting at the edge of a clearing

1

picking his teeth with a rabbit bone when he had seen a solitary rider on a magnificent warhorse emerge from a thicket and weave his slow unhurried way through the narrow stretch of open ground. Donal had scuttled off to fetch his brothers and all three, keeping well out of sight, had observed the leisurely passage of the rider passing by. The horse alone must have been worth more than the entire catch from a summer's toil in their fishing boats. They had resolved to take possession of the animal, and everything else the horseman might have of any value.

The temptation was not to be resisted. The mounted man slouched drowsily in the saddle, apparently oblivious to his surroundings and allowing the grey stallion to pick his own path over the broken ground. The huge beast trod his steady measure along a deer trail, relieved to have emerged from the dappled shadows of the trees that were so oppressive to his equine nature, enjoying the sense of freedom engendered by the bright daylight. The feathered feet of the warhorse strode in easy motion, the rider nodding soporifically.

Crouched low in the jumble of brambles along the edge of the clearing the marauders had waited expectantly, breathing in the wet earthy smells of rot and pine needles that mixed with the spoor of animal musk and the aroma of wild-grown berries. They gave no thought as to how one horse might be divided amongst three thieves, but then their appetites invariably roamed far forrard of their judgment. Wanting preceded taking, and taking preceded having, and having preceded decisions as to entitlement. They would argue the toss of ownership later. The old Heurtslin way was to favour the elder but it was seldom honoured these days. Perhaps they would find a buyer for the horse.

Remaining concealed within the wood, by dint of hard running they had circled around in advance of the horseman searching for trees that could be climbed. Pine were of no use for ambush. They tended to be bare trunk without foliage for the first thirty feet, besides which the thick, scaly bark of the pine would often flake under a climber's weight and scatter a warning debris of wood chips on the ground below. Luck was with them and they found some Wych Elm; leafy giants over 100 feet high but with plenty of foliage lower down. *Wych* meant 'pliable', so named because the tree gave good flexible reddish-brown wood for carpentry that was tough enough for the keels of boats and cart wheels. The Wych Elm was ever an old friend to the fishermen of Loch Mòrothne. There was a cluster of Elm just where the small glade ended and the forest closed in again.

snorted and breathed streams of clouded air and increasingly took on the aspect of a wraith rather than a natural beast of flesh and blood.

A seven foot spear of well-seasoned ash was attached by a hanging saddle-sheath along the side of the horse. The head of the weapon was eighteen inches of polished iron but, in addition to this, thin strips of metal extended a hand's breadth further down the length of the smooth wooden shaft of the spear to minimise the risk of the spearhead being chopped off during battle. Closer inspection would have revealed that the spearhead also had a circumference of tiny spikes at its base set at an angle so that once the blade had entered an opponent's body, removing it would rip bloody carnage in their flesh. Alongside this fearsome weapon, the hanging sheath contained two short javelins for throwing, similar in design to the spear but only half its length.

From the pommel of the saddle hung a wooden buckler made from hardened teak and reinforced with a raised half-sphere of iron in the centre and four satellite half-spheres around it. This style of buckler identified the country of the rider for it was typical of an Aenglian spearman; a small circular shield gripped in the hand to be used in conjunction with his spear or his knife in hand-to-hand combat. As a shield it was too small to offer much protection against missile weapons, and it was worthless under an arrow storm, but it could be highly effective in deflecting the blow of an enemy's sword, axe, or mace in personal contest. A skilled practitioner could catch his opponent's blow with the buckler and turn their attack aside, opening them up to a counter thrust from his own spear or knife. The raised half-sphere of iron in its centre, called a boss, not only strengthened the tool defensively by adding metal to the wood without adding too much to the weight, but it also had an offensive advantage in making the buckler a useful punching weapon.

It was obvious, given the armoury he carried readily to hand, that the figure at the stranger's gate was a fighting man of some description; a disquieting thought for a rural agrarian society. The hamlet was as quiet as the grave. The feeling of foreboding and uncertainty in the air was palpable. The menacing-looking stranger sat his horse in patience. Then, from the central building amongst the various dwellings, one that was noticeably larger than its neighbours, a man emerged and strode forth, approaching the horseman directly. This would be the village herdsman. Amongst men of the warfaring class, the head man in any village in this part of the country was often, in a derogatory manner, called the herdsman, for the common villagers were but cattle. This specimen of the breed was a big, strapping fellow in a cambric shirt and rough wool breeches. He had dried cow's blood splattered across his leather apron and a splash of it had dried in the greasy mass of his wiry black hair. This would have made it natural for him to be carrying a butcher's cleaver but, in fact, he was empty-handed, deliberately and conspicuously displaying no hostile intention. He was perhaps thirty years of age; sufficiently mature for the position of authority he held in this hamlet and broad enough in the shoulders to impose himself physically upon any amongst his herd who might challenge his seniority.

Walking to within twenty feet of the traveller the herdsman could now see the face under the hooded mantle and realised that this foreigner was a good deal older than might have been supposed; his visage lined and creased with hardship. The herdsman supposed the fellow to be a decade older than himself and felt considerably relieved at this turn of events. A fighting man of twenty or twenty-five would have been more worrisome. Despite this, as he spoke up to open negotiations the herdsman was careful to demonstrate the humility of his deference to the well-armed stranger.

"This be the village of Ceadham, named for our river, the Ceadda, and I be the Holder of the Manor here. My name is Selwyn. What be your name and people, my Master?" enquired the herdsman.

"Ealdræd," said the horseman, "of the Pæga; a clan of the Aenglians. I seek a night's lodging."

The voice was neutral, revealing nothing of the speaker except his accent which hinted distinctively of those lands that occupied the westernmost portion of the Ehngle Peninsula; the extreme north-western tip of the continent that was the known world; country so ferociously fought over that they still had no kingdoms for no war chieftain had ever grown strong enough to subdue all his rivals. It confirmed what the horseman's weapons had already told them and what the man himself had now declared; he was of the Aenglia, a close-knit coalition of inter-related tribes who collectively held the territories between Merthya and the great western ocean. They shared a language with the folk of Merthya but each had its own very distinct dialect.

10

The voluptuary nations in the far south and east of the continent held the Aenglians, along with many of their neighbouring races, to be barbarians. This was both true and false. For those who view the barbarian as an untutored savage contrary to all forms of social propriety, civilization and decorum, it was not true that the Aenglians were barbarous for they had a cultural heritage that was as ancient and decorous as could be found anywhere and they had long developed a truly sublime artisanship in the most skilled and sophisticated techniques of handicraft. But if by the term barbarian is meant a race that favours booty, loot and plunder over a submission to the degradation of the soul inherent in the life of the municipal citizen in her caged domesticity, then those who numbered themselves amongst the free people of the Aenglia would take the name of barbarian with honour. Theirs was a culture of personal autonomy and adult respect, not one of castration through the deceit of politics and the infantilism of gentility, nurturance and niceness. This Ealdræd of the Pæga, with his stone face and his martial bearing, was typical.

The name Ealdræd was comprised of two words, *eald,* which meant 'mature or wise', and, *ræd,* meaning 'counsel or adviser'. The veteran surely looked the part of the wise old counsel. He wore his long hair and beard in the Aenglian style, plaited in thin braids. There were streaks of grey in those braids as they swung like writhing snakes around his grizzled head. He was still a vigorous man and due the respect owed to a warrior, but at passed forty years of age he would soon be thought an old man. Already he lived with the many and uncharitable aches and pains that come from the harshness of a life spent without any resource but the strength and dexterity of his spear arm and the tolerance of his body to bear pain and endure; sleeping out in all weathers and waking wet with dew, the days, weeks, and even months of malnutrition during the years of famine; the drunkenness, lechery and feasting in the years of plenty; the wounds received that healed but never healed entirely; a man who took pride in knowing that all his scars were carved on the front of his body, not the rear; a life as hard as the frozen clods of winter earth, as parched as the summer drought.

"I follow the River Wven, travelling south." explained Ealdræd. "I hear that mercenaries are needed in the Marches of the Wehnbrian Lordships."

Selwyn the herdsman said nothing; t'were a likely enough reason for a man of this stamp and kidney to be on the road. The constant skirmishes betwixt the vassal Duchy of Oénjil and the kingless Lordships of Wehnbria meant that mercenaries were always wanted by one side or t'other, and more often by both. This fellow on the devil horse certainly had the look of a professional soldier about him and was likely telling the truth; it was reasonable to believe him that far, at least, though he must have pressing reasons to risk riding alone. Four or five men might ride together in search of a soldier's pay, but what chance would a friendless, isolated individual have if set upon by a parcel of villains?

Still, that was no business of the good people of Ceadham, and be that as it may, anyone in the mercenary's trade who had lived to see his fortieth year must be a wily old bird indeed. Not that he need be thought a threat to the village. One man, no matter how fortified by weaponry, was a manageable proposition. Six stout-hearted lads with pitch-forks could see him off, if it came to that. All things considered, in the herdsman judgement, it was safe to allow the veteran to bide betimes in the village. It was the arrogant young bucks who caused the trouble not the battle-scarred grandpas. Anyhow, this old hand might have some coin on him that he'd be willing to spend, or some other things of value he might be willing to part with under the inducement of a full belly and a country wench. Having decided so much it was a short step to conclude further that if anyone was to benefit from this fellow's coin it should be the chief of the village and the only resident with the backbone to come out and face the man who had called upon them so unexpectedly in the dusk.

The herdsman's appraisal of his prospective guest was knowing and shrewd, yet miscast in certain telling respects. This Ealdræd was a soldier of fortune and more. His reasons for travel were pressing but they were the same reasons as had kept him in the saddle for most of his life and they were reasons that he kept close to his conscience. He did not share them for they were the consequences of his youthful folly and if he had not closed his mind upon them entirely it was only because banishment is a fire whose embers smoulder long. But although he had wandered far and seen as many tribes and nations as there are leaves on a tree, his own culture and ethnicity stayed strong within the exile.

The spear was the weapon of his clan; his kith and kin. Swords were for the posturing nobility and axes were for wood-chopping peasants. Ealdræd was neither nobleman nor farmer, he was a fighting man of the Aenglia and they had been spearman for a hundred generations, since before history was. The wielding of the spear had been engrained in him since he could walk, and its use was as much a part of his being as the use of his hands. This was especially true of his clan of the Aenglians, the Pæga, for whom there was a spiritual union between man and spear. Not that he despised all other armaments. Though the axe was undeniably a crude tool, a hacking and clubbing weapon, Ealdræd had learned respect for the skilled deployment of the axe long years ago when battling against the formidable Wehnbrian shield-wall, for the men of Wehnbria employ a combination of double-headed axes in a rank of warriors in which each combatant's shield covers not himself but the man next to him. The shield-wall was an engine of death for those who stood against it and earned a man's admiration in his own blood. So whilst Ealdræd did not practice the use of the axe, he knew of its redoubtable character.

Nor did he entirely scorn the sabre or the cutlass but he had little respect for the broadsword. Leave those to the sons of Thegns and Eorls and similar popinjays who liked to make an extravagant show. The swords of the aristocracy were overly heavy, ostentatious, clumsy two-handed things that took all a man's strength to wield at all. Consequently they were slow and of no use on horseback. Their design had outgrown their function. The men of Aenglia made proud boast that they were the greatest cavalry on earth and when engaged in equine combat Ealdræd's spear became a lance, and its extra reach over the sword, mace, axe and other handheld weapons was one reason for this supremacy. The spear used as a cavalry lance could lethally unseat an opponent without the spearman ever coming within range of the enemy's shorter weapon. Much the same was true when fighting on foot; he could get the razor-sharp iron tip at the end of his seven foot shaft of good Aenglian ash through the throat of a man with a broadsword whilst the swordsman was still hefting his weighty blade overhead for a downward stroke that he would never have the time to deliver. Ealdræd's spear was a thrusting weapon, and struck the target with pin-point accuracy. When he needed a long-distance weapon to be thrown as a missile, he had his javelins. He also carried a twenty-inch knife across his belly in a scabbard at his belt, worn openly, not concealed. A knife was essential for close-in fighting when the reach of the spear became a hindrance instead of an asset. Ealdræd was extremely proficient with a long knife, which went some way to explaining why he was still alive and healthy at his age, but his clan-culture made spearmanship his love and his pride.

He had some skill with the longbow but notoriously the bow was generally a poorly made weapon because it was commonly crafted by the archer himself from whatever wood was available to him. Primitive construction and a poor choice of wood meant that bows were often under-powered and inclined to break. Knowledge of the correct manufacture of the longbow was the close secret of the true bowyer, especially the Heurtslin woodsmiths, whose carpentry defied replication. Ealdræd respected a well-made longbow with its draw-weight of over 80lbs that could skewer an enemy in mail and even pierce plate armour; capable of bringing down an unarmoured man at a distance of more than a hundred and fifty yards. Such a bow was a worthy armament for a soldier and he would cheerfully have carried one but, due to the scarcity of true and reliable longbows, so rare a weapon was a lure to footpads. It was highly prized by roadside brigands because it enabled you to kill from a place of concealment. Many a half-hearted outlaw had been enticed to chance his arm by the security of camouflage that a bow afforded, so generally Ealdræd did not carry one. It made a man too much of a target.

Another reason was that archers, especially those employed as mercenaries, tended to be sacrificed unduly on the battlefield by high-born generals who viewed the bow as the weapon of the base-born peasant; the man of low degree. Consequently, the nobility who employed bowmen were spendthrift with the lives of their inferiors. When those of the chivalrous and iron-clad cavalry of the opposing army who had survived the volleys of arrowshot eventually reached the ranks of archers who had been raining down death upon them, the mayhem that ensued soon routed the unfortunate bowmen. Lacking any defence against the hazards of either horse or rider they had no other recourse but to flee. Ealdræd had lived with death for two decades and he had enough reverence for it to not wish to meet it with a longsword in his back or a lance up his arse.

Reverence for death was a lifelong companion. The schools of war had perforce taught him innumerable methods to deliver it, and not a few to escape it. Ealdræd had a chainmail shirt folded in his saddlebags and a simple four-plate iron pot basin helmet that fitted snugly enough that he could wear it under his mantle. These would not save a man from the direct cut or thrust of a sharpened iron blade but they would turn a blow which struck at an angle, and what might have been a mortal wound would instead be a contusion. It was adequate to his needs.

Few professional soldiers cared overmuch for heavy armour. Since its weight and convoluted design meant that it could not be thrown on quickly it was largely irrelevant to the majority of fighting that a man might be called upon to do in his own defence. Full armour was strictly for organised warfare, but even there its deficiencies were greater than its advantages. It exhausted its wearer long before the battle was over and slowed him down so much that he became ineffective in anything other than a pitched battle of full-scale armies in massed lines. On top of which it was unaffordable. A full suit of plate armour, with visored helmet, gorget, pauldron, breastplate, gauntlets and greaves was so immensely costly that it was the exclusive privilege of the very rich, besides being popularly believed to be proof of cowardice; proclaiming the wearer to be afraid of being killed in battle.

No, Ealdræd preferred a mail shirt that permitted free movement but still offered some protection, especially when worn over the quilted sleeveless gambeson that was his habitual tunic. The gambeson, a thick, padded garment worn underneath armour or chainmail, not only cushioned the bruising weight of the iron but reinforced the mail so as to reduce significantly the risk of broken bones and ruptured organs, even if it couldn't withstand a clean cutting or piercing blow. Apart from his helmet, the only piece of plate armour that Ealdræd owned was the iron cod-piece which he took care to utilize in military encounters larger than a skirmish.

Yes, Selwyn the herdsman had summed up this visitor to his village fairly accurately as far as was revealed by outward show and now looked up at the horseman warily, still assiduous in exhibiting no provocative antagonism. When a man encountered another unknown to him, undue aggression could get him killed. Cautious parley was the rule, and a wise one.

"I shall need stabling for my horse and clean forage-feed before he sleeps tonight," continued Ealdræd, "bran and fresh oats, if you have them."

As was the case with any sensible man, Ealdræd put the health and well-being of his horse ahead of any concern for himself. The only times when a man might favour himself over his mount were those of starvation when it might be necessary to eat the beast, or when fleeing from deadly pursuit when it might be unavoidable that the horse be ridden to death. But Ealdræd had eaten once already that day, if only dried biscuits of whey-bread and cheese, and he perceived no danger from the farmer in front of him. The man's name, Selwyn, meant 'a friend in the manor' from the words *sele*, meaning 'hearth or manor', and *wine*, meaning 'friend'. It was a good name for a host and right fitting for the circumstance. Ealdræd was inclined to take it as a good omen.

"Do you intend to depart in the morning?" asked Selwyn. "There is but a servant-byre in my manor for you to bide till dawn. Shall you be gone tomorrow?"

Here was a warm welcome. The man would have him gone before he had properly arrived. So much for omens.

"At first light," confirmed Ealdræd.

"Then do you set down, my Master, and I shall provision you. We have wooden floors in my dwelling and good comforts."

The Aenglian dismounted. He had been in the stirrups almost continuously today from sunrise to sunset, yet when he swung down from a horse seventeen hands high the movement of his supple form was as smooth and fluid as a Murgl gypsy dancer. And now that he was on his feet it became apparent that the mercenary was rather taller than Selwyn had realised; loftier than was Selwyn himself and he was two yards tall. It had not been solely the horse that had made him ride so high. The man was undeniably daunting, with bulging shoulders and arms like tree-limbs, but long and sinewy from the ribs down. Perhaps it had been a trifle premature to invite him to reside the night. But the herdsman had no leisure to retract his offer of lodging, for to do so now would be considered an insult. Whatever else this man was, he was not a person to insult unnecessarily. Selwyn did not call his field-boy to come lead the horse to its night's stabling, for he knew the boy would not have dared. He turned and bid the traveller follow. Let the foreigner stable his own horse.

Ealdræd was surprised to find that the stable was of a respectable size and strongly made with stout walls of wattle and daub; strips of wood woven together and insulated with clay. It even had a rudimentary roof of thatch. More surprising still, there was already a horse inside, a young bay that retreated skittishly to the farthest corner at the approach of the roan blue-grey monster. For one man to own an enclosed shelter for stabling and a horse to keep inside it

16

was really quite impressive for a settlement of this size, so far removed from the nearest town. Farmers generally cared more for pigmeat to eat than for horseflesh to ride.

While Ealdræd removed his saddle and weapons from the horse, Selwyn remained outside washing the blood off himself at a watering trough, having removed his butcher's apron. A civilized man does not bring the stink of death into his home and hearth. Ealdræd took some time settling his steed, murmuring to it affectionately and stroking it. The gigantic brute took precedence over anything else. He had named the animal Hengustir, after the fabled charger that pulled the war-chariot of the legendary giant Ffydon in the time before the Well of Mægen gave birth to all the races of the world.

A latticework wicker bowl full of oats and grains had somehow been left at the stable gate although Ealdræd had seen no sign of who had placed it there. No doubt the field-boy knew his duties and had the sense to know that fulfilling them unseen was the most dependable route to a trouble-free life. Ealdræd brought the bowl into the stable and Hengustir devoured the oats in haste, as if there might be some possibility of the bay trying to steal them; although Hengustir knew better than anyone that there was no possibility of that.

The two men walked over to Selwyn's manor together in the murky gloom of nightfall, all the hidden eyes of the village upon them, Ealdræd carrying his own possessions. He would sleep with them to keep them safe. Not only were they property of real value, they were also all that stood between him and a relentlessly perilous environment. Without his weapons his life expectancy could be measured in weeks, or even days, or as it may be, hours. He would not be without spear, javelins and knife, even in the herdsman's homestead. There was a surprise here, too, for whilst the building was constructed mostly from shaved oak planks with a roof of thatch, the gabled manor was fully thirty yards long and incorporated stonework corners. The windows had sturdy shutters modelled on the same pattern as the robust oaken door. All in all, it was a substantial house and worthy of a Holder of the Manor.

Having taken a step inside Ealdræd stopped to accustom his sight to the darkened interior. The common practice for such a residence was for it to be one large room but here there were indications of a desire to present the manor more in the style of a Lord's estate house. The hall had been partitioned at each end by wattle screens to create sectioned-off areas. There were also some additional rooms built as extensions on the side of the main building, including the bower that was the bedroom for the master and mistress.

The night fires were already lit creating pools of light in various places throughout the hall. There were some genuine wax candles, whilst others were merely rush-lights; rushes from the river that had been dried and dipped in animal fat. They burned as well as candles but smelt strongly of the beast whose body oil was aflame. The central fire directly below the conical chimney-hole was not a simple open fire but was contained within a huge stove that maintained a steady heat to warm the hall. The chimney above it was widest at the bottom to catch the smoke and narrowed to a much smaller hole at roof level. For the ordinary folk whose hearth fire was open, the Merthyan chimney was a great blessing in keeping the air indoors breathable.

Despite his soldier's distaste for those whose livelihood was earned grubbing in the soil, the Aenglian cavalryman considered, as he surveyed the room, that it was a commendable resting place and worth the price, although naturally he expected that they would try to rob him blind when it came time for payment. Well, they would see about that on the morrow. For the moment he would attend to his physical needs by acknowledging the religious. Each dwelling place had its own house-fetish and it was the strict ritual upon entering to give praise to the fetish. Still standing at the doorway, Ealdræd declared in a firm voice:

"I honour the fetish of this manor and seek its blessing while I bide here."

Selwyn nodded his shaggy head appreciatively; it was well-spoken. There was many a man of arms who knew nothing of the ways of decent folk and who scorned to act in accordance with civil standards and laws. As a landowner Selwyn was gentry and therefore he naturally despised a landless killer-for-hire, but at least this braided greybeard knew enough of religion to conform to the rules of basic decency.

Like all of his people Ealdræd naturally believed in the Well of Mægen as the origin of the human species and in Wihvir Lord of Hálsian as the commander and corruptor of spirits but in the privacy of his soul he was merely agnostic toward domestic fetishes.

Perhaps there was something in them, perhaps there was not; who could say for certain? What mattered was that it was both polite and politic to make observance in another man's house and Ealdræd would not have risked his habitation for the night by omitting such a necessary ceremonial.

A woman in the attire of a lady appeared from behind the nearest wattle screen. Fair-skinned, well-proportioned and of middle height, she was in the flowering of her youth, no older than twenty and of appreciably patrician deportment. It was the first thing that Ealdræd noticed about her, the noble quality of her demeanour, for she held herself very erect and returned his appraising gaze with a rare self-assurance. She wore the petticoats of her long linen undershift all the way down to the ankle; a little lower than her woollen dress so that the richness of both the embroidered linen and the brocaded wool could be seen and admired. She wore no cloak indoors but the pair of enamelled brooches that would hold her cloak in place, one at each shoulder, decorated her dress. Her coif, a cap without which any woman would have been assumed to be of low birth no matter how expensive her raiment, was covered not only by a head-mantle of a costly woven fabric that Ealdræd did not recognise but also by a torse, the crown-like headgear that for the very wealthy were fashioned in precious metals strung with silk. This lady's torse was worked in willow-reed however, although it was adorned with velvet. Her bodice was tight and raised her bust quite fetchingly, the upper portion of which had quite daringly been left bare. At her girdle hung the keys of the house, displayed as a mark of her rank. She wore leather shoes, the toes of which curled back upon themselves in the courtly manner.

The lady gave a little bow rather than a curtsey, which would have been presumptuous of her had Ealdræd been anyone of civic importance but, as he was only an old mercenary from the uncultured west, the finer points of etiquette could be assumed to be wasted on him. As happenstance would have it, Ealdræd was quite aware of the lady's presumption but forbore to comment upon it. He returned her bow, dipping a little lower than she had in the prescribed manner, thereby making the point that he knew the drill. It wasn't a soldier's drill but he knew it all the same. She softly spoke a few words of formal greeting, welcoming her guest, but the obsequiousness of her language was not matched by the knowing sparkle in her green eyes. The Aenglian responded with an equally respectful salutation. It was manifest from her clothing that this was the lady of the house and the foremost personage of this humble

19

little hamlet of Ceadham; this was the reason her husband spoke of the place as a village and would soon doubtless be declaring it a town. Selwyn the herdsman who, a few minutes earlier, had identified himself as the Holder of the Manor, the senior man in the community who occupied the manor house, now introduced this lodger for the night to his wife, Gelwyn.

Although the stranger could know nothing of their history, so plainly was the story of their lives written upon their conduct that he could have guessed the larger part of their biography, if not the precise details of it. The actual truth of the matter was that the wife had formerly been Gelfrith, youngest daughter of Belwnfrith, a Thegn to the Shire-Reeve of Gewn, although as the youngest female she was the least of his progeny. Even so, it had been something of a coup for Selwyn, a commoner with social aspirations, to claim her as his own. It was the custom amongst the tribes of Merthya for wives to adopt the form of their husbands name; thus upon her marriage to Selwyn the former Gelfrith had become Gelwyn, but with the casting off of her father's name she had by no means abandoned her love of prestige; her sense of her own magnitude and eminence. Her husband must one day grow to be the man her father was or she would know the reason why. She would not submit to bear the shame of having married beneath for one day longer than was necessary. Allied to her spouse, they made a lively pair.

The introductions completed, the lady withdrew once again to the portion of the hall behind the screen, though whether this was due to wifely modesty at the presence of a man or to imperious disdain for the company of a common throat-slitter, Ealdræd was unable to judge.

The lady's fine apparel set the tone for this manorial establishment, for the world over the same social convention applied: the higher a person's rank, the more many-layered and voluminous their clothing; the lower a person's rank, the more meagre and sparse their flea-bitten rags. When in public ladies wore both undershift and dress along with their coif and mantle even in summer, for this went with the status of ladyship; a gentleman of substance would generally be cloaked and wear hose or breeches along with his tunic or doublet and boots. By the caste of their garb were they known. So, too, was it with the dregs of society; the poorer the person, the scantier, the more paltry and derisory was their clothing.

20

Thus it was in keeping with both his wife's wishes and his own burgeoning pomposity that, his days labours done, Selwyn replaced his cambric shirt with a brushed woollen tunic to smarten himself for his evening's diversions. Then, in his role as the host, he performed his duty; somewhat grudgingly, but he performed it.

"What be your pleasure, my Master?" asked Selwyn.

"A meal, a bed, and a woman," Ealdræd informed him, "and make sure that the food includes plenty of meat and ale; none of your peasant's parsnip gruel," he added with an unfortunate lack of refinement. It was clear to the herdsman of Ceadham that whatever the veneer of the social niceties with which this foreigner was coated, really he was an ungracious clod.

But Ealdræd knew whereof he spoke. It would be the meal that would cost the most of the three, and he wasn't about to pay a price for a pottage-stew from the kitchen garden. For all the prominent display of comparative affluence, this would be a penny-pinching household, in his estimation; aye, and not despite their show of prosperity but because of it. Those who had garnered a little wealth and wanted a great deal more were always the most reluctant to part with a farthing or a groatæ that might have been saved instead of squandered. But there were cows penned outside and his host, so recently stained with the blood of butchery, was equipped for feasting so Ealdræd expected a goodly portion of the slaughtered animal on his plate. And at this time of the year there would be little left in the local farmers' barrels of cider and home-brewed beer, which would as like as not make Selwyn disinclined to be liberal in dispensing the restoring draft, so it were as well to remind the fellow that Ealdræd required service for his coin.

Selwyn went through a door to what was presumably the kitchen for Ealdræd could hear him shouting at someone and the sound of a few stinging smacks. Some slattern was being set to work. Good; let the drudge comprehend the need for speed and manly proportion. With his innards rumbling in anticipation, Ealdræd crossed the room to put a wall at his back and then sat himself down on a stool facing the main door to await his sustenance. He was not a man it was easy to approach by stealth. The victuals duly arrived and all was satisfactory; thick slabs of hot roast beef and potatoes in their skins flavoured with onion and served in a wooden bowl almost the width of Ealdræd's buckler and twice the depth. It was good tasty ballast for an empty belly and washed down with two tankards of Merthyan beer; a nut-brown cask fermented ale that was as strong as it was delicious.

These nourishing splendours were brought to him by a comely blonde serving wench who possessed a few splendours of her own. Hers were of the fleshly variety, sensually hedonistic and bawdily flaunted in her flimsy domestic apparel. The girl's main garment was a threadbare, nearly transparent flax-linen shift that fell from her shoulders to her thighs and which had been cleaved open at the front to expose her considerable breasts. Aside from this, all she wore was a constrictive corset made of bone and sack-cloth that squeezed her waist so fiercely that it emphasised the overhanging breasts all the more, and a pair of Merthyan clogs. This footwear was as merciless a form of gratuitous torture as had ever been invented. The clogs were made entirely of wood, encasing the whole foot, and were built up with a three inch block under the heel to slant the foot sharply down and force the wearer to walk upon her toes. It was said that this made a woman's walk more pertly feminine, flirtatiously cheeky, and pleasingly tart, but it also tended over time to break the girl's toes, collapse her arches, and cripple her ankles. Consequently, it was generally the servant-maids who were obliged to wear clogs, not the leather-shod ladies whom they served.

The kitchen-slut was almost as appetising as the steaming victuals she carried to him for his repast. As she had laid the meal before him on the small half-barrel table, her splendid breasts had eased through the gap in her inadequate attire most appealingly, and when she curtseyed to him those youthful bosoms had all but bounced out of her linen. She remained at his side while he noisily did justice to his appetite but she did not meet his eyes; instead staring askance at the floor and just catching sight of him in her peripheral vision. This warrior with the barbarous plaited braids and imposingly muscular arms was too intimidating to face directly. Neither did his table manners ease her agitation.

Could this be the herdsman's daughter, wondered Ealdræd, attending to her familial chores? But surely the fine lady in the brocade dress would not have her own daughter serve an outsider when she was wearing nothing but her linen shift and corset? Unlikely, but it might be so, for there were many who used their female offspring as scullions and betimes as whores. Families with a multitude of daughters would hire them out as daily chattel or even sell them outright. It was commonplace enough but not, he decided, in the manor house of Ceadham. The girl lacked even a coif and her blonde hair tumbled freely to her shoulders in a cascade of loose curls. Yes, it was a deal more liable that this curvy hussy was the hard-pressed maid of all work in the homestead of Selwyn and his lady. In which case she would certainly be for sale and it would be she that would be forcibly pressed into further service later to supply the third element of Ealdræd's order of a meal, a bed, and a woman.

Had Ealdræd been less engrossed in his voracious gorging he would have realised that the maid could hardly have been the daughter of this establishment because she was of about the same age as her mistress and for Selwyn to have sired her he would have had to have done his manly fornication at around the age of ten. But the mercenary's mind was full of the excellence of the meat, the thirst-quenching restorative powers of the beer, and the sauciness of the trollop's barely covered bottom. As for the girl, she continued to stand at his convenience, tremulous and all-aquiver, awaiting his permission to curtsey and scurry away, leaving him to his meal. But Ealdræd was enjoying her discomfort and mused erotically on the bareness of her legs, the painfulness of the clogs and the extreme tightness of her corset. As for the shift, it was probably the last vestiges of one of her mistresses old cast-offs, suitably abbreviated as befitted the servant's lack of status. In fact it was so reduced in size that the girl was almost spilling out of it and Ealdræd wondered if she were not a paid domestic after all but of a still lower social standing.

"What are you girl, servant or slave?" he queried.

Under Merthyan law the penalty for raping a slave was a fine of seven groatæ and Ealdræd could hardly be expected to pay more for the girl that it would cost to rape her. If the perpetrator of the rape did not possess the coin, then a payment in kind would be deemed acceptable, such as comb made of horn or a wooden belt-clasp or anything else that was worth approximately seven groatæ. If she were a paid servant, however, the fine for raping her might be as much as twenty groatæ. It was a significant difference. In this as in everything, social standing mattered, and the price of a night's pleasure with a whore was usually set accordingly; being kept just under the cost of rape for fear that otherwise no trade would be forthcoming.

The trembling girl flinched at his question, for she was shyly aware of the implication behind it, but she did not reply. She appeared to be incapable of utterance. Perchance she had been born mute or simple-minded. More probably she was merely too scared to speak. All strange men were a threat to a scullery baggage such as her. It might well be fear that made her shiver, though it could as easily be cold, for her clothing was scanty enough to pass for a city tapster's madam. If she were a slave it would be probable that she'd be naked; few in these parts wasted clothing on slaves. Yes, since she was not nude she must be either a servant or the herdsman's own daughter. Ealdræd hoped she wasn't the herdsman's daughter. She would cost more if she were.

"Answer me, trollop."

"Corynnelia, begging your pardon, my Master; a servant of this manor." she lisped in a voice husky with hesitation and trepidation.

The Aenglian barked out a short laugh. The name was a conflation of two: Corynn, meaning 'maiden or girl', and Cornelia, meaning 'taken of a horn'. So the strumpet Corynnelia was, quite literally, a girl taken of a horn. Notwithstanding any previous failure of omens, he took this as a fateful portent indeed.

He gnawed on the beef bones to clean his strong yellow teeth. He was meticulous and systematic about it. For someone of his age to still possess his own teeth was akin to the miraculous when so many had mouths full of blackened stumps and empty gums, and it would have struck an observant person as proof that here was a very unusual fellow and no mistake. In the midst of the human abattoir of war he had outlived his contemporaries and still had teeth to bite with whilst the friends of his boyhood mouldered in the grave. One of the more effective weapons in Ealdræd's arsenal was the habit that the rest of the world had of underestimating him.

While the guest had been eating, two of Selwyn's neighbours had met with a willing reception when they had called at his home for a game of dice. They were a couple of likely lads, well set-up and willing to take a chance. They both measured what property they had in yards of dirt and chickens' eggs, but they reckoned they could sit down with a passing soldier and a pair of dice and get up the richer without having had their fingers burnt or their noses slit. With these local reinforcements Selwyn felt keenly disposed to try his hand also. Gambling was an honourable way to steal a man's purse. But to their intense and ill-disguised disappointment Ealdræd refused their invitation to join them in a game. Moreover, having nothing to say to a rabble of peasants and not wishing to be kept late in conversation, Ealdræd spoke only briefly with his host after dinner. He might have dallied a while with the peasant's proud wife had the lady cared for the companionship but the lady was nowhere to be seen; closeted with her weaving or spinning or sewing, doubtless, or at her prayers. As soon as good manners permitted Ealdræd asked to be conducted to his bed and sure enough it was Corynnelia who was dispatched to this task. Good enough, thought Ealdræd.

With a disconsolate air she led him off to the servant-byre, which turned out to be a small room about the size of a three stall cattle shed and smelling much like one too, attached to the kitchen of the main hall. It was the girl's own sleeping place. He dumped his gear and fell gratefully down on to the bed. It was comfortable; a real bed made of cattle hides stitched together and deeply stuffed with dry straw. This was luxury. The bawdy baggage was pampered. It certainly meant that Selwyn must be an occasional visitor to these quarters for he would not have considered the expense of a mattress if he were not using it himself from time to time. The Lady Gelwyn would certainly have no objection to such night-time visitations because it was everywhere understood that the sexual use of servants was irrevocably a part of the natural order of things.

This thought recalled his mind to his present business. Ealdræd sprang back up to his feet with an agility that caused the girl to recoil half a step. He swept her up in his arms and she felt the enormous strength within him. The girl made no pretence of resistance. It was not her place to have an opinion and past experience with her master had taught her that if she were to oppose his will, matters would quickly turn ugly and violent. If she showed reluctance to play the whore, her Lord Selwyn would be enraged that she had failed to please his guest and she would end up suffering a beating from each of them. Better to comply without protest. It was not the first time she had reasoned thus; nor the one hundredth time.

As the mercenary's rough hands stripped her, the extraordinary contours of her body seemed to roll like milk in an urn, slopping this way and that. Disrobed, she was a breathtaking exhibition of female sensuality and concupiscence. He took his time exploring every inch of her. Predictably, her back was covered in a tell-tale criss-cross patchwork of fine scars that told of a lifetime of floggings inevitably entailed in the routine existence of one who was born to servitude. It explained everything there was to explain about her. She would be whipped for punishment; she would be whipped for sport; she would

25

be whipped for her master's sadistic carnal pleasure; and she would be whipped merely to remind her of her station in life; she would be whipped by her Lord and she would be whipped by her Mistress. She was as much livestock under the burden of the yoke as any oxen that pulled a cart, but she would fetch a far lower price at sale. She accepted floggings the way she accepted the sky overhead and the earth beneath her agonisingly clogged feet. Life could not be other than it was. Anything else would be inconceivable; unimaginable. Those empowered to beat her would do so; why should they not? Tonight would be no different.

Ealdræd growled a laugh, snatched up his belt in one hand and grabbed hold of a handful of her abundant hair in the other, his fingers entwined in the coiled locks. Guiding her down to her knees he let the strap hang eloquently down by the side of her docile face for a moment, then with the same hand he raised the skirt of his tunic. Something of yet greater silent eloquence swelled forth from beneath it.

"Get it down your throat, wanton, and if you don't serve to my satisfaction," he warned, "I'll lay stripes on your backside with this," and he gestured meaningfully with the belt.

*   *   *

An hour or two after the Aenglian had retired with the maid of all work a torrential rainstorm brewed up outside that rattled the window shutters and sent Selwyn's gaming companions scuttling off to their own hearths. There being no further entertainment to be had that evening, the herdsman betook his wife to their own bower and the manor house settled into quietude. Cuddled up in Corynnelia's byre, the girl's newly chastised and welted bottom radiating heat against his groin, Ealdræd drifted off into the cloister of sleep listening to the persistent drumming of the pitiless rain against the roof and congratulating himself on having found this sanctuary when he could so easily have been enduring nature's tempest outside squatting under his cloak tonight. The girl moaned gently and turned over, her floppy-haired head resting against the expanse of his chest. Tranquil, he finally relaxed all the tension from the muscles of his lean, hard physique, and he slumbered. Another hour or more after that, with the storm still raging, the bell rang at the stranger's gate.

Ealdræd was snoring contentedly using Corynnelia's soft naked body as his blanket, yet something inside the warrior that had been keeping him alive when others had surrendered their souls to Wihvir Lord of Hálsian now made him aware of the tolling of that bell. It was a sound that was no natural part of the storm and his brain, sleeping peacefully though he was, registered the abnormality. Any such jarring note was a potential danger and a man preserved the beating of his heart by sensing any latent or impending peril that might threaten, waking or otherwise.

He stirred and threw the girl from him. She rolled over under the impetus of the shove and groaned an unconscious enquiry but dozed on. Taking his knife but not bothering to don his clothes, Ealdræd went to the byre door and opened it a crack, no further; just enough to see and hear what transpired without. Then he waited. In no kindly temper, the Holder of the Manor came staggering forth, flushed red and cursing, carrying a lantern in one hand and stuffing the tails of his nightshirt into his knee-length breeches with the other. Abandoning any further pretence at sartorial affairs, he bore up a cudgel from a box on the ground and, brandishing this as if he were eager to test its mettle, he crossed the width of the main hall and went out barefoot into the night. Woe betide what he found there. Ealdræd waited. Nothing stirred in the stygian hall for a long while.

The return of the herdsman was a very different story. Carrying his lantern high and soaked to the skin, he re-entered his own imposing dwelling-place with an abashed, haunted look on his normally square-jawed features. His broad shoulders drooped as if in defeat. His head was lowered meekly. Ealdræd's curiosity was piqued to a sharpened point. The sinister figure that followed behind him gave the reason for this transformation. Selwyn's second lodger that night was covered from scrawny neck to bony ankle in a rain-drenched monk's habit but was plainly thin to emaciation; his cadaverous head shaven and his sunken face beardless. He had arrived on foot for his sandaled feet were caked in wet mud and the skirts of his habit were thickly splattered with it. Ealdræd caught his breath in his throat and made the sign of the sevenfold preservation of Buldr. Here was an unforeseen stormy-petrel. A necromancer!

Selwyn led this newcomer over to the glowing remains of the hearth fire, opening the oven door to let the heat out. In the yellow circle of the lantern-light they sat huddled close to the stove, baking their sodden clothes until a fog of steam poured off them. The magus muttered a string of guttural words none of which Ealdræd could discern clearly enough to understand but the dialect made apparent that this latest arrival was born north of the cloud-laden mountains of the realm of Bvanwey; a god-ridden sorcery-plagued territory of dark-wassail and chant-mantra. If ever a land were infamous for the breeding of magicians, seers, charm-speakers and leech-healers, then Bvanwey was that land, particularly north of the mountains.

The braided man with the knife who loitered in the deep shadows of the unregarded doorway of the servant-byre was paying close attention. It was hard to tell with those who professed to be enchanters and soothsayers whether they be true practitioners of herb-lore and the divine arts or nothing more than charlatans. Some had the sacred knowledge, that was beyond question, but there were many who traded upon the public's terror of such mysteries to fleece the gullible. This was not so very difficult, for most people, from the highborn to the commoner, were well-primed by folklore and chose to believe the claims of any such witches and scholars of the arcane wisdom that they had the misfortune to meet and treated them as being the genuine article for fear that it might be so. Better to be fooled by a swindler than to disrespect a true priest adept in mystic divination and wizardry who, if displeased, might conjure mischievous sprites to shrivel the transgressor's genitals or, in their righteous wrath, employ Talismans to revenge the insult by inflicting the torments of seductive enchantment upon the wives and daughters of the impious one. Their ability to speak to the dead was a proven fact and it was popularly believed that those gifted with the facility of shape-shifting could turn themselves into the forms of animals; the beasts of the field and the birds of the air.

Selwyn the herdsman was typical of the type most prone to faith in the sending of the hex and the calling of the fetch, spell-craft and auguries, the summoning of goblins and journeying to the netherworld. Farmers, of course, lived in constant dread of sickness amongst their animals and adverse weather blighting their crops, so any safeguard afforded them by supernatural means was swiftly grasped at. But in Selwyn's case his predisposition to superstitious faith was made more acute by his aspirations to self-betterment. The temptation of exploiting some clandestine insight into the penetration of the veil as a means to personal advancement was a snare that had caught many. This gale-tossed soothsayer's rhetoric had obviously convinced the Holder of the Manor even before the two of them had attained the house from the stranger's gate.

Suddenly the hair at the nape of Ealdræd's neck stood up. He spun on his heel and the blade of his knife cut a vicious arc through the air, poised to strike, only to find himself confronted by the dim silhouette of a drowsy and stark nude Corynnelia as she stumbled lethargically from the warmth of the bed to find out what was going on. She huddled in close to him and he whispered to her that they had a seer of the mystic arts on the premises and the girl shook at the very mention of such unnatural things. She watched and listened with him for several minutes and Ealdræd could feel the shrinking of her body with revulsion every time the warlock's rasping speech was loud enough for her to hear.

The necromancer took a pouch from the sack that contained his few belongings and from the pouch poured a small quantity of salt on the ground at his feet, flattening it out smoothly. He then proceeded to write with his forefinger the strange witchcraft of the runes; written symbols by which those with a knowledge of the secrets of their patterns could communicate with each other even when they were not in the same place together. This was one of the most compelling instances of true magic and one of the most inexplicable. One sorcerer could speak a message to another who had not been physically present when the words were spoken. Ealdræd had actually seen this done once when a warlord's magus had received a scroll heavily spotted with hieroglyphic devices from a fellow sorcerer who was accompanying another wing of the army fully ten leagues distant. The magus had read the script to the warlord, the latter had acted upon it, and the magus had been verified correct. Somehow his fellow sorcerer had invested his voice into the parchment so that the warlord's magus could hear it when none other in attendance could. Ealdræd had been right there in the room when the scroll was read and he had heard nothing but a rustling of parchment. Yet the magus had heard the other priest's voice clearly from thirty miles away. Ealdræd had not slept easy for a week afterwards, for it was uncanny. It made his flesh creep.

He was not the only one who appreciated this power that the priests exerted and kept as their own prerogative. Selwyn had turned dreadfully pale. For the writing of the runes to be performed in *his* house, and in salt – for everyone knew the magical properties which resided in salt – that would make the influence of the spell so much stronger. The pallid face of the Holder of the Manor was cast in apprehensive premonition. Those in thrall to the wizard's arts were said to have been inveigled by illusions to sail amongst phantasms in the ship that traverses the great spaces of the underworld until

29

their spirit has drained away. Selwyn most assuredly had all the visible signs of the seduced, as if his will was no longer his own but a mere apparition of the serpent's tongue of the conjurer.

The girl could bear it no longer and slipped from Ealdræd's embrace to retreat to the refuge of her bed. Ealdræd maintained his vigil at the door. Slowly the voices by the stove grew too soft to be intelligible at all. The two men sat tomblike until their voices ceased and all movement had come to an end and Ealdræd concluded that they had both fallen asleep in the cosy warmth of the hearth-fire. He realised that he was himself chill with cold from standing naked for an hour. He hurried back into bed, warming his cold hands on Corynnelia's wriggling body and making her squeal. They snuggled down close together and in less than a minute both were again snoring happily.

The relaxation of their slumbers gave good rest but after the commotion of the magician's dramatic entry into the house the Aenglian warrior's unconscious alertness for danger was hyper-sensitive. His sense of hearing and of smell operated sleeping or waking with a canine responsiveness to the slightest disturbance. When, shortly before the break of dawn, the door of the servant-byre eased open, the sleeper's eyes opened with it, not knowing what it was that had unsettled him yet vigilant and searching the darkness. His ears felt as much as they heard the movement of the stealthy footstep inside the room. Something sly, something furtive was present.

The warrior's prodigious knife, which he had not returned to his kit but which instead he had planted in the wooden boards of the floor next to his head, was in that instant in his hand. The total absence of light in the byre meant that there was no revealing glint from the twenty inch blade. Death awaited the unknown intruder in a razor's edge.

As Selwyn, with cudgel raised high, shuffled fast toward the unsuspecting sleeper, prone and defenceless, he was certain that he had his man. Not daring to risk a light, there was no means by which to differentiate between the two bodies on the mattress, but he had no qualms about killing both Corynnelia and the uncivilized rascal if needs be. The likes of her was easily replaced. He launched his burly body at the vague shape on the mattress and yet when the cudgel thumped brutally down at the vulnerable human flesh it connected only with the straw-filled cowhide of the pallet because incredibly the intended victim was no longer there. The weapon pounded like thunder just four inches from where Corynnelia's upturned countenance slept oblivious. The cry of frustration that would have burst forth from the herdsman's throat was choked on its own blood. The mercenary was somehow at his enemy's back, one fist in the man's hair to snap back his head, the blade was at his neck, the throat erupted not in a cry but in a shower of blood, and hideous slaughter had come to house of Selwyn. The fountain of the man's life poured forth, the body crashed down on to its knees, and what else remained was dead before it crumpled to the floor.

Corynnelia, awoken by the impact of the cudgel upon the bed, came to consciousness amid the splashes of hot blood spraying over her. She could not see it but the smell of the gore told her what it was. Her mouth opened to emit an ear-splitting scream but Ealdræd fell upon her and smothered her mouth with his hand. His big bear's paw of a hand totally covered her face. But a pool of blood was smeared all over her breasts and her abdomen was slick with the stuff. He held her down in the vice of his arms while she struggled in a paroxysm of disoriented, terrified, mindless panic, as if in a fit, at the horror of it. Her vigorous young body was fired by the vitality of sheer fright but he pinned her to the bed until eventually her convulsions subsided and the paralysis of petrification took over. Immobile, she quaked and shuddered feverishly as if with the ague, twitching in the palpitation of her distress. As the two of them lay there in the pitch dark all he could hear was the staccato rhythm of her shocked panting; the rest of the house was noiseless, apparently undisturbed by the few brief sounds of the sudden attack and its equally abrupt dissolution.

Ealdræd made soothing noises until her frantic breathing slowed and slackened; he caressed her as tenderly as he might have stroked his horse to calm it after an upset. Corynnelia slowly recovered her self-control and some measure of composure. But she desperately wanted to leave this terrible room of death. She undorotood nothing of what had happened and wanted only to flee.

She was unlucky. Ealdræd was desirous of further dealings with her first. For the danger and violence and triumph of the killing had aroused the Aenglian and now in lustful victory his excited passions became directed toward the tantalising, tearful strumpet with the provocatively bloody breasts who, murmuring close to his ear, bleated in imploring whispers for mercy and relief from the torment

31

of her apprehensions. He had a rampant erection brought on by the nearness of mortality and the glory of his foe's defeat. The swollen phallic begetter of his progeny needed to be buried in the wench. With the malodorous yawning wound of the stiffening corpse stinking only a yard away he climbed on top of the disbelieving Corynnelia, pushed wide the squirming girl's firm thighs, wrapped them snugly astride his narrow hips, and drove himself solidly into the moist warm haven of her.

*   *   *

Forty minutes later Ealdræd strode boldly out into the vivid daylight of the morning dragging the unwilling girl behind him by the arm. He was dressed for riding and wanted to be on his mount and away before the Lady Gelwyn discovered the corpse of her husband. Not that there were any in the local population who could seriously threaten him in physical combat, nor any five, but if they sought to bar his progress he would have to cut a swathe through them, and a discreet departure was the preferred option, being on this occasion the better part of valour. He bethought him to take Corynnelia with him for the first five miles so that she should have no opportunity to wake the household with alarms before he was well away. Having provided himself with so considerable a head-start, the girl could then be released to find her own way home.

There was no one abroad in the village as he hastened toward the stable, despite the sun having risen. This could only be because his demonic-looking horse was still within the village wall. Normally the whole hamlet would be buzzing like a hive from the first rays of a new day. Yet, aside from Selwyn's two dice-playing cronies the evening before, none of the villagers had shown themselves at all since Ealdræd's arrival; nor would they until after he left. Perchance they were aware also of the second arrival in the midst of the storm? The clanging of the stranger's gate would not have passed unnoticed. Two visitors in a single night, both of them summoned by witchery from some druidical hell or fiendish pit as like as not, was a cause for consternation and best kept clear of.

The girl had not been permitted to dress. She stumbled along behind him, nude and half out of her mind over the fate of her master. She could not quite believe that he was dead. On top of which, the fresh welts on Corynnelia's backside were aching abominably. She had been thrashed twice during the night, once before the slaying and once afterwards, and her poor lacerated bum was sorely complaining by dawn. But she had surrendered to the absolute dominance of the man who now hauled her through the gate and into the stable and she only came up short when confronted by his charger.

The immense monument in horseflesh stood in his familiar braced legs pose in the centre of the stall, clearly agitated. He was nervous, as any horse would be, by the stench of death in his quivering nostrils. Amongst the filthy straw scattered on the hard ground was the limp and lifeless body of the necromancer. Half his head was missing; spread all over the floor between the corpse and the stable door. Corynnelia choked, whined, and collapsed at the sight of it. Her once orderly, strictly proscribed and minutely regulated world had lost its senses utterly.

The mercenary soldier gazed down at the shattered carcass, its spindly arms and legs splayed and broken and twisted all awry. Now all was plain. The wizard had wanted Ealdræd's ghostly blue roan horse. No doubt he imagined that he would cut a finer figure upon the broad back of the mighty Hengustir, and his holy sandals might be spared the dirt of the roads. In the early hours of the morning, in the darkness before dawn, he it was who had convinced Selwyn to sneak into Ealdræd's bed-chamber and murder him in his sleep. Who knows what impish faerie reward had been promised? It mattered not. And while the herdsman was busy at the carnage of his cudgelling, the wizard went to take possession of the stallion.

The horse-thief had attempted to cajole the animal away but Hengustir had known better. Just as Ealdræd had killed his assassin, so too had the horse killed the magician. Rearing high the brute had lashed out with his front feet, catching the man in the side of the head with his iron-shod hooves, and caving in the fellow's brains more surely than any blow from a mace. The rag doll which had so short a time ago been a man lay beneath the great barrel chest, in amongst the very hooves which had done it to death.

The girl, all but overcome by the events of the last few hours, was staring saucer-eyed in appalled marvel at the ripped and shredded remains of someone whom she had feared as she feared the fires of the afterlife, but who's terrifying command of the supernatural had come to nothing but a crushed skull against the natural violence of the horse.

"The power of the wizard lies in the persuasions of his tongue and the manipulations of his voice," muttered Ealdræd, "The animal was proof against it, having not the faculty to understand it."

But the girl, cowering back against the stable gate, had her own more convincing interpretation of events.

"The demoncraft of the devil-horse be stronger than that of any manly conjurer. O Lord Ealdræd, I do humbly beseech you, take your unholy demon from this place of death and from our village, and you shall have all our blessings and any such vittles and comforts as you wish to take with you."

Ealdræd smiled warmly in pleasure at the trembling strumpet and led his mount outside into the bright sunshine of the fresh spring morning. The night had brought pleasure to some and mortal demise to others but the day looked set fair for all. He turned to Corynnelia and with something like affection he counselled:

"Then remember this night's work, you wanton baggage, the next time some necromancing dog conjures you to slit the throat of an honest soldier and steal his steed. Have naught to do with the blandishments of witches and enchanters, girl."

"Aye, my Master," she affirmed energetically, with sincere conviction, nodding her head till her breasts wobbled. "Be it so, my Master."

He swung up into the saddle and, before her fear of the beast could cause her to draw back, he pulled the bare wench up behind him. She flinched a little as her flagellated hind quarters slapped down heavily upon Hengustir's own meaty rump. Then she was greatly surprised to discover that the horse's muscular flesh was warm, like that of any other animal. She had imagined it would be as cold as the mists of Hálsian. She steadied herself with her hands round Ealdræd's waist and with a squeeze of his heels he prompted the blue roan forward.

Chapter 2

The Aberstowe Brethren

Built half-indoors and half-outdoors so that business should not be hindered by the vagaries of the weather, the Weeping Cuckold tavern was one of fifteen thriving hostelries in the small provincial township of Dunstan in that lateral strip of land known as the Sæx, a territory no more than two hundred miles from north to south although it was more than five times that distance from west to east, which constituted a sort of border country flanked by Merthya in the north and Wehnbria to the south. The town's name was taken from the rocky hill atop of which it had been built; a brooding, menacing mound of basalt whose appearance belied the cheerful prosperity of the town upon which it had bestowed the title of Dunstan or 'dark stone' from the word *dun* meaning 'black or dark' and *stan* meaning 'stone or rock'.

It stood on and above the Herebeorht road, that mercantile highway which swept almost the entire length of Sæxyny from Heurtslin in the north east to the River Wven, where it turned sharply south as far as that notorious stronghold of thieves, frauds and swindlers the city-state of Cerdyc, a protectorate of Wehnbria. Dunstan was but seven leagues from the walls of the city-state and so was well situated for foreign trade on all sides. Its domestic population was upwards of five hundred, supplemented by a twelve score of itinerants and passing traffic, and since the Treaty of Herebeorht between the warring Sæxyn princes Godmir and Hereward the Exile had opened the road east of the Herebeorht Passage, commerce in the township was flourishing.

Sæxyny had been ruled these several decades by old King Leof, a fine sovereign in his day, now grown enfeebled. Though his grip had weakened he was not yet dead and his sons, as is the way of sons in such circumstances, had wearied of waiting. The two royal brothers had split the kingdom under force of arms the year before and had left the east of the realm riven by famine and the threat of plague. This region of the country being Hereward's dominion, he had been compelled to yield to Godmir insofar as he had signed a treaty which had preserved the feudal integrity of his lands at the price of his own banishment from them. He had found refuge in the

Flitan Eþel, the disputed territory which was nominally Merthyan but which Sæxyny claimed on the grounds that its population had a Sæxyn majority. The *Flitan Eþel* was far from Hereward's feudal hearthland and the army of Godmir stood between them. And so the exile sat and brooded and nursed his ills, and then turned his restless mind to the promising enterprise of securing the Merthyan *Flitan Eþel* for Sæxyn rule under his own lordship.

Godmir, now the sole heir apparent in the kingdom itself, received the favour of his father and ruled Sæxyny as Reagent in all but name. In these young days of Prince Godmir's ascendancy, the Sæxyn talent for commerce had re-asserted itself with renewed confidence; nowhere more so that in Dunstan. Its marketplaces were lively and its streets busy. There were many foreigners, especially impoverished labourers from the south west of Heurtslin, venal Cerdycite traders whom many suspected of ulterior political motives, and exotic-looking caravans of the Ymbærnan, the travelling nation who had no country of their own.

The extraordinary influx of migrants in recent years was causing much dissent and controversy in the country. Those who welcomed this as a source of cheap labour spoke loftily about the union of nations and the interplay of peoples whilst saying nothing of the financial benefits they received personally. Those who paid the price of cheap migrant labour, the Sæxyn artisans and peasants, had a low opinion of such falsely elevated and condescending talk that concealed economic self-interest. Impromptu meetings in the streets, in the fields and in the workshops discussed issues of cultural integrity, of their very identity as Sæxyns, and the demand that their ethnic heritage should not be cast aside without the consent of the common folk. They spoke of *se eard*, meaning 'the country' in the singular. Their affluent opponents spoke of *þa eardas*, meaning 'the country' in the plural. One realm could not be both. But those with the power and the money favoured *þa eardas*, and so the commoners found that they must bear what they could not change, as usual.

Meanwhile the taverns did good business and wherever there is prosperity there is also thievery. A trio of down-at-heel brigands had noticed a veteran mercenary seated in the Weeping Cuckold at his breakfast that morning, paying for his dumpling eggs, apple-seasoned pork and brandymilk from a tidy leather purse of coin that tinkled disconcertingly in the ears of the hungry un-breakfasted thieves. The mercenary occupied a table in the outdoors half of the premises, sitting in the pleasant early morning sunshine, chewing hugely on a pile of vittles weighty enough to sink a ship. He wore a sleeveless gambeson tunic of thick padded Hessian which fell to the thighs to form a skirt below the wide belt on which a broad-bladed twenty-inch knife was sheathed. Though he consumed his food like the verriest glutton, the hard curves of his naked arms had an intense muscularity that bespoke many years of weapons training. Over his shoulders was draped a hooded mantle, the hood drawn back from his head on which an iron-plated pot-basin helmet sat snugly. His leggings were cross-gartered with thong to just above the knee in the manner of the western folk. His origins were confirmed in the way that he wore his shoulder-length hair and beard plaited in braids, in the Aenglian style.

The loitering thieves watching him eat were not about to take any precipitant action however sorely their bellies rumbled. Despite the recent civil war, the King's Writ still ran in Dunstan. King Leof had laid it down that the penalty for robbery was the amputation of the hands, and the three brigands were understandably chary of perpetrating robbery in a town where their names and faces were known to the magistrates, as well as to their sundry informers. So the three cut-purses were on the alert for travellers passing along the Herebeorht road who might stop to spend a night in the comfort of a bed in some accommodating hostelry before continuing on their way and whose covert disappearance outside the town walls would not be noticed. The guzzling foreign mercenary looked a distinct prospect.

From the serving-wench who had brought him his breakfast and whose bottom had been bruisingly sauced by his lustily groping hand, the brigands had learned nothing. But from her husband, swain to the landlord, they had been informed that the Aenglian was riding south down the trail of the River Wven, taking the old well-worn slave-monger's route from Cerdyc known as the 'turnkey's turnstile' into the peaceful western lowlands of war-beset Wehnbria before turning eastward to the still distant Marches of the Wehnbrian Lordships where he hoped to find a soldier's pay in the ranks of their Lordships mercenaries.

Last autumn the Wehnbrians had suffered a grievous loss in the field to a Geulten army from Oénjil, supported by Bhourgbon irregulars, at the battle of Fontónil. The onset of winter had called a halt to further hostilities but it was certain that the frog-eating bastards would return this summer to pursue the greater glory of the three crowns of the Geulten Alliance. So the word had been spread throughout the Ehngle nations from the valleys of Merthya to the pinewoods of Heurtslin for a great mustering of the available soldiery. Men learned in the skills of combat were much needed. This old mercenary was one such who was answering the call.

His reasons for travel counted for nothing to the three brigands because, although they too were of the race of peninsula peoples known as the Ehngle, it is not the way of low thieves to concern themselves in matters of politics. They leave that to more high-born cutthroats. However, his direction of travel was of consuming interest to them. It would be a simple enough matter to take the road a little ahead of him and lay in wait at some convenient place, if the prize were sufficient to the risk. When the swain identified the fellow's horse, this question seemed to have been answered.

Better than his purse was his mount. The Aenglian's horse was tethered nearby where it could readily be watched over by its owner, and it was a sight to stir the marrow of any sticky-fingered felon. Not only was it a war-horse, massive and powerful, but the animal was also a genuine blue roan; the colouring of its hide was grey-white tinged with blue. Only at the fetlocks did it have the black hair of its sire. It was a ghoulish-looking beast and likely to be ill-luck to the unwary, but mightily impressive. The horse stood impassively at the hitching rail of the tavern, its thick legs seeming to be rooted into the very earth. A horse as magnificent as this would be worth a high price at auction. Not that so distinctive a stallion could be sold here in Dunstan, but six leagues away in the market town of Baucáster, a habitation that only existed one day in seven when the market traders created it afresh each week to trade and barter, the sale of any horse could be managed without difficulty.

The brass-bedecked military saddle on its back was far from new but of skilled manufacture and good quality, and hanging from that saddle was treasure indeed. Two short javelins for throwing, each about a yard long, and a seven foot spear of well-seasoned ash which had clearly seen service but was well-maintained. The iron head of the weapon was polished till it shone, even to the circumference of tiny spikes at its base that were angled backwards to ensure that once the blade had entered an enemy's body, removing it would scour their flesh. Added to these, from the pommel of the saddle hung a buckler made from teakwood reinforced with a raised half-sphere of iron in the centre and four smaller satellite half-spheres around it. All in all, the retail value of both horse and armaments combined could provide three deserving highwaymen with months of ease and comfort.

The tempting lure of all this notwithstanding, there had been some discussion amongst the vagabond band as to the advisability of waylaying so heavily-armed a gentleman-of-fortune. True, once he was dead those weapons would sell for a good price, but first the death must be accomplished. He was a big man right enough, very tall and with arms and shoulders that might well lend caution to faint heart. But they were three and he was but one man, and there was grey in the woven braids of his beard and hair. For all his muscle and the litheness of his movements, he must have passed forty years of age. They were three bold young brigands in the first flush of their youth and the equal of anyone. He was an old man. He should have been dead and mouldy and done to dust a long time since. Well, they would see to that. They would not falter and what was his would soon be theirs.

Of the three, the youngest was called Aedheúrt which was akin to a joke by whatever gods had cursed his begetting since the name was composed of *aed* meaning 'prosperity or riches' and *heúrt* meaning 'of the Heurtslin', so that he was 'a prosperous Heurtslin'. In fact, Aedheúrt had lived in abject poverty since his misbegotten birth two decades ago and had never been able to steal enough to put himself in funds for more than a few days at a stretch. Never having known his Heurtslin refugee parentage, he had been dragged through a childhood and adolescence of unspeakable abuse and misery until recently his circumstances had improved somewhat when he had taken up with his new family of cut-purses. He had even managed to acquire his first ever piece of serious weaponry, a forty inch two-handed iron mace with a striking head in the shape of a spiked ball. Each of the multiple spikes that stuck out in all directions was two inches long. It was a grotesquely fearsome weapon and the previously much-bullied Aedheúrt had developed a definite swagger in his stride since it had come into his possession. The mace required very little knowledge of the techniques of weapons-handling and in his only skirmish with it to date, a rowdy melee between the three brigands and a couple of drunken liverymen outside the Stag and Hounds public house, Aedheúrt had swung his mace so wildly that eventually he had made contact with something and the spikes had literally ripped the face off a fellow who, as luck would have it, turned out to be one of his opponents.

39

Aedheúrt's clothing was of the plainest; a cambric tunic with a woollen cloak, and whilst this was an improvement upon the past, he still went barefoot and hatless. His only protective apparel was a cuirass of hard leather of which he was so proud that he even slept in it. His mangled growth of a beard was permanently crawling with lice.

The second brigand was by way of being their leader. He was a local Sæxyn man, Winfrid, whose parents had most certainly been liars because *wine* meant 'friend' and *frid* meant 'peace' yet never once in his twenty-five years had he proved himself a friend to any or brought a minute's peace into the world. He had been born a ceorl, but although common he was yet a freeman who owed fealty to none. It was his boast that he had lived free all of his life, giving his oath of allegiance to no thegn or liege-lord.

Not as undernourished as his younger companion, he had a thin but sinewy frame that suggested considerable physical endurance. His shirt was a woollen hauberk which he wore with sack-cloth breeches and a pair of boots so decrepit that they were held together with twine. Over his head and neck was draped a chainmail coif and on his right shoulder he wore a pauldron; an articulated series of plates that armoured the area between neck and biceps, thereby lending some useful protection for the shoulder of the sword-arm. His own weapon was a single-edged sword with a slightly curved blade reminiscent of a cutlass such as the sailors of the Canbrai Isles in the western ocean were famed for using. It hung from a scabbard at his waist. Both were the booty from a raid upon a Wehnbrian merchant's caravan last year and despite the dangers entailed in their appropriation they were all the plunder he'd had from the affair, the best of the loot going to others in the raiding party. It was shortly afterwards that he'd left that troop of cut-throats and sought out a light-fingered crew of his own where he might have the ascendancy and be the one to corner the richest pickings.

Winfrid had the fair hair of his Sæxyn lineage and he, too, like all men was bearded, but he had shaved his upper lip in the fashion of his people. The Sæxyns were recognised across the eight kingdoms for this characteristic style of barbering, though none of the neighbouring races could make sense of this odd practice of cutting off a part of their manhood. Priests and women wore a smooth face, and beardless boys, but for a grown man to barber his moustache struck those who resided outside of Sæxyny as perverse. In addition to which, whilst priests kept special razors for the removal of hair as a religious observance, any common folk who indulged this perversity would have to use such blades as they happened to possess for use as a shaving knife. Consequently, the Sæxyn men were distinctive not only for the partial reduction of their whiskers but further for the red rashes that ornamented their skins from scraping away at their flesh with a tool too blunt for the purpose. This drawback notwithstanding, Winfrid was assiduous in shaving his upper lip, but if he had washed since puberty the fetid smell of him gave no evidence of it.

He owned a tired, scrawny pony whose experience of the world had been no better or worse than young Aedheúrt's and whose probable future gave no cause for optimism. Winfrid's otherwise dubious ownership of this animal was not in dispute because its prior owner was deceased.

The third brigand was a thick-set woman as tall as her two cohorts and just as flea-ridden, if not as bushily bearded, though as blonde as her Sæxyn kith Winfrid. In age she was somewhere between the other two and, being more cautious by nature as well as a more prolific thief, she was more heavily armoured than were they, with a gorget to protect her neck and upper chest, below which was strapped a miss-matched back-and-breastplate that did not fit together securely and left a space between the plate armour and the gorget. For a helmet she had a padded hard leather chain-mesh cap and, like a sensible thief who wanted to keep her hands, she wore a linen scarf wrapped across the lower half of her face to confound easy identification. Naturally she favoured male dress and wore a thick wool doublet and breeches with a pair of patchwork slippers so split and peeling that they made Winfrid's boots appear quite serviceable by comparison. Her only noticeable weapon was a six foot halberd with an unsuitable pine shaft but a reasonably robust if small barb-point and axe-head combination. If she had other tools of dealing death, they were not manifest to the casual observer. What was obvious, however, was that she had been the ninth child in her family because her name, Noni, meant 'ninth'.

Having conferred on their course of action the three rogues decided that with age and numbers on their side as well as surprise, they would ambush this snake-braided foreigner as soon as he was beyond the sleepy vision of the guards at the town gate. When the Aenglian recovered his horse from the tavern rail and walked it off in the direction of the town wall, the gang of brigands set off at a run for the gate and the road south. They maintained a good speed on the main road and when they reached a location that they had made use of before for the same purpose, they felt confident that their intended victim was still too far in the rear to have noticed them.

Winfrid's pony was induced to lay down thirty yards or so from the road amongst some scrub bushes in the neighbouring field, whereupon they staked down his bridle to ensure that he would not get up. The pony out of sight, they had only to hide themselves. On this road there was but one place of concealment that was close enough to a passing traveller to be able to dash forth and reach him before he spurred up his horse to canter away. This near to the town, the rough road still had ditches on both sides and it was in these that the three vagabond-highwaymen lay in wait. There was a good deal of rain in the ditches from the preceding night and all three cursed this misfortune for they were immediately soaked in the cold brackish water as they stretched prone on their bellies in the filthy ditches to secrete themselves from view. Why could the old soldier not have got himself drunk and collapsed senseless in his cups in some convenient place where they could have killed him quietly and filched his belongings without all this lying about in ditches? Instead he had gorged himself on fresh eggs and succulent pork swilled down with rich brandymilk, a mixture of hop-brandy and cow's milk that was a speciality of the Sæx, until his stomach must burst. Consequently, they now found themselves in the only available roadside hiding place, covered all over in wet mud, with their faces perforce hangdog in the swill because they dare not raise their heads for fear of being seen by their approaching victim. At least the road was blessedly deserted this morning so that there would be little chance of mistaking their target, it being the thirteenth day of the month, *wóhlic dæg*, and bad luck to travellers, so that the Aenglian was alone upon the road, and soon to suffer the penalty of his foolish irreligion. After an eternity of waiting, the dull thud of the war-horse's feet tramping in the damp earth, heavy and rhythmic, foretold the mercenary's approach.

The rider, Ealdræd of the Pæga, a clan of Aenglia, sat tranquil atop his steed, contentedly digesting the substantial meal he had just enjoyed, swaying gently along to the animal's rhythm, reflecting upon the pleasures betaken of the tavern wench the night before. Her cockless swain of a husband in his own barren marriage bed had been passed over by his audacious slut of a wife whose preference had been to cuddle up with the hard body of the mercenary in the guest-room that he occupied for ten groatæ a night, and at no extra charge the adulterous pair had copulated enough for a whole warren of rabbits. By Buldr's balls these alehouse slatterns could ride the shaft! And when for his sport he'd trimmed her up with a leather strap across her whipped and welted hind quarters, why, she'd fairly purred with satisfaction, the randy baggage.

It was pleasant to muse upon such things, with the town behind him and a straight road ahead. The weather was fine, both he and the admirable example of horseflesh beneath him were hale and hearty. His stomach was sated and there was still plenty of coin for the long journey east to the Marches. The old wound in his calf was not, Buldr be praised, proving troublesome for once, nor the ache that sometimes plagued his joints. Life was good today. His disposition was benign. Tomorrow was tomorrow's concern.

As the superb blue-grey stallion, Hengustir, reached a pre-agreed place on the road, all three outlaws emerged from their hidey-holes at the same instant and rushed at the rider from both sides. Aedheúrt attacked from the right, Winfrid and Noni from the left, bellowing their battle cries to add to the shock and the suddenness of the assault. They were sodden wet from the ditch and angry as a hive of wasps at the Aenglian whom they blamed for their discomfort. The two men had naked sword and mace hoisted aloft but it was Noni's halberd, the longest of the assailants' weapons, which reached the rider first, used in a straight line like a lance and clouting him with a tremendous buffet to the side of the head. The soldier's helmet saved his skull from cracking but he was tipped unceremoniously off horseback, grabbing at his saddle as he went down.

He landed messily but managed to cushion the fall with his hands and feet, rolling over on to his back to face the closest assailant. Somehow he already had a javelin in his fist. His grab at the saddle had not stopped his fall but his hand had seized one of the two javelins that were suspended on hanging sheaths from the saddle and he had come away holding one of the short throwing spears, his practiced hand finding the correct grip even as his tumbling body came crashing to a halt. He had come down on Aedheúrt's side of the horse and as that worthy ran at the man on the ground, his hideously spiked mace held double-handed high overhead preparatory to bludgeoning his way to riches, Ealdræd sat up sharply and brought one arm over to throw the javelin from a distance of perhaps four feet. The iron and ash went through Aedheúrt's throat with such power that it very nearly went all the way through, the tail end of the javelin just getting snagged in the man's windpipe before it could rip free, and so the first brigand was consigned to Wihvir Lord of Hálsian the commander and corruptor of spirits.

The great size of Hengustir meant that Aedheúrt's two confederates had not witnessed his fate. Confident still, Winfrid circled the horse while Noni sought to grasp its bridle and gain control of the excited beast. Ealdræd, with the veteran's instinct for spontaneous tactics, dived under the stallion's great barrel chest and when he emerged once again into the sight of Winfrid and Noni it was with his spear in his right hand and his buckler in the other.

Winfrid, having discovered the butchered remains of Aedheúrt, understood the mistake that had been made but, the die cast, knew there was nothing left to do but make a fight of it and look for the opportunity to escape. Recklessly he lunged forward, thrusting with the cutlass at his opponent's belly. Ealdræd parried with his buckler, the small round shield deflecting the sword out of harm's way. Winfrid sought desperately to twist his upper body aside to evade the expected attack form the poised spear in the soldier's calloused fist but instead Ealdræd brought the buckler up in his left hand to punch the rogue full in the face, the raised iron boss in the centre of the buckler breaking nose, teeth and jaw all in one crushing collision of bone and metal. Stunned by the impact of this hammer blow, for a moment Winfrid hung in the air suspended by his own insensibility. A moment was all that was needed. Ealdræd kicked aside the robber's sword which fell uselessly from numbed fingers, but the spear thrust that would have killed the man was knocked down by the third ruffian's halberd as Noni joined the fray, coming in fast to clatter shaft on shaft and spoil Ealdræd's strike. Misdirected, the spear went point-first into Winfrid's foot.

The momentum of this misdirection caused Ealdræd to spin but rather than resist the motion he went with it, turning a complete circle and so flailing round with the buckler to catch Noni on the back of the head, thumping her clean off her feet, and sending her plunging headlong into the mud. Leaving the wounded bandit to totter back screaming through the shattered remnants of his broken jaw and smashed teeth, Ealdræd turned upon this third enemy, and with his creased visage grinning a smile of baleful reckoning the veteran swept down upon his helpless foe like the despotic hordes of Prince Leofric the Beloved when they laid waste to the city of Mðen. Many are the tales told of the sacking and pillaging of Mðen by his esteemed royal highness but in no single one of them is the word 'mercy' ever once used.

The brigand was shaking her dazed and dented cranium, rising to her elbows in the dirt and pitching over clumsily to the side to turn herself over right-side up. But then she flattened herself upon her back on the ground in terror as Ealdræd loomed over her, spear hefted high for the killing stroke. One second from death, she snatched the scarf from her face and appealed for quarter, crying out "I'm a woman!"

Had the Aenglian warrior had the leisure for reflection he might have wondered why this reprobate villain had chosen such bizarre last words for the final seconds of her life. Their utter irrelevance would have been a bafflement to him. Doubtless it must be some inexplicable eccentricity of the ethnic clan within the Sæxyn culture from which she came. Perchance she had been reared in a society so perverse that it had different standards for women and men in the matter of killing. Many and winding were the oddities and foibles of disparate cultures in the wide world and much amused entertainment may be garnered from the contemplation of these peculiarities. So might it be considered by the learned and the wise. But Ealdræd thought none of these things for there was no time for philosophising in the midst of battle. He simply thrust down powerfully with his spear at the half-inch gap betwixt the brigand's gorget and her ill-fitting breastplate. With unerring accuracy the fatal point found this weakness in her armour, breached the crack, and the eighteen inches of iron that was the razor-sharp head of the spear cut deeply and fully through the meat and organs of the torso of his enemy before being instantly wrenched back out again, taking some goodly portion of her innards with it.

Thick blackish-red gore exploded from her mouth and her whole frame went limp as the spark of animation departed, but Ealdræd wasted no precious time in watching her choke to death. He had dispatched her from his mind as he had dispatched her from this world. Two he had delivered into Wihvir's cold bosom, but three there had been who had taken up arms against him. There was one brigand left, but where?

Winfrid of the Sæxyns, his face ruinously mangled and his foot sliced from toes to ankle, stumbling and reeling frantically, had limped his way bloodily to where the pony was tied, had cut the restraining rope that tied it down, clambered and hauled himself awkwardly into the saddle, and now the dastard was a-horse and galloping for his life.

Ealdræd delayed long enough to quickly recover his javelin from the neck of Aedheúrt and clean it rapidly on a loose fold of the outlaw's clothing before giving chase to the one who had yet to suffer the fate that justice demanded. The weapon was worth more than the life it had taken and Ealdræd would never have conceived of abandoning so beautiful a piece of craftwork in the heat of the pursuit. Only when his armoury was safely re-sheathed did he ride on to hunt down and execute the remaining scoundrel who owed him a life, for the man must die.

It was an entirely necessary action. The attack upon Ealdræd, like any offence committed against the person, was more than just an attempt to do injury, it was at the same time an insult to the person against whom injury was attempted, and insults must be punished. This was not something that it would have occurred to an Aenglian to doubt, the morality of it being self-evident to those who value personal honour.

Elsewhere amongst lands indolent with conceit and blind with self-congratulation there were benighted souls who, failing to understand such concepts as dignity, respect and honour, would have indulged themselves in the vanity of immoral mercy. Ealdræd had been to these lands and seen their ways and pitied them the infantilism of their deformed and distorted social code; for an ethics which neglects dignity through justice is no ethics at all. He had marvelled that these wretched folk could not see how an act of mercy thwarts justice in that it deliberately refrains from the implementation of a due penalty, so that the perpetrator is not shown the respect of being held accountable for their own actions, and the victim is not shown the respect of having the insult avenged and their dignity restored. What could be more obvious than that an act of mercy is an act of injustice?

Some of these warped and misshapen cultures actually went so far as to praise the practice of clemency. When he had first come across this perfidious and heretical fallacy, Ealdræd, still a comparatively young man and new to the perversities of foreign climes, had been astonished and repulsed by such self-debasement in the guise of false goodness. To treat those who had insulted you with forgiveness was, unquestionably, more immoral even than mercy because in addition to its refusal to act in accord with justice, it elevated such premeditated injustice to the status of a virtue. It was the poltroon's masquerade that what was in truth an act of cowardice, was in their self-pretence believed to be an act of moral rectitude.

Whilst Ealdræd had ridden the roads of such countries in years past, he had held steadfastly to his own tribal and clan-ethnicity and armoured his mind against infection from the pusillanimous. He was not one of those to neglect his own dignity. Nor was he the type who would have let the fleeing thief ride off and be damned to him; grateful to have bested two enemies and lived to tell the tale with a whole skin. It was not the way of the Aenglians to sell the integrity of their unrepentant self-esteem as the price of an easier life. An insult diminished a man, and to tolerate the insult and be diminished by it was to surrender a portion of oneself that could never be recovered.

The thief was riding a pony whereas Ealdræd was riding his massive warhorse, seventeen hands tall, whom he had named Hengustir because the gigantic brute was built like the fabled charger of the legendary giant Ffydon. When Hengustir was at the gallop he was like a small army on manoeuvres. He was not built for cross-country races and could hardly be expected to keep pace with a pony half his girth, especially when the lighter, nimbler beast had been permitted a considerable start. But expectation was confounded, for the brigand's animal was a poor specimen; a broken-winded, bandy-legged cow of a worthless nag, so that Hengustir – whose own fighting blood was up with the smell of fresh death in his quivering nostrils – not only kept the fleeing ponyback miscreant in sight but actually narrowed the distance between them, slowly but steadily gaining ground, with the brass buckles, rings, and terrets of his harness creating a percussive rattle and clatter in time with the thunderous drumbeat of his hooves.

The country hereabouts was far from barren, being grassy and lush, but it was unusually scarce in trees and moderately level going for the most part, so that the quarry was distinctly visible from several furlongs behind. Ealdræd did not seek to spur Hengustir into feats of alacrity that were beyond him but kept the chase at a brisk canter that would not exhaust his wind or threaten his shanks; a pace at which the great war-horse could rumble onwards without faltering for half a day, if needs be. Hengustir was still young enough to enjoy his own strength and intelligent enough to appreciate that they were chasing the pony and rider ahead. He had no understanding of why this was so but he needed none. The horse lived in a world of facts not reasons; it was a fact that they must apprehend their enemy and the immense warhorse thrilled with the desire to run down the foe. Ealdræd need not even whip up or spur his beast forward; Hengustir sought to catch the quarry for the sheer excitement of it. The Aenglian had only to moderate his horse's speed to suit the distance. Inevitably the flustered prey must tire and then retribution would overtake him. The race was not always to the swift.

Winfrid, in contrast, was driving his animal with the clear intention of killing the wretch to secure his own safety. It was not that the thief was craven; he was simply pragmatic. Had he and his comrades hit their victim with a fatal blow in the first rush, or if they had battered him sufficiently to befuddle his senses and render him defenceless, then they would now be congratulating themselves on their cunning and their daring. But things had not gone well, they had gone badly, so that there was nothing left to do but to find some way to survive the mistake that he had made.

Survival did not look particularly promising. His pursuer was only five furlongs in the rear, a mere thousand yards. And in this cursedly flat country there were no bolt-holes or hiding places to afford him the chance to disappear. Unlike the forested and mountainous Merthya to the north or the vast acreage of woodland in Wehnbria to the south, the wide belt of Sæxyny between was broad meadowland. Oh for the alleys and back streets of his native Dunstan where he could lose a pursuer within five turnings amongst the canopied and zigzag lanes. He had always detested travelling further than a mile beyond the town walls, for there was little but hard labour and starvation to be had from the country, and now this damnable rustic's pastureland would be the death of him. His undernourished nag rattled across an expanse of rockier ground and pressed on towards the brow of a low mound, which was all that the area offered in the way of a hill. Winfrid swore vociferously at his misfortune; there was no woodland that might camouflage him, no escarpments or embankments to delay the hunter in the pursuit, nothing but the peaceful, benevolent, gently undulating countryside. The Sæxyn could feel the hot eyes of the Aenglian burning into his back. He ground his heels into the bleeding flanks of the labouring pony to force the poor beast to press on though its neck was already white with lather. There was a single chance, if he could but reach Aberstowe.

A narrow river banked with willows cut across the valley bending the road to the east. The despairing pony, all ribs and sweat, shied away from the uncertain footing by the trees. Winfrid, as if heedless of where his flight might take him, followed the curve in the path, looking over his shoulder as often as he looked to his front, the pony determining their route as much as the rider, losing the cadence of its gallop as it tired but dashing along as best it could in parallel with the little river. In fact the man had a very definite destination in mind, if only the pony did not die before they came upon it; the Abbey of Aberstowe , a place of dark reputation, rightly shunned by all but the peasants who served the needs of the Sibling Brethren who resided there worshipping who knew what foul evils and pestilential mischiefs. Even so, they were a holy order and might offer shelter to the penitent wayfarer. Winfrid could just see the distant dull shapes of a gaggle of buildings on the horizon where the tributary river emptied into a much larger waterway; one substantial structure in stone surrounded by a motley collection of peasant dwellings. His mount shivered beneath him and for one dread instant Winfrid thought the pony would drop or trip but somehow the exhausted nag recovered its balance and continued its frenzied flight. Slowly, slowly, the village drew nearer.

Winfrid's pony, its lungs bursting, distended eyeballs glaring, and its legs cracking with the strain, could scarcely raise a trot as it lurched and floundered into the village of Aberstowe where the stately Abbey lifted its turrets high into the midday heavens to lend its name to the local community, *aber* being the mouth of a river and *stowe* the name for a sacred habitation or holy place. The Abbey had been erected at the juncture of the minor Wyenveny River and its very much bigger elder brother, the River Wven.

The pony stumbled with terminal fatigue; he could carry his master no further. With base ingratitude Winfrid whipped the pony on, though it was upon the edge of collapse, to the very door of the Abbey. He fell rather than dismounted, hobbling to the mammoth wooden door that was the height of two men one atop the other, which in keeping with the luck he had suffered all day, was firmly shut.

His cracked jaw made intelligible speech impossible but, pounding on the great oaken door, he roared a garbled incoherent alarum to wake the dead:

"Sanctuary!! I crave sanctuary!!"

Winfrid placed his back to the oak and searched the distance for the mercenary. He had no need to search far, for there was the braided bumpkin astride his devil horse, the immense stride of the blue roan devouring the half-mile remaining between the soldier and his vengeance. Winfrid blasphemed every god he could think of and then damned himself for getting into this fix when there was no necessity. Why had he not taken heed of the demonic aspect of the bastard's horse? No one who rode such a hellish-looking ogre could be anything but bad cess to those that crossed his life's passage. A blind Murgl gypsy fortune-teller could have told him that for the price of a hair ribbon and a couple of beads. He should have noted these omens and with a sly wink to the faeries of fortune he should have passed up the tempting target and selected a poorer but an easier victim. Aedheúrt and Noni were dead and bargaining for their souls with the Lord Wihvir, whom none could cheat, and soon Winfrid would be joining them; rot the idiocy of his greed.

Behind him the enormous door opened and the self-reproachful brigand turned to see the monkish gatekeeper, a portly wine-inbiber with a liverish complexion whose vacuous smile bid the newcomer inside with unexpected invitation. Not having said a word of explanation as to his appeal for sanctuary, Winfrid was careful not to spoil with speech the things that are there for the taking, and he accepted the chubby brother's silent welcome with haste. The bright sunshine outside did not penetrate the doorway to light the gloomy darkness within but the Sæxyn stepped through into shadow without pause and the door closed behind him so ominously that from the outside the Abbey took on the aspect of some gargantuan organism that had swallowed him.

Ealdræd's arrival a minute later in a cacophony of hoof-beats and equine snorting disrupted the quiet of the village a second time. Henguslir was in fine fettle after the excitement of the fight and the stirring rigour of his exercise, his temper roused and his ire awoken. Let those who dare approach him in this mood. Ealdræd could safely leave him here alone; there would be none in this farmer's hamlet who would seek to steal a blue roan with his hackles up. The warrior swung down and walked briskly to the Abbey door. That his quarry was inside was evidenced by two compelling facts; the dying pony lay expiring in the dust, breathing its last gasp, and there was nowhere else that the man could have gone.

He thumped the door with the heel of his palm and demanded entry. Splinters of wood broke off the panels of the door. Fortunately, this time the gatekeeper was prepared and there was no delay; entry was granted. Met by the same tubby inebriate who had succoured Winfrid, the Aenglian asked for the name and fetish of this house. The little monk told him that his name was Sibling Bertolf and that he was pleased to serve so virile and courtly a nobleman; that the house was the Abbey of Aberstowe, and that the gods of the house were so numerous as to be too many to name. Also, many of them had no names.

"Then I honour the many fetishes of this house of worship, both named and nameless, and seek their blessings while I tarry here," said Ealdræd, brusquely but judiciously. "Where is the wounded man who arrived here just ahead of me," he added with an air of menace.

"Do you follow me, my gracious lord," said Sibling Bertolf with a degree of obsequious servility that would have turned the mercenary's stomach had his mind not been occupied with other matters, "and I will straightway conduct you to your heart's desire. It shall be my privilege to escort a fighting man of such palpable martial fortitude."

Ealdræd followed in impatience but in silence, having little wish to engage in conversation with this honey-tongued toady. As they walked from the gate across a tiny courtyard into an echoingly empty Hall of Contemplation and from thence into a similarly empty Assembly of Meditation, Sibling Bertolf explained in a querulous voice that the Abbey was home to the Brethren, a monastic order, of whom he had the intense fortuity to be a member. He spoke with a degree of pride that betokened an overweening conceit and for all the overt flattery with which he had greeted the braided mercenary soldier, the rotund cleric was plainly not one to neglect his own heart's desires. Whatever religious devotions to their nameless gods transpired within these walls, they did not preclude drunkenness and frequent inebriation; the gatekeepers rosy red nose was a flower that took a good long while to grow with regular watering. His very sweat smelt of wine.

They passed by two or three other clerics, all dressed in the same style of monk's habit that was thrown so scruffily over Sibling Bertolf's short but ample frame, all with the shaved heads and shaved chins of priests the world over, and it was difficult not to notice that all the siblings had a figure fully as corpulent as that of their brother Bertolf and that, despite the somewhat spartan

51

furnishings, the whole Abbey was positively redolent with an air of a lifestyle of sensual over-indulgence. As Ealdræd strolled along fingering the knife at his belt in hasty zeal he neglected to pay much heed to the route they were taking but he did become conscious of its complexity and he fell to wondering why Winfrid, presumably a stranger, had been transported so deeply into the inner recesses of the Abbey. That was not the way of religious orders. The clergy guarded their secrets most jealously as a rule.

Moreover, he could not help but observe that there were quite a number of young women of the peasant class working at various domestic tasks about the place, more than one of whom were heavily pregnant. The slatterns were dressed in nothing but their thin cotton shifts, so there could be no mistaking their fecund and expectant condition. There was no one to have impregnated these women except the Brethren themselves, and this was surely the case. Not that such a circumstance was in itself so very surprising, but what was genuinely mysterious, so puzzling as to be almost disturbing, was the total absence of children in the Abbey. A living space in which three dozen men and their trollops were daily fucking and, at routine intervals, spawning their progeny would very naturally have a large litter of snot-nosed bastards running about underfoot. Aberstowe had none. It was curious.

Finally, Bertolf stepped through a strangely smooth-fitted undersized door in a wooden wall and bid Ealdræd do likewise. The latter, his every sense starkly alert for treachery, slipped through nimbly in one quick motion and looked about him. The room, if it could properly be so called, was unique in the well-travelled soldier's vast experience. It was a kind of indoor circular arena of about fifty feet circumference, made of wooden planks all the way around its one continuous circuit of a wall. The floor was flagstone, worked so smooth that it almost appeared polished, but it was the roof that captured and held the imagination. It was made of very fine, very thin red silk and with the midday sun burning down directly upon it from above the whole arena was bathed in a preternaturally red light.

There was a small sacrificial Alter raised on a plinth in the very centre of the circle with a thick crust of dried blood caked on it and a deeper, darker stain of older blood beneath. This amphitheatre of wood and silk was their chamber of sacrifice and its good standing as a temple of the abattoir was beyond question. But the Alter, an oval dish no more than thirty inches wide atop a column forty inches high, was much too small for the sacrifice of human adults. Was it that the Brethren offered up to their gods the lives of chickens and dogs and rabbits? Or was this sinister Alter the true explanation of why there were no children in Aberstowe Abbey?

There were twelve sibling brothers in the room. Ealdræd was careful to count them accurately because mayhap he would have to kill them, and it was a wise to know the number of the enemy or else be caught napping when another appears from behind. Then he saw Winfrid, seated between two of the Brethren whilst a third bound with bandages the awful cut in his foot that was still seeping prodigiously. Little could be done about the ruin of his face. Ealdræd's grip upon his spear tightened and as he began to move toward the man he had come to this place to kill, one of the twelve brothers stepped forth, raised his arms in salutation, and said to the two adversaries:

"I am Sibling Amleth. I congratulate you on being granted the sublime favour to participate in today's ceremonies. I do assure you, it is an honour far beyond your comprehension. But, never you mind our transcendent spiritual concerns; let us return to your own reasons for being here. If you good sirs are at dispute, then you have the remedy at hand." He referred, of course, to the weapons both carried. "We of the Aberstowe Brethren place this hallowed chamber at your disposal for the carriage of your wills. Let he whose power is superior, unleash it."

At which all the members of the Brethren dramatically shouted "Unleash!" collectively. It was a safe wager that the word was oft-used in these halls. Sibling Bertolf was still close by the Aenglian and Ealdræd observed that the fellow's former fawning sycophancy had completely disappeared, and been replaced by a malicious triumph that bespoke of quite another side of his character. Sibling Amleth spoke again in his overblown declamatory fashion:

"One sword; one spear, two men; one life."

Winfrid was to have only his cutlass and Ealdræd only his spear. In the ordinary way of things the mercenary would not surrender his weapons to anyone, but here he need only lay down his buckler and knife by the Alter and, having slayed his foe, recover them. It seemed politic to accede to this piece of theatre rather than be put to the trouble of having to slaughter half the brethren in order to reach the thief who had insulted him. The old soldier was unconcerned; his opponent was much the inferior man and already seriously wounded besides fearful, for the Sæxyn was no fool and fully aware of his terrible disadvantage. Armed with the favoured weapon of his clan, the Aenglian could not fail.

The two combatants prowled toward one another as the sibling brothers faded into the background. Ealdræd adopted the fencing position with his spear; one hand cradling the butt whilst the other balanced the length of the ash shaft so that the point, seven feet away, circled and probed for an opening. Limping and nauseous from pain, Winfrid felt as if his enemy was insolubly beyond the reach of his sword-edge. Each time he attempted to step in close enough to reach the wily old mercenary, that spearpoint flashed out to chew a lump out of the swordsman's vulnerable leading arm. Once, twice, three times Winfrid's sword arm was bled by that ever-circling, ever-dancing spearpoint. He could barely retain his weakening grip upon the hilt any more. Frustration and despair overwhelmed him. How could a man over forty move with such swiftness? Had not the man the decency to be crippled with age like the rest of his generation?

With precious little choice in the matter, knowing that all was lost with him anyway, Winfrid decided not to play out this farce. Summoning up the tenacious valour of his Sæxyn forebears that was his heritage, he gripped his sword in both hands, whirled it in a high circle and as the energy in the motion of the iron pulled him toward his opponent, he launched himself off his one good foot in wild abandon, lunging gamely but hopelessly, gambling his life on somehow dodging inside the poised, hovering spearpoint to bring the sword-blade down upon the Aenglian's damnable head. In doing so, he left himself wide open to a counter. Against a mercenary as experienced as Ealdræd the Aenglian, it was suicide. The veteran's refined and developed fighting awareness had made him alert to the wounded Sæxyn's shift in balance preparatory to the lunge, and the old man had been waiting for it. His response was instantaneous. Powered by the pushing arm of the hand that cupped the butt of the ash-shaft, the spear was driven smack into the centre of the brigand's chest with such strength that the spearhead tore right through the breastbone and burst out in a welter of blood from the middle of his shoulder blades.

The impaled thief fell to the floor as dead as mackerel. There was a collective gurgle of gratified revulsion from all the Brethren watching; an audible cringe of pleasure at the grotesque. Sibling Amleth stood smiling complacently like a magistrate who had just seen a death sentence he had passed carried out with unusual efficiency by a particularly proficient executioner. Aside from the few preliminary scratches to the Sæxyn's sword-arm, Ealdræd had killed Winfrid with a single devastating blow. But it took him over half a minute of pulling and tugging to wrench his spear back out of the rascal's chest.

Brief though it had been, battle is always warm work and when a comely young wench, noticeably less pregnant than the majority of her sisters but conspicuously endowed for the suckling of the young, brought him a pewter goblet the size of Ealdræd's helmet filled with a restorative draught of the local ale, the parched soldier quaffed it back eagerly, and good beer it was too for a man with the thirst to relish it, though it was rank piss in comparison with the giddy slop-house tankards he had enjoyed while the troubadours had warbled to their gut-strings in the Weeping Cuckold the night before. By all the gods of the boudoir, he was in a mood to disport himself again with that swain's harlot, after all this morning's killing. And why shouldn't this busty Abbey scullion serve in her place? The baggage had a pleasing shape. The light shift she wore, which revealed so much of the sensuous contours beneath, testified to the fullness and the soft ripeness of her body. The plain cotton dress was cut very low to conceal almost nothing of her firm, unspoilt breasts, for it was understood at the Abbey of Aberstowe that a woman's flesh was the incarnation of the will of the gods, named and unnamed, so there could be no shame in the public display of the gods' creation. It was only human vanity that made a fetish of concealment. For the same reason the hemline of this spare garment fell no further than the top of her thighs. She wore nothing underneath. Indeed, she wore nothing else at all, not even shoes. She was a child of nature, clean limbed and elemental. Her hair was uncut and reached almost to her waist. The girl had an astonishing natural beauty that needed no Jezebel embellishments. She was radiant with the first flowering of her sexual maturity.

Ealdræd drained the remainder of the goblet. He scowled at the poor quality of the ale. But then, what did priests know of the tapsters' trade? That notwithstanding, the ride here from Dunstan had been dry and the brandymilk of breakfast felt long overdue for reinforcement and, his mood greatly improved, he was just fetching the serving girl a friendly squeeze of her splendid tits and enquiring as to her refilling his goblet when he noticed a numbness in his fingers and a lack of focus in his vision. Taken unawares, he did not at once comprehend the reason for these strange sensations. Then the swirling mists swept over him. His drink had been dosed with some narcotic substance and the potion with which the beer had been imbued quickly clouded his mind, dimmed his senses, deprived his limbs of volition, and in less time that it took the deceitful whore who had drugged him to slip from his lecherous grasp he had tumbled all unconscious to the floor.

The confused babble of the prayers of the Brethren were the first thing he became aware of as he returned to consciousness, loud and importunate they prayed, all speaking at once as the pious revelatory zeal seized them, kneeling in raggle-taggle conclave, begging their divinities for success in their endeavour on this sanctified and illustrious occasion. Not that Ealdræd had the least idea of what all their demented howling and wailing was in aid of. All he need comprehend was that he had been fool enough to deliver himself into the hands of those who had now revealed themselves to be his enemies. For he was seated on the ground in the sacrificial arena and there was an iron fetter bolted around his left ankle by which he was chained to a link embedded in the floor. The full length of the chain was only a yard, so he was limited to a maximum two yards of movement; nary more than a step to either side. Apparently, he was to be a votive offering to the arcane shades and magical forces worshipped by these fat-bellied devotees of the mystic obscurities, for he had been stripped of all clothing and weapons. His kit formed a small unregarded pile up against the wall, except for his spear which was held in the podgy hands of one of the Brethren nearby.

Ealdræd looked around the circular room, glowering ferociously at all and sundry. The men of Aenglia knew how to hate, aye, and how to bear a grudge, and the tribe to which Ealdræd belonged, the Pæga, were sometimes called 'the aggrieved' by their neighbours because of their reputation for carrying a feud and bearing a rancorous animosity for years, betimes for generations. The malevolent enmity of the gaze which Ealdræd turned upon his captors was chilling. The sibling brothers had best hope that the links of the chain were strong. But the Brethren were unaware of the Aenglian's spleen for they were preoccupied with something of much greater significance than the venomous resentment of a shrewd veteran who had been shamefully bested by a simpering wench with a pair of bouncing tits and a jug of drugged ale.

A procession was underway, three stately clergymen slow-marched majestically toward the central Alter, now freshly dressed in red silk draperies of the same colour as the canopy overhead. The priest in the middle of the three moved with the slow gait of a sleepwalker. He towered over the other two, who acted as prop-supports under each arm, holding up the central figure like human crutches. This august gentleman was the foremost member of their community, the most exalted of the inhabitants of Aberstowe Abbey, and he had come amongst them for the celebrated day that all here assembled had been praying for since Sibling Dyfed had first translated the writings contained within the Sacred Tome of Bedwyr, alchemist of centuries past, which disclosed sound biological knowledge of rarefied metaphysical mysteries undreamed of by less daring philosophers. This very day the Brethren would immortalise the genius of the Blessed Bedwyr, their spiritual ancestor, and in doing so acquire a power that would elevate them to a national stage. Religious vindication and political authority awaited them. The beating heart of all their faith was to be demonstrated on this stupendous, memorable day, and the ceremony was about to begin.

The Senior Cleric had taken his place at the Alter and the sibling brothers took up their allotted places in a circle around the room, each man equidistant from the next. The Senior Cleric was dressed in the same simple habit that all the brothers wore but in other respects he was utterly unlike them in every way. Where they were soft, he was hard; where they were slothful and self-indulgent, he was ascetic and self-mortifying; where they were obese, he was angular. He was an extraordinary person physically; a tough, raw-boned fellow of at least seven feet in height and of haughtily aristocratic bearing. He was a head taller than Ealdræd whose own stature was well-above the average. Added to which, the priest had globular reptilian eyelids that had the appearance of being bulbous slits through which dread portents, vile prognostications, and polluted auguries could be envisioned.

But, perchance, the soporific quality in those heavy lids had a more tangible cause, for however austerely frugal and abstemious the Senior Cleric might be in his normal way of life, today's esoteric rites had required the ingestion of potions in plentiful number. Even now he raised a clay jar to his lips and drank from it some milky fluid. It wasn't only the folk stripped naked and trussed up for ritual sacrifice who were drugged in the ceremonials of the clergy of Aberstowe. The Senior Cleric was so thoroughly intoxicated with the many holy brews and sacred medicines that he had consumed that he was stupefied with the concoction. So anesthetized was he that whilst his juniors set up a low moaning chant in unison which then grew in volume and fervour as the inspiration rose in their breasts, he in contrast stood tomblike in their midst, as still as a statue.

The euphoric revels of enchantment continued apace and the name "Okhrun, Bánfæt Wæpenbora" was shrieked repeatedly. Ealdræd had never heard the name of Okhrun before but then he was far from being schooled in the ways of sorcerers and diviners, wizards and astrologers. His only dealings with such occult conjurers had been kept firmly at arms length, plus the twenty inches of his broad-bladed knife. But that did not leave him in total ignorance of the proceedings because all the Ehngle peoples, Aenglian, Merthyan, Sæxyn, Heurtslin and Wehnbrian, all spoke a common language and he knew plain enough that the grisly title of Bánfæt Wæpenbora meant 'knight cadaver' or more literally, the 'corpse who bears arms'. That bode ill, particularly as it seemed probable that he would be martyred to this thing, whatever it might be.

Each sibling brother in turn left the circle to fetch one piece of ancient armour and carry it reverentially to the Senior Cleric, and to solemnly place it upon his body as if the act were hallowed. Yet at no time did the mournful mantra of their hymn of summoning let up. One by one they brought to him poleyn and cuisse, vambrace and cowter, breastplate and greaves, until the seven foot giant was encased in full armour. When the bassinet helmet was lowered onto his head no part of the Senior Cleric was visible; instead a knight stood there, a creature of metal. One brother remained; he brought forth a monumental broadsword the blade of which was over four feet long extended by a hilt that, necessarily, was designed for a double-handed grip. This priest, the guardian of the most holy relic, was Sibling Dyfed, the translator of the glorious Bedwyr's consecrated and sacrosanct writings. He carried the sword laid across his outstretched arms, grunting audibly under the weight despite the solemnity of the occasion, to submissively proffer the antique brand in awed and worshipful humility. It was taken from him and held aloft by the knight. Somehow it was no longer possible to think of the man in the armour as being the Senior Cleric. From where had the previously torpid and unresponsive priest found the strength to hoist up so heavy a blade? The music of the congregation's intonation became immediately much more urgent and insistent. Sibling Dyfed cast up his radiant countenance and declaimed:

"Hear us, Lord Okhrun, deathless soul of the knight whose incorporeal life cannot be claimed by the legions of Wihvir, we offer you this vessel for your return! Fill this host with your essence. Incarnate yourself!!"

Ealdræd was doing his best to follow this deranged ranting. The 'vessel' could only be the body of the Senior Cleric, since no one was paying any attention to the Aenglian. They were weaving the spell of revitalization to raise the disembodied soul of this Bánfæt Wæpenbora, the spirit of the long departed Lord Okhrun. Let the dead stay dead, was Ealdræd's view. But not of these priests, who were intent on resurrecting this Okhrun's soul and housing it in the abstinent flesh of their own Senior Cleric.

As if in response to Sibling Dyfed's ringing invocation the knight sprang into action, writhing and growling profusely. The Brethren sang their holy joy at such irrefutable proof of the visitation of Okhrun's ghostly presence, invested in the very bones of the leader of their conclave. For his part, Ealdræd wondered if the compound in the Senior Cleric's potion was hallucinogenic for he raved like a madman, or could it be that he was truly crossing over the astral planes of existence from one material dimension to another, immaterial?

Despite his earnest scepticism, Ealdræd felt the icy shiver of gooseflesh on his skin as the fanatical Dyfed threw himself upon the ground, followed by all his Brethren, and ardently importuned Okhrun's acceptance of their gift.

"Whilst we live, so will you live. Not until the breath of life is stilled in all those who utter this pledge, shall your reign on earth be ended. Our souls are the guarantor and for as long as they are ours to command you shall have governance upon the earth."

The knight was shaking like a man in a fit, the broadsword across his shoulders in a pose of crucifixion. The dedication was reaching its peak as the enthusiasts became fevered in their earnest entreaties for the ethereal apparition of the Bánfæt Wæpenbora to materialise. And then it came. The soul of Okhrun, the knight-cadaver, raised incarnate in the mortal tissue of the Senior Cleric; resurrected in his body by the prayers and enchantments of the Brethren.

The armoured figure stepped jerkily forward like a puppeteer's toy, its limbs answering to a will not it's own. In mindless malignancy it swung the finely-honed edge of the gigantic sword to the left and to the right in devastating arcs, sweeping the sharp iron from side to side blindly. Something had seized control of those arms and legs and turned the human mannequin into a threshing machine of imminent fatality. Ealdræd muttered an obscene profanity and made the sign of the sevenfold preservation of Buldr. This was no creature born in the Well of Mægen, the baptismal font of all that is natural. This travesty had been drawn up from some reeking charnel pit of damnation, and it was reeling its way toward the naked man who was chained to the ground. Trapped without hope, the Aenglian knew he had met his end. He could but stand and spit at the harbinger of death. But then the podgy priest who had possession of the mercenary's spear snapped out a word to attract the old soldier's attention and hurled the spear over to him. Ealdræd caught the weapon in flight, whirling it expertly around and down in one smooth trajectory into the on-guard position.

And so all was explained. The Brethren must test and understand the success of their spell. They had wanted a fighting man so that they could test the destructive power and invincibility of the Bánfæt Wæpenbora against an opponent of serious worth. Two candidates had obliging arrived, Winfrid and Ealdræd, so the sibling brothers had encouraged them to settle their quarrel in combat as this would confirm which of the two was the stronger so that he might then face their resuscitated dweller of the netherworld in mortal combat; if mortal were a word to be employed of such a spectre, to test the indestructible mettle of the resuscitated Okhrun. The Brethren knew perfectly well it would kill Ealdræd, of course, they merely wanted to witness what an armed man of skill and experience could do against their unholy champion before being severed in twain by that colossal broadsword. Nothing, was their expectation. It was also their fervent hope.

For the Aenglian, such explanations no longer counted. He was chained to the ground right in front of something that purported to be the undying essence of a dead lord inside the iron-clad frame of an armoured man. There was no choice; he had to fight.

The Brethren set up a chorus of exuberant chanting, rasping and repetitive, and the creature took a step toward the man with the spear, its physical control over the body it inhabited more assured now. The sibling brothers were ecstatic, enraptured; their divinely conjured animated corpse was certain to make them the most powerful order in the land, from the endless mists of Northern Bvanwey to the twilight dunes of the Torvig Steppes. They would slay their enemies without limit though they depopulate the world, and glory in their righteous ascendancy. Kings would kneel to them and potentates grovel. Grasp would exceed ambition. Their dirge resonated in their hearts. It all began with the destruction of this uncivilized oaf for the wonder and grandeur of god.

The phoenix leviathan that was the Lord Okhrun rushed at Ealdræd in a fury, bringing down the broadsword two-fisted overhead as if to cleave the world apart but the reflexes of the seasoned warrior meant that when the iron descended it crashed uselessly into the stone ground with an ear-splitting clang. Having side-stepped the blow, with the daemon's arms still extended, the Aenglian drove his spear at what he knew from his long experience of military affairs was one of the two weak points in such otherwise all-protective armour; the seven foot ash pole with its razor sharp tip drove up under the arm, into the armpit and up through the shoulder. It struck home true. It could not reach the heart from that angle but it tore through the muscle and bone of the shoulder with a fearful shredding of flesh. But the colossus spun round as if unharmed and drew back its sword again. Was it the numerous strange potions that the Senior Cleric had drunk that made him so oblivious to pain, drugged insensate and sedated? Or was it that the Bánfæt Wæpenbora was not a thing of nature and one cannot kill that which is already dead?

The next blow cut laterally from right to left at chest height and had Ealdræd been struck by it he would have been cleaved to the spine, but dropping instantly to his haunches he felt death whisk by inches above his head. There was no chance for him to counter because the behemoth was sent running forward by his own momentum which took him right passed the crouching spearman. And then a bizarre and incredible thing happened. Having staggered several steps beyond Ealdræd the wraith did not turn again to face him but blundered onwards in heedless rampage to slash the throat out of one of the priests and then stamp his head to a pulp as the man was savagely trampled underfoot.

The fiendish soul of the zombie, acting in unreasoning blind hostility to everyone and everything, driven by an inchoate malice and the insatiable urge to kill, had no masters and took no sides. All that was mortal was its enemy. It swung the biting iron blade in huge sweeps, scything down the adherents of Bedwyr in a blizzard of hellish destruction.

The broadsword sliced through Sibling Bertolf, cutting the man literally in twain. Another monk, frozen in disbelief, was decapitated in one lethal swipe of the sword. The undead Lord Okhrun, the knight-cadaver returned from the shadowless transparencies of the void, was not a weapon to be used for the political machinations of men; it was purest hell-spawn, killing whoever was in front of it. It had attacked Ealdræd because he was the closest but once its first target was out of sight, it addressed those newly presented to it. Sibling Amleth was the next to die, with a terrible stab through the bowels. In mere seconds the chamber of the sacrificial Alter was a heaving, seething mass of terrified clerics, screaming in abject horror as the berserker slaughtered its way through the Brethren.

Sibling Dyfed ran to the Alter and with the strength of stark fear lifted it high and dashed it to the ground, splintering it into pieces, then started chanting the prayer of undoing, only to be stopped short when one of his legs was hacked off. He collapsed shrieking and pouring blood from the appalling wound. The remainder of the Brethren were too petrified and disorganised to recite the necessary enchantments to break the spell and de-animate the corpse, they thought only to flee but for all their efforts to do so, they could not escape through the single door in the wall of the arena because there were three bodies piled up against the door, killed in the act of trying to open it, and they were blocking the door with the solid weight of their mortal remains.

The butchering of the other priests was a massacre witnessed by Ealdræd alone, their puny bodies rent asunder. The mercenary, wise in battle-craft, had the good sense to stay crouched low and inconspicuous in the midst of the chaos. But it would matter little in the end. Shackled as he was, the implacable wraith must reach him eventually; he might be the last to die but death was none the less certain. When the final sibling brother had been hewn to pieces the giant looked across the room at the mutilated and dying clergy whose obscene sorcery had brought it into being and saw only the one living thing left to kill.

The Aenglian had no more leeway than a step of two yards in either direction but three times the dead knight swung at the man and three times the lithe soldier of fortune dodged aside, his spear primed to punch home should a target open up, making no attempt to parry the oncoming blows but gambling on sheer speed to evade the attack and stay alert for the possibility of a decisive counter-strike. It came when the colossus steadied itself to regain its balance after a particularly powerful cut at its frustratingly elusive enemy's head had gone astray. The groin, the second of the weak points in the otherwise invulnerable armour, was momentarily unguarded. As fast as human muscle could propel it and as accurately as human eye could guide it, the spearhead tore into the target and Ealdræd had skewered the foul thing through the lower abdomen, a grievous wound ripping up through the pelvic bone and cracking through the hip. It was an injury that would have disabled any living man, but to Ealdræd's resigned desolation the wound seemingly had no effect upon this filth of sorcery, this creation of necromancy and witchery; it barely even slowed the monster. The Bánfæt Wæpenbora was yet on his feet, cutting and swiping in all directions with the four-foot broadsword and the man could not avoid this threshing machine for long.

It was at that moment that the hideously maimed Sibling Dyfed, whose lifeblood had been draining from him all the while from the stump that was once his leg, finally expired from loss of blood. He was the last of the Brethren to die. With his decease all who had cast the enchantment of the resurrection of the Lord Okhrun breathed no more.

The suit of armour that stood before Ealdræd went flaccid; then in a bizarrely fluid dissolution, wilted and crumpled to the floor as if all the bones had been removed from it. Suddenly there was nothing to hold it up and it slipped noisily into a heap. The Aenglian glared down at the irregular pile of metal as if expecting it to rear up in homicidal rage like all the furies of the underworld. But there was no hint of any activity within the metal shell; all action ceased. It was an incomprehensible mystification; a perplexity beyond solution. But then something was recalled to his mind; something that Sibling Dyfed, the fanatic, had said just minutes earlier.

"Whilst we live, so will you live. Not until the breath of life is stilled in all those who utter this pledge, shall your reign on earth be ended."

But the pledge-makers were no more, and with their demise so too had departed that which they had conjured. Could it be so? Could such an obscenity to raise the hackles be true? Had it simply been the Senior Cleric's absolute faith, his passionate, obsessive belief that Okhrun would cease when the brethren were dead, that had caused him to perish? Or was it their magic that had truly animated the soul of the Bánfæt Wæpenbora within the cleric's mortal shell and once those that had summoned it were all dead their spell had ceased to be in effect and the corpse who bears arms had returned to the unspeakable void of the netherworld from whence it had come to await its next conjuring?

It was more than a simple soldier could fathom and Ealdræd vexed not his head with such conundrums. It was sufficient to be whole when the Brethren were dismembered. His stars had been with him. Saved, by lucky happenstance!

But how to release himself from the chain? His spear would snap like a twig if he were to attempt to use it to burst the iron that held him. The infernal giant's sword, however, just within reach of his eager fingers, was more suited to the task. He placed the point of the blade under the last link of the chain, embedded in the stone at his feet, and using it as a lever he threw his full weight and strength upon the hilt. The strain of iron upon iron set up a banshee wail of tortured metal grimly in keeping with the execrably diabolical events just witnessed and the broadsword bowed but did not break. Exerting himself to the utmost in his desire to be gone from this cursed place, he hauled for all he was worth and slowly a slight crack appeared between link and stone. Encouraged, he laid on with renewed will and with a rending and a buckling sound he wrenched the damnable link from its rock, sending himself crashing to the floor as he did so. He was up in a trice and, somewhat encumbered by the shackle and chain, dressed himself from the pile of his clothes that were still where they had been left by the wall. Properly attired and armed once more, he gave not a glance to the tangled debris of jumbled carcasses scattered about the chamber but pulled aside the bodies that barred the little wooden door and thence made a swift exit into the rest of the Abbey.

He stomped ferociously through the deathly silent monk's habitation, his face as dark as thunder, all ears and eyes to catch any sibling brothers who might yet remain. It was certain that there would be apprentices, novices, and lay-brothers about the place somewhere. These religious orders were always a nest of rats. There was nothing he could do about removing the fetter bolted around his ankle nor the yard of chain still attached to it; that would take a smithy's tools and skills to remove. He must first recover his horse, thereafter to ride in search of a blacksmith. So, trailing the chain behind him he made his noisy way through the corridors, wishing he had paid more attention to the route he had taken when he had followed Sibling Bertolf through this maze just an hour before.

He cast about various passages hoping to recognise one of them and taking the opportunity to help himself to such portable valuables as he happened across, including some nice ornamented candlesticks that would fetch a tidy sum in whatever town he rode through next. As he finally struck upon the hallway that he realised would lead him back to the main gate he heard a startled yelp from the rear and turned to see a couple of pregnant wenches scampering off down an adjacent corridor. It put him in mind of the injury he had received from one of their number and for the time it took him to trudge, chain clanking, to the gateway and freedom he repeatedly cast a jaundiced eye about him for the ghost-worshipping strumpet who had brought him the drugged ale but there was no further sign or smell of any of the women. A pity. He had a score to settle with that harpy.

Chapter 3

Witchery in Wehnbria

The urgently rhythmic slap, slap, slap of flesh on flesh was driven by the one thing more frenzied and mindless than fear; it was driven by ecstatic sexual pleasure. On a splintered wooden bedstead, its timbers creaking like a banshee in a high wind, closeted in a shuttered private room upstairs at the Pint Pot Tavern in Ockerham, a self-gratifying indulgence in copulation was being enjoyed in as much quantity as a common soldier could afford. The voraciously carnal greybeard, his braided hair and beard marking him out as an Aenglian from the north west of the continent, was sating his barbarous desires with a trollop of the town. His broad chest heaved and his pelvis rolled under a whipcord waist as he pandered to his ripest inclinations, piling lustily into the soft, yielding hind-quarters of the compliant tavern wench, driving his bucking loins rhythmically like a war-horse at the gallop. His muscular buttocks flexed and pushed his groin forward in potent thrusts with such speed and venom that one might almost expect the woman kneeling face down on the mattress to be dislocated at the hips. The slattern moaned and gasped as she clutched at the bedclothes, took the weight of it on her braced arms, arched her back to ease his passage inside her, and bore up under the strain in a womanly fashion. She was experienced in harlotry and could likely have taken an actual war-horse from the rear had occasion demanded it.

Still, her customer was no youngster, she judged him to be past forty in the maturity of his years, and she had thought when she had first taken his coin earlier that week that she would barely notice a fuck from such an old man. But the veteran had turned out to have a sting in his tail. He had arrived at the Pint Pot wrapped in a long woollen cloak against the chill of the night and she had neglected to pay attention to the glint in his eye and the spring in his step when he had followed her up the rickety staircase to the overnight rooms. When she had seen him stripped, however, it had been plain that she must revise her initial opinion. Brawny in the arms and across the shoulders, he was lean and sinewy everywhere else, carrying numerous scars but looking as tough as an Ahkrani ox-gristle steak. He had bought her four times since his arrival in Ockerham, aye, and bought her sister in prostitution, Noemie, just as often, and each time the alehouse whores had been forced to ride the whirlwind. But being girls whose interest in their trade was not limited solely to the acquisition of hard currency, they had found their service to him had more than pecuniary advantages. He had rapidly assumed the mantle of their most favoured client and the two young women had commenced to engage in some slight competition over him.

The baggage currently surrendering her comely flesh to his appetites was called Annis, meaning 'chaste', a name to which she had lost all honest claim in her adolescence as soon as her breasts had grown, but such were the times. Now in her early twenties, she was a ruddy-complexioned country wench, naturally voluptuous and built for her trade. Annis was a native of the town of Ockerham and sported the red hair and fair freckled skin so common in that part of the world.

The second girl of the house was Noemie, whose name meant 'pleasing' or 'pleasant' which she undoubtedly was to look upon. A natural beauty she had only to pout those tempting lips and flaunt those provocative breasts to have her clients feeling like colts in springtime. Dark haired and dark eyed she had a sensuality that bespoke an inclination to find delight in carnal wickedness and a tantalising willingness to submit or to dominate as her gentlemen required. As her name disclosed, Noemie was of Geulten heritage, having been born in a small fishing village on the coast of the Barony of Langelais and taken as slave during a raid by buccaneers when she was hardly more than a child. Brave souls those buccaneers must have been to risk the wrath of the famous 'sea-barons' of the noble House of Langelais with a pirate-raid on their shores, but taken she had been along with many another and Noemie had spent the rest of her young life in the brothels and trollop-shops of Wehnbria. The inn-keeper here at the Pint Pot Tavern, a jovial rogue by the name of Oeric, had bought her two summers since and she had settled in to make the place her home. She did not know exactly how old she was but was approximately the same age as Annis. Certainly, the two girls were in their physical prime.

As the landlord and host of the establishment the mendacious but cheerfully bright and breezy Oeric ruled the roost with a paternal bonhomie. He was a friend to all his customers and if he was paid out for his friendship in coin of the realm, well, his many regulars didn't seem to mind. To the effete gentry of Amsburgh no doubt the Pint Pot, had they been burdened with the misfortune of patronising its malodorous premises, might have seemed a three-story rabbit hutch for the bog-trotters, villeins and serfs who spent their misbegotten lives up to their knees in muddy ditches to harvest the produce for which the gentry were pleased to underpay them. But to the hard-labouring residents of Ockerham in the Eorldom of the Marches the Pint Pot Tavern was a rollicking, beer-swilling, song-chorusing palace of gaiety and revels. When not attending to patrons in one of the two chambers upstairs the buxom Annis was a rather fine singer, although she invariably warbled songs that were in the coarsest of taste, and the high-stepping Noemie would dance upon a table top flashing her legs flirtatiously till the cheers rumbled in the rafters.

When the degree of inebriation had reached sporting levels the challenges would be proposed amongst the company for a sally at *þa cnifas*, the Sæxyn game of 'knives'. This was a pastime which arose from the Sæxyn habit of shaving the upper lip. Whereas elsewhere in the world only priests, women and boys wore a hairless face, it was the long-standing practice of the Sæxyns to barber their moustaches, although they retained their beards. Consequently, every Sæxyn man had a knife which he used for the partial removal of his whiskers. In the game of *þa cnifas* these shaving knives would be thrown blindfold at an opponent, the two competitors, their heads masked by hoods of thin sackcloth, taking turns to throw until one of them was struck. The knives being generally fairly small, wounds were usually very slight. It was only rarely that someone lost an eye.

There was a variation on this form of contest that was especially popular in Ockerham. It was called *sagol* or 'cudgels' because it was played with solid wooden clubs about the size of a wine bottle and it was the more damaging form of the game because the clubs were hurled quiet hard enough to bruise ribs and break noses. Oeric the landlord had once had most of his teeth smashed out during the course of a particularly exciting bout of *sagol*. He bore the injury without complaint, it having been acquired in the noble cause of sport.

The Pint Pot Tavern was easily the most entertaining and pleasurable hostelry in this quarter of town and Ealdræd of the Pæga judged himself fortunate to have stumbled across a watering hole so full of concupiscent sex, liberality of drink and flavoursome belly-stuffing after his long drought in all three respects. If he did not go so far as to make a pig of himself, he at least took a good look long around the sty.

Four days earlier the dissolute veteran had taken up temporary residence in the Pint Pot to spend whatever remained of his money because he had almost reached the end of his long journey from his native homelands in Aenglia to hire out his spear-arm in the war that was shortly to be fought between Wehnbria and the Duchy of Oénjil; or rather, in the war that was shortly to be *resumed* between Wehnbria and the Duchy of Oénjil because the two nations had been at each others throats for generations.

The purpose of his journey was written on him for all to see. Travelling alone on horseback, of necessity he wore his weapons openly. A seven foot spear of well-seasoned ash with eighteen inches of sharpened iron at its head hung from a saddle-sheath at the side of his horse. The sheath also contained two short javelins for throwing. On the pommel of his saddle was hung a scratched and scarred wooden buckler made from hardened teak and reinforced with a raised iron boss in the centre. A twenty-inch knife snuggled against his belly in a scabbard at his belt. These armaments were as typical of his race as the long plaited braids of his hair and beard.

From Aenglia he had come but not the tribal territory of his own clan, the Pæga, from which he had been formally banished into permanent political exile some twenty years previously, and in which he had not since set foot. Still the rest of his own country was open to him and, despite all his constant wanderings throughout a life spent as a mercenary which had encompassed nations and provinces that were as unimaginably remote to those he had left behind as was the moon, places scarce heard of or believed to exist by any but those whose horse's feet had trod their soil, he had repeatedly found his way back to Aenglia and the home of his heart. But never to tarry there long. Soon enough he would be a-horse once again, as now, to find wages for his services as a professional throat-slitter wherever there was mass murder that would pay.

There was a need at present in the Wehnbrian Marches for the likes of Ealdræd of Aenglia. In that southernmost land of the Ehngle peninsula, where the populace lived under the rule of the three kingless Lordships of Wehnbria, there was constant skirmishing along the border, for to the east lay the Duchy of Oénjil, a vassal state of the great Geulten kingdom of Bhourgbon under its ten-year old monarch, Henri, the boy king. The duchy was sworn to a feudal obligation of homage, fealty and allegiance for which it received its honour as a nation-state and sworn pledges of mutual protection, not only with Bhourgbon but with all three royal crowns of the Geulten Alliance.

The realms of Aenglia, Merthya, Heurtslin, Sæxyny, and Wehnbria were all of the race of peoples known as the Ehngle, who occupied the great peninsula in the north west of the continent, all of whom shared a common language, though with a multiplicity of dialects. The realms beyond Ehngle territories to the east that occupied much of the central portion of the continent were the three powerful kingdoms of the Geulten and their colonies, dominions and dependencies, all of whom also shared a common language, of which they were inordinately proud and of which there was an even greater diversity of accent. The Geulten were the hereditary enemies of the Ehngle and they used the two smaller vassal states of the Fiefdom of Vespaan and the Duchy of Oénjil, the two Geulten lands immediately adjacent to the lands of the Ehngle, as a buffer betwixt their own grandiose kingdoms and the hostile Ehngle to the west.

Because Wehnbria and Heurtslin, the country to the north of Wehnbria, were the Ehngle nations that shared an eastern border with the Geulten nations, they were the ones who were most frequently at war; the Heurtslin against the Vespaan forces, ruled by their feudal liege Count Gustave du Sanhk, and the Wehnbrians against those of the Duchy of Oénjil, ruled by the Duke Etienne en Dieu. Sporadic warfare had erupted recurrently and persistently during the whole of the last turbulent century until it was largely seen as inevitable and was accepted as a fact of life amongst the populations of those four nations.

King Håkon of the Heurtslin had fought the forces of Count Gustave to a standstill a decade ago and since then an uneasy stalemate had existed between them, broken only by intermittent skirmishing. This was possible because the circumstances in the north were not so conducive to warfare. The length of the border between Heurtslin and the Fiefdom was a mere three hundred miles and in places it was too impenetrably thick with trees to allow for the passage of an army. The immeasurably tall silver-fir trees that flourished there shrouded the terrain in the permanent darkness of shadow at ground level. Some reckless Generals had tried to burn a way through with forest fires but had succeeded only in getting themselves a scorching. A large body of men could cross the frontier only by marching over one of the rocky passes at altitude where the wall of timber thinned out. The situation was made still more obstructive for Count Gustave because the Heurtslin capital city, Skælig, was located directly in the path of any army approaching from the east and it was one of the most heavily fortified and militarily armoured cities in the world. No Geulten army had ever seriously threatened it.

Historically the ale-sodden whiskery belligerence of the Wehnbrian Lordships towards the Geulten of Oénjil had told mostly in their favour, to the considerable detriment in reputation of the Duke's ancestors. Sovereignty in kingless Wehnbria was exercised by three Eorls of illustrious stature, each of whom had his own province; Eorl Caridian of the Eorldom of Shrewford in the western region, which included the immense mercantile Port of Chiltegn where the River Wven emptied itself into the ocean; Eorl Aykin of the Eorldom of Chestbury, who ruled over the rich harbour cities of Milcombe and Tarhampton on the southern coast, and inland across the central section of the country; and Eorl Atheldun, the great March Lord whose word was law for the full length of the Eorldom of the Marches. Wehnbria was a maritime nation, making the realms of the Eorl Caridian and the Eorl Aykin prosperous indeed, but they paid generous bounty in cash and men to the March Lord for it was he who stood between them and the enemy in the east so that all their wealth was dependent upon him for its security. The term 'March' was derived from the ancient term 'mearc,' meaning 'boundary' and it was understood by all, for what could be more obvious, that the armies of the Marches were a bristling boundary of spiked and bladed iron that represented and defended not merely the Eorldom itself but all of Wehnbria. From grandfather to grandson, aside from an occasional lapse, it had stood firm against the Geulten.

Last autumn this traditional Wehnbrian dominance had been badly fractured when the army of Oénjil, its ranks swollen by a prodigious influx of Bhourgbon irregulars, had scored a major success for the Geulten at the battle of Fontónil; one which they had been unable to capitalise upon cololy due to the onset of winter. But they were expected back this summer to continue to press their advantage. Buoyed by the prestige of the previous year's victory Duke Etienne had found himself able to attract further military support from both Philippe, King of Guillaime, and wily old King Béri of Eildres himself, so that the army of Oénjil could truly be said to be a coalition of the three crowns of the Geulten. To make matters worse for the Ehngle domains, there had been ruinous political upset in Wehnbria these twelve months past and this had seriously undermined that country's capacity to defend itself. Thus there was an urgent need for mercenaries to reinforce its beleaguered border and defend not merely the Marches and Wehnbria, aye, but even the Ehngle peninsula itself.

The word had gone out northward and westward as far as the mountains and valleys of Merthya, the pinewoods and lakeshores of Heurtslin, even to the deep forests and seaside villages of Aenglia, until many a likely lad had kissed his weeping mother a sad farewell and left the barren dirt of his family's farm or the impoverished hovel that had been his home since birth, and set his hungry footsteps to the faraway south for the mustering. But not all were callow boys and beardless youths. Amongst them were men of experience and ability; hard men with the skill of combat in their hands and quick death on the points and razor edges of their spears, axes, swords, and knives.

As Ealdræd had journeyed down from Aenglia, through Merthya and into Sæxyny the shortest route to the mustering point of the Wehnbrian army in the Marches had lain directly southeast but there had been much talk of a plague in eastern Sæxyny during the winter, and with pestilence came famine, so Ealdræd had opted for the longer but safer route joining the Herebeorht road south as it ran parallel with the River Wven through Sæxyny as far as the provincial protectorate city-state of Cerdyc on the borders of Wehnbria before he finally turned his horse's head southeast.

Cerdyc was built right over the Wven so that the river actually formed part of its defensive walls. The waterway also served as the perfect merchant's highway for the Cerdycites to trade along, all the way from Lake Rhen in central Merthya to the port of Chiltegn in south-western Wehnbria from whence their trade goods could be transported overseas. In addition to which Cerdyc sat squat like a bloated toad catching flies at the western end of the Herebeorht road, the primary mercantile artery to the east, a road that traversed more than half the length of Sæxyny and extended all the way into Heurtslin. No trade route was more profitable.

The city of the Cerdycites was a notorious den of trickery and double-dealing, full of thieves and swindlers, cheats, frauds and charlatans. The protectorate was an autonomous political state protected both diplomatically and militarily against Sæxyn incursion by the Wehnbrian Lordships in exchange for which the strategically useful protectorate accepted stringent obligations of trade and political support. Officially it retained its sovereignty but in real terms it was caught between its two more powerful neighbours and could hope for no better than to play one off against the other. Over time this circumstance had fostered an ethnic Cerdycite society that valued and celebrated fraudulence, dishonesty and treachery as civic virtues, and had bred a culture of deception and duplicity that seemed to infect the character of every last citizen of the city.

When Ealdræd came within sight of the thick stone walls of Cerdyc he met with a caravan of more than three dozen long-axle coach-wagons, four-wheel drays, and two-wheel tumbrels laid up upon the road. They were Ymbærnan, the nomadic folk found all over the continent, whose fancily-painted carts were their only native soil and whose camp-fire oratory was their only government. They were a travelling nation who had no country of their own, though it was believed that their origins lay in such impossibly faraway places as Tehlitz and Ahkran and the Murgl tribes of the Khevnic Steppes; lands so distant that they were close to mythical in the minds of the western peasantry. Certainly the skin colouring of the Ymbærnan had that swarthily walnut brown tint that could not be mistaken for mere sun tan.

This particular band, a transient community of one hundred and fifty or so, were spread out across both sides of the road, having spent the last two days there. The gaily dressed men sat at their ease while the darkly enshrouded women scurried busily among their cooking pots and the skylark children ran hither and yon babbling excitedly in their own tongue. Ymbærnan rarely learned more of the language of the countries they occupied than was needed for them to sell and barter their craft goods. The exotic caravans of the Ymbærnan were perhaps the most conspicuous of the extraordinary influx of migrants making colonial inroads into the western lands in recent years, generating much dissent from the indigenous populations, and they were met with a distrust fuelled by the Ymbærnan's own flaunted refusal to accommodate their ways to the ethnicities of the lands they settled in, retaining the overtly alien character of their presence with a pointed rejection of western ways that seemed deliberately provocative to those whose national identity had been rejected. This was especially true of the women of the Ymbærnan who were heavily veiled so that nothing but their eyes could be seen, and this was a constant affront to the cultures of the Ehngle and the Geulten. Not only was such self-concealment highly suspicious in a dangerous world, but it was also an abusive insult to everyone they met, for it declared publicly that the veiled one would not tolerate the unworthy eyes of other people to stain her with their odious gaze.

The Pæga warrior on the enormous warhorse felt the provocation as much as anyone else. But Ealdræd was a traveller here too, albeit as an individual not as a people, and so he would stretch a point and meet the Ymbærnan half way. It would be different if he found them rattling their cartwheels over Aenglian soil, but here in Sæxyny it might be said that they were all foreigners together, so to speak, so if their scabrous children refrained from throwing stones at him, he would refrain from cutting their throats for them.

The Ymbærnan caravan had been forced to curb its progress because no foreign traffic was being permitted to enter the city of Cerdyc at present on account of this week being a holy festival during which the citizens purged themselves of all impious taints of alien culture. Although Cerdycite merchants and traders roamed freely through Sæxyny to such an extent that many Sæxyns feared some darker political purpose behind their ubiquity, the city-state itself had strict regulations upon the number of foreigners they would permit to enter their own sovereign territory. This hypocrisy they felt legitimate due to the special circumstances of their position as a small power surrounded by much stronger nation-states.

For the holy festival the entire population spent four days and nights continuously fasting and praying. When not so engaged, they participated in numerous civil processions in which everyone crawled on their hands and knees through the streets in penitence for their sins. As an Aenglian, Ealdræd would have to wait upon the completion of these devotions before he would be allowed to enter the city for provisions. He decided not to tarry. Truth be told, he was pleased to have a reason to ride on by without stopping for even a single night in so a wicked a place as Cerdyc, so steeped in perfidious piety. Instead he turned his mightily dignified blue-roan stallion, Hengustir, away from the river that they had been following for almost a month and out across the broad grassy pastures and wildflower meadows of Wehnbria, for they still had many long miles of riding before they would find the army at muster.

Most of the countryside that the man and horse negotiated in their steady progress directly eastward was a tranquil expanse of hill and dale, dotted hither and yon with the numerous fields and plots of

74

agriculture, tillage, orchards and animal husbandry that made this region the food basket for the rest of Wehnbria. It was as pleasing to the eye as it was made for easy riding. For a dozen days or more the roan horse, who stood a mammoth seventeen hands tall and whose blue-grey colouring could instil fear in a superstitious peasant from the first snort of his nostrils, clip-clopped his way unhurriedly in peace and comfort. All the inhabitants to be seen in these fertile valleys were invariably peasants; farm labourers tilling the fields and strongly inclined to avoid conversation with the menacing-looking stranger riding by on a steed of such demonic aspect. This ostracism suited the mercenary, for he had no proclivity to converse on the subject of turnip-blight or worm-pest with the tribe of slow-witted mudlarks who spent their lives digging in the dirt. He continued easterly into the open scrub landscape of the Wehnbrian moors, wearing nothing but his gambeson tunic and cross-gartered leggings as the spring weather turned warmer, swaying gently with the ambling rhythm of the metronome walking pace of his giant stallion.

The preponderance of the major cities and urban municipalities of Wehnbria were in the southern shires of the country, especially along the sea-coast, rich from the maritime trades. Ealdræd's route now took him over the northern stretches of the Eorldom of Chestbury, sweeping tracts of unenclosed acreage extending to the horizon; a part of his lordship's domain to which the Eorl Aykin paid less heed than elsewhere, the vast moorland being poor hunting grounds where civilized dwellings were scarce. The Eorl's subjects hereabouts were scattered wide amid the unsheltered heath that was fit only for the grazing of cattle and the herding of sheep that gave the local folk their living. Ealdræd took a further fortnight to navigate this unregarded district of Eorl Aykin's jurisdiction, the majority of this section of his journey again undertaken in uneventful solitude.

The one conspicuous exception to this isolation on the moors was the fact that there was a deal of disorder and unrest every few days as another and yet another column of refugees rattled westward in carts and wagons piled high with their belongings and the detritus of city living, fleeing the imminent conflict with the Oénjil and their allies. It was by no means unusual for merchants, tradesmen, and similar cowardly scum to relocate their stock and businesses to safer locations when war threatened, but these fellows were rife with disconcerting rumours of the certain fall of the border defences and the inescapable loss of the Marches to the swarthy perfumed dogs of Geulten who, the refugees swore, would meet no opposition if they should invade this year. All of the convoys of migrants carried tales of how the capricious and vacillating Wehnbrian nobility had fallen into the coils of internecine conflict at the very moment when they should be bound faithfully together in steadfast union for the conservation of their homeland.

One name in particular he heard repeated by each new procession of refugees as they swore the culpability of those who had beset them with sore miseries. It was a name he had never heard tell of before but in the days to come he would hear of little else. It was the name of Maev de Lederwyrhta.

A courtesan from the Duchy of Bhel, this woman had apparently raised an uproar throughout the realm. Already notorious amongst the kingdoms of the Geulten, she had now cast her shadow over the sweet green fields of Wehnbria, and a black, gloomy crow's beak of a silhouette it must be, to be sure, if the talk of the asylum seekers were to be believed. From all the cities, towns and villages between here and the picket lines of the tents of the army of Duke Etienne en Dieu came an intermittent stream of refugees all of whom had heard some version of the terrible truth about the siren seductress and occult conjurer, Maev de Lederwyrhta.

"A spectral wraith of a woman from the icy catacombs of Hálsian," warned a stonemason from Cabham, "and a true bride of the Lord Wihvir, the corruptor of spirits."

"The most beautiful woman on earth", declared a Thornford silversmith in rapture, "and the most evil".

"Where natural women had a vagina," insisted a weaver from Penbury, "it was said that the Bhelenese jade had a pit that was the entrance to hell. That was how she had been able to claim the hearts and minds of gentlemen of worth and power throughout the Geulten nations, aye, and of the crowned heads, too."

"She had a collection of men's souls stored in clay jars," swore a Tunlow potter conspiratorially, "their cork stoppers sealed with wax."

"A banshee apparition in the form of a woman," whispered a baker of the town of Sodmoor emphatically, "with no blood and no heartbeat."

There seemed to be no limit to the immensity of the supernatural abominations of which this Maev de Lederwyrhta had been guilty in her machinations to do down the Eorldoms of Wehnbria, and if there was one person on the road to the Marches who had a kindly word to say about her, Ealdræd never met him. Exactly how this foreign fiend's witchery had brought the country to its present low position, none were quite sure. But then who could fathom the secret ways of the wizard's craft? It was publicly known that she had done this deed, and that was enough. And now there was nothing but defeat and destruction ahead for the Eorldoms and honest folk had no choice but to flee for their lives.

Ealdræd had heard stories of this sort all his life in sundry assorted languages in as many different places in the world, whenever the citizenry was gripped with foreboding at impending war and resentful about the disruption to their money-grubbing businesses. It gave him neither worry nor amusement. Indeed, the journey had become wearisome in its monotony. He stopped at farmsteads to eat and sleep but the food was as tasteless as the women were ugly. They reminded him of their own herds of ponderously bovine hornless cattle. There was nothing to interest or succour an old mercenary who, as his journey proceeded over tedious weeks, had sore-developed a mood for a little distraction and disport.

So little in the way of entertainment had presented itself along the road that by the time he was once again riding through a slightly more populated area where perchance there was diversion to be had for the purchase, Ealdræd found himself at a rough guess all but thirty miles or so from his final destination and still with money in his purse; too much money. He did not want to have any coin in hand when he signed up for soldiery as he would only lose it in the gambling that beset all armies, no matter what the war, and the Aenglian veteran, who despised the false optimism of the gratuitous wager, begrudged the waste of good coin in a pastime from which he took no pleasure.

It was in this state of mind that the frustrated man in the saddle of the ghost-pale horse had ridden into the small township of Ockerham, about thirty miles short of the muster in the Marches, determined that when he rode hence it would be with no more than a few coppers in his possession; just sufficient for a meal or two before he reached the army. Thus, in a spirit of libertine resolution, he had embarked upon a four day debauch crammed with drinking, eating, fornication, and all manner of playful amusements and frolicsome delights. He had quaffed, chewed, and shafted his way through his purse of coin, a good two thirds of it spent between the spreading thighs of Annis and Noemie, the two flatteringly eager upstairs-wenches at the Pint Pot Tavern until the head of his cock was red raw from fucking and his knees had lost their sap. He had not stinted, nor had he regretted a groatæ's worth. It was money well spent in an uncertain life.

His debauch had been glorious but ultimately it had run its course, as all pleasure must, with the depletion of passion coinciding nicely on this occasion with the emptying of his purse. He had used up the last he could spare of both his coin and his semen on a final lusty merry-go-round with Annis, and if he didn't fuck her till he broke her back it wasn't from want of trying. This being as satisfying a farewell as could be wished, he resolved to leave Ockerham, a place of fond memories and a town likely to foster an Aenglian bastard or two come winter.

Or so he assumed. But at the very point of his departure in the pallid light of the first glimmerings of dawn he was disturbed by an unforeseen interruption in the tavern stables as he saddled the majestic Hengustir with a meticulous precision and ensured that all his weaponry was securely sheathed and draped in chamois leather against the adverse weather that had blown up last night and which still plucked petulantly at the tree-tops outside. The veteran's ears detected, before his eyes could see it, the muffled figure lurking in the dim shades of the horse-stalls.

Not wishing to be throttled by mistake in the semi-darkness of the stables, the girl coughed demurely to announce her unobtrusive presence, then a tearful Noemie crept out of a stall and scurried quickly over to lean in close to the tall soldier as he stood intrigued by the side of his blue-roan monster of a horse. Dressed for travel, his hooded mantle of soft leather cast his face into shadow and draped over the great girth of his shoulders, giving his lofty bearing a more than usually daunting quality. She looked up into his granite grey eyes, her characteristically serious expression one of earnest entreaty and supplication. The girl did not seek to delay him or curb his departure. On the contrary, she begged to be taken with him.

Knowing of his intention to leave at daybreak, she had risen very early and kept vigil for him. Her nubile form, still warm from her cosy bed, was wrapped around in a woollen travelling cloak over her cotton bodice and skirts but she still wore her domestic slippers. She probably owned no walking shoes. She carried a clutch-bag concealed beneath her cloak; its contents were, doubtless, not strictly speaking her own. As a slave she had no legal right to possessions whatsoever but perhaps a trinket or two had come her way during her two years in Ockerham. Her alarm and excitement was causing her to pant a little, breathing through her soft-lipped mouth. She laid a girlish hand upon his chest as she held his eyes with her own.

"Oh Sir, do you ride for the army? Let me accompany you and you shall find me a faithful and thankful servant."

Her voice was rich with the promise of deferential sexual subservience and it was pleasant to hear the lie so well told. Ealdræd knew perfectly well that the slut would be off without a backward glance the first time she met a better prospect, and with an army of lusty lads and copious quantities of virile officers carrying heavy purses it would not be long before that better prospect presented itself. A grizzled old cavalryman had little enough to offer. But that was all right with the mercenary; he did not resent her perfidy, for she was as entitled as anyone else to look to her own interest, and good luck to her. Besides, to expect honesty and trustworthiness in a whore was an absurdity. She was very likely tired of the crowd of country bumpkins and peasant oafs that made up the regular clientele of the Pint Pot and relished the chance to find others amongst the army who might improve her life's condition. As the slave of the tavern landlord her prospects were, to say the least, poor.

"And what of your lord and master, Oeric?" enquired the Aenglian mischievously.

The girl looked a little shameful but troubled at the same time and close to tears. Her sensual lips formed a tight line as if she were reluctant to let any words pass through them. Her only reply was to shake her head sharply from side to side.

The braided warrior broke into a hearty grin, gave her tits a lively squeeze, and readily agreed to her proposition. He was not averse to a few days more attention from her skilful and extensive boudoir technique. It was no hardship to the Aenglian to extend their fruitful relationship further. It would cost him nothing but her food and he knew from recent experience what it would gain him. She would soften the road ahead for as long as she lasted. Hengustir would hardly notice her additional weight.

Noemie reflected his grin with one of her own, stretching up on her tip-toes to kiss him on the cheek. Then, her anxiety getting the better of her, she glanced over her shoulder to where the daylight was creeping in through the stable doorway and pleaded:

"My love, do not let us tarry, I fear discovery!"

With the wench nestled in close behind him, a gratifying warmth from her breasts radiating steadily into his spine, the small war party set off from the Pint Pot, through the slumber-shrouded and still empty lanes and byways that led to the main road out of Ockerham, and thereafter pointed their horse's steps eastward for the battle grounds of the Marches. Last night's storm had almost blown itself into passivity with the rising of the sun and the day looked set fair for a swift journey and a good chance of reaching the mustering grounds thirty miles thither before nightfall.

They had scarcely got a mile and the sun hauled itself clear of the horizon to bathe the world in its crisp daylight before the urgent sound of rapid pony hooves caused Ealdræd and Noemie to turn in the saddle to see Oeric, the inn-keeper, thundering up behind them on a bedraggled mare that was evidently unfamiliar with such early morning exercise. The jocular landlord was not his usual humorous self this fine morning, nor anything like it, but instead his cup was brimful of froth and fury. The way he dug into the mare's flanks with his heels she would be sure to suffer bruised ribs.

There was little need to ponder the reason for the whoremaster's haste, it was written in the hunched ferocity of his body on the pony's back. The road cut in a straight line through the woodland offering an unobstructed view and at a distance of fifty yards Ealdræd could already discern the beetle-browed anger that creased and distorted the publican's visage. The fellow had a profitable business to run and he wanted his Noemie back. Ealdræd could appreciate Oeric's feelings in the matter, as far as any warrior could comprehend the workings of the mind of a parsimonious merchant, but be that as it may, the opinions of rapacious, grasping tradesmen meant not a piss in a waterfall to an Aenglian man of the spear.

Noemie, by contrast, appeared considerably exercised by her pimp's brisk arrival and Ealdræd imagined that she must be concerned as to the hard flogging she would receive if her former owner succeeded in winning her back. Ealdræd set the girl on the ground out of harm's way and moved Hengustir into the centre of the narrow dirt road. Then he sat his mount calmly to await the onslaught of the outraged tapster. The Aenglian cradled a javelin in one calloused hand.

The tavern-keeper was a hefty brute, fleshy but brawny. His bald head and rotten gums belied his comparative youth, at less than thirty years. Perhaps it was this that caused him, with ill-advised confidence, to charge headlong at the greybeard thief who had run off with one of his girls. The mare was not given a moment to pause but was driven hard straight at the giant roan who stood rooted in its path. At twenty yards the professional spearman whipped his right arm forward, pulling the javelin he had been holding through a smooth movement that resembled nothing more than the uncoiling of a snake and which projected the missile with blinding speed and force toward the oncoming foe. The weapon would have struck the rider in the dead centre of the torso except that the unfortunate mare lifted its head at the decisive moment and as a result the lethal shaft drilled deep into the animal's forehead and felled it like a slaughtered ox.

As the beast's head dropped, its neck folding under it, the still moving but quite dead carcase collapsed into a heap, and the man on its back was hurtled off his mount into a helpless dive that grounded him face foremost into the earth with a jolting force that should have snapped his neck clean through. Oeric was made of stronger stuff however, and his neck survived the impact. Bellowing in pain and frustration the beefy publican lurched blindly to his feet, reeling around to locate his enemy. The man had no teeth to lose but the fall had smashed flat his nose in a red abundance of gore that ran over his mouth and dropped onto his goat-leather jerkin. When he spotted the soldier still sitting placidly on his grey horse the lust for revenge fairly glittered in Oeric's eyes. The thick fingers of his strong hands flexed mechanically as he shuffled toward his rival. If he could but lay hands upon his quarry he would tear the fool limb from limb. He stooped to seize the long-hafted axe from where it lay by the sprawled and steaming mare and his battered countenance curled into a toothless grin. Cradling the axe-haft like a lover he jogged forward into a slow run at the horseman.

81

Without fluster or panic the mercenary slid down from the rose leather saddle and eased his twenty-inch knife from the scabbard at his waist. He wore a sardonic expression that betokened martial contempt. He was sufficiently scornful of his opponent not to bother to unsheathe his spear. The knife would be adequate. He bore this Wehnbrian pimp no malice, nor wished any ill to his trade, but the girl had made her choice and it was a decision that suited the Aenglian. The tavern-keeper would just have to purchase himself another girl when next the buccaneers brought the plunder of their pirate-raids ashore.

Bleeding profusely from the nose and spitting crimson but gripping his axe white-knuckled in both fists, the younger man paused in his rush a few yards from the soldier, stood tall with his chin outthrust, and hefted his weapon high, roaring:

"That wench is my Langelais slave bought and paid for in full these twice twelvemonth ago and well fed at my own expense ever since. Pray to whatever black gods cursed your birth, freebooter filth; you die today."

The mercenary said nothing. He felt no need to justify himself. The man's claim was one of law, and the law was nothing. Pillage was an Aenglian's cultural inheritance. If the lawful sought redress, let them do it with a naked blade.

Oeric showed every willingness to do so, closing in with the axe raised up and to the side, tilted for the scything blow. Ealdræd's defensive posture readied him for the evasion that would position him most effectively for a decisive counter-attack. He already knew when and how he would place the knife when this public house bully-boy made his crude swipe. The mercenary was almost able to observe the combat dispassionately as a matter of purely professional interest, as if he were not personally involved.

Then something grabbed hold suddenly of Ealdræd's left arm, clasped very tight, dragging at him, pulling on him with frantic energy. In the split second it took him to register that it was Noemie clutching and hauling on him with potentially deadly consequences he had already dismissed the question of why she was acting thus in favour of dealing with it; lurching backwards to hit her with his left elbow, a solid thump in the midriff which doubled her over. Even as her scratching hands released their grip upon his arm his whole concentration was once again on the large body lunging at him from the front, its axe sweeping down and across with murderous intent, but the girl's interference had left the veteran totally off-balance.

Lacking the mobility for his intended manoeuvre of evade and counter-stroke, all pre-arranged strategy was abandoned and he acted simply from conditioned instinct as he dropped flat to the ground. The axe whistled impotently by overhead close enough to lop the tail off one of his braids and whilst its considerable weight and momentum now took the Wehnbrian's arms into the backswing, upwards and to the left, Ealdræd from his prone position at the man's feet brought his knife around behind Oeric's right knee and cut clean through his hamstring. The burly publican was bringing his wide circular swing back around and cutting down vertically for a fatal blow when Ealdræd rolled aside to leave the axe-head to bury itself eight inches into the mud.

Oeric tried to pull the weapon clear but his severed right leg gave way underneath him. He collapsed to an involuntary kneeling position and held on to the axe handle to support himself, bewildered as to what had happened to his knee, but by then the Aenglian was on his feet and moving to the man's rear, reversing the long knife in his grip to plunge the iron point-first into the back of the kneeling Wenhbrian's neck to hack its way out through his throat before the big man even knew that he was as dead as his mare.

The bunched muscles of the bloody ruin of a face went slack and the weight of the corpse slumped further down upon its haunches. Then as his killer ripped the knife free back out of his neck the leather-clad tapster hit the dirt of the road for the second time that day and this time was to be the last time. The butchered meat did not so much as twitch. At which Noemie, who had recovered her breath, screamed in funereal sorrow and bitter heartache. Flinging herself extravagantly upon the dead man she wailed her misery and woe at his demise. Then rising in a boiling fury she began spitting like a cat in vehement rage at the Aenglian, swearing her love for her martyred Oeric, declaring him her own, for all the world championing the very pimp she had but a moment since been deserting.

Her fevered breathing and guttural, rasping expletives filled the morning air as she proclaimed before all the world that the dear departed was worth any ten-score uncouth barbarians from the demon-infested forests of foreigners and oh how she implored the gods to intervene to make sure that this villainous murderer from the black north would be slain by the Geulten in the forthcoming war, and that most torturously and with much suffering at his end.

This tirade explained her grabbing his arm during the fight but as to her change of heart in her attitude toward the tavern-keeper, switching from runaway slave to adoring lover in the space of a heartbeat . . . . that was not so easily explained. Had her escape from the Pint Pot been nothing but scheming fakery from the first? A mere ruse to prompt Oeric into chivalrously risking his life on her behalf by heroically reclaiming her from the mercenary? Had all this been naught but an amorous child's romance? Did the slut not understand her own status as property?

It was not a mystery that the put-upon and disgruntled soldier was going to give his mind to or expend any time upon at present. There was a measure of justice to be dealt out first. He moved swiftly to snatch her up in his arms but the slender wand of a girl, as lithe as the cat whose temper she shared, scampered away thirty yards in a few seconds and it occurred to the Aenglian that catching the bitch would be not dissimilar to fishing for eels with your fingers. Of course, it wasn't necessary to actually catch her. He squatted down over the pony and started to wrench free his expended javelin from its forehead.

"Begone, you wayward baggage," shouted the exasperated and uncomprehending veteran, still capable of being surprised at the fickleness of humanity even at his age, "or I'll slice the ears from you."

The incensed Noemie was so taken in wrath that she seemed not to know what she was doing, dancing about and ranting wild abuse, snarling homicidal curses and insults of quite staggering obscenity, yet some sense of self-preservation must have remained for even as she called down the pestilence of a whore's revenge to pox his cock and blight his balls she was none the less careful to stay out of the killing range of his javelins. Or what she believed to be the killing range. Pulling the short spear free, and with it still dripping the mare's hot blood, he hurled it full force at the girl who was skipping and hopping around forty yards away. It went through the trajectory of an arc like a volley of arrowshot and then fell out of the sky as if directed to its target. She felt it swish through her black hair no more than an inch from her left cheek and upon the instant she was running for all she was worth. Perchance the muscular barbarian could slice off her ears at forty paces after all.

But when she was twice that distance away she turned again to sing out her grief for the wonderful man who had shown her so much kindness and who would have proven his true love for her if he had not been so treacherously murdered by a pagan outlander. The bemused Aenglian could hear her still seething volubly at her former owner's vile assassination as she stomped back down the road by which they had come, presumably returning to the Pint Pot Tavern.

God rot her and let her go. Ealdræd found himself too baffled to bother to pay her out as she deserved. He rode on alone shaking his head with incredulity.

*   *   *

Traffic on the road was a good deal busier as he drew close to so enormous an assembly of people as were gathered in an army camp. Consequently, there was a profusion of street merchants, peddlers and hawkers who had set up shop along the highway, duplicitously singing their fraudulent wares. Most ubiquitous were the roadside food stalls selling all manner of sweetmeats whose succulent aromas set many a belly a-rumbling; hot chestnuts, strips of roast pork on wooden skewers, toasted rolls of rye and barley bread, stewed pottage, any of which could make a welcome variation in diet to the cheese and wafer-biscuits usually carried in a traveller's sack. Each stall inevitably had its small band of filthy half-starved children clustered around it begging for food and ducking out of the way when the proprietor, red-cheeked with outrage, swung a fist at them to chase the impecunious little brats away. Street vendors purveying foodstuffs had two perennial pests to contend with; flies and orphans. The more intelligent traders encouraged the urchins to beg passing wayfarers to buy them food; their smudged little faces turned up imploringly as they begged a foot-sore wayfarer to buy them a jellied eel or a fried oatcake that the wretched pedestrian couldn't even afford to procure for themselves, let alone for some strumpet's discarded illegitimate offspring. None the less, this was a shrewd manoeuvre by the retailers because it did sometimes work, adding to sales, and even when it didn't, it at least got the brats away from the stall where nippy infant hands could grab and steal whenever the vendors back was turned. No solution had yet been invented to get rid of the flies.

The first sign that one is about to enter an army muster is the smell. It isn't any smell in particular but, on the contrary, is a mixture of a thousand different odours, none of them especially fragrant and chief amongst them the delicate bouquet of unwashed bodies and the scented fragrance of the cess pool. This forewarning can reach the approaching traveller five or six miles away. The second sign is the murmur and hubbub of noise that is the faraway rendering, drifting on the wind, of a multitude of voices all speaking at once. Ealdræd smelt it and then he heard it, and then finally when he topped a hill which overlooked the valley of the Tamarlaine he saw it. It was, as always, a tremendously impressive sight.

A mustering town is not a real town at all but simply an impromptu habitation thrown up for the purpose of mustering the army in one place. Ealdræd reined in Hengustir on the summit of the hill and paused a moment to soak it all in. Ahead of him was upwards of thirty thousand men women and children spread out in a chaotic disorder of tents and blankets and cooking fires and wagons and horseflesh right across the Plain of Tamarlaine; from end to end they must have comprised ten furlongs of seething wriggling humanity, a congregation as long as it was wide, like the gods' own colony of ants. This maelstrom of shouting, marching, eating, farting, laughing, arguing, singing, sleeping people had been drawn here from every land in the Ehngle peninsula and they had settled down upon the flat of the plain to prepare for the battles to come. When the army eventually departed on its campaign it would leave behind it nothing but a copious and imperishable litter of its residual rubbish. For this reason the 'town' had no proper name but was straightforwardly called what all such temporary army towns were called: Muster. This one was situated a few leagues outside the city of Amsburgh, the capital city of the province of the Eorl Atheldun of the Marches. After three months on horseback, Ealdræd had arrived.

The blacksmiths were hard at work, naturally, for they could be naught else on the eve of battle, beating out the enormous piles of arrowheads that would take the gravest toll of death once battle was enjoined. For every enemy slain by one of the sword-wielding, armour-encased aristocracy, fifty would die under the arrow-storm. And, indeed, to look out across this extraordinary human panorama of society, be they thegn, archer, halberdier, page, pikeman, squire, woman, child, or militiaman, all busy about their business amidst the sharpening of lance points and the stitching of leather and the repairing of chain mail the overarching sense was that they were set within a glistening metal ocean of blades and breastplates, quarterstaffs and billhooks, harnesses and helmets, all sparkling in the sun.

Living conditions were typical, field sanitation being something of an afterthought. There were apparently too few slaves on hand to dig latrines of a necessary depth and length. Such latrines as there were had been dug with the reluctance of soldiers pressed into service. Consequently they were too short, too shallow, and were filling apace. If the army remained mustered here for another few days it would become dangerously unsanitary; the pits would overflow and cholera would fester. Parasitic disease was a constant threat with so many foregathered and when contagion struck in these circumstances it could be a devastation. Ealdræd noted, as he rode by them, that the Heurtslin had pitched their kitchen tents too close to their sewage pits as usual. They were a people who kept their mouths too near to their arses for an Aenglian's liking. Still one of their women was combing through an infantryman's hair searching for lice, so they hadn't entirely abandoned all good sense.

Happily, the oxen looked to be labouring so the supply carts must be well-provisioned. That was a comforting sight to see. Before now, Ealdræd had been in camps where the starving soldiery had been reduced to eating horse fodder.

Riding slowly through this mass of confusion, the Aenglian spearman wasn't aware of it but he had a wry smile on his battered features that was equally as sincere and affectionate as it was cynical and knowing. This improvised shanty town, wherever it was situated, in whichever country and speaking whatever language, was always some kind of a home-from-home to so experienced a fighting man. If he belonged anywhere at all, it was here.

Yet, as if to prove the contrariness of the world, a little deeper into the settlement he came across the unexpected. Just as everything seemed so familiar, an unusual note was struck: a lively and sporting gathering of soldiers and harlots attending a witch-burning. Although these were a not infrequent feature of urban life and an intermittent facet of rural life, they would normally be frowned upon by the officers of any army because of the uncertain effects of so volatile an exhibition upon a rowdy soldiery. The enlisted man, it was universally acknowledged, had a tendency to get carried away and not know when to stop. This present incident, therefore, was far from being typical of an army camp and hardly what the veteran would have expected to find on the eve of so significant a campaign. A festive and expansive crowd had gathered expectantly in audience for the event. A witch burning was always a popular form of entertainment because it combined a self-aggrandising sense of justice with a socially acceptable form of sadism and an element of scientific curiosity; a fairly potent combination. Ealdræd dallied a while to watch the spectacle.

A woman of perhaps thirty five years of age, stripped nude, was bound with rope along the cross-piece of a timber frame which suspended her at a height of three feet over a pile of faggots and logs. Despite the discomfort her head was drawn up so that she could look at her executioners. She had been screaming her protestations of innocence for many minutes before Ealdræd had arrived upon the scene, raving passionate avowals of her guiltlessness all the while they tied her in place, but by the time the Aenglian had joined the throng the accused woman had fallen silent apart from a gagging incoherent grunting. The mask of terror that had replaced her face was fixed and rigid. The expression in her wide eyes was that of a trapped creature driven stark mad by uncontrollable fear. Her legs were wet with her own piss. All the muscles in her naked body were twisted tight, yet a persistent shudder shook her frame, as if some giant hand were shaking her. A low enfeebled feline whine drooled from her contorted mouth.

The faggots were lit and with the help of some grease from the cooking pots to act as an accelerant the bundles of sticks burned with remarkable speed. The witch was soon enveloped in flame, screeching her agony in a deranged, mentally dislocated way, her voice cracked and shrill. The convivial and jubilant audience, in contrast, fell utterly silent and remained very quiet now that the fires were actually lit; subdued by the hideousness of it, humbled by the horror. The sound of the shrieking from inside the sheet of flame was so piercing that some of the animals nearby shifted uneasily, but the people appeared rooted to the spot. The woman's skin began to blister and bubble; then her flesh turned black. Her screaming ceased when her lungs were too internally scalded from breathing in the superheated air to function any more. The stout timber of the cross-beam and the strong rope still held her peeling cadaver in place over the fire long after she was dead.

The charge of witchery had arisen because an artisan's wife, heavily pregnant and in the first throes of labour, had called for a midwife and a local widow who made her meagre stipend from the provision of such services had been brought to attend upon her. The birth went badly and the baby had been still-born. The artisan's distraught wife accused the midwife of having killed it deliberately and, calling upon all present to witness the pathetic corpse of her dead child, she swore that the midwife must be a witch.

That alone might not have condemned the widow, for still-born babes are a common occurrence and there are not that many witches in the world, but the artisan was friendly with a sergeant of pike from the Eorl Caridian's regiment who was fond of his friend's wife and took her sworn word as proof. A man of summary judgement he demanded justice. His large and powerful regiment in its entirety had come up to the Marches from the Eorldom of Shrewford in the west of Wehnbria to assist in the Ehngle defence and they were consequently very popular with the rest of the army. Nobody was going to argue with the Wehnbrian sergeant of pike. The midwife had been adjudged guilty and set to the burning.

In this part of the world witches were most commonly known as 'aglæca', a name given to them as a group meaning 'fiercely combatant miscreant monster' or 'an enemy of fierce deviltry'. The whispered word "aglæca" on the hasty wagging tongues of the impulsive could set whole villages aflame. It was an incendiary word, quite literally.

The stench of dead human flesh frying in its own body-fat was getting unpleasant and the crowd started to break up and drift away in all directions, returning to their disparate tents and camping grounds. Hengustir was eager to be gone and Ealdræd had to report to his brigade and hopefully discover just who was to be his commanding officer, the man with power over his life in the forthcoming conflict, so he leaned down from the saddle and enquired of a likely-looking Merthyan archer where the mercenary camp was. The man pointed a stubby finger toward a mass cluster of bedrolls and blankets on an earthen mound about half a mile upwind. It was just possible to discern a red flag with a black cross in its centre, the usual mercenary standard, fluttering on a mast. Ealdræd thanked the Merthyan and rode on. Trust a mercenary brigade to have the good sense to pitch their camp upwind of the rest of the army. Ealdræd smiled to himself again.

He positively grinned when he discovered who it was that had been given charge of the mercenary brigade. There was a sergeant of arms distributing brigade favours to new recruits; canvas ribbons in red and black like the mercenary flag. The ribbon would identify each man to his comrades as one of their own. When neither army wore uniforms of any kind in a battle that was sure to swirl around and lose cohesion, without some form of identification a soldier was as likely to get killed by his own side as the enemy. Even against the Geulten, whose attire was distinctly foreign, it was as well to take no chances. As Ealdræd, having taken the shilling and officially joined the brigade, tied a ribbon on to his four-plate iron pot-basin helmet that fitted so snugly over the top of his head he would often forget that he was wearing it, he asked the sergeant who they were serving under. The answer was music to his ears. It was Eádgar Aeðlric, the low-born but highly respected Heurtslin cavalryman who had been appointed by the Eorl Atheldun to be his Captain-General of Mercenaries.

This was good news! Ealdræd was personally known to Eádgar from past campaigns and despite the difference in their military rank, if they were to meet during this campaign they would meet as peers and comrades. Eádgar was a few years younger than the Aenglian but they were approximate contemporaries and, both fighting for pay, had hacked limbs and splintered bones on the same battlefields in a few wars. The name Aeðlric or 'noble ruler' had been conferred upon Eádgar, the son of a wine cooper, by those men who had served under him at the battle of Ásgautr ten years ago. It was an honourary title which Ealdræd considered to be fully deserved. Eádgar had won a conflict that day which only one General in a hundred could have achieved, and in doing so he had saved the lives of the five thousand mercenaries under his command who would certainly have been consigned to the icy shades of Wihvir, Lord of Hálsian, corruptor of spirits, if any other General had been leading them.

Ealdræd had not forgotten; he had been one of the five thousand. The meandering path of Ealdræd's life-journey had crossed that of Eádgar Aeðlric only infrequently since then and if they could not rightly be called friends, they could at least be said to share the deep mutual respect of men who had fought alongside one another and seen the valour and personal worth of their comrade-in-arms proven by the testimony of their own eyes.

No such honourable value would Ealdræd expect to find in the heart of the pious and scrofulous god-worshipping vermin whose thin, reedy voice was carrying on the wind over the top of the constant murmur and hubbub of the muster. The cadence was undoubtedly

Merthyan and the ranting, carping tone could only have belonged to a priest. Again, here was perplexity. How was it that a necromancer was permitted to show his shaven head amongst good honest soldiery? The whispering insinuations of wizardry could take the guts out of an army with a single malign rumour. Ealdræd would happily wring the scrawny neck of any magus who came within the precincts of a muster, on principle.

"Be not seduced, my children!"

The voice was strident in its appeal to the motley ragbag of listeners who had gathered around the speaker, a tall skeletal creature who stood on an outcrop of rock with his arms aloft and the light of sanctified zeal in his animated visage. The boulder was not large and it was irregularly shaped so that his footing was uncertain; his sandals sliding on the stone. The robe he wore made sense of why he was at liberty to speak in the camp; it was the robe of an Andredsweald acolyte, a hedge-priest.

The Andredsweald was the common name for those many areas of verdant forest and extensive woodland that still covered the majority of the terrain of the Ehngle peninsula and in recent generations a religion had sprung up and spread like a sneeze at the winter solstice which adopted the Andredsweald as its fetish. Those druidical-minded worshippers of the natural flowering of the soul became its acolytes; spreading wide the message to bide a life within the forestry and woodland of Ehngle. This was not a god-worshipper at all, but a celebrant of the liturgical rites of the nature ethic, a devoted attendant upon an ethnic faith for the Ehngle which advocated the people's dwelling amongst the wood. Its rites involved no gods at all and it was fanatically opposed to witchery and hexcraft. Many witches claimed that their craft was based upon nature-lore and this incensed the acolytes of the Andredsweald whose secular faith believed itself sullied by such claims.

"Do not betray your Ehngle souls to the bastardisation of foreign corruption, my children!"

As Ealdræd strolled up to join the edge of the throng the acolyte was already in full flow, agitating and persuading for the cause. Spit-flecked and exultant, he was carrying his audience in his skinny arms on the words of his emotive rhetoric. It was from this loquacious fellow that Ealdræd again heard the name of the notorious Maev de Lederwyrhta. It was a name and a reputation of

91

which he was already becoming accustomed to hearing. The orator roared at the crowd:

"A debased debauchee, abandoned of all shame, this courtesan from Bhel originally came to prominence in her youth as the lover of the Grand Duchess Griselde, a woman of over sixty at the time! Oh, what wanton defilement and warped perversion was not committed amongst the depraved sexual profligacy of the rulers of that damnable Grand Duchy!"

The long road that Ealdræd had followed in this life had never taken him to the Grand Duchy of Bhel. It was a semi-autonomous state to the north of Guillaime and Eildres, protected from both by the enormity of the Cordennes Mountains. Behind this gigantic natural barricade of rock the Grand Duke Belaric could rule his realm as king in everything but name. The three crowns of the Geulten alliance were, unsurprisingly, grossly offended by such upstart presumption but it would not have been worth the cost in gold and ordnance to clamber a martial expedition over the frozen peaks of the Cordennes to put the Grand Duke properly in his place. Nor could an army approach through the bogs and marshlands of the 'Marécage' in northern Eildres, whilst the boiling whirlpools of tidal cross-currents off the western coast of Bhel, known to the despair of many a seagoing vessel as the 'Mariners Cauldron' made a naval assault unfeasible. As a result of this felicitous impregnability bestowed by nature, Bhel was the one minor Geulten nation that operated relatively free from the coercive influence of the three crowns. Not that the Grand Duchy actually did much in the way of operating, though, as the hedge-priest had rightly said, the dissolute and licentious Bhelenese ruling caste were terminally degenerate to a deplorable degree and the Grand Duke Belaric took no interest in anything but the breeding of lapdogs, a study in which he was said to be a leading authority. It was this political diffidence that made it acceptable for the three crowns to tolerate Bhel; its impact upon the rest of the civilized world was so negligible that it hardly mattered what it did or failed to do.

"But even the reprobate wickedness of that degraded place was yet insufficient to the ignominious tastes of Maev de Lederwyrhta!" bawled the priest. "Having subsequently made her way south over the Cordennes in a Piccolian travelling bordello, she thereafter fucked and fornicated her voluptuary's path through the members of the multitudinous ruling houses of the three crowns like a dose of syphilis, until finally setting up home in Oénjil, just across the border of our own dear Wehnbria."

The crowd bellowed their raucous approval of this fine and praiseworthy nationalistic sentiment, and the hedge-priest wiped a salty tear from his eye in a manly fashion. When the hollering finally subsided he lowered his voice to a resonant rumble to convey the importance of what he was about to say next. His audience were instantly hushed in their desire to know all that he would reveal to them of the world that so sorely threatened them from without.

"Then, it was, that Maev de Lederwyrhta, the Bhelense mademoiselle, was offered redemption for her foul sins by our towering champion of moral rectitude, Eorl Atheldun, the High Lord of the Marches!" The cheering that this induced drowned his words but as the yelling died away he was saying ". . . . But what did she do, the foul harridan? She spurned this soul's salvation and betrayed our most honourable liege lord. And how was this treachery performed, you ask? Witchcraft! Damnable witchcraft! Having inveigled her way into subverting a fine and generous lord's true judgement by means of fraternisation with dark powers, she employed those obscene conjurements for the ruination of the country!"

Someone in the mob shrilled "Burn the aglæca!" and many fervent throats took up the cry. The hedge-priest smiled down upon them, then gesturing for silence with one imperious hand he gave them judgement on Maev de Lederwyrhta:

"Physical evidence of her witchery has been produced; irrefutable proof. The object used for the enchantment was a menstrual towel which none but the most decadent and dissipated ladies of the court would employ; a napkin of sewn linen stuffed with a thin layer of wool fleece. To make use of this device for sanitary purposes is deviant enough, but to use it in the black arts is the height of human depravity! Aye, and perchance something other than human! One such towel was found beneath the bed of each of the three Eorls and it has been ascertained, by undisclosed means, that they belonged to the Bhelenese courtesan. This must assuredly be a singularly powerful charm upon which to work her craft for it carried her secret blood . . . ."

The mob was growing restless at this. They wanted no talk of menstruation and the sanitary habits of ruling class ladies; they

93

wanted to know the villainy of their enemy and the justice of their cause. He was losing their enthusiasm and immediately sought to set matters to rights.

"But be not demoralised, my brave children. Let not the abusive and debased foreigner brutalize and deflower our green lands! Stand true and steadfast to thy gracious and heroic lord, Eádgar Aeðlric! He will lead you to a glorious victory against unclean forces. Let not the bestial pollution of the Geulten, their spies and their witchery pervert your Ehngle souls!"

Amid wild cheering and triumphant hurrahs the crowd responded by hoisting the speaker up on to the shoulders of two stout Heurtslin corporals so that the whole pack of them could march around in a circle singing the praises of decent fellows of Ehngle stock and damning all rascally Geulten pig-buggerers to a pit of their own making.

Ealdræd withdrew. The speech had put some small fortitude into the flagging spirits of a pessimistic legion, that was certain, if only momentarily. But it left the Aenglian uneasy. He made the sign of the sevenfold preservation of Buldr. It wasn't the hedge-priest's convictions that had put his mood out of joint; it was the mere presence of such morale-boosting tomfoolery. For the tainted blandishments of religion to be preached so publicly was a bad sign. That a wise General had given his accord to this hinted strongly of desperate measures. Ealdræd, who had once seen Eádgar Aeðlric kick a priest up his bony arse for preaching when Eádgar was preparing his men for combat, wondered privately to himself just how bad the situation here in the Marches must be for the Aeðlric to be permitting a canting ranter to spout his self-aggrandising and profligate sputum within earshot of all in the brigade camp of the mercenaries. It did not bode well.

Ealdræd betook himself over to the large tent which flew the General's personal banner in the red and black of the mercenary flag with a mailed fist emblazoned upon it. The Aeðlric was not the type of senior officer who would resent an unannounced intrusion from a common soldier for he knew the value of them. Besides Eádgar had not grown so high and mighty as to forget that the had sweated into the same mud of war as this particular braided spearman and that they drew their pay in the same service.

The tent was a circular pavilion with a canopy, the individual sections of canvas from which it had been made were again a chequerboard of red and black. There was no one on guard outside and the Aenglian entered without ceremony. Besides the General's camp-bed and personal accoutrements, the pavilion contained a substantial table littered with maps, cups, plates, and eating forks. But the Aeðlric was not present. The only man inside was a splendidly dressed youngster with a faint wisp of beard sitting on an upturned barrel sipping from a pewter goblet. His doublet was fashionably elaborate with the button sleeves that all the rake's favoured. His breeches were pleated in the latest style but his hair had been shaved to the temples in the traditional manner of the Wehnbrian aristocracy. He wore no armour or weapon.

The Aenglian strolled into the pavilion and nodded a greeting toward the elegant gentleman, smiling amiably. He received a sharp expression of reproach in return. The youngster rose imperiously, as if from a throne rather than from a lowly example of the cooper's art, and demanded to know what Ealdræd thought he was about, walking into the General's pavilion as if he owned it.

Although only twenty years of age Athelwin Godricson, the decorative youth who now confronted the hard-bitten veteran in the Aeðlric's pavilion, was the Castellan of the Eorl Caridian's castle at Hove, the city on the lagoon in the Eorldom of Shrewford. This post conferred upon him the duties of Governor, responsible for the shire around the castle and its military administration, when the Eorl was not himself in residence at the castle. So signal an honour had been conferred upon him at so young an age because he was born an Atheling, having the status of a noble of the blood royal, albeit a minor branch. Such a prestigious lineage still meant something. He would have been eighteenth in line as heir to the throne had the monarchy not been abandoned these two hundred years past.

Athelwin Godricson had been in the foulest of moods ever since the Eorl had ordered him to take up his current ignominious duty as liaison officer to the Captain-General of the mercenaries, Eádgar Aeðlric. Eorl Caridian wanted one of his own to be close at hand to monitor the activities of the professional soldier. General Aeðlric was a man of very considerable reputation but to Athelwin the role of holding the hand of the chief bandit of a rabble of mercenaries, paid men who fought for money instead of feudal duty in vassalage to their lord, was far from befitting his status as the Castellan of Hove castle.

"How dare you intrude amongst your betters," spat out Athelwin Godricson, more than ready to vent his spleen on this old man with the vulgarly braided grey-flecked hair. Such an affront could never have taken place in a decent Wehnbrian brigade.

"This is a mercenary regiment, boy" purred the Aenglian benignly. "We don't ply the forelock as a rule. The Aeðlric knows me of old and would not begrudge me a word. I came only to pay my respects."

That word "boy" spoken in Ealdræd's soft burr of a rural accent was the only word Athelwin heard in the whole sentence. It struck him like a slap across the cheek. This peasant was patronising him; him, an Atheling of the royal line.

"Villein filth, I'll have you flogged!" shrieked the outraged noble, flinging his pewter goblet at the Aenglian. But the braided man had shifted sideward and neither the goblet nor its contents hit their target. Ealdræd's smile broadened. This boy was evidently used to throwing things at social inferiors who were too respectful to get out of the way.

In a fury now, Athelwin drew up his fist to strike the impertinent oaf backhanded across his face. The veteran stepped in crouching low under the wasted blow and then punched his assailant three times hard and fast in the guts. The youngster would have collapsed but Ealdræd caught him and kept him on his feet to deliver a swift thump with the side of the hand to the fellow's windpipe. The Atheling choked for air as the mercenary dumped him face down over the barrel and said:

"Don't you worry, boy, I won't hit you where it shows. I'm sure you'll want to keep this little encounter a secret between ourselves."

Then he crashed a fist with all the force he could muster into Athelwin's kidney. The Castellan of Hove jerked full length and puked hugely in reaction. The vomit smothered his scream of pain. For good measure Ealdræd repeated the punch into the dandified youngster's other kidney. With a bit of luck the boy would be passing blood in his piss for a week. It would serve as a timely reminder every time he went to the latrine.

"There are no villeins in Aenglia, boy," said Ealdræd with emphasis, "nor any other form of serf. We've killed all our masters long since."

With that the Aenglian turned on his heel and departed the pavilion. It had not been his intention to abuse the hospitality of the Aeðlric. But then the General had not been there. Still, it would certainly come to nothing; Eádgar Aeðlric would hear no word of the matter. That aristocratic popinjay would never tell a living soul about the incident. He could never have endured the shame.

* * *

The woman and the man, both naked, were hanging upside down from the crossbeam of the gallows-like scaffold by ropes fastened to their ankles. Strong twine, half an inch thick, tied to their wrists was pegged into the ground below them to keep their arms extended at full stretch and thereby ensure that their writhing bodies were as defenceless as could be contrived under the bullhide ox-whip that the burly Heurtslin sergeant was lashing into their naked backs and buttocks, carving great bleeding welts into their flesh.

They were thrashed steadily and evenly, with the unhurried methodical patience of the military superintendent of punishments. Every impact of the whip sounded an equal, uniform crack against tormented human meat. The softness of the woman's pale body was forced to suffer and withstand in equal measure a laceration that was cutting deep into the more muscular frame of the man who hung inverted beside her. No privilege was bestowed upon her on the specious and counterfeit grounds of her sex. The Captains of the Guard cared not a whit for an offender's gender. Her agonised shrieks were appalling as the tough, abrasive bullhide racked her with stroke after stroke that raised of mass of crimson lines from her shoulders to her thighs. The man screamed no less and his pleadings for mercy interlaced with ferocious curses and blasphemies had not lasted beyond the fiftieth strike of the whip. Each of the bleeding wretches had been condemned to three hundred lashes at the public gibbet. In keeping with the character of their offence, the floggings were undertaken simultaneously, the Heurtslin sergeant alternating his laying on with the whip, first across the woman, then across the man, then across the woman, then across the man, and so on. The glistening droplets of sweat stood out on his tattooed forehead and a second sergeant from the same regiment stood close behind, ready to take over when his seemingly inexhaustible arm eventually tired. For the punishment would continue until the whip's end had been thrown into the two torn and shredded bodies fully six hundred times. The solidly-built sergeant was held in high esteem by his peers for the vigour of his good right arm and his manful endeavour this day fully merited his enviable reputation. Only when the count had reached two hundred for each miscreant did he pause in his labours and pass the gory instrument of chastisement to his brother sergeant behind him, who then stepped forward to take up the infliction of the remainder of the flagellation with fresh energy. Both of the condemned were still conscious when they were eventually cut down.

Military corporal punishments on parade were normally witnessed in a state of subdued silence, each man in the audience thinking of how easily it might have been himself being beaten senseless for some slight misdemeanour or another. But on this occasion the mood was very different. The witnesses numbered some hundreds of both men and women and, ironically, the congregation had been brought together initially at the behest of the two gallows bait now bleeding into the earth, for the pair who had been hanged by the heels were the leading actors in a troupe of a dozen or so strolling players.

Wherever an army musters troubadours, mimes, dancers, minstrels, lyric bards and the like are sure to follow, with caps doffed to catch coin. So it was here. Newly arrived, the troupe had spent the morning walking around the camp advertising to all and sundry the amusements to be had at that afternoon's Jests and Pantomimes featuring a morality play entitled 'The Vengeful Deviance of Lord Poltroon' or 'The Cuckold's Perversity'.

In due course the wassail was conducted. Singing and the playing of musical instruments had begun the show. This was always the case as it was the best means by which to announce the opening of the proceedings and draw a crowd. Certainly the almighty percussive squawking rattle of the rebec, crumhorn, viol, drums, whistles and cymbals which announced the onset of the revels had soon enticed several hundred smiling faces to the improvised wagon-cart stage until the blaring of the music was crashing impressively to wash over the craning heads of the audience.

It had been a splendid performance, with juggling and acrobatic dance while a variety of tiny dogs scurried on and off the stage for no apparent reason or purpose, and there had been a skilful display of fire-breathing, a Merthyan speciality, although in the present political climate the fellow had been wise enough to leave out the conjuring tricks that normally graced his act. But, as ever, it was the buffoonery of the jesting which had pleased the crowd the most. The highlight of all was the lewd badinage between the Lord of the Jest, a clown by the name of Uwen, and the Lady of the Jest, his wife and leading stooge Bronwyn. These two experienced mummers knew the tastes of a military audience and did a thirty minute version of 'The Cuckold's Perversity' that had lampooned, complete with elaborate gestures and exaggerated facial expressions, every possible sexual act that a woman and a man might engage in together, along with several more borrowed from the farmyard.

Though costumed and painted to look older, both were in their mid-twenties. The woman was a prime example of a soldier's fancy, all bouncing tits and smacking lips, being amply proportioned and cuddlesome in her tawdry mock-affluent dress, its fake richness all the better by which to satirise the gentry. Her comic artistry was matched by her brazenly pornographic indelicacy as she slyly winked and groped various portions of her own body to accentuate the profanity of her dialogue. The obscene lewdness of her gesticulations had an audience of underpaid soldiers and cheap whores cackling with delighted mirth, for the saucy baggage on the stage was the very embodiment of the randy bawd that folk the whole world over knew to reside inside the façade of gentility painted upon the supposed lady of high-breeding and social refinement.

No less was her husband the personification of the vulgar, pompous, coarse, affected cultured gentleman of gracious manners that all shoeless infantrymen and common men-of-arms heartily despise and denounce with relish in every language under the sun. The mask which covered the top half of his face had bulging goggle-eyes and a drunkard's purple-veined bloodshot nose that was fully a twelve-inch long, and below his padded-out bloated glutton's belly swung an enormous pink dildo twice the length of his nose. Repeatedly he bent his Lady of the Jest over at the waist to thrust the giant dildo in-between her legs, at which she would throw up her hands, simulate a licentious flutter of her eyelids as she rode rhythmically upon the gigantic phallus, and cry aloud "Oh, the fiend, the fiend!" to chortles and whoops of hilarity from the assembled motley.

With every puffed-cheeked look of shock on Uwen's ruddy face and every concupiscent immodesty from Bronwyn, with each lecherous debauchery from the Lord of the Jest and each bawdy riposte from his Lady, the audience guffawed with laughter and roared their approval. Coins were thrown and the children, presumably the offspring of members of the troupe, scampered around much like the dogs to harvest this largesse in their tiny, eager hands. The jesters progeny were kept busy for this adaptation of 'The Vengeful Deviance of Lord Poltroon' proved very popular.

Less than an hour after the completion of the entertainment Bronwyn and Uwen had been strung up by the army authorities for a public flogging as penalty for their injudicious humour and the selfsame mob of soldiery and harlots who had hooted approbation at their revels just a short time before were subsequently treated to a further leisurely diversion, not to be found on the original programme, of seeing their erstwhile favourites being whipped into raw slabs of mutilated tissue.

A well-educated Adjutant of the Eorl of Shrewford's Irregulars had complained to the Captains of the Guard that the performance had been outright cant and a doctrine of infamy. His explanation of exactly why this was so would have been lost on the common soldiery but it struck home with some force on the Captains.

In times long past but far from forgotten a warfaring liege-lord known to history as the Duke Gilbert en Dieu had ruled over the Duchy of Oénjil, and he was assuredly one of the more successful ancestors in the exalted lineage of the current Duke Etienne. This noble forebear, the Duke Gilbert, had seized possession of a stretch of land in the northern region of the Wehnbrian Marches and when the cartographers had drawn up a map of the revised border it was seen that the newly won ground was in the shape of a laughing profile with a large upturned nose. It so happened that the Duke Gilbert himself had a nose of a similar protrusion; a monstrous appendage that reared out from his pox-ravaged countenance in identical fashion to this small but impudent increase to Oénjil territory that he had won, and which flew the banner of Oénjil to this day. In Wehnbria this stretch of their border with Geulten lands was known as *Feónd Nosu* or 'nose of the fiend' and it constituted a provocation to their honour.

Thus it was the pantomime of the woman being raped by the giant dildo was the cause of all the trouble for the unfortunate mummers.

The man had been wearing a huge false nose and the woman had been heard to cry "Oh, the fiend, the fiend". Consequently, as the Adjutant of Irregulars perceived the matter, the laughing Uwen had ravished Bronwyn whilst he was in the guise of the *Feónd Nosu* and this was tantamount to his having portrayed the ravishment of Wehnbria by the damnable Duke Gilbert. The Captains of the Guard had decided that this was a little too close to treason to pass unpunished. But, in acknowledgement that the guilty were Merthyans who may have erred due to ignorance and folly rather than having committed the pre-meditated evil of political dissent, the Captains had not hanged nor quartered the upstart actors, merely had them flogged to a bloody ruin for the enlargement of their education and the improvement of their characters.

Ealdræd, a cavalryman in the brigade of mercenaries, had greatly enjoyed the wassail and, like so many of his warrior brothers, he entirely failed to understand the nature of the crime that had earned the two leading players a flogging. But it was the way of things for actors to cause offence to those in power, so he supposed that they must be guilty of some transgression and, if they were not, then it was no concern of his. He was at the muster in preparation for war, not to lend ear to the advocacy of lawyers.

The mercenary brigade that Ealdræd had joined was the much-maligned 'raggle-taggle'. Despite the implied disparagement in the name bestowed upon them due to their muddled assortment of ethnic types and their irregular appearance in regards of clothing, weaponry and armour, the raggle-taggle were in fact a fearsomely skilled mercenary force of multitudinous talent and ferocious warlike intensity. In addition to their pay in coin, which was supposedly paid out by their captains at each waning of the moon's cycle though seldom was coin available so readily or regularly, they were quartered and fed at the expense of their lordly employers. But a mercenary was expected to supply his own arms and armour. So whereas a troop of Wehnbrians or Heurtslin or Merthyans would have an ethnic uniformity of dress and choice of weapons, the mercenaries displayed a wide degree of diversity in both.

The advantage of a mono-ethnic troop was precisely that they fought as a cohesive whole, having an ardent sense of community which united them as a body of men in loyalty and kinship. There was no better example of this than a shield wall of Wehnbrian axemen. The prime fighting force of Wehnbria was their lordships' Household Guard of Huscarls, the trained soldiers from amongst the general population each of whom served their Eorl in time of war as a feudal duty in vassalage to their overlord. According to age-old tradition each Huscarl's feudal contract to their Lord could be renewed or dissolved at the winter solstice but in practice this was honoured only in the breach and feudal service was invariably treated not only as a lifelong commitment but one which was passed down to the next generation, from father to son. Even so, the oath of loyalty was formally sworn each year as a part of the solstice ceremonials and was a ritual of civic joy and celebration. The captains of the Huscarls were those amongst their number who held estates of over 20 hides; a hide being the quantity of land required to support one family, the same measure as was used for taxation. It was the Huscarls' pride that their shield wall held the place of honour in the front and centre of the Wehnbrian army in both attack and defence formations; it was a pride that had been earned, proven, and re-proven from father to son, and from father to son. Only a social bond as strong as ethnicity could unite individuals to this extent, teaching a consistent method of combat down the ages and generating so powerful a personal commitment, constancy and fidelity.

Whilst each mercenary had a heritage of his own individually, they had neither of these advantages collectively, lacking a communal heritage. But where they had the advantage was in their talent and experience as warriors. They were men who earned their livelihood by the slaughter and would have been dead long since if they hadn't been superbly efficient killers. And although it was impossible for so mismatched a jumble of ethnicities to ever have a common sense of community, they did at least have a strong sense of fellowship; the brotherhood of the blade, and that was a fraternal affinity that stood a man in good stead amid the horrors of combat.

Within the raggle-taggle there were many who could claim the honour of entry in the *Wyrtgeorn*, the guild of the 'tempered in combat', the strictly disciplined union of warriors who constituted the absolute elite amongst professional soldiers for hire. It was understood, in light of these considerations, that although the name raggle-taggle was in widespread usage, few would risk using the term within the earshot of the *Wyrtgeorn* for mercenaries took grave personal insult at the name in that it seemed to confuse them with the ragtag and bobtail gathering of unskilled arrow fodder known as the *canaille*, that great flock and assemblage of peasants and ordinary common folk who had for one reason or another signed up to fight in the campaign though they carried little in the way of weapons beyond rusty and corroded swords or axes that were liable to shatter if subjected to serious impact, or otherwise bore smithy hammers, kitchen knives, homemade shields and spears, along with scythes and assorted other farming implements. To conflate the ill-tutored and cack-handed rabble of the *canaille* with the experienced men of the brigade of mercenaries, knowledgeable in all the arts of war, was to abuse worthy fighters who knew their trade like few others.

Nightfall saw Ealdræd at his ease. All over the Plain of Tamarlaine there was a general bustle of cooking for the evening meal. As there were men of all stations in life, so were there meals to match them. There was partridge and roast coney for those that could afford it; there was beef sausage and black pudding made of sheep's blood, too, and there was hare stew or smoked eels and water-fowl for the poorer sort. But there was honey-mead, Wehnbrian ales and Sæxyny wines for all.

A veal pie and half a bottle of new red wine, still with the tang of the fruit in it, fell to Ealdræd as his portion. He received them from the quartermaster of mercenaries who was provisioned to give each man a meal on his first night in camp. Money was being spent on this campaign all right, and Ealdræd fancied that the three Eorls of Wehnbria would have to demonstrate the depth of their pocket-pouches before this war was over.

Hengustir was tied loosely by the bridle to a peg, there being no stabling erected for horses, and his master was sitting by a roaring bonfire with a motley crew of his brothers who were amusing themselves by swapping tales and boasting. The talk turned to the peculiar character of the forthcoming war, with regiments supplied by countries that would in other circumstances be at war with each other. Ordinarily it would only be the mercenaries who constituted the multi-national element in an army but with this mustering they had Merthyan bludgeoners pitching their tents alongside Sæxyn pikemen and Heurtslin archers breaking bread with Aenglian spearmen and lads from the Wehnbrian militia sharing their salt with chainflailers from the western fens of Merthya, and where would it all end? How long would it be, they wondered, before old foes and present comrades became foes once again? Ealdræd said that his Aenglian kith and kin did not need to stir from their own forests if they wanted combat; the many clans of Aenglia had so many feuds and conflicts that the bloodiest fighting he'd ever known was between one clan and another. His own people, the Pæga, were at spearpoint with almost all the other clans and likely to remain so.

A young Sæxyn halberdier of the raggle-taggle whose name was Herebeorht but who was known as Hob, had a lot to say in the matter of the instigation of the current threat presented by these bastard Geulten. He was a rangy lad whose stringy muscles bespoke a good deal of stamina, and he was attired in a sleeveless belted tunic, the hem of which reached his knees, and a pair of clogs with leather uppers but wooden soles. The top half of one of his ears was missing, and the fringed halo of his fair hair and beard lent him a prophetic aspect. There was an air of the enthusiast about him, heightened by the ready animation of his mobile features and constantly shifting eyes. With considerable dramatic gusto and with much shaking of his shaggy blonde head, he enlightened all and sundry on the subject of the deficiencies of Wehnbrian politics and the dire set of circumstances that had led to a war which could now only be prosecuted successfully if strong and lusty Sæxyn lads like himself stepped up to save the Ehngle folk from the degenerate Geulten trash; which fortunately he was perfectly happy to do.

Hob began with a denunciation of the diabolical and hell-spewn Maev de Lederwyrhta, of whom nobody had a good word, and Ealdræd was inclined to think that he was in for the warmed-up leftovers of the meal of fire and brimstone that the hedge-priest had served up yesterday, but t'were not the case at all. Hob may have been no partisan for the Bhelenese whore but his theme was decidedly critical of the ruling caste in whose service they were all enjoined. Mockery of one's masters is always a popular sport and as he warmed to his subject his audience grew eager to hear more. He was a charismatic speaker and seemingly well-versed in matters above his station and conversant in the doings of his masters, so that the others seated in the warm circle of the fire fell to listening as the Sæxyn got into his stride and held forth. Most informative he turned out to be.

Employed in the cause of the Eorl Atheldun and his lordly cousins the Eorls Caridian and Aykin, the delightful mademoiselle Maev de Lederwyrhta had been employed in the capacity of an important spy amongst the Geulten aristocracy for several years and had demonstrated her value in the role. As such she had been held, if covertly, in high esteem by her paymasters for a space of time. But following the disastrous defeat on the field at the Battle of Fontónil, for which may all the guilty Generals be torn between trees, Maev had made the serious error of responding to a summons from the Eorls and no sooner were her dainty feet on Wehnbrian soil than she had been arrested and accused of being a double agent and, somewhat predictably, a witch.

The accusation of witchery was bound to be laid against her on the grounds that it was the only conceivable explanation as to how she had been able to fool their Lordships for so long. Their rank, the most noble in all Wehnbria, meant that they must necessarily be considered to be also the most intelligent, insightful, physically and intellectually gifted persons in the kingless realm, and consequently logic dictated that they could only have been deceived by the spy if she had worked enchantment upon them by supernatural means.

Maev de Lederwyrhta had been imprisoned and tortured. No one but the Eorls' lawyers and witch-finders knew for a fact what had been done to her there but t'was certain sure that her sufferings had been intense and comprehensive. She would have been set to walk upon the coals, and put to the pressing, undergone trials by fire and water, and suffered the ripping of the nails and the impalement needles. Doubtless she would have been sat naked upon 'the cradle', an ordeal to break the strongest spirit, where the accused sits astride the upturned edge of a triangular wooden anvil so that the whole weight of her body drives the anvil's edge into the vagina and anus, and then the interrogators add to the pressure by attaching heavy bags of sand to the victim's limbs. It this were to prove insufficient, the lost soul on the cradle can be rocked to and fro. There was a seemingly infinite number of such torments in the dungeon's of the mighty, and none could doubt that the queen of all the witches, Maev de Lederwyrhta, must have been subjected to them all.

But, like others before them, their noble lordships had underestimated the redoubtable Maev. A woman of intricate and indefatigable resource, she had found a way to turn their own weapon against them. She had publicly confessed. She had confessed unsparingly, naming as her confederate witches dozens of prominent ladies from all three of their lordships courts of state. She confessed arcane conspiracies involving a vast international network of witches that had perforated Wehnbria like a cheese. She confessed unspeakable treasons and diabolically contrived spells committed by so many persons of such high quality in positions of unimpeachable respectability that the finger of accusation threatened to fracture like dried wood the very social structure that maintained their lordships in their ascendancy.

Understanding too late the error they had made, the Eorls of Wehnbria used the same methods of persuasion to try to force a retraction. But once given, Maev would not retract her testimony but held to it implacably through a grotesquery of subsequent torments, no matter what was done to her, and much was done to her. Everyone was convinced that Maev de Lederwyrhta was lying but no one could take the chance of not believing her. How could her confession be accepted as the truth at all without being accepted in its entirety? Controversy raged, and a wave of divisive political disputation shook the country across all levels and ranks of person. The three Eorls cautioned their subjects that only the spy's confession of her own guilt should be believed. They admonished with a firm rebuke any suggestion that Maev de Lederwyrhta's mischievous deceits about the high-born and genteel should be listened to or lent any credence. Punishments for dissenters were strengthened. It did no good. The poison was in the system. It was whispered on all sides that it was well-known to be true that practitioners of witchcraft and the dark arts did not commune alone with the were-creatures of the netherworld but congregated with other blasphemers to perform their conjuring of obscenities in covens. How could Maev de Lederwyrhta not be believed?

Old scores and rivalries surfaced and persons of quality began making hearsay accusations against each other. It was all too easy to mention that this or that fine lady had been seen in the company of the dastardly Bhelenese spy and, because Maev was indeed on very intimate terms with nearly all of the ladies of the court, how could the obvious conclusion not be drawn? It began with the imprisonment of one or two of the politically weakest members of the court, who were insinuated and gossiped into incarceration in the state inquisitor's dungeon. These refined ladies had, under the inducement of serial agonies, implicated numerous other persons of both sexes from amongst their social circle. The dam began to crumble and the waters broke. Those accused were put to the rack, the branding and burning, the thumbscrews and the 'iron glove', until they in their turn implicated others of their acquaintance. The floodgates opened.

With bewildering speed the arrests, imprisonments and confessions under torture had escalated out of all proportion. So many of the high-born were being condemned as witches even while almost everyone felt certain that all were innocent. It was the revenge of Maev de Lederwyrhta. The ruling caste was being laid waste by its own senior members and seemingly nothing could be done to halt the mayhem. An hysterical witch-hunt was in progress at fever pitch throughout the patrician class in their seats of power the whole length of the southern coast, all the way from Ebb, where the last king of Wehnbria has lain buried these two hundred years, to Hove, the city on the lagoon. If Maev de Lederwyrhta was indeed a spy for the three crowns of the Geulten kingdoms, she had most definitely found a very novel method of decimating the ruling caste of their nearest enemies. Wehnbria was not merely in turmoil, the splits and factions between various barons, thegns, minor lordlings and their respective followers were such that it was riven by social discord and politically rent asunder in utter disarray.

All of this Ealdræd and the others sitting around the fire heard from the young Sæxyn called Hob and, finding themselves much affected by his compelling rhetoric, when he paused in his narrative to wet his whistle with a draft of Merthyan cider they fell into a brooding and solemn meditation in the privacy of their own thoughts. Not one to neglect an audience for long, the Sæxyn set down his empty flagon and took up the tale afresh with a few thoughts on the correct method for determining whether an accused person be a witch, and how Wehnbrian techniques were not to be relied upon. But a sergeant of the raggle-taggle strolled up, eavesdropped awhile upon the lad's discourse, and then interrupted to advise the incautious Hob to shut his insubordinate mouth if he didn't want to receive a hundred stokes punishment at the company whipping post next morning for disseminating defeatism and sedition. Hob, who'd already had the top of one ear loped off for some prior indiscretion, stopped abruptly in mid-sentence like someone had put the cork back into the bottle.

Next morning there was not yet any news of the army of the Duchy of Oénjil having crossed the border so for most of the assembled soldiers there was little or nothing to do. Their Generals had no choice but to wait. The Wehnbrian army was not itself in any condition to take the initiative and loose the dogs by taking the war to the enemy. Morale was at rock bottom; with so much talk of the country being riven by witchery and the aristocracy at odds with themselves, the common soldiery spend a deal of their time grumbling that they were certain to lose the battle when it was finally engaged. Only the morale of the mercenaries was high. They fought for pay and for the Ehngle peoples against oily dark-eyed bastards

107

of foreigners, and in the meantime they were at their leisure. They wanted no more than that from life, so all was right with their world. If they were to live or if they were to die; that they left to Waðsige, God of Wars and Lord of Chance.

Waðsige was not the God of War, a deity to *instigate* war and enjoy its conduct. Rather, in the midst of the ill-chance and mixed fortunes of warfare, Waðsige was the God of Wars and it was to him that a man prayed for the *luck* that caused the arrow to strike the man standing next to you instead of yourself. Whether you gambled your purse on a roll of the dice or wagered your life in the lottery of battle, it was the Lord of Chance that you called upon for your salvation.

There were no orders for mobilisation so the camp was idle. The Aenglian knew how dangerous that could be. Having had the foresight to spend all his money on his debauch at the Pint Pot Tavern in Ockerham, Ealdræd was in no danger of being enticed into the gambling pits that the unoccupied troops had set up all over the camp. Soon after breakfast it began and would last for as long as the money lasted. The gaming was still predominantly friendly this early in the day but by noon quarrels would have started and it would be a rare novelty if by dusk at least one man hadn't been stabbed in the vitals by a companion of the dice who had lost and was dissatisfied in the manner of his losing.

With only his recruitment shilling in his purse Ealdræd was also disinclined to join his comrades in drink, for his coin would not last long and he was not of a disposition to accept a drink from another man which he could not return. Nor would he whoremonger with them. He passed a momentary thought for that contrary bitch Noemie who had begged to be allowed to accompany him on his journey to muster with the army but betrayed him for the sake of the man she loved. She had been a comely wench although more than halfway barmy. Still, she would have been a warm and welcome distraction now. But you can't carry water in a cracked pitcher, as the Piccolians say. The fickle slave girl had made her choice as she saw fit. The Aenglian only hoped that whoever owned her now was smartening her up with regular doses of the whip. A hearty smile crossed his weathered face as he imagined it. All the same, with an empty purse Ealdræd's whoring was done with until the war had brought him some plunder or more pay.

So instead he saddled Hengustir and decided to take himself off to the capital, Amsburgh, a big bustling market town that was the commercial hub of the entire region. It was not far to ride, less than a few hours. He had not had occasion to visit a city in a six-month. He would see the sights and smell what was on the wind, and then return to muster for the evening meal.

Leading the massive blue-roan by the bridle he strolled through the camp, toward the southern perimeter. A poetic soul in blonde moustaches was sitting in the back of an open cart playing a mournful tune upon the bellows pipes, accompanying himself as he sang in pigeon Wehnbrian. He had by no means mastered the language as yet. The bag of the bellows pipes was pumped by the elbow, leaving the hands free to finger the notes of the two reed pipes attached to the bag. The musician was a Cambrain islander. The Cambrai Isles were a cluster of small islands at the furthermost western point of the continent; westward even of Ealdræd's own native Aenglia and whilst it was commonplace enough to see their ships along the coastline all around the Ehngle peninsula, it was quite unusual to find a Cambrain alone and making his living on land. It was often said that the men of Cambrai choked to death if they had to breathe air without salt in it. Doubtless this musician would have a long sad story to tell of the misadventures which had led him hither, and no doubt it would end up being retold in one of his songs; suitably dramatised. How the young folk would weep when they heard it, and how they would sweat in their passion at the romance of it.

Further along the mercenary paused to watch with interest an organised boxing bout that was underway between two soldiers. One was a cudgeller who was obviously from Heurtslin for he was covered in tattoos in keeping with his ethnic culture. As a folk, the Heurtslin were sometimes called the picture-people due to their many tattoos in blue ink, especially on the face. The second man was identifiable from his plaited hair and beard as a compatriot of Ealdræd's, an Aenglian. Ealdræd knew from the tiny bronze beads woven into the boxer's braids that his clan was the Glæd, meaning 'bright', named for their gaudy hair decorations. They had been the ferocious enemies of Ealdræd's own clan, the Pæga, for generations but only within Aenglia itself. When meeting in alien territories, the clans of the Aenglians felt a kinship for one another that they entirely lacked within their own borders.

Both boxers had clearly been waging their mutual struggle for long enough to have made a sorry mess of each other. Ordinarily such a gratuitous bloodletting would be proscribed by the sergeants and

109

captains, for there was little point in ruining a brace of useful men at the advent of battle when good men were needed. It was a sure sign that all was far from what it should be at this muster that the officers were prepared to sanction a sporting bout at such a time. The reason was not far to seek; they hoped that a sterling example of martial pride and physical endeavour would stir some kindred feeling of the sort in the spectators.

Both men were naked but for the leather wrapped around their lower arms and the genital wrapping that cushioned any blow to the groin and so helped to ensure that bouts were not disappointingly curtailed by quick victories due to boxers being rendered unconscious through a kick to the testicles. Boxing audiences preferred their fights long and bloody.

Boxers wrapped their hands in strips of supple leather to protect the knuckles of the fist which might otherwise be badly broken during the course of a long fight. This stout leather wrap usually extended up the forearm to make a defensive shield out of the lower arm. There were no settled rules about such things; they would be agreed by the contestants prior to the bout. Aenglians had developed a style of boxing which employed a good deal of kicking to the opponents legs before following in with fists and elbows. For this reason, Aenglian boxers often wrapped their elbows in leather also. This particular Aenglian had tied his braids together to hinder their being grabbed during the fight, although this was not a tactic very frequently attempted because the leather wrapping on their fists made grappling techniques difficult. For the most part it was a matter of clean strikes, blocking and evasion.

As Ealdræd paused to watch their progress, the hulking Heurtslin missed with a head-butt and so took a heavy punch to the throat that he caught unprotected as he lurched forward and which came close to breaking his windpipe. Choking, he reeled back and his adversary stepped in to club a fist into the side of his head, knocking him down on to one knee. But as he knelt the tattooed fighter threw a hooking punch into the side of the Aenglian boxer's thigh and the violation of nerves was so severe that the whole leg went numb from hip to calf. The Aenglian went down hard on his shoulder but rolled away, scrambling for distance, while the Heurtslin clutched at his throat and tried to breathe. The two men, both on their hands and knees, glared menacingly at one another.

110

Slowly they both regained their feet and circled, looking for an opening. The Heurtslin feinted a grab but the Aenglian was not fooled and let the bogus opportunity pass. As the pair revolved within the arena they inched closer and closer. The Aenglian lashed out with an ankle sweep that the Heurtslin only managed to avoid by leaping up into the air. Both men were left off-balance and each sought to exploit the other's disadvantage, causing the two to crash together chest to chest in a windmill melée of short jabbing punches and elbow strikes. A spray of spit, sweat and blood from one or both of the fighters splattered part of the crowd nearby. The Heurtslin threw his thick arms around his opponent in a bear hug, straining with all his might to crush his adversary. The captive wriggled for all he was worth but to no effect. He could not make use of his knees for his enemy held him too tight, and the tattooed man had his head tucked in beside the Aenglian's ear so that the braided man could not attempt a clash of heads. The latter, momentarily nonplussed, felt his lungs unable to draw breath. There was a chuckle of satisfaction from some amongst the audience. No amount of flexing and straining from the Aenglian of the Glæd clan affected the determined Heurtslin's implacable grasp. Scenting victory the Heurtslin squeezed as if to snap his man in half. The Aenglian could feel his mind blackening from lack of air as his constricted lungs could find not an inch to open. But then he planted his left foot on top of the Heurtslin's right foot, and pushed hard with his own right foot against the inside of the Heurtslin's right knee, against the joint. A roar of pain was ripped from the Heurtslin as the pressure on the bones of his knee increased beyond toleration. Staggering he sought to shake the hold that the other's feet had upon his knee but to no avail. Slowly, like some great tree of the Heurtslin forests, the man of the north was felled, toppling over to the right, taking the Aenglian with him in his arms, the pair smashing into the ground together, the impact permitting the Aenglian to break free. The crowd cheered approvingly and once again the combatants rolled clear to glower furiously at each other from their positions on the ground.

A timekeeper gave a great shout of "Rest!" and both men reared wearily to their feet and limped back to their respective corners. Fights were separated into rounds, each lasting the time it took for a 30lb bag of sand to drain into a vessel. Fights were won by knockout or lost by surrender. Deaths were rare but not unknown. Any part of the body was both a legitimate weapon and a legitimate target.

The fighters puffed and panted, sipping from water bottles, whilst the officials went about their business. The sandbag was tied off at the base and refilled from the vessel. The apparatus having been reassembled, the string was pulled untied, and the timekeeper shouted "Box!" for the next round. The fighters shuffled out to confront each other in the centre of the ring of enthusiastic onlookers. The two men were very evenly matched and it took a further two rounds of pummelling and pounding, during which the Aenglian suffered a wide gash across the cheek and the Heurtslin had his nose broken, before the Aenglian boxer's tactic of repeatedly kicking the Heurtslin's legs and ankles made it almost impossible for the tattooed man to move about quickly on his feet. He was too numb from all those bruising kicks. Lacking mobility he became an easier target and it became clear to all watching that from this point on the contest would be a matter of how much punishment the big fellow could endure before he capitulated or collapsed. Having too much pride to accept defeat whilst still standing, the Heurtslin was in for a fearsome beating.

The spectator's enthusiasm increased in anticipation of the brutality of the bloodletting to come but Ealdræd's interest waned with the certainty of the outcome and he turned away from the spectacle. There was a small gratified smile on his lips at the success of the man of the Glæd who had so skilfully bested the Heurtslin giant. Let none question the fighting prowess of the Aenglians. It was a fine thing to see his countryman display their superior proficiency and expertise in fair contest. He enjoyed the combat but he cared little for the butchery of the denouement.

*   *   *

It was still morning when he arrived in Amsburgh. The reputation of the capital was of an enterprising and modern community. Some of its roadways had been paved, which all agreed was as sophisticated a piece of civic conceit as could be found anywhere. Its public squares, where residents congregated, were not simply open spaces flattened by the casual impact of innumerable feet; they had been intentionally designed by beating a square of ground with the ends of logs until the earth was flat and hard, and then covering it with a layer of ash-gravel. Any inquisitive foreigner who was about to enter Amsburgh might, therefore, reasonably find his spirits lifting at the thought of what else he might see within its precincts.

Ealdræd had not been within its city walls for over ten years and he was curious as to what changes there might have been in the interim.

Changes there had been, but not as he had imagined. When Ealdræd arrived in Amsburgh the city was in uproar. It appeared to be more disorganised than was Muster, and an army's mustering town is a byword for chaos and disorder. Everyone appeared to be in haste and small groups of Amsburghers were gathered in urgent discussion on their renowned public squares. Keeping to the saddle, the Aenglian rode forward at random. He passed the town crier who was proclaiming injunctions laid upon the citizenry by the Burghermeister. Strangely, various houses in the streets he wandered down had been burned out; totally gutted and razed to the ground by fire. Yet it was evidently not by accident. Left to its own devices wildfire is indiscriminate; blazing its way along a whole row of residences, so that swathes of housing is razed on the whim of the prevailing winds. That was not the case here. Rather an individual house had been burned down to its foundations whilst the houses on either side of it remained untouched. These were fires that had been set deliberately. These were the former homes of Amsburghers accused of witchcraft. All the talk was true, then; the rumours of a country tearing itself apart.

Ealdræd let Hengustir pick his own road as the horse and rider made their way deeper into the maze of streets, attentive to the curious panorama of paranoid fear all about them. It was soon apparent that the whole city was scarred with the burnings. It gave the place a wounded feel; a crippled atmosphere. With so many house burnings the streets looked like a mouth full of pulled teeth. Yet aside from the unusually large number of buildings reduced to smoking ruins, what struck the Aenglian cavalryman most forcibly about Amsburgh was the exceeding luxury of the profligate use of silk in female attire. It could hardly have been a bolder contrast to the smoking ruins of ravaged dwellings but against this backdrop of selective devastation the ladies perambulated in their lush finery. Sumptuous and costly, silk was paraded here almost as if it were as commonplace as linen. The dyer's art was also much in evidence indulging the Wehnbrian's predilection for bright colours, with vivid hues of blue from the leaf of the herb woad along with moss greens and yellows from the juice of the weld. Besides this he witnessed at first hand a revolutionary feature of current fashion that, unbeknownst to him, was the choice topic of reactionary chatter and salacious tittle-tattle from here to the walls of Cerdyc.

The sartorial development in question was that unlike the Ehngle cultures further north and west the women of Wehnbria had taken to often leaving their heads uncovered. The coif, the simple head covering that all ladies of worth used to cover their hair in public and which was so ubiquitous in the lands of Merthya and Sæxyny, was only an optional feature of a woman's apparel amongst the better quality of person here. It was a major source of serious political discord. There was a vocal body of opinion that saw in this the seeds of the destruction of the race, insisting loudly that all of the peoples of the Ehngle peninsula had long held the tradition of the coif for their womenfolk. None but servants and the lowliest of women went without a coif out of doors. All this notwithstanding, the use of the curling tong amongst women to shape their hair by singeing had caught on and become popular, and nowhere more so than in the Marches.

It was a style heavily influenced by the decadent etiquette and manners of the courts of the three crowns of the Geulten alliance. For this reason it was frequently claimed that to wear the hair in the Geulten style was tantamount to treason, since it implied a woman's belief that the Geulten would be victorious in the present war and these treacherous baggages were preparing for a Geulten ascendancy over Wehnbria. Some blamed this fashion on Maev de Lederwyrhta also. To hear some folk talk a person might conclude that all the woes of Wehnbria could be laid at the door of that scandalous and disreputable woman. Be that as it may, it was certainly true that a conspicuous number of the more finely apparelled ladies sported their tresses in beaded or crocheted hair-bracelets, and not only that but often chose to have it curled and piled high in a tower. A few of the really daring ones even had their long hair worn loose and left to fall as a drapery to their shoulders like some slattern of a scullery maid. Critics said that this was tantamount to walking naked in the streets.

In opposition to this new fashion, ladies of an expressly patriotic bent had started to wear the 'milven', a wide-weave net or mesh of elegant spun-thread which contained ladies' long hair in a latticework as intricately constructed as a spider's web. It was named for the Baroness who had originated the wearing of this type of hair covering at court. In a milven a lady's tresses were visible but not blatantly so. On the contrary, the latticework was a sublime example of the weaver's art. The milven was said to demonstrate that the hair of the ladies of Wehnbria was every bit as handsome as that of those in exotic foreign parts and they were not ashamed to prove the fact but, unlike their less morally discerning sisters in far-off lands, the women of good Ehngle stock had the social delicacy, cultural refinement and personal honour to display their beauty within the necessary limits of due propriety and modesty.

The success of the milven had led to a further development of nationalist fervour in female clothing, in the guise of the 'canbril': an ankle-length gown, generally in silks, with wide sleeves to the elbow, sleeves so voluminous that they hampered the use of the arms and hands; a most genteel affectation. Customarily the edging of the wide sleeves as well as both the hem and the collar line would be worked with dense embroidery in the colours of the Wehnbrian flag, blue and gold. The body of the gown was closely tailored to frame the bust, which was left three-quarters exposed to draw the eye of the male observer; something which increased the ardour of the many gentlemen who spoke flatteringly of this patriotic style of dress and recommended it zealously. The canbril had been promoted by a rival baroness who did not wish to be outshone by Baroness Milven; a rival who happened to be the possessor of as splendid a bosom as could be observed in the Eorldom.

Ealdræd knew as much about the subtleties and nuances of transitory fashionability as he knew about the bottom of the ocean but he was always interested in the latest mode of feminine sexual regalia, besides being a enthusiastic observer of the absurdities of the more bizarre foreign customs if seldom a participant in them, so he took careful note even if he failed fully to understand the political niceties involved.

All such frivolities were banished from his thoughts, however, when he reached the great central square of Amsburgh in the shadow of the majestic Cathedral of Wrecan, the holiest vessel of the religion of *godcund hie wræcon*, the divine revenges. This edifice had been erected throughout the previous century and was justifiably illustrious as an architectural achievement. Built in stone, in a world of buildings constructed in wood; rising four stories high, in a city whose structures for the most part didn't climb above two; the Cathedral of Wrecan was the pride of Amsburgh even amongst those who were not disciples of *godcund hie wræcon*. When Ealdræd had set eyes on this a decade ago it had been during the annual flower festival and the entire square had been festooned with strewn petals. The cathedral monks had been distributing the largesse of alms and the Amsburghers themselves had been in gala mood, the Morris-men dancing in carnival.

Not so today. There was a militant gathering of townsfolk upwards of two hundred strong, but there were precious few of the social elite in their milvens and canbrils to be seen. The women were respectably adorned with the conventional coif and there were even one or two of the very elderly who were traditional enough to be wearing the wimple; the ancient predecessor of the coif. The men were in working habiliments of sackcloth and leather. This was a crowd of the commons and the truculence of their mood matched their political purpose. They were taking charge of the pestilential contagion of blasphemous occult divination that was wrecking their country and they were doing so with the sword of holy flame.

In the centre of the square had been erected a ducking stool for accused persons to be tied to a plank on a pivot which would lower the plank into a huge tub of rainwater. Next to it stood a seated foot press, a device furnished with two horizontal iron plates which compressed the foot so that the bones would break when the plates were tightened by the operation of a cranking mechanism. This device had been set over a low brazier so that the feet could be roasted as well as crushed, the soles of the feet smeared with lard to facilitate baking over the smouldering cask. Neither of these instruments of questioning was in use at the moment. But nearby a girl of about eighteen, surely not more, was hanging from a witch's pillory.

The apparatus known as the witch's pillory consisted of hinged wooden boards that closed to form holes through which the hands and wrists of the suspected witch were inserted. The two boards locked together to secure the captive and were set at a height of twelve feet above the platform on which the pillory was built. They were positioned so that the accused hung below them, suspended by the wrists alone. It was usual to attach some sort of weight to the captive's ankles and it was so with this girl. She had a three gallon barrel of beer tied to her feet and the barrel must have been full because it was stretching her out till her joints cracked and her ligaments snapped in crippling elongation. She groaned through the gag that had been stuffed into her mouth.

Although she was the person most directly concerned with what was happening, the attention of the large and disputatious crowd was not focused upon her but on a disfigured character in the woolen cap

116

and coarse cloak of an apprentice in the Craft Guild of Artisans who was haranguing the mob with much exercise of his arms and energetic pacing up and down.

A trial was underway. This young apprentice had suffered an appalling outbreak of massive pustulant boils across his face and neck; an eruption of unsightly swellings and abscesses so extreme that he was deformed grotesquely by it. Ironically, he looked much as a person might who had been subjected to interrogation by hot coals upon the question of witchery and it was this that he argued was the clearest indication of the true state of affairs; that the girl had inflicted this fate upon him by the devilish processes of witchcraft. It must be she, he contended, because the boils had broken out on his mutilated flesh very soon after he had raped her. He had paid the fine of twenty groatæ in compensation for the rape but the girl had not been satisfied and had sworn revenge. There was no other soul in the world who bore him any ill-will or held any grudge against him. It *must* be she.

Witnesses had been called to testify that the apprentice had previously had an undisturbed complexion but the judges were undecided. Six burghers of the town council had been appointed to determine the rights and wrongs of this matter and despite the vindictive mood of the multitude, these stout-hearted fellows refused to condemn without stronger grounds. With no further evidence to hand the mob started to grow very restless so the judges decided to supply themselves with some evidence; they directed the authorised officials of the court to burst his boils "to see if the pus that doth flow thenceforth be healthy and natural or be corrupt with witch's bile".

The young man was horrified at this ruling and protested most violently but all to no avail and against his remonstrations he was held down by the public executioner and one by one all the boils were burst with an iron spike. He squealed in pain and bellowed in rage as the throng winced to see the revolting discharge of oozing excreta that seeped sluggishly onto the gravel of the market square, but it had to be done. Unfortunately, there was then disagreement amongst the judges as to the health or corruption of the pus.

There was long and vehement dispute as the correct colour, constitution, and texture of bile but as the panel of six burghers divided equally, three for and three against, no decisive judgement could be reached. In the end a compromise was affected. It was decided that, for the security of all, both the girl and the boils would be put to the flames.

As the girl, already half-unconscious from her ordeal in the pillory was taken down from there by willing hands from amongst the mob to be tied instead to an upright stake to await execution in the purifying inferno, a torch alight with that very same cleansing conflagration was fetched by the executioner and set to the young man's witch-infected face and neck. The apprentice had himself testified that the boils were the outgrowth of evil magic so he could not now object if they were sanitised by the only means available. At least, that was the judges' opinion. It took four men to hold the arms and legs of the howling, pleading, wailing apprentice and another fellow to secure his head steady with a strap in order for the executioner to be able to apply the torch to his swollen head. The withering pustules were scorched off taking all but a thick crust of what was left of the flesh of his face and neck, but it was necessary to be thorough when expunging the corruption of hellish conjuring that lay therein. The apprentice was insensible when his friends from the Craft Guild of Artisans took what remained of him off to the apothecary. They did not even stay behind to watch as the faggots were lit at the stake of the young woman he had accused.

Ealdræd did not remain to look at it either. He had seen a burning only yesterday and it held little novelty for him. Of necessity all witches must be burnt, no one but a fool would question the morality of that, but the righteousness of it did not detract from the ugliness of it.

His attention was drawn by a slim figure scurrying quickly across the street. Something about this individual's physical bearing suggested the clandestine, the furtive. Perhaps it was what she had been wearing; a white fur-trimmed brushed sheepskin fleece cloak that enveloped the whole body down to the knee, needing no pin or brooch to clasp it in place, and which had a large hood completely concealing the bowed head of the wearer. Fleece hoods and mantles were not the custom this close to summer, and the weather had been decidedly too warm for the last month to warrant so heavy a garment. And, of course, only the very wealthy would ever wear a cloak in white. Or maybe it was a servant maid in the stolen habiliment of her mistress?

Just then, this person dropped something and had to bend down to recover it from the road. In doing so she looked about her from side to side, as if concerned that watchers might have her under surveillance. She failed to notice the tall Aenglian doing precisely that, but he did not fail to notice the delightfully delicate beauty of her pale and anxious face as it peeped forth from the hood. What loveliness; a perfection of symmetry and bone structure. And skin like milk. It quite swept from his mind all thoughts of roasting witches and pustulant boils.

As she huddled inside the bulky concealment of the cloak, all that was visible of her to the world were her shoes. These too were contrary to her surroundings. The typical footwear of the natives of Amsburgh, as in most parts of the world, was stitched together from durable stiffened animal hide; flat-soled ankle boots, fastened above the ankle-joint with laces, or soft boots to the knee that were held up by knee garters fashioned from strips of leather. Leather tanning meant that boots for both sexes were dyed in various colours, and for those that could afford it shoe buckles of engraved brass or carved bone provided ornamentation along with function. But this lady had her elegant feet decked out in curled doe-leather slippers filigreed in gold with silver shoe-hooks. If this golden decoration were genuine, a single slipper must have been worth double what Hengustir would fetch at auction. The beautiful maiden darted stealthily down an alleyway and out of his line of sight. Who was it that could have such expensive feet and yet scuttle through the town like any uncouth goodwife? What if she should perchance suffer the misfortune of losing a slipper in her haste where an enterprising soldier might happen to find it?

With no calculated plan of action, or even any definite idea of what his interest might be in doing so, he followed in pursuit. He had come to town, after all, in quest of leisurely activity to occupy his day. This enigmatic madam might supply it in one form or another. If the chase turned dangerous, or dull, he would simply abandon the hunt and pass on by.

As he set off after the mysteriously mantled woman the sudden and piercing high-pitched shrieking of the witch enduring the sacrificial penance of immolation behind him was loud in his ears as the conflagration charred her legs and worked its way up her torso, but thankfully the sound of the ghastly caterwauling lessened as he turned the corner into the alley.

Like anywhere else, most of the residential lodgings in Amsburgh were single story dwellings, although many had a cellar below but there were some that were built on a slightly larger scale to include a second story. This district of the city, close to the centre, had a surprisingly large number of abodes of the latter sort, giving evidence of the wealth of the city in clay and timber. The alley led to an intersection which the lady negotiated with the same air of surreptitious illegality as before. She fluttered through a public garden, took a side lane that was as narrow as a footpath between what smelled like animal stalls and emerged into a discreet private courtyard shielded by trees. Ahead was a generously proportioned mansion with an upper floor and a covered entranceway into which the lady shot like an arrow from a Heurtslin longbow.

Ealdræd loitered in the courtyard wondering to himself what he thought he was up to. He had pursued the maiden on a momentary whim; the merest fancy. Was he now to go prying into a private manor motivated purely by inquisitiveness and that blind but intuitive sense of the underlying importance of apparently banal events which is sometimes the consequence of a keen eye and a lively intelligence? He decided that he was. With the justified arrogance of a man who had killed hundreds of enemies in personal hand-to-hand combat in a life devoted to violent self-reliance, he was not to be daunted by fear of social embarrassment or the mewling outcries of the gentry for the sanctity of their property. He would pry as he pleased for whatever reasons he felt were adequate, no matter how fanciful.

Tying Hengustir's reins to a rail in an enclosed but empty space at the back of the mansion, it struck him that so fine a dwelling ought to have more commotion about it in the middle of the day. Why did it seem so deserted? Again, it roused his suspicion. Ealdræd placed his spear and javelins, which were the most valuable items amongst his possessions, on the ground between the huge roan's iron shod hooves. Let those thieves foolhardy enough to dare, when tempted, attempt to steal his belongings from there. The horse understood the meaning of his master's action and would trample upon the foolhardy, should any such volunteer themselves for trampling. The animal would faithfully stand guard, its mighty legs rooted to the earth.

The manor house was built not in clay but in stone and looked solidly impregnable, its downstairs window-holes tightly shuttered. If anyone were at home, they must be using candles or cressets during daylight. The maiden had entered so there was someone inside. The locked wooden shutters must therefore be for secrecy.

But the shutters had been left open in the upper story and the damaged remnants of an old carriage had been left discarded against the rear wall which indicated a possible means of entry. The occupants of a house, if at work upon underhand dealings, would expect any intruder to enter from below not from above, so Ealdræd scaled the wall by standing on the carriage and leaping up to catch hold of the sill of a window-hole on the upper level, then hauling himself up by the strength of his arms. Climbing in through the circular aperture in the stonework was tricky for a man of his breadth but he managed it at the cost of a graze to the skin of his shoulders.

The room was comfortably furnished but uninhabited. Creeping to the door he opened it gently and looking out he found that he was at the top of a flight of steps that descended to the main hall of the manor. The soft murmur of sprightly discussion stopped him in his tracks. Dropping to one knee he paused in the doorway to listen to what transpired below. The upper landing of the stairs masked him from view by these queer folk who used candles during the day so as to avoid unfastening their window shutters, but unfortunately it also hid them from him and by now his interest in their identities and purposes was so piqued that he wanted to get a good look at them whoever they were. He lay flat on his belly so that only the top of his head extended over the edge of the landing as far as his eyes. The picture presented to him fully met and then far exceeded whatever fantasy he might have imagined.

The intriguing young woman who had led him into whatever this was had joined a group of imposingly magnificent personages in the main hall. There were three men and another woman, in secret conclave. Although as far as they knew they were alone, they none the less spoke in hushed tones, all except a burly grandee in a velvet tunic and cloth of gold skirt whose vocal intonation was so imbued with the familiarity of command that his briefest utterance had a rhetorical ring to it. His loud, hectoring voice carried easily to the Aenglian's hiding place on the upper floor and it was sufficient to identify so celebrated a personality to anyone who had been involved in Ehngle military concerns in the last twenty years. Ealdræd's sharp eyes opened very wide when he realised who it was: His Lordship the Eorl Atheldun of the Marches.

Behind him was a lithe youngster in the uniform of the Household Guard who positively radiated physical power and whose hand never left the hilt of the broadsword in the scabbard at his waist. A bodyguard, plainly. The sword was so long that its point almost scrapped the floor even though the guard was well over two yards tall. The third man was obscured somewhat by the intermittent shadows generated by the candlelight. Then he shifted his position and the light showed him clearly. Ealdræd was astonished to see the balding head, the belly-length beard, and the stockily muscular form of a gentleman not normally associated with the type of double-dealing and duplicitous liars who wrap themselves in the coils of secret conspiracies; a man for whom Ealdræd had the deepest respect: Eádgar Aeðlric, the Captain-General of Mercenaries in the Wehnbrian armed forces.

But then even this revelation was superseded by another still more surprising; one to cause the woman seated in the chair around which the others were gathered to claim all of the Aenglian's attention from that point on. The March Lord referred to her by name and it made a simple soldier's head swim.

Her raiment was of the very finest silks and velvet, puffed and frilled, laced and latticed, a harmony of glittering greens overlaid with bejewelled brocade and enhanced by gold sewn trim woven into an edging of ermine. The girdle tightly bound around her waspish waist was extremely constrictive, with diverse decorative charms and fetish objects of protective incantation swinging pendant from it. Though her plush dress was so long and trailing that it covered her feet, the low cut of the bodice was very bold permitting a proud flaunting of her fine bosom.

One thing completed her ensemble, and it struck a note unreservedly at odds with the rest of her appearance; it was a 'scold's bridle', a locked iron muzzle that caged the head and inserted a metal plate into the mouth to hold down the tongue and prevent speech. It was a device much-favoured by husbands who had committed the error of marrying shrewish wives; nagging matrons whose insolent and disrespectful mouths needed to be suppressed. This particular bridle was of Vespaan design, where the plate in the mouth was studded with tiny spikes which inflicted an additional measure of pain if any attempt were made to speak. The intention in the use of the scold's bridle was to bring punishing humiliation upon a woman who caused trouble with the wagging of her tongue, and if the Eorl Atheldun had put a bridle on this particular woman, then it seemed to Ealdræd that his Lordship had a point. The woman was the infamous Bhelenese courtesan, the mademoiselle adventuress, the intriguer and spy, Maev de Lederwyrhta.

It was very obvious that Maev de Lederwyrhta was being held prisoner in the mansion but why this was so, rather than her being buried in Milord's deepest dungeon or set afire at the stake on the executioner's scaffold, the reason for that only came to light from the pieces of information that the Aenglian overheard as he lay breathlessly still on the landing, quietly meddling in matters that did not concern him.

The noble Eorl Atheldun was in need of some way to restore the morale of his fighting troops or all would be lost. With the army of Duke Etienne en Dieu of Oénjil likely to invade within the next few weeks, the absolute necessity was to be able to meet the Duke on the field of battle with warriors who would hold their ground and irrigate the mud with Geulten blood, not turn tail and run in the sorry belief that the war was hopeless. This essential measure took precedence over everything else; it took priority even over his desire to publicly and painfully execute Maev de Lederwyrhta with the ritual of hanging, drawing, and quartering, as it was the fond hope of his heart to do.

The sorely beset Eorl had come around to accepting that he must negotiate some agreement with Mademoiselle de Lederwyrhta or lose his lands to the enemy. A public statement from her that in some way explained away her former statements so as to quell the paranoia of the witch-hunt that had disabled the country was the last chance left to him of saving his power and his position.

Ealdræd could scarce take it all in. He could not help but wonder what Hob, the Sæxyn halberdier in the raggle-taggle, would make of all this. Would he speak more respectfully of the lady from Bhel in future? For what could be said of Maev de Lederwyrhta that would do her justice? From unspeakable ordeals on the jailer's wheel of pain and the scalding of his branding irons, from the dislocation of her limbs upon the rack and the contrary compression of her body in the 'scavenger's daughter', from the midst of a mortifying hell on earth, this extraordinary courtesan had proposed and carried out a strategy of mass incrimination by which, it would now seem, she had saved her own life and confounded her enemies. Ealdræd could not take his eyes off her.

The explanation of what Ealdræd found the most perplexing element in this political stew, his Captain-General's involvement in these backhanded dealings, turned out to be simplicity itself. The Eorl

Atheldun had chosen to conspire with Eádgar Aeðlric because there was no one else of significant stature that he could trust. So terminal had the internecine strife amongst the Wehnbrian nobility become that the Eorl must look to an outsider to assist him. Eádgar had thousands men at his word of command, his honourable reputation was exemplary, and Eorl Atheldun had known him personally for years; not as social equals, naturally, for the son of a wine cooper could never truly rise above the status of a commoner in any civilized culture, but Eádgar had been well known to the Eorl and what had been known was all to his credit. Besides which, needs must when the devil drives.

So now the Captain-General was accommodating himself to the unfamiliar role of conspirator and political schemer with the Eorl Atheldun. The lad from the Household Guard said almost nothing, for he did not count, of course. Neither did mademoiselle's breathtakingly gorgeous lady-in-waiting, who had unknowingly drawn Ealdræd to this house when he saw her acting so suspiciously in the street. She answered any questions put to her about her mistress but did not presume to speak unprompted. As for Maev de Lederwyrhta, she was hardly in a position to contribute much to the conversation. The General, who had the good sense to appreciate the lady's exceedingly high intelligence, whatever her morals, had suggested removing the scold's bridle to see if mademoiselle could offer any thoughts, but the fury on the Eorl's scarlet countenance had required no words to express his feelings as to that proposal.

With Eádgar Aeðlric having no disposition or talent for politics outside of the politics of war, and with his Lordship possessing no creative imagination to speak of at all, the discussion was not progressing well. They had been over the same tired ground several times but had found no plausible plan by which the poisonous damage to the Eorldom could be reversed. They had talked their tongues dry and the angelic lady-in-waiting was sent to fetch more wine from a back room but the Aenglian was no longer paying any attention to her since the other much more fascinating dignitaries in attendance were of a social radiance to eclipse even her maidenly allure. It was for this reason that it was not until he, and those below, heard her frantic cries of alarm that he remembered Hengustir. The lady-in-waiting rushed back into the hall babbling frantically of the horse tethered to the rail outside.

In the two seconds Ealdræd wasted on withdrawing his head from the edge of the precipice and closing his eyes tight shut in the effort to think of what to do next for the best, the situation was pre-empted by the tactical military brain of the Captain-General. From where he stood Eádgar Aeðlric could not see the hidden Aenglian but he looked up directly at Ealdræd's hidden perch as if he knew any intruder must be there and said with emphatic self-assurance:

"Come down, fellow, I can reach your horse seconds before you could possibly hope to and those seconds will cost you your life! Come down. Come down and speak with us."

It was a damnably awkward moment. He was not a spy, yet it was foolish to deny that appearances were against him. He had intended no espionage, yet he had eavesdropped with rapt concentration. If he were to bolt back out the way he had entered, that would only confirm the false impression; who then would not believe him a spy? Besides which, one of the party assembled below was a man whose good opinion the Aenglian would not wish to lose. It was this last point that was the most telling. Better to brazen it out. With a nonchalance that he did not entirely feel, the veteran mercenary rose to his feet and sauntered down the stairs.

The young guard's sword was in his hands, using a double-handed grip to take the weight of its colossal blade, and the Eorl Atheldun was holding a contraption which was totally new to Ealdræd despite his long experience of weaponry; a small bow held horizontally with a thick iron arrow strung in place and ready to fire. The bow was held by a handle built into which was a metal trigger. Ealdræd was later to discover the name of this improbable mechanism; a crossbow. It was the latest technological development from the cream of the Heurtslin woodsmiths whose genius led the world in the construction of the bow. Both the sword and the arrow were pointed at the intruder.

The seated mademoiselle gave no indication of being at all troubled by this unexpected development, though her lady-in-waiting cowered behind the chair as if Ealdræd were a whole troop of cavalrymen rather than one lone soldier armed only with a twenty-inch knife which he had left unthreateningly in its sheath out of harm's way. As he strolled down the last few steps the embarrassed veteran smiled sheepishly at his General.

"Ealdræd of the Pæga" said the mercenary General, recognising the interloper and noticing the canvas ribbon in red and black, the banner colours of the mercenaries, that was tied on to the Aenglian's four-plate iron pot-basin helmet, signifying that the tall spearman had taken the shilling and officially joined Eádgar's own brigade. "This is most injudicious. What do you here, Aenglian? How is this contrived?"

"Chance, by Waðsige, the wanton perversities of fortune, Lord Aeðlric," asserted Ealdræd. "Yesterday I took the coin from the recruiting sergeant's hand to serve at your pleasure, and today I sought diversion by following the skirts of a pretty maid." He gestured with his head toward the lady-in-waiting, who blushed crimson and contorted her exquisite features into an expression of ingenuous disassociation. "By this blameless procedure have I placed myself in a dilemma I could not have conceived and would not have believed had it been told to me."

Eorl Atheldun had heard enough. The fool was some blundering clod and the sooner he was dead the sooner they could return to issues of importance. He raised the crossbow to shoot.

"A moment, Milord," interjected the General.

"Why so, Eádgar?" the other queried.

"Good man with a spear," muttered Eádgar Aeðlric meditatively to himself, though whether this was meant as warning or mitigation it was impossible to be sure.

The uniformed guard spoke up in hasty intemperance, his hand twitching upon the hilt of his weapon: "My Lord, give me the word – at your single word, My Lord."

"Easy boy, easy," smiled Ealdræd at the impetuous youth. "Wiser heads than yours have the vision to see further."

"I need no assistance to despatch this fellow," asserted Eorl Atheldun, aiming the crossbow at the dead centre of the braided warrior's chest.

"I will vouch for this man." It was Eádgar Aeðlric who had spoken.

The finger trembled on the trigger of the crossbow.

"You do?" said the Eorl doubtfully. It was difficult for his lordship to lend credence to the idea that anyone in his own circle of acquaintance would willingly place their own reputation at stake for the likes of a grizzled old mercenary of cavalry. If Ealdræd were to prove false, Eádgar Aeðlric would be accountable. By vouchsafing the Aenglian, Eádgar Aeðlric had placed his rank as Captain-General at risk.

"We have dropped sweat into the same killing fields in our time; and spilt our blood there, too. A man's character is written plainly upon him when he faces death continuously from the first clash of arms to the ceasing of the struggle, and that may be from sunrise to sunset. This man is true, I believe, and if he is not I will answer for it."

Since Eádgar Aeðlric's affirmation was so very definite, there was little the Eorl could do but accept it. To do otherwise would have been an insult to Eádgar, and Atheldun needed his Captain-General of Mercenaries. So, willy-nilly, he must have the Aenglian as well.

"Very well, I take your word of course," manoeuvred his cautious lordship, "but we cannot send this man on his way and have him free and at his leisure. If he is to be a part of our undertaking, he must be with us with a whole heart. We must keep him close. Having stumbled upon our little conspiracy, he is obliged to serve it because to have knowledge of a plot of this magnitude means one of two things; to join it if you may, or to be silenced instantly and permanently if you may not."

"Agreed," said the General. He did not consult Ealdræd. Why should he? He was saving the man's life and he was the mercenary's commanding officer. "Let him stand with me to watch my back, as your own guard stands with you. He will be an asset to our endeavour, in any case, to judge by past experience."

The Eorl nodded his consent, albeit grudgingly, and lowered the crossbow.

"Well, fellow," barked the Eorl Atheldun, addressing the Aenglian in his customarily brusque tone, "it seems you are to be a member of our company. I can only say that you may have blundered into more than you bargained for . . . ."

*   *   *

127

Ealdræd sat murmuring quietly in close conference with his Captain-General of Mercenaries, Eádgar Aeðlric. In the absence of anyone who cared for matters of social status, they spoke together as equals and comrades. Both these hard-bitten and lethal gentlemen of the quartermaster's shilling had earned the respect paid him as his due by the other. They spoke in low voices for the hour was very late and the tall burgundy-coloured candles had burned low in their pewter candlesticks. The guttering wax would soon burn out their wicks but still the two sat drinking steadily together from a jug of honey-mead, leaning forward in their chairs, elbows rested on knees, their conversation frank and sober. The only folk left awake in the house, they yet sat in discreet proximity for they were conspirators and the role was new to both. It was an occupation that neither of them relished.

The Eorl had retired for the night and, lacking an entourage in this secret business, he was having to shift for himself. The imprisoned lady around whom this whole conspiracy was to be affected, Maev de Lederwyrhta, had likewise taken to her bed although she had her decorative lady-in-waiting to act the maid and dance attendance upon her needs. The only other member of the plot, the athletic if overconfident youngster in the uniform of the Household Guard who was the Eorl's personal bodyguard, was sitting hunched on a soft couch nodding dreamily in half-sleep at his post by the front door.

Although Ealdræd was a man of no rank, being naught but a cavalryman in Eádgar's brigade, the old campaigner was apparently quite at his ease amongst his betters. He was man of at least forty years of age in an army where the average age was barely five and twenty, but the muscular arms which he leaned upon his knees were eloquently powerful and as skilled in battle as four decades spent living in a world of constant violence could make them. He may have been twice the age of the strapping young man dozing lightly by the door, but this was no enfeebled dotard; rather a lithe and vigorous combat veteran built and honed for his trade. For longer than the guardsman had been alive Ealdræd had been entitled to claim membership of the *Wyrtgeorn*, the guild of elite mercenaries.

Eádgar Aeðlric was physically quite dissimilar to his companion, being a good deal shorter, with the hair on his balding head cropped short and his ruddy face above the belly-length beard displaying the tattoos that were so distinctive of the men of Heurtslin. He was of middle height but his exceedingly brawny and solidly thickset build gave the misleading impression of his being squat. This entirely false intuition was due chiefly to his being disproportionately wide. It was said his grip was such that he could crack walnuts in his fists. His knowledge and experience of warfare was fully the equal of the Aenglian and this Heurtslin cavalryman had proven far more successful in the acquisition of military rank. Whilst in the years of their acquaintance the two men had seen too little of each other to really be called friends by any serious meaning of the term, their richly tapestried life-paths having taken them in radically different directions, they yet shared an undisguised mutual respect that had nothing at all to do with social position.

Eádgar, a natural tactician, had made no mention in front of the others in the company of his feelings at Ealdræd's unexpected intrusion into their dark fellowship, but as soon as all but the two mercenaries had gone to bed the Heurtslin had rapidly expressed himself in no uncertain terms on the subject. The exasperated Captain-General had sworn vociferously at the Aenglian's suicidal folly in meddling in matters that were no business of his, and had muttered several heartfelt comments on the subject of "gawping, over-curious, interfering, bastard sons of Pæga pig-farmers", while Ealdræd had grinned in good-humoured acknowledgement that he was entirely at fault in the matter. Such abusive comments as these were no insult between comrades-in-arms. Eádgar's true opinion was evidenced in the fact that he had saved the Aenglian's life where any other General would surely have had him flogged in brigade field punishment for his crime, aye, and maybe have taken his life by having the sergeant lay on with the whip till the bones showed through. He was grateful for the leniency of his general's judgement. Yet Ealdræd was aware that this clemency was not because Eádgar was in any way soft in his approach to military discipline; he could hardly have earned his place at the top table if he had been slow to inflict the necessary judicial severity. No, it was simply that he was far too realistic and sensible a soul to waste time and manpower on meaningless rituals of formal punishment that benefited no one.

Eádgar Aeðlric had not been given his rank by right of birth; he had started as a common soldier and earned his several promotions to his current stature and authority. Consequently, he had not received his command over men as a social privilege but had instead had to *learn* the command of men by the *practice* of it. As a result, he had a method of discipline that was wholly and in every particular pragmatic. If there had been any practical advantage to having the Aenglian whipped, the General would certainly have so ordered it.

But he knew well enough that a flogging would only antagonise the big Pæga spearman and make him less useful not more so, and if there was one thing the General in his wisdom had an absolute aversion to, it was the wastage of talent. Besides which, they were not presently at muster with the army; they were closeted away clandestinely in a townhouse in Amsburgh where military rituals would not be so easily accomplished if any fool were to try. In any case, more importantly than all these several considerations, Eádgar Aeðlric was secretly pleased with the Aenglian spearman's inadvertent inclusion into the conspiracy because it gave him at least one person in all this meddlesome deceit upon whose honesty and loyalty he could trust as a man after his own heart.

The Aeðlric's assessment of the battle-scarred veteran's disposition and temperament, based on the first-hand evidence of past deeds, was sound. But Ealdræd was about to prove his value by means of his sagacity also. For though the celebrated Eorl and his mercenary General along with the woman at the heart of all the trouble had been foregathered within this house for the purpose of conspiring together, they had as yet formulated no coherent plan of action by which their ends were to be achieved. On the contrary, they had conceived of no way forward whatsoever. This deficiency could not, in all fairness, be laid at the door of the scheming and brilliant Maev de Lederwyrhta, since that lady's tongue had been imprisoned within a scold's bridle throughout, at the vengeful insistence of the Eorl, thereby rendering her incapable of uttering so much as a single word. Neither the young guardsman nor the lady-in-waiting would have presumed so far as to offer an opinion in the presence of their superiors, so that the only third party to bring a fresh mind to bear upon the issue was the wily Aenglian, perspicacious in his maturity and ready enough to volunteer a suggestion in the company of as worthy a fellow as the Aeðlric.

The difficulty to somehow be resolved was that of the deplorably low morale in the Wehnbrian army and in the wider country on the eve of war with the Geulten army of the Duke of Oénjil. The Eorl Atheldun's former spy, Maev de Lederwyrhta, having been unjustly accused of witchcraft by the Eorl in bogus explanation of the Wehnbrian defeat at Fontónil the previous year, had found for herself an ingenious method of revenge; she had confessed to witchcraft in coven with most of the ladies and many of the gentlemen of the Wehnbrian ruling caste. As a result, the country had been ripped apart by fanatical witch-hunting amongst the aristocracy and this had led inevitably to an air of intense defeatism in the army. As things stood, the Geulten armed forces would be able to walk into Wehnbria at a stroll and with little or no trouble speedily overcome any puny opposition that might be placed in its path. If a Geulten army could establish itself in eastern Wehnbria, the whole Ehngle peninsula would be threatened.

Having talked around the problem for an hour or more until they had certainly exhausted all the conceivable military options and found each one wanting, the two knowledgeable warriors had convinced themselves that a solution of another nature must be sought. Eádgar had argued thus far earlier in the evening with the Eorl, too, with as little success. But Ealdræd now had an alternative strategy of sorts to propose for his General's consideration:

"Lord Aeðlric, you are more familiar with politicking than am I, but it has been my experience of people in all the cultures that span the world that they will seldom believe anyone who tells them the truth in counter to a lie but they will often cease to believe a lie if they are given an even greater, more overblown lie to believe in its place."

Ealdræd's voice was level and evenly paced. He sat drinking strong mead in his barbarous braids and sleeveless gambeson tunic, a broad-bladed knife tucked into his belt, every inch the uncouth and brutish professional throat-slitter from uncivilized climes, yet his thoughtful words were the careful wisdom of the intelligent strategist. Eádgar said nothing in reply, having the good sense not to interrupt.

"The most straightforward solution", Ealdræd continued, "is to counter one piece of cowardly gossip with another. It must be put about that the Eorl Atheldun has convinced the Bhelenese mademoiselle to undo the damage she has done and that she, convinced now of the godly righteousness of the Wehnbrian cause, has placed a curse upon the Geulten army of Duke Etienne en Dieu; that she has ordained by black witchery that they shall never leave a field of battle victorious."

The impassive face of Eádgar Aeðlric revealed nothing of his incredulity at such a plan being described as "straightforward". Yet it was the most creative piece of thinking anyone had so far managed to concoct in this middling-indifferent conspiracy of theirs. It was as imaginative as it was bold.

"I know of one fellow amongst the mercenary brigade," said Ealdræd, "who might be the very man to sell this particular tale convincingly. Doubtless he will know of others of a similar kidney and convey the romance to them. Once the word has spread through the brigade it would not end there; gossip is a grassfire in a high wind."

The man he was referring to was the youthful Sæxyn halberdier of the raggle-taggle called Hob. A charismatic speaker and keen to talk of politics despite already having had the top of one ear loped off for his unruly and occasionally mutinous chattering. But Ealdræd did not mention Hob by name to the General because he was, after all, speaking of someone whose usefulness consisted in their being exactly the kind of insubordinate, tongue-wagging troublemaker that Generals are wont to look at askance. Ealdræd had it in mind to exploit Hob's penchant for insolent rhetoric but he did not wish to bring any subsequent misfortune down upon the loquacious Sæxyn firebrand's head. It was a measure of how Ealdræd and Eádgar were so much alike in attitude and conduct that Eádgar did not even ask for the name of this person who was to play so pivotal a role in their undertaking.

"What we need to convince the troops of this fabrication is for some genuine malady to strike down the Geulten soldiery; some pestilence that might plausibly stand in for a curse. This presumably could only be achieved by some noxious poison introduced into the Geulten camp. I know nothing of poisons myself but thought, my Lord Aeðlric, that perhaps the lady of infamous reputation who is sleeping upstairs . . . . . ?"

Eádgar let out a long aching relaxation of a sigh. Then he slapped the palm of his hand down upon his thigh and barked out a canine laugh.

"Ha! You are well-named, old cousin of the killing floor, for if I mistake not *eald* means 'wise' and *ræd*, 'counsel'. Sooth, you have proven yourself the wise counsel this night. By the wounds of my dead father, who would have thought to find such duplicitous machination in a man of the spear and buckler? It is an admirable plan and if the gods of humility do not send us stark mad with their laughter in ridicule at our presumption, it may even succeed!"

*   *   *

132

Breakfast had been a desultory affair of smoked kipper and plain bread rolls. The larder of the kitchen had not been provisioned, so the guardsman had been sent to "forage for fodder" as the General had phrased it. The lad had returned with the victuals a half hour later looking somewhat crestfallen. It had transpired that the current disorder in the city in addition to the wholesale removal of food produce to the muster of the army had combined to leave precious little to be had for purchase from the local shops that was fresh, and amongst the preserved foodstuffs still available pickled herring and smoked kipper were the least repellent of a poor selection. He had bought a sizeable portion of each but feared that his master the Eorl would not be best pleased.

Ealdræd, a typical Aenglian in the matter of diet, was a lover of the kipper from boyhood and took considerable pleasure in grilling a copious plateful for himself which he consumed as if t'were ambrosia. Eádgar was well-used to making do with whatever could be had in the circumstances and so he joined the veteran in a slightly smaller plate of fish, swilled down with the remains of the honey-mead from the night before. As much was true of the guardsman and his portion of herring. But the Eorl Atheldun and the two ladies upstairs were, as predicted, a large measure less than satisfied with such commonplace fare, and it was the lord's displeasure that lent a lacklustre atmosphere to the breaking of their fast.

The conversation which followed it, however, was decidedly lively; indeed it became quite agitated. This was because, having explained Ealdræd's unorthodox plan to the company, the Captain-General, who spoke on the Aenglian's behalf, proceeded to advocate the removal of the scold's bridle from the Bhelenese lady. Up to this time the bridle had been removed only during the hours of sleep and for the consumption of meals, both of which took place upstairs in the absence of the Eorl. His lordship was far from tolerant to the idea that she be permitted to speak in his presence.

As the calm and reasonable persuasion of Eádgar Aeðlric slowly drew the recalcitrant Eorl to relent, the woman in question sat very erect and almost tranquil in her chair despite the discomfort of the bridle. Much of her petite face was covered by the solid iron harness and Ealdræd for one was impatient of his lordship's resistance to the removal of the metal gag for the mercenary was keenly curious to see the lady's face revealed. Her upright carriage was not merely good posture, it was an act of will; the privations of her body that she had suffered under the long months of torture had left her permanently damaged, as was plainly evident when she walked, but while seated she portrayed the carefully composed poise of a queen. Ealdræd was fascinated by this physically diminutive woman whose extraordinarily giant character had been written across half a continent.

Both she and her lady-in-waiting were costumed differently from the previous evening, a fact which betokened her status as prisoner being more discretionary than absolute. If the mademoiselle were allowed a servant and a wardrobe of clothes, then some accommodation must already have been reached. There remained but the question of her freedom to speak.

Her apparel this morning was as silken and velvet as when Ealdræd had first seen her, and again the frills and lattice-lace were abundant. But this time the harmony of rich colour and texture in the garment was predominantly of a sunset red and the bejewelled gold brocade by which it was enhanced made that sunset seem to shimmer. The girdle was as tightly constrictive as before with, if anything, an even greater abundance of decorative charms and fetish objects of protective incantation hanging from it. The provocatively low cut of the bodice was again so daring as to brazenly flaunt her fine bosom but the dress was once more of a length to conceal her feet which caused the Aenglian to wonder if her feet had been so badly injured that she wished to disguise the fact. It would explain her difficulty in walking.

The coif and torse she wore gave no sign of what her hair might be beneath it, and Ealdræd suspected that her head may have been shaved during her extensive and comprehensive torture by the Eorl's enthusiastic witch-diviners. Her face was nothing but a pair of exquisitely expressive blue eyes behind the scold's bridle which muzzled her in a locked cage that inserted an iron plate into her mouth to hold down the tongue and prevent speech. The Eorl had chosen a Vespaan bridle which had the subtle addition of rows of tiny spikes on the plate that gripped the tongue to ensure immediate pain if any attempt were made to speak.

The fashionable ensemble of her extraordinarily pretty lady-in-waiting reflected that of her mistress except that it was quite properly of less grandeur and more restricted in its puffed and befrilled splendour. It had been the beauty of this maiden that had caused the Aenglian to follow her into this misadventure in which he was now embroiled but as he gazed upon her loveliness this fine morning he could not find it in his heart to reproach her for it. She appeared always to be in a state of blushing embarrassment even when there was no apparent cause for bashfulness. A girl of less than twenty, this servant with the flaxen tresses escaping from her coif was addressed by the rest of the company only as Mistress Bryony, which prompted the Aenglian's excitable curiosity for this was a name found frequently amongst the Ehngle but very rarely amongst the Geulten. How came it that the Bhelenese mademoiselle had an Ehngle lady in attendance? The meaning of her name, Bryony, was a 'vine with small blossoms'. Ealdræd gave thanks that she was so misnamed for assuredly the girl's blossoms were fully as developed as those of her mistress if less extravagantly exhibited. It went against all civilized custom for the attire of the mistress to entail a more blatant sexual display than that of the servant. Yet Maev de Lederwyrhta evidently wished it so. This in itself would have informed the shrewd observer that here was a woman who defied convention as a hearth-fire defies the winter chill and a refreshing breeze defies the enshrouding fog.

With a discourteous expletive the Eorl Atheldun finally consented to Eádgar Aeðlric's urgings and the guardsman was instructed to remove the scold's bridle. As he levered the device apart and then tossed the infernal contraption aside, the pale oval of the diminutive visage beneath retained its placid equanimity. She was perhaps twenty-seven or twenty-eight but there were lines of prolonged pain etched into that dainty face that would not have been there a mere six months ago, for dungeon life ages a person rapidly. Yet the sublimity of its proportions and contours were undiminished and Ealdræd could only wonder at what such an awe-inspiring countenance must have been before the Wehnbrian torturers had set to their grisly work. That this woman had conquered the crowned heads of the Geulten alliance required no stretch of the imagination. Nor would she have needed any recourse to witchcraft to do so either. Ealdræd banished from his mind any suspicion that the stories of her witchery might be true. What needed she of hex-craft, her sexual allure alone could sway the course of kingdoms.

"And lo, madam," said the Eorl resentfully, "your serpent's tooth is returned to you."

"Mademoiselle," she corrected huskily, still feeling the imprint of the bridle on her flesh.

"A title for innocent maidens, surely," shot back the Eorl, "and not for those harlots whose perfidy has sent seven thousand men to their deaths."

Those devastating eyes turned upward toward her jailer and captured him in their magnetism. In a controlled tone, yet with a rising inflection, Maev de Lederwyrhta spoke to the Eorl Atheldun thus:

"You and your lordly cousins, the Eorls Caridian and Aykin, picked me for your scapegoat and blamed me for your defeat on the field of battle at Fontónil. You would not blame yourselves; you would not blame your soldiers; but the infamous Bhelenese whore, ah yes, she you can blame. And so it is Mademoiselle de Lederwyrhta who must be imprisoned; it is Mademoiselle de Lederwyrhta who must be tortured; it is Mademoiselle de Lederwyrhta who must be executed! But no, you failed at the last did you not? My little stratagem undid all your plans for my so very public and so very ignominious death, did it not? And so to your current misfortune; one you have brought upon yourself, for the only fraud here wears a coronet. There was no magic worked for your undoing on the battlefield, and no magic was needed; your own vainglorious conceit in refusing to heed my warnings about the strength of the reserve troops at Fontónil was the begetter of that military calamity."

For all the primly articulated diction, for she was speaking in a language not her own, the speech was a quickfire burst of contained fury and not a word of a lie in any of it. The Eorls' actions had been just as she described. Her head was set back and she had him fixed in the gleam of her eye. Maev de Lederwyrhta was a traitor to her people, a spy for her country's enemies, and a whore to all the crowned heads of the Geulten nations, and yet here she sat, upright as a bantam cock, positively taking the high moral ground. And getting away with it, too, for she was in the right. Ealdræd could not help but admire the adventuress from Bhel.

Predictably outraged at the foreign strumpet's audacious scolding, the Eorl Atheldun stepped forward and struck the seated woman venomously back-handed across her fatally entrancing face, snapping her head round sharply. Nobody in the room reacted. The Eorl commanded here, and a fist in the face was a trifle in comparison with all that the mademoiselle had endured in the last half-year.

"Keep your viper's tongue behind your teeth, madam," hissed the Lord of the Marches, "you will speak only to answer our questions and no word more."

As the Eorl strode off to the table in the centre of the room to pour himself a goblet of wine from the jug, Eádgar Aeðlric tried to get the wayward conversation back on track. His patience was wearing damnably thin with these puerile political intriguers whose every action seemed to be motivated by childish spite rather than being governed by practical deliberation toward a clearly defined objective.

"Lady," he said gently, "you know well the situation for which we must find remedy. Can you afford us the means to pursue the plan we have devised?"

In calculated contravention of the Eorl's command that she should speak only when spoken to, the defiant mademoiselle did not respond to the Aeðlric's direct question but instead asked of Ealdræd:

"The General tells us that this plan is of your devising, Aenglian. How is it that such artfulness is to be found in one of no social rank?"

Her seductive voice held only a slight trace of playful, teasing condescension but without that austere disdain which would have made it offensive; rather, if it held any particular spice, it was that of the subtly flirtatious. The man so addressed had been known in his time to break the bones of those whose tone veered too far into the supercilious. On this occasion, as if suspending his final judgement of her until later, he answered plainly and without emotion:

"If a man lives a goodly while in the business of the world and keeps his ears open, he hears many things. Some of those things may be of use to him. During the time that I was soldiering in Ahkran . . . ." without exception every single person in the room, even the Eorl Atheldun, raised their eyebrows at this casual mention of so impossibly remote a country; to be in conversation with someone who had actually seen the place with their own eyes was unusual in the extreme ". . . . the senior officers in the defence militia of the Ahkrani prophet-vizier undermined an opposing army from one of the Gathkar Queens by insinuating a poison into the Gathkar forces' water supply. The Gathkarees died like flies from the resultant plague and were convinced that it was an act of the Ahkrani gods.

There were many religious conversions and the Gathkar Queen was sold into slavery for three hundred camels. It was considered a bargain by the Ahkrani tribal chief who bought her because . . . . but that is besides the point. The use of poison and superstitious fervour worked very effectively in the cause of the prophet-vizier and it seemed to me that you might well try something of the sort here if you did but have a supply of a suitable source of poison. It is not an art of which I have any knowledge but I thought that perhaps you, Lady . . . ." and then he grinned cheerfully in gesture towards Maev de Lederwyrhta as he had, in effect, branded her a poisoner.

The mademoiselle took full notice of the braided northerner properly for the first time, looking long at him directly in the face. He returned her stare calmly, and although she said nothing further to him for the moment there was sufficient communication in her fluently evocative eyes for personal contact to have been established between them. Maev de Lederwyrhta now turned back to Eádgar and said matter of factly:

"The wise counsellor is right in his expectation; I can indeed place my hand upon a suitable toxin," her lips curled into a malicious smile as if she were anticipating the lamentable calamity that she was about to unleash upon an unsuspecting humanity, "but it will be necessary for someone to actually enter the Geulten camp to put the potion into their communal cooking pots. It is usual for half the army to fill their eating bowls from those enormous soup-kettles and their Bhourgbon mulch stew tastes so foul that a heavy dose of blightworm can only improve the flavour."

The Eorl Atheldun had taken a severe dislike to the Aenglian from the instant of his arrival the night before, and this dislike had deepened further at the barbarian's gross presumption in daring to propose a stratagem; an impertinence that seemed to his Lordship perilously close to being an insult to his betters. What *was* the fellow, after all, but one of a thousand nameless bodies to be advanced under the arrow storm and thereafter left on the field of war as meat for the carrion crows. Yet this commoner had put himself ahead of his own General in planning their tactics? And now their whole enterprise, a matter of the greatest possible consequence, was to be invested in this fellow's strategy for lack of any other. It did not sit well with the Eorl at all.

So, suppressing with a wave of his hand the young guardsman's fidgety desire to volunteer for the dangerous job of infiltrating the enemy camp, his Lordship turned from the woman he so despised to a man that he liked little better and took this gratifying opportunity to enlist him in the task.

"Adequate, mademoiselle, for we have just the fellow here for the manoeuvre you describe. Well, Ealdræd of the Aenglia, you have played the spy with us, now you can try your luck with the Oénjil."

There was something in the big veteran's expression, a slight shadow of annoyance or provocation, which suggested that his mind had returned to thoughts of the breaking of bones for those guilty of an injudicious tone in their speech. The Captain-General of Mercenaries had noticed it and, exercising his new-found talent for diplomacy, he spoke up quickly to settle the matter. The Eorl's bland assumption that Ealdræd was his to command might cut little sway from the Aenglian's perspective, but if the Aeðlric so ordered it, the mercenary would comply. To help smooth the waters, he added a bonus to a soldier's pay:

"I quite agree, my Lord Eorl," concurred Eádgar, "but this man is, like myself, a mercenary who fights for money. I thought, perhaps, twenty pieces of gold . . . . ?"

". . . . upon his *return*, his mission accomplished," completed the Eorl, for whom so small a purse of gold was trifling but he wasn't about to send the fellow off with his saddlebags full of coin and expect the Aenglian trash to do anything but abscond with it.

"So be it, my Lord," confirmed Eádgar. "The army of the Duke is mustered two days hard riding from here. The infiltration of their camp must necessarily take place during the night, and if he does not accomplish it at the first attempt, there will certainly be no chance of a second. Therefore the entire journey should take between four and five days. We may expect his return on the fourteenth day of *tocyme tilung*, the advent of husbandry."

*   *   *

Having seen as much of the continent as he had, Ealdræd was not dismayed at the duty which had fallen to his lot. The mission was not, in his view, as perilous as it might at first appear. No matter what the nation, army camps were riotously disordered places, not

139

least at night, where a man might walk at will with little chance of being challenged so long as he acted with nonchalance. As a soldier for pay, Ealdræd had been a foreign mercenary in many an army betwixt the weeping cliffs of the Canbrai Isles and the turreted towers of Piccoli. He would not feel so very out of place sauntering through the rows of tents of the Duke's men.

Ealdræd spoke the Geulten language with a broad East Bhourgbon accent for that was the region within the alliance of the three crowns in which he had spent the most time during the wandering course of his life's travels, having spent many months there recovering from near fatal wounds in his younger days; and if a man from the Ehngle peninsula is to spend any length of time in such a place then he had better lose no time in learning how to speak in the local dialect or be ready to brawl on a daily basis. Given this dialect, it was no more than common sense for Ealdræd to dress himself in the East Bhourgbon style to adopt a rough and ready disguise. There was little difficulty in this since the male fashion in those parts consisted chiefly of farmer's knee-length woollen breeches and cambric shirts, items that could be found anywhere on either side of the border.

That said, there was one measure that needs must be taken to disguise himself. In none of the Geulten realms was it the custom to plait the hair except for the Barony of Langelais where, in the inexplicably perverse manner of custom, the practice was exclusively restricted to women. Consequently, before setting off the Aenglian had to disguise himself by unplaiting his braids. With a slyly mischievous smile Mademoiselle de Lederwyrhta instructed her lady-in-waiting, Mistress Bryony, to assist him in this. The girl acquiesced with an engrained reflex of spontaneous obedience but her excruciating embarrassment at being in such extreme proximity to the fearsome Aenglian savage as he sat on a stool and she so very delicately unlaced his braids was almost as much a pleasure for Maev de Lederwyrhta to witness as it was for the Aenglian to enjoy, and the eyes of the mercenary and the courtesan met severally during the long process in shared good humour.

With his hair and beard worn loose, the northerner somehow appeared to Mistress Bryony to be even more wildly uncivilized rather than less, and when he slipped an arm around her waist and pulled her down onto his lap she shrieked and struggled away instantly, his laughter ringing around the room.

"If you've quite finished teasing and playing the coquet for your soldier, Bryony," mocked the Lady Maev, "you can let him be about his errand for the Lord Eorl."

Mistress Bryony, her milk white skin blushing scarlet from scalp to throat and her tender lips speechless with incredulity at this smirking injustice, looked reproachfully at her superior and curtseyed modestly.

But the Aenglian did in truth have a duty to attend to. The Aeðlric gave Ealdræd a roll of paper with the General's personal seal imprinted upon it so that he might have safe conduct through the Ehngle advance picket lines, especially upon his return journey when he would be coming from the direction of the enemy. The seal of Eádgar Aeðlric commanded respect wherever it was seen. With that, and a casket containing a bottle with the Bhelenese courtesan's poison in it, the tall spearman took to horse.

First he rode only back to Muster. There he found stabling for his mighty blue-roan charger Hengustir with a troop of Aenglian cavalry of the Wreocan clan, known amongst the clans of Aenglia as 'the oath-takers' because of their fidelity to their vows. One ruddy-cheeked lad amongst their number agreed for a fee of one gold sovereign to tend the roan until Ealdræd returned within the week. Ealdræd would be in a position to afford this because he was confident that he would be duly paid his own reward of twenty pieces of gold; for if the Eorl, a man of ambiguous honour, were to renege upon the debt, then the Aeðlric would certainly feel honour-bound make good out of his own purse. Meanwhile, the Wreocan would defend the horse with his life rather than be in breach of promise, and the safety of Hengustir was worth a gold sovereign fifty times over.

What made all this necessary was that the Aeðlric, for reasons known only to himself, had given Ealdræd no more than five days to complete his task, and this would mean ruining the horse which was to carry him hence. So much continuous hard riding would break the animal's wind. Ealdræd had no intention of damaging his faithful Hengustir so wastefully. Instead he stabled the magnificent brute with the Wreocan and, using the General's seal, he commandeered an army horse from the quartermaster. He harnessed it with his own saddle so that he might take his weapons with him in the hanging saddle sheaths, then he put the animal to its heels and headed at speed for the border of Oénjil.

Clovis Ascelin of the city of Charibel in the region of Montesauril was in as foul a mood as any archer of King Philippe facing battle within the month had a right to be. The army was riding high on the crest of the wave of last summer's victory, the Ehngle filth who opposed them were in disarray as a result of their own cowardly reliance upon witchcraft, and with the enemy in such poor order the Geulten victory in the forthcoming campaign was a foregone conclusion, yet here he was as penniless as an Eildressian goatherd whilst all evening and well into the night there had been gambling pits all over camp where he might have plucked a fortune from the dirt-farmers and dung-slingers with whom so much of this Oénjil army of the Duke Etienne en Dieu seemed to be composed. It was heartbreaking to be encamped amongst so many fools whose money was there for the taking and not have a paltry stake to get him started. He had twice attempted to sit in with a game on credit, but not even the hayseeds would tolerate that.

It was just as he was advising himself that sterner measures were required that he spied one such old farmer trudging head-down through the ropes of the tents, dressed in his bog-trotter's breeches and the grey in his long curtain of hair glinting silver in the moonlight. The oaf was carrying a casket. Ascelin knew what would be in that casket: a bottle. It was a disgrace to the embroidered tabard that Ascelin wore so proudly in the colours of King Philippe of Guillaime for some old farmer to have the price of a bottle when he, an archer of the colours, had none. Upon the instant, Ascelin knew what he would do. If the casket contained a decent Guillain wine, he would drink it himself and if it were some inferior foreign bilge he would sell it and use the cash as a stake to wager. The archer from Charibel circled around to intercept the bumpkin at a point where the lights of the torch fires didn't quite penetrate the shaded areas between the baggage tents.

Ealdræd was walking unhurriedly through the Geulten muster so naturally that he would hardly have been noticed at all by anyone who hadn't a strong reason for doing so. Yet by mischance, Clovis Ascelin, his mind festering on his resentments toward the hog-breeding peasantry, was precisely of a mind to take note of a fellow in a baggy cambric shirt and mud-splattered breeches carrying an object of likely value, whose greying hair suggested that he might be an easy target. Ealdræd had deliberately contrived to appear innocuous, very far from the daunting fighting man that was his normal aspect, but now the very success of that disguise had told against him. As he stepped from one shadow into another, a man in a Guillain emerald green tabard challenged him for his casket.

"You, there, dung-shifter. Surrender your burden to the pride of King Philippe!"

The old farmer paused and looked about him. It was evident that the Guillain had no confederates close by. Despite mention of the king's name, the man's voice had been hushed, from which Ealdræd correctly deduced that this was not a guard challenging a suspected intruder. That the fellow had demanded the casket seemed to confirm that this was a mere thief. The Aenglian had no leisure to contemplate the irony of this light-fingered bully-boy wishing to steal a bottle that, had he but known it, contained enough poison to kill him a thousand times over. All that mattered was to dispose of this interference as swiftly and as silently as possible.

Ealdræd had buried his spear and javelins wrapped in chamois leather just outside the pickets of the Geulten muster, for they would have seemed incongruous had he been seen carrying them, and so he was armed now only with his twenty-inch knife. The man facing him was bearing a double-edged sword, short enough to be held in one hand. The man from Guillaime eased forward on the balls of his feet and, deciding that the old fellow was either too deaf or too stupid to save his life by surrendering the casket, he lunged with the point of the sword darting directly toward his victim's face.

Ealdræd dodged aside with such nimbleness that to the Guillain he seemed to simply vanish into the air. The would-be thief swung round in the direction that he assumed his prey to have fled and the Aenglian's counter strike with his knife was a flash of polished iron in the dark. The weapon would have embedded itself in the Guillain's chest to the hilt but the man's reflexes were fast enough for him to raise an arm to block the blow. However, this meant that the knife point was driven solidly right through the meat of the fellow's forearm which caused him to drop the sword as the shock of the penetration of his body seized his mind. The knife blade caught on the bone and Ealdræd couldn't pull it free before the fellow had staggered back, saucer-eyed with astonishment and disbelief, taking the knife with him, his arm impaled at right angles.

With both men effectively disarmed, the combat became more primitive still. Clovis Ascelin's mind had yet to come properly to terms with his circumstances, these being so at variance with his expectation, when Ealdræd's unexpected low stamping kick buckled the Guillain's knee and as the man lurched off-balance the Aenglian got a hefty punch into the fellow's startled face, missed with a kick to the balls that none the less did damage to his adversary's thigh, hit him low to the kidney, then spun him around and grabbed him from behind in a hold used by the wrestlers of the Heurtslin; Ealdræd got his hands under his opponent's arms and round the back of his head. From that position he could apply pressure. Enough pressure and the man's neck would break. The disoriented, pain-drenched Guillain archer heaved up, then squatted down, and threw himself from side to side in the effort to break free.

All this while the man in the embroidered green tabard still had Ealdræd's broad knife sticking grotesquely through his arm as they fought; both fighting in silence for the Guillain was a thief and would be hanged if caught, whilst the Ehngle warrior was a spy who, if identified as such, would be flayed alive. But with the neck-lock in place the Aenglian spearman's massive shoulders and upper arms could be brought into play upon the straining vertebrae of the Guillain archer's spine and amid the frantic gasps and grunts of their life and death exertions there came a loud crack and the Guillain fell limp in his killer's calloused hands. The city of Charibel in the region of Montesauril had lost one of its sons.

Rather than waste time hiding the body Ealdræd left it in the deep shadows where it was unlikely to be found before morning unless someone tripped over the bastard when ambling off for a piss in the middle of the night. When daylight led to its discovery Ealdræd would have long since departed or be already stripped of his skin, and the Guillain's death would be attributed to some random quarrel.

It took only a few minutes more to find the central cooking area with its enormous communal cooking pots. They were unguarded. The fires were out and the vicinity deserted. Most of those still awake were gathered around their company bonfires, swapping lies and sleepily singing songs. It would not have occurred to anyone to think of bothering to protect cooking utensils. Ealdræd proceeded to take the bottle from the casket and slop a large dollop of the mademoiselle's potion into each open kettle.

Hidden in the tops of his boots he had a pair of rustic leather gloves. Maev de Lederwyrhta had warned him in deep seriousness not to allow a drop of the toxin to make contact with his skin and to discard the gloves immediately he had finished using them. He was also advised not to breathe too close to the open bottle. Ealdræd took all her warnings as soberly as she had delivered them. Poison was no weapon for an honest soldier and as he slopped the virulent muck from the bottle in a gloved hand he held it as far from himself as his arm would reach, and he had a fold of his shirt stretched across his nose and mouth. This was pestilential work. He dropped the bottle into the final pot, thinking it unlikely that anyone would bother to look inside before making their next fifty gallon batch of potato-stew stomach liner.

Making away from the cooking area he threw the gloves into the first unattended fire he passed. Ealdræd was careful not to hurry as he took his leave of the Geulten camp; just another drunken reveller staggering off to find a blanket to sleep under. One of thousands. He made it passed the drowsy picket guards without further incident. Before dawn he had dug up his weapons and was a-horse riding west as fast as the tired nag could run.

*   *   *

Ealdræd had been uncertain when he had first formulated this plot as to how he would convince Hob to play along with it, because the recalcitrance of the man might cause him to react against any scheme that had been hatched in the interests of those prominent Wehnbrian politicians of whom the young halberdier had such a low opinion. But by the time Ealdræd reached the sentries of the Ehngle muster in the growing darkness of the evening he had entirely revised his thinking on the matter and decided on the substitute plan of keeping Hob out of any knowledge of the conspiracy, for the man was less than discreet, and simply tell him of the supposed cursing of the Geulten as if this were a prevalent rumour that he had heard when in Amsburgh. He would approach Hob in the manner of one seeking counsel from the politically astute Sæxyn as to whether this rumour, widespread in the city, was to be believed or not.

The impromptu subterfuge worked a good deal better than he could reasonably have hoped and Ealdræd's judgement of Hob's character proved fully justified. Hob, flattered that so seasoned and

145

experienced a veteran as Ealdræd should call upon him for advice, seized upon the story at once, finding it easy to lend credence to so twisted a narrative, and was earnestly believing the story almost before the Aenglian had finished the telling of it. Not that Hob spoke of his acceptance straight away. First he pulled a few faces to express judicious scepticism before finally confiding in Ealdræd his judgement that the rumour was undoubtedly a true one and that he, Hob, could give Ealdræd the reason why; it was because none in the ruling caste could restrain for long their slothful addiction to their basely debauched appetites and the villainous Bhelenese trollop was too insidiously one of their own kind for the likes of Eorls and Barons to deny themselves her hex-craft for very long.

What was really persuading the normally sceptical Sæxyn into credulous belief, and perhaps the boy did not even realise this himself, was that Hob was simply the kind of person who is always ready to believe a good story. He was more than just receptive to the idea; he *wanted* to believe it for then he could have the satisfaction of relating the tale to others around the camp to the general astonishment of all, along with a few permissible embellishments here and there to add a frisson of still greater scandal to the drama. It was too good an opportunity for a man like Hob to let pass by. No, no, the story had to be believed true.

Although Ealdræd was convinced that the seed had been thoroughly sewn, he guaranteed that it would bear fruit by whispering to Hob, as he left the young Sæxyn for a much needed night's sleep, that they had best keep this matter to themselves so that when the hazardous and possibly seditious story broke, as it soon would, it would have nothing to do with either of them. Ealdræd could almost see Hob twitch at the thought of someone else getting the credit for having first knowledge of a tale as absorbing as this of machination and artifice in high places.

The next afternoon in camp Ealdræd recovered a healthy-looking Hengustir from the Aenglian of the Wreocan clan, paying him out one gold sovereign from the twenty that Ealdræd had collected that morning from a brusque but plainly satisfied Eorl Atheldun. His Lordship was not so much a fool that he did not rate ability in his underlings. Ealdræd had risen in the Eorl's estimation, if not in his liking.

As the Aenglians took the time for some conversation together, a passing Wehnbrian squire's page greeted them cheerily, paused beside them, tapped a dirty finger along the side of his nose in a signal of secret communication, and informed them both of the good news. The bitch from Bhel had been taught the error of her ways by the Eorl Atheldun's torturers and had now smote the bastard Geulten with a black curse that would ensure an Ehngle victory. Ealdræd feigned ignorance and the squire's page confided with a knowing wink that besides the torments of the noble lord's dungeons, it had also been the sexual favours of a particularly handsome and lusty jailor's apprentice which had convinced the insatiable strumpet to switch sides.

Within the hour Ealdræd overheard two soldiers arguing the matter heatedly because one had heard that Maev de Lederwyrhta had agreed to curse the Geulten on condition that she could have the pick of the Wehnbrian Household Guard as her male harem of lovers until the war was won; whereas the other fellow had heard that despite the witch-harlot relenting and agreeing to curse the Geulten to atone for her misdeeds, his lordship still wanted her punished for past treacheries and had decided to give her to the Household Guard for their sexual use until she had been raped to death. Each was convinced that his version of the story was the correct one, and the two men came to blows over the question.

Three days later reports started coming into the muster from multiple sources that spoke of a rampant dysenteric pestilence amongst the Geulten that spread like no natural disease. It was being said that one in ten of the Oénjil and their allies were afflicted already, and the death toll was rising faster than could be calculated. Ealdræd, thinking back to how close he had been to the contents of that bottle, shivered in disgust and aversion. If these reports were even half true, then it demonstrated the abominable potency of Maev de Lederwyrhta's casket of plague. It was hideously contagious.

In fact, had Ealdræd but known it, the ferocious outbreak of dysentery that was ravaging the Geulten army was absolutely as deadly as had been reported. In the last few days they had lost hundreds of their soldiers to a form of dysentery so severe that it was always crippling and very frequently fatal. The bloody flux was a gross disorder of the belly and bowels that caused an arse-shriveling diarrhoea so abominable that should death carry off the sufferer, they went willingly to escape the lacerating mortification of their innards. The infection attacked the intestines and caused profuse internal bleeding that saturated the constant diarrhoea, hence the name 'bloody flux'. Incessant dry vomiting, sweltering fever and crippling abdominal pains added to the sufferer's incessant agonies. No wonder that so many wished themselves dead before they actually died.

Hob's gossipy agitation had set a brigade of tongues wagging and with the word coming out of the army that the Bhelenese whore had turned upon the Geulten and smote them with a curse, the first accounts of a devastating plague amongst the Oénjil was seen to definitely confirm this in every particular. Thereafter the story spread as fast as lips could tell it and no one doubted the origin of the flux, for once the news had gone abroad that this deadly ailment amongst the Geulten was the work of witchcraft, whom else but Maev de Lederwyrhta could be believed to be behind it? The pestilence soon acquired the name of 'Maev's Malady'. Even so, this alleged change of allegiance in the mademoiselle's sympathies won her no forgiveness amongst the Ehngle. The soubriquet, though spoken of jokingly by the Wehnbrian soldiers, carried no affection in it. And, naturally, when this explanation for their sufferings eventually reached the ears of the Geulten soldiers, the name of de Lederwyrhta was uttered only with the foulest insults. If ever a woman was hated on all sides, that woman was the courtesan from Bhel.

And in regard of the poor suffering Geulten with their arseholes afire and their guts all awry, spewing and dying on the eve of battle, perhaps they had some cause to hate the lady who had inflicted this upon them for she was, or had been, one of their own folk. But then, the loyalties of Maev de Lederwyrhta shared with the fickle caprice of the weather the characteristic of being at best uncertain.

*   *   *

The coalition army of the Duchy of Oénjil under the command of the Duke Etienne en Dieu in person took to the field in something approximating good order and they even looked smart enough from a distance, bolstered as they were by regimented infantry from Guillaime, sent by King Philippe, and light cavalry from Eildres sent by old King Béri himself. The lances of the Eildressian horsemen were as pretty as a parade ground. The Duke Etienne's victory at the battle of Fontónil the previous year had prompted this martial bounty from the allied Geulten crowns. But closer inspection revealed that their ranks were full of men so gravely weakened by the pitiless dysentery endemic in their army that many of the footsoldiers could barely march to the front and stand to, whilst there were cavalrymen who could scarcely maintain their saddles.

The field of conflict had been chosen. It was a narrow valley between steep hills on either side so that access to the ground to be fought over was from the west and the east only. To the north and south they were hemmed in. No elaborate flanking manoeuvres would be available to either of the commanding Generals, with the valley funnelling the front lines of the massed soldiery of each army directly into their oncoming enemies so that they could advance or retreat but they could do nothing else. It seemed that the ground had been selected to ensure a decisive result, for the army that turned in rout would be at the mercy of the opposing cavalry.

Above the open canopied pavilion tent of the Ehngle Commander-in-Chief could be seen the fluttering banners of all three of those matchless noblemen who exercised sovereign power in kingless Wehnbria: Eorl Caridian of the Eorldom of Shrewford, Eorl Aykin of the Eorldom of Chestbury, and Eorl Atheldun of the Eorldom of the Marches. All had brought regiments into the field and all had stumped up the monies to pay for the defence of their imperilled lands. In truth, however, the Eorls Caridian and Aykin were on hand purely politically, not militarily. They paraded themselves in glistening plate armour to inspire their troops but this was entirely for the sake of appearances; neither would under any circumstances engage in the actual fighting. Their role was as figureheads. Only Atheldun would play an active part. It was the great March Lord who would personally command the massed army of the Ehngle as its supreme general in the imminent conflict.

At the Eorl Caridian's right hand was the youthful Athelwin Godricson, the Castellan of Hove, an Atheling of the blood royal in the lineage of Wehnbria's long dead monarchy. He was there at the Eorl's insistence. Having not the wit to properly appreciate Eádgar Aeðlric's quality, the presumptuous Caridian had wanted an aristocrat to oversee the actions of the low-born Captain-General of mercenaries. Atheldun had thought it politic to comply and had appointed the noble youth to the position of liaison officer, but had privately informed the Castellan that he should not impose himself upon the Aeðlric in any way and, all things considered, it would be best if Athelwin Godricson just adopted the role of an observer and tried not to get underfoot. The vanity of the Atheling bristled like a hog's back at being compared unfavourably with a man who, whatever his merits as a professional soldier, was none the less merely the son of a wine cooper. The squinting of Godricson's imperious eye had more to do with the bitterness in his soul than with the dazzlingly bright sunlight that swept the field of conflict panoramic before them.

When finally the Wehnbrian forces had mobilised from muster and headed eastward, they had covered no more than fifty miles to reach this battlefield. The name of the place was Proctors Wæl, named for some ancient steward whose responsibility it had been to watch over this stretch of land near the Wehnbrian/Oénjil border. That the name was in the Ehngle language gave telling evidence as to which side of the border this battle was to take place and which of the two nations was on the defensive.

Without the need to forage for supplies as it went, the Wehnbrian army had been able to move twenty miles a day, whereas it would have made little more than ten or even five miles a day when foraging on the march. But they had been well-stocked by Amsburgh. This also kept the cavalry, who did the lion's share of the foraging, on the road and out of the habitations of the populace, and so it minimised the problems that habitually arose from the killing and raping of peasants, which was a consideration when travelling through friendly territory. Although when in enemy territory, of course, looting and pillaging were actively encouraged so long as they didn't disrupt the line of march too much. Leaving aside the issue of the violation of local peasants, if anyone were of such delicate sensibilities as to consider this an issue, the main consequence of the Wehnbrian army having so short a march to Proctors Wæl was that it meant they were fresh for the fighting when they arrived. And now that witchery appeared to be involved in events rather more in their favour than against them, their morale was relatively good and they were in fine fettle.

Ealdræd, who had spent the last few months of his life travelling down from Aenglia specifically to participate in this war, was ironically not to take part in it after all because he had been commissioned, with an additional purse of twenty pieces of silver from Eádgar Aeðlric to match the gold he had received from the Eorl Atheldun, to escort the now superfluous Maev de Lederwyrhta to wherever she wished to go. The lady had played her role and would be of least embarrassment to all concerned if she were simply to disappear from the scene with as little fuss as possible. When charging the Aenglian warrior with this political embassy the Captain-General of mercenaries had expected a verbose show of reluctance from the bloodlustful veteran but Ealdræd had surprised him by accepting the task as "an honour, Lord Aeðlric". Eádgar put this unexpected attitude down to the extraordinary erotic charisma and personal charm of the intoxicating witch. What else could it be?

The lady could find no safe haven now in either the Ehngle lands or the Geulten kingdoms so she had opted to attempt to return to Bhel. Despite the considerable distance involved Ealdræd had readily agreed to take her at least as far as the Heurtslin coast where she might take ship, or if no vessel could be found to navigate the treacherous waters of the 'Mariners Cauldron' then as far as the great barrier of the Cordennes Mountains where she might find a guide to carry her over. The battle of Proctors Wæl would have to be fought without him.

Ealdræd, Maev de Lederwyrhta, and Mistress Bryony set off north at once, and with the valley full of two great armies there was no choice but to ride up over the hills to the north. This would of necessity be a slow progress because Maev de Lederwyrhta and her lady-in-waiting were to travel in a small carriage pulled by a single horse. Ealdræd had just drawn breath to make the obvious point that they would make better time if the women each rode a horse when Maev de Lederwyrhta forestalled him by confiding to her Aenglian escort:

"I was once a fine horsewoman and took some pride in the fact. But several of the tortures practiced upon me by the witch-diviners of the Lord Eorl have ensured that I shall not take the saddle again for a very long time. Nor shall I be able to enjoy congress with a man; something else for which I once displayed a certain talent."

She spoke apparently lightly, yet there was an ocean of darkness just below the surface of her words. Her temperament was remarkably resilient but still a shadow had been cast over her normal personality that would not easily lift. Ealdræd, who knew of the coals, the pressing, the trials by fire and water, the ripping and the impalement needles and the cradle and a catalogue of similar atrocities, said no more on the matter.

One consequence of their initial snail's pace was that they had the opportunity to enjoy a perfect view of the battle in the valley below as their small charabanc crept and climbed the steep slope. The carriage horse was led uphill by a junior member of the Eorl's retinue on foot, so there was no need for the ladies to guide the animal with the reins, leaving them free to crane their necks behind them to watch the grand spectacle of war spread out for their entertainment every step of their passage uphill. Hengustir needed no direction from his rider to follow the carriage in from of him, so Ealdræd too could look to the rear and focus his attention on the orchestrated carnage that was about to unfold.

The Bhelenese courtesan, half in jest and half from the genuine interest of a specialist, asked the Aenglian if he saw any sign of illness amongst the Geulten that might be the consequence of the toxin that she had supplied and he had delivered. Since they two had been the actors in that drama, she was curious to know the outcome of their efforts. The veteran scanned his experienced eye over the prettily uniformed army of the Duke, its proliferation of armaments sparkling in the sun, and nodded his head in slow sagacity.

"I see cavalrymen standing in their stirrups; doubtless the scalding conflagration of dysenteric combustion in the ring of their arses does not permit sitting. And there are scores of infantry whose posture suggests that they have shit their britches. Aye, I believe you may compliment yourself on the efficacy of your potion, mademoiselle."

The lady smiled sweetly at this salty congratulation with the innocence of an immaculate virgin. She might have been twelve years old and just taken in holy orders. Mistress Bryony sat next to her with an expression of profound tragedy upon her lovely face, as if understanding the unforgivable gratuitousness of what was about to happen.

On any battlefield anywhere on the continent an army would be split into three basic divisions: the cavalry, the archers, and the infantry. So it was on both sides today, with the devastating Ehngle archers slightly behind and to the sides of the solid barricade of the Wehnbrian shield wall, firmly in its place of honour, front and centre. The cavalry were friskily held in reserve behind the shield wall. The Geulten forces were almost an exact reflection of these lines of battle except that in the place of the shield wall they had lines of infantry many ranks deep.

It was common practice for mercenaries to be incorporated into these divisions. However, if the Eorl Atheldun was knowledgeable on any particular subject it was that of the organisation of an army and he was fully aware that mercenaries could be more effective when permitted to engage the enemy independently as a cavalry/archer/infantry force of their own. This could only work, of course, if they had a strong and charismatic leader who could guarantee their obedience to orders when in combat. In Eádgar Aeðlric they had such a man, and so the March Lord had given him the mercenary brigade as his own division with a roving commission. Let the mercenaries find their killing grounds were they best pleased. This state of affairs was extremely welcome to the common soldiery of the brigade because although these were paid troops who fought in the cause of their paymasters they had a strong sense of themselves as professionals and so greatly approved of a strategy which permitted them to retain their own separate identity as a regiment both on the field and off; with their own rules of conduct and a code of mercenary justice which left them largely free from civil law, for they were answerable in all such matters directly to their own Captain-General. Eorl Atheldun was again wise enough to know that the mercenaries would fight all the better with their morale boosted in this way.

Seventeen thousand men stood sweating in the sun for most of an hour awaiting the off. This preamble of delay always preceded battle though no one for the life of them could have given an adequate reason why. Then the Wehnbrian archers loosed the first of the dozens of arrow storms they would unleash before the sun set, and the Duke Etienne ordered his infantry forward and suddenly the Geulten footsoldiers were charging for all they were worth at the shield wall, trying to cover the three hundred yards or so between them and their enemy before the Ehngle bowmen riddled them with those murderous iron-tipped shafts.

But they were not as fleet of foot as they might ordinarily have been and their bone-crunching impact upon the wall of shields failed to force the Wehnbrians to take a step back. Maev's malady was already working to undermine the best efforts of the Oénjil but stark terror can motivate even those with vomit-empty bellies and ruptured bowels, and the enraged ferocity with which the Geulten tore and slashed at the Huscarls of Wehnbria spoke volumes of their desperate fear and desire to kill. Even so, the Geulten infantry could not split the Wehnbrian shield-wall, though they hewed at it with their maces and cudgels like massy hammers, and with swords sharp from the grinding that cut grievously but futilely against the implacable wall of wood. At the same time the shuffling half-step forward march of the Huscarls in unison moved them slowly but steadily toward the rest of the Geulten army, though shields splintered where sword-blades struck. The long-hafted axes of the Huscarls smote down through the momentary gap that would open between two shields for just long enough for the axe to hack homicidally into a Geulten body before the shields closed tight together again.

The Ehngle archery squadrons kept up a withering diagonal cross-fire from as far to each flank as they could manoeuvre to discourage a cavalry advance that might smash through the centre, while the Geulten archers concentrated their fire to arc over the shields to fall upon the Wehnbrians from above. Shuffling their insistent half-step forward march over the ripped and shredded corpses of the first wave of the Oénjil, the shield wall of the Huscarls pushed onward stoically all morning, foremost in the advance, as stout as oak and as solid as rock, inching forward step by step in an impregnable line. Before them fell whatever stood in the way of their relentlessly grinding and unyielding momentum. The glorious Huscarls, as befitted their descent from ancestors of courage, defended their land in the slaughter of battle against the hostile horde of Oénjil and rejoiced that their enemy perished in such copious quantity, as they were fated so to do, said many, by the dark witchery of the malign Maev de Lederwyrhta.

As the forward motion of the Ehngle front line began to increase in speed, the Oénjil foot now falling over one another in the attempt to withdraw to a stronger position, the Duke sent in all the regimented infantry he had received from Guillaime to support his own troops, but the Aeðlric had brought his mercenary archers forward in a wedge formation from the side. He had placed his pike in amongst the archers to ward off any potential counter-strike from the Geulten. The arrows of the mercenaries whipped across the short intervening gap between them and the enemy and in true mercenary style their shafts were kept low, less than a yard off the ground, to fly under the raised shields of the Geulten to feather viciously into their legs, slicing them down to be finished off later. The Guillain infantry had to turn to meet this new threat from their right and this took all the impetus out of their advance.

This soon got bogged down into a stalemate between the infantry and Eádgar's wisely positioned pike whose long weapons kept the infantry at bay whilst the mercenary archers regrouped. All in all, this meant that the Duke's foot reserve had been committed to no visible effect. From now on it would be a battle of attrition. With both the initial and reinforced attacks against the Wehnbrian shield wall failing so conspicuously, there was no longer any question that the plague amongst the Geulten had left them seriously weaker than expected. The Wehnbrian army took heart. It was perhaps at this point that the battle turned decisively in favour of the western army for with his infantry giving ground continuously there was no real opportunity for the Duke to commit his cavalry. But were he to draw his cavalry back he would be leaving his soldiers afoot to an inevitable fate.

When the Huscarls' shield wall drew level with the Geulten archers, the lightly armoured bowmen had little choice but to take to their heels and the sight of their own comrades fleeing took away whatever heart remained amongst the Oénjil and Guillain infantry. As they turned in flight the Wehnbrian front line was no longer shuffling its interminable half-step forward march but instead was running in pursuit, and that was when the Eorl Atheldun commanded his cavalry forward. The thundering avalanche of heavy horseflesh that pounded toward the frantically escaping Geulten poured through the opening that suddenly appeared in the centre of the shield wall and the Wehnbrians on horseback rapidly overtook the scurrying, scampering enemy in seconds.

The mercenary cavalry joined in the hunt and, had he not been otherwise occupied, that was where Ealdræd himself would have been at this moment, in close order with his Captain-General, using his spear as a lance, the long wooden shaft of hardened ash bloody for half its length. Instead, Ealdræd, watching from his vantage point on the hill, could just make out a fancily beribboned Sæxyn, not so much dressed as costumed, on a fine black mare keeping pace alongside the Aeðlric and attempting to wield a long double-handed broadsword that well-suited his affectation of noble status but which was quite the wrong choice of weapon in the saddle. As the old Aenglian mercenary shook his head in censorious disapproval the sartorially flamboyant fellow with the unwise taste for ornamental weaponry flailed wildly at a footsoldier, missed, and failed to haul his too-heavy blade back into position in time to prevent impalement upon an out-thrust Geulten pike. The peacock was unhorsed and went down into the cloud of dust at ground level to be trampled to death by the ranks of cavalry rattling along behind him. Should've got himself a good serviceable spear, thought Ealdræd. Then the Aeðlric was lost from sight as the mayhem surged forward.

By mid-afternoon the battle was over and the Geulten retreat had cost them nearly all of their soldiers on foot. Their cavalry managed a staged withdrawal to the relative security of the moated trenches of the Nanthil Dyke some twelve leagues distant over the border into their own lands but that was small comfort for the Duke. The day could not be considered anything other than a shameful and calamitous loss for the House of Oénjil. His army had been the larger but it had been forced to concede the ground and at a terrible loss of life.

A vast legion of broken humanity lay in clusters across the valley floor, destroyed by arrow-storm, axe-bite, sword-impalement, lance-point and spearhead. But most especially it had been the axes of the Huscarls that had broken the Geulten. The archers may have killed more men but it was the Huscarls who had smashed their spirit. The field flowered with the rose red corpses of the slain and the grievously wounded warriors who, hacked about mortally, would soon to join their number. The countless dead, in their grim mortality, bearing an awful, honourable testimony to the weary and the war-sated army of the Ehngle as to the dread strength of the Wehnbrians, the Sæxyns, the Merthyans, the Heurtslin, and the Aenglians in the trading of blows.

But there were dead on both sides. The ruddy-faced Aenglian of the Wreocan clan who had taken care of Hengustir in Ealdræd's absence lay with his head caved in and his belly rent asunder. Bereft of his kinsmen, fallen in midst of the mightiest strife, he had found an unsought resting place in the charnel house of slaughter, hewn and hacked to pieces, with the crows partaking of carrion flesh.

But not so with a certain young halberdier of the raggle-taggle. Hob, his blond beard splattered bloody under his Sæxyn's shaven upper lip, had suffered a sword point through the shoulder some time since but now as he sat in recline on a dead horse like a triumphant war-god at rest he felt little pain from his wound for a woman from amongst the baggage-train had brought him a flask of ale and he was relating to an exhausted Merthyan cudgeller nearby the story of how he had buried the blade of his halberd so deep into the skull of one Geulten pig that he had lost his weapon but continued in the thickest press of the fight with a hand-axe and poniard recovered from the ground with which he had skewered an armoured knight of the Oénjil who had been so remiss as to open the visor of his helmet so as to breathe in the crush and thereby taken Hob's poniard full in the face. The Merthyan had seen no armoured knights amongst the infantry but lacked the energy to comment upon the fact. Hob meanwhile was modestly admitting that the noble knight had been just the cream of the half dozen lives that he had ended this day, and where was there another tankard of ale for a Sæxyn hero of the fighting men of Ehngle who had earned strong beer by the cask for the deeds of valour he had performed . . . . . ?

Then amongst the carnage, riding slowly and majestically in unstained armour on unwinded horses under their colourful banners, came the Eorl Caridian of Shrewford and the Eorl Aykin of Chestbury. They hailed their fighting men as they rode, commending one and all for an historic day's work. They were seeking the Ehngle Commander-in-Chief, Eorl Atheldun of the Marches, who was somewhere in the midst of the cavalry where, unlike his noble cousins, he had laboured gallantly in his country's service. The Eorl's were keen to congratulate him on his victory. Alongside Caridian, seated stiff-backed on a fine bay stallion, was the Castellan of Hove, Athelwin Godricson. Despite his not having stirred from the side of his lordship throughout the butcher's engagement, he had somehow contrived a conspicuous smear of enemy blood across his breastplate. And very dashing it looked, too.

High above the valley of Proctors Wæl, on the rim of the hillside, Ealdræd was riding escort to Maev de Lederwyrhta and her lady-in-waiting on the road north. They had waited to witness the outcome of the battle, of course, and to see the fulfilment of the Aenglian's plan, albeit one for which Maev would get all the credit and all the blame. As if thinking of this very thing, the mademoiselle said to her escort:

"I would as lief both armies had destroyed each other utterly, for whilst I have burned my bridges with the shallow, rascally knaves of the three crowns it affords me no pleasure to see a triumph for the beggarly whoreson, rogue and pander of an Eorl you serve."

"Not I," answered Ealdræd with a sprightly demur, "I have taken the mercenary's shilling under the Lord Aeðlric. I serve none other."

"Then you chose wisely when taking your payment, my sagacious greybeard counsel," said the mademoiselle with an open but good-natured mockery upon his name.

The Eorl's retainer, somewhat shocked by the conversation he had just overheard, was happy to depart from the company of these disrespectful foreigners and return to his master in the valley below, uncertain as to what to report to his lordship in regard of the potentially treasonous comments he had heard spoken. It was not always wise to be the messenger.

The three travellers then turned reflectively from the scene of devastation, leaving the mutilation and entrails of the butcher's yard out of sight and beginning a journey by which they sought asylum somewhere in the world for the notorious Bhelenese. Behind them as they rode off was the battlefield; ahead they knew not. Ealdræd observed sardonically to his companion:

"Now that you are popularly believed to have split one country in twain by your witchcraft and shattered an entire army with a single curse, you shall be more feared that ever before. If you live, there will not be many who will dare to cross you after this."

"That thought had occurred to me as long ago as our introduction in Amsburgh," replied Maev de Lederwyrhta with a chuckle.

Ealdræd laughed with something like affection and confessed: "I do not doubt it, Lady, I do not doubt it."

Mistress Bryony, somewhat less self-conscious now that it was merely the three of them alone on the road, spoke up to ask: "Will the Geulten be pursued into Oénjil, mademoiselle?"

"Neither country is in particularly good condition for a prolonged campaign," was Maev's opinion. "The Oénjil have suffered a shameful defeat and the Wehnbrians, despite their splendid success today, still have crippling political problems back home." She smiled as she said it; she the architect of those woes. "I suspect that there will be no further battles this summer, both ruling castes being happy to await better circumstances next year."

"Poor pickings for a professional man," added Ealdræd in accord with her analysis.

"So after all that terrible horror and all those poor men killed, no one is really the victor," concluded Mistress Bryony sadly.

"For a politician like myself, perhaps the only victory is survival," said Maev de Lederwyrhta.

"Aye, mademoiselle," agreed Ealdræd, "it is the same for mercenary soldiers."

Chapter 4

Mercenary Justice

The wide road known as the 'Archer's Furrow' that ran directly north from the Wehnbrian Marches to the border of Heurtslin, and in fact beyond it all the way to the capital Skælig, was a long-established and well-frequented thoroughfare. It had to be. This was the highway up and down which troops patrolled the long border between the great peninsula of the Ehngle peoples and the Geulten nations to the east who occupied the centre of the vast continent that was the known world. Unusually straight and broad in its construction, the Furrow cut an orderly swathe through the leafy rural woodland of the Northern Marches. Someone walking along it might pass by fellow travellers as frequently as twice an hour, which meant that there were also occasional hostelries upon the road, there being sufficient trade to justify their existence, if not to ensure their prosperity.

Lacking something of the fame of the Herebeorht Passage, its Sæxyn equivalent that ran almost parallel to it for many leagues, it could claim to be just as important and perhaps more so. For where the Herebeorht was a highway of commerce and trade, the Archer's Furrow was an extended parade ground for the soldiery of Wehnbria and Heurtslin on their respective sides of the border, and a lifeline for the security of the peninsula.

Our grandfathers' grandfathers would have seen the great Ehngle hero, Beornheard, lead the rump of a once proud army along the Furrow to face the flower of Guillain chivalry and set their lives to the chance. Beorn meant 'bear' and it was at the battle to which the hero gave his name, the Bear's Sacrifice, that a motley of Wehnbrian longbowmen supported by a meagre force of Sæxyn infantry put to shameful flight the massed knights and nobility of Guillaime, though the bold Beornheard himself had fallen in the struggle. Having set the fletchers to the task of making ten hundred score arrows, all of which were used in the eight hours that the conflict lasted, the hero had proven to the world that the archers of the Ehngle nations were the most destructive military power on the planet. They had been rightly feared ever since.

Two generations later this road would have witnessed the 'Congregation of the Iron Anointed' when two hundred Merthyan fanatics, inspired by the ecstatic preaching of their necromancers of mystic divination, had stormed on horseback across the Duchy of Oénjil and the tail of the Fiefdom of Vespaan to turn south into the Kingdom of Bhourgbon where they had set every town, village, and hamlet to burning, slaughtering indiscriminately all classes of persons that came before them and raising an enduring legend of horror, until eventually all two hundred of them were butchered by the Bhourgbon army that halted them outside the city of Crichlé.

And as recently as this very summer the Archers Furrow had been the path down which so many Heurtslin regiments had marched and ridden as allies to their southern neighbours on their way to support the Eorl Atheldun in his desperate conflict with the coalition Geulten army under the Duke Etienne of Oénjil at the battle of Proctors Wæl; a clash of arms gloriously victorious for the Eorl who was now being spoken of openly as a successor to Beornheard.

It was on this exalted martial route so redolent with history that now, making their peaceful and sedate way up the Archers Furrow, was a party of three. A man in the distinctive braided beard of the Aenglians rode on a massive blue-grey roan horse. He was riding escort upon two ladies who sat side by side in a small but expensively made carriage. Superficially, they were unremarkable women typical of their station in life, and if t'were not for the radiance of their beauty they might cause little in the way of a stir. Yet one of these two had been ritually burned in effigy in cities across all the lands of the three crowns of the Geulten Alliance, and in many a township across Wehnbria, too. There was, in truth, nothing typical about the woman in question.

Her travelling raiment would have beggared most ladies' choicest finery. She wore the very finest Guillaime silk and latticed velvet, laced with frills, bejewelled and brocaded. The girdle squeezed so tightly her waspish waist that it was a wonder that breathing were possible in a garment so constrictive in the extreme. It was adorned with a multitude of highly decorative fetish charms of protective incantation pendant from it, which swung as the carriage proceeded along the irregular road. Her gown trailed so low that it covered her feet but the low cut of her bodice was very daring indeed, permitting an extravagant flaunting of her prominent bosom. The torse upon her brow was a beautiful construction of silverwork, worn with a coif made not of linen but of white silk. She was a woman that many thousands of men in both the Ehngle and the Geulten armies, particularly the latter, would gladly have crucified if they could have laid hands upon her. Many there were who would have had her torn between trees or flayed alive at the first opportunity. She was the notorious Bhelenese courtesan, the infamous adventuress, the political intriguer, witch and spy, the Mademoiselle Maev de Lederwyrhta.

Her guardian on the ghostly warhorse could have counselled her against such a flamboyant show of wealth whilst travelling, it being an unnecessary invitation to robbers and brigands, but there seemed small point. This delicate, enchanting lady was perhaps the single most hated woman of the century. Her reputation for treachery, deceit, infidelity, and most of all witchcraft, meant that should her identity be discovered she would immediately be swept up by a swarm of her enemies. The splendour of her appearance might perversely work in their favour as perchance she would be taken to be an eminent member of the local nobility taking the air close to home so that she need be attended by only two servants but with others of her retinue within call. Not that Ealdræd, the custodian with responsibility for the preservation of her life, placed any faith in such hopes. Her security consisted in his speed and accuracy with the javelin, his considerable capacity as a throat-slitter with the twenty-inch broad bladed knife sheathed at his belt, and with the lady's own astonishing and brazen ability to command those around her with the overwhelming power of her personality. To see her sitting with the poise of a queen, so upright and self-composed in her well-sprung carriage, few would realise that this was a lady whose head would fetch a price almost anywhere betwixt here and the smugglers' coves of Langelais.

Each time that other users of this famous highway drew toward them on the road Ealdræd would ease a javelin from its saddle sheath and lay it casually across the muscular neck of his horse until the other travellers has passed by on their way. The sight of the enormous roan blue stallion was enough to arouse superstitious terror in many a wayfarer, and the brooding menace in the face of its battle-hardened rider would provide a similar sense of intimidation in those who lacked religion.

The extraordinarily pretty younger woman sitting beside Maev de Lederwyrhta, the girlish maiden who held the reins in her dainty hands to guide the single coal black mare which drew their carriage, was less ostentatiously clad, for she was lady-in-waiting to the other.

But if the girl's gown was less stimulating in design and somewhat more subdued in the pomp and puff of its grandeur, less revealing in its exhibition of the exposed portion of the bust, it was a no less fashionable ensemble. Whereas the erotic fascination of the mademoiselle was an intoxication of omniscient sexual wisdom, that of her servant was the delightful attraction of modest naïveté.

It was in defiance of civilized custom for the attire of the social superior to exhibit a more blatant display of the bosom than that of the servant. Everywhere the convention held that the lower down the social order a person was, the more insubstantial was their apparel, especially in the case of female servants who would, as a matter of course, expect to raise a bastard child or two. That Maev de Lederwyrhta should flout social etiquette in this way said something as to the lace-covered iron of her character.

This unconventional party of three had left the field of the battle of Proctors Wæl a week behind them and the magnificence of this military victory for the united forces of the Ehngle nations guaranteed that there would be no risk for the time being of army manoeuvres this far up the Archers Furrow by either side in the war. The attention of the world was focused upon the flight of the Geulten cavalry to the moated trenches of the Nanthil Dyke and the problems that Wehnbria would now have to cope with as a result of having a large mustering of idle and therefore riotous Sæxyn, Heurtslin, Merthyan and Aenglian soldiery visited upon it. For these were the stalwart hearts of oak who had turned back the vile aggression of Geulten imperialism and they would be basking in the glory of it a while yet. No doubt, within a month they would be fighting each other again instead of their common foe.

Ealdræd would, in the normal way of events, have been among their number but his esteemed Captain-General, Eádgar Aeðlric, had commissioned him with his current duty and he had not been loathe to accept it. His dealings with the mademoiselle had fostered a healthy respect between the two, and such camaraderie was rare in the mercenary's rather solitary lifestyle. There were other considerations also. Despite being twice her age he was already sharing his blanket with Mistress Bryony.

The young woman was finding this a mixed blessing. She had known the pleasure of a man's body before this, but never one who could rattle her bones with quite such vigour. For a personality as bashful as that of Mistress Bryony, it was a blush-making embarrassment to be aware that her great lady, the Mademoiselle de Lederwyrhta, could hardly be in ignorance of her sexual involvement with this barbarian brute; a person scarcely fit for a lady's company. But Bryony had rapidly developed an appetite, a positive hunger, for the exhaustingly hard ride that she received from her ill-bred paramour each night, for it was a physical exhilaration undreamt of in her sheltered upbringing, and she would have bravely born the shame of consorting with a man of no social status if that were the only price of the sheer rapture of the sensual pleasure he afforded her, especially as her mistress appeared to actively approve of such goings on.

However, it was not the only price by any means. Sadly, the mercenary savage was also in the habit of lashing the young women who shared his bed with a leather strap during the course of his night's sex play, and the stainless ivory of Bryony's formerly unspoilt posterior was now welted and sore by the dawn. Each day as she rode in the carriage with her lady, every time the wheels passed over a bump in the road the shaking of the carriage caused her a moment's discomfort from the stripes on her backside.

Her mistress disdained to suppress the smirk that crossed her diminutively feminine countenance each time her lady-in-waiting flinched, and Bryony could not help but think, disloyal though it may be for a lady-in-waiting to have such thoughts about her superior, that the mademoiselle took pleasure in her servant's discomposure specifically because of the way that these tender aches had been acquired.

The fact of the matter was that from the very commencement of their journey the mischievous Maev de Lederwyrhta had taken every opportunity to employ her consummate skills at flirtation, even flirtation at one remove, to encourage a sexual dalliance between her timid but obedient lady-in-waiting and the big mercenary soldier who had been accorded the duty of guarding them safely on the first leg of their journey. Ealdræd was as yet still uncertain as to why the lady took such an interest in orchestrating this amour but, in the sagacity of his life's experience, he reckoned upon making a fair guess.

Maev de Lederwyrhta's own admission to him several days earlier that the reason she must make this trip north by so slow a means of conveyance as a carriage, when once she had been a fine horsewoman, was due to the physical damage she had suffered

164

under the tortures of the March Lord's witch-diviners. Many months she had endured the grotesque atrocities of the Eorl Atheldun's cruelty whilst he tried to force from her a confession of witchcraft, and then subsequently to force from her a retraction of her confession after it had implicated a whole strata of the Wehnbrian aristocracy and caused a political crisis in the country, just as the Lady Maev had intended. By such agonising procedures, she had admitted to Ealdræd, the vengeful Eorl had ensured that she would not be able to ride a horse or enjoy sexual congress with a man for a very long time; two things, she had said rather wistfully, for which she had formerly "displayed a certain talent".

With this admission in mind, it seemed likely to Ealdræd that, no longer being in a position to use the weapon of sex herself in her relations with men, she was having to settle for second best and make use of her lady-in-waiting to stand in as deputy for her in this regard. He doubted that the mademoiselle had any specific reason for plying him with young Bryony's considerable erotic charms at this stage of their acquaintance. It was more probable that the wily Maev simply considered it a wise and good practice to have this means of influence in play in case it should prove useful in some later circumstance which was at present unforeseen.

The weather had been blessedly warm and dry these last several days and they were making reasonably good time. Ealdræd had wished to press on during the first week to ensure that they put many leagues between themselves and those irate folk back in the Southern Marches whose minds might turn to wondering as to what had become of the villainous harpy and iniquitous spy from Bhel. But the road had been uncommonly quiet up to now and there was little to do but let Hengustir, his massive warhorse, stroll along steadily at five leagues a day.

Maev de Lederwyrhta, a politician to the marrow of her bones, was incapable of silence for any length of time and passed the journey in an endless didactic soliloquy that was much more of a monologue that a conversation. It caused Ealdræd to ponder on how sorely her loquacious spirit must have chaffed all the while that the Eorl Atheldun had kept her tongue curbed by the scold's bridle. Now that her tongue was absolutely unfettered she gave it free rein and her subject was always the thing which was her sole interest in life: politics, and most especially international politics. Mistress Bryony knew little of such matters and showed not the least desire to expand her knowledge, so Mademoiselle de Lederwyrhta directed her musings toward the Aenglian.

Although he was at times taciturn, being a man who spent long periods of time alone with only his faithful Hengustir for companionship, Maev had already seen evidence that he was knowledgeable of the doings of the wide world and that beneath those snake-like braids that hung in a curtain around his head there was a shrewd brain. She knew from a comment that Ealdræd had made when they were both conspiring with the Eorl and the Aeðlric that the Aenglian mercenary had seen service in the remotely distant lands of Ahkran and the Gathkar Queendoms and it was his first-hand experience of these places, of which Maev herself knew nothing but myth, that she was particularly eager to hear tell of. But, in keeping with her character, she concealed her eagerness and proceeded surreptitiously.

Her current theme was the perfidy of monarchy. For the best part of twenty minutes she had been denouncing Philippe, King of Guillaime, for a whore-mongering bugger whose life revolved around the prosaic fantasy maintained for his highness by all his courtiers that the gracious reign of the romantic King Philippe was the absolute summit and perfection of courtly love when really, as Maev had occasion to know, it was a sodomites paradise where a female courtesan like herself had best place her cunny in mothballs, cut her hair like a boy, and make the best use she could of her anus. Not that she had any objection to sodomy, or to the pretty boys who made their living from it and by wearing out their knees in the private chambers of the lordly; not she. No, her distaste was not in any way for the sexuality involved but for the double-standard the king practiced in making homosexuality in women a capital offence. Now where was the justice in that, Maev wanted to know, for the boys to be indulged and even sanctified by licentiousness whilst the girls who wished to find pleasure in one another were suffering decapitation under the headsman's axe by Philippe's royal order of execution.

At this point she enquired of Ealdræd whether it was true, as she had heard, that in the Gathkar Queendoms lesbianism was compulsory by law. When the Aenglian answered her cheerfully in the negative she shrugged her feminine shoulders and observed that perhaps it was just as well as she would not like to think that a girl had only other girls to look forward to in life. Men certainly had their place, she opined, and besides it was no joke to get embroiled

166

with some bitch who got stricken with lockjaw every time a girl fancied sitting on a face . . . .

Whether any of this was said merely for shock value or to test Ealdræd's capacity for broad speech, he neither knew nor cared. The doings of kings and queens were nought to him and he had little appetite for salacious gossip or the toilet secrets of the celebrated. What he was enjoying was the animated chattering of the lady's charming and bell-like voice. Her vivacity was attractively coquettish and he was content to bathe in its tinkling musicality regardless of the content of her discourse. The uncomfortable but resigned expression on Mistress Bryony's porcelain features spoke volumes as to how unladylike she found this symposium on contemporary sexual morés, and how frequently she had heard the sermon before from her Bhelenese mistress' soft pink lips.

Returning to her theme of duplicitous royalty, Maev launched into a prolonged oration on the self-serving baronial back-stabbers who occupied the positions behind the throne in the great Geulten kingdom of Bhourgbon under its ten-year old monarch, Henri, the boy king. The child was a monster of course, spoilt and indulged until he believed himself to be a god upon the earth, and probably even worse that his father when it came to ruining the kingdom by playing favourites amongst his senior nobility. His royal sire had exercised a preference for a certain Marquis that betimes had all the other nobles united in opposition against the throne. The regal brat, with similar prejudice, would split the realm in twain before he reached manhood; civil war was always a possibility when the pre-pubescent were permitted to wear the crown.

They passed by a circle of standing stones; fourteen stones, each the weight of fifty oxen, reared up out of the ground with such precision that astrologers and the casters of bones could tell the character of the next year's harvest by occult consultation within the circle at sunrise on the solstice. These stones were a landmark on the Archers Furrow and by them Ealdræd knew that their expedition had drawn level with the castle-fronted land of the *Feónd Nosu*, just a few leagues to the east over the timber hills. They had covered a little over half the distance to the Heurtslin border from Proctors Wæl where their journey had started.

The *Feónd Nosu* or 'nose of the fiend', was named for the upturned nose of the Duke Gilbert en Dieu, a ruler in times long past of the Duchy of Oénjil, and an honourable ancestor to the present Duke

Etienne. The Duke Gilbert was known to his enemies the Ehngle and to history as 'Gilbert Kellogg', meaning Gilbert 'the killer of hogs', for having been born a lowly younger son he had slaughtered several members of his own family in order to become the Duke. This did not in any way detract from the lustre of his memory for he it was who had stamped his very face on to the land of the Wehnbrians.

In a successful campaign one summer in those long gone days he had taken possession of a stretch of land in the northern region of the Marches and claimed it as his own. When the cartographers had drawn up a map of this slight extension to the Duke's dominion it transpired that the newly won ground was in the shape of a laughing profile with a large upturned nose. By chance, the Duke Gilbert himself had just such a nose protruding monstrously from his unsightly pox-ravaged face, and so from that day to this the small but impertinently provocative extension of Oénjil territory that thrust out so impudently into Wehnbria had been called *Feónd Nosu* or 'nose of the fiend'.

It was the furthest west the Geulten could boast as their sovereign soil and more than one generation of March Lords had sworn to cut the bastard's nose off. They had never managed it. The impertinence of Duke Gilbert remained, his nose a perpetual insult to their Wehnbrian Lordships, and although the terrain in those parts was so heavily forested to be generally useless for farming or the rearing of livestock, it was none-the-less the most fought over blood-soaked patch of worthless good-for-nothing dirt between here and the Heights of Turghol where the Torvig goat-herds kill one another over the bartering of fetid cheese-milk.

Maev de Lederwyrhta had fallen silent as they passed the circle of stones, as all were hushed in awe who laid their eyes upon that ancient mystery, but once the prehistoric monoliths were out of sight, her happy tongue commenced to chatter like a bird in summer once again.

Having dispensed with the King Henri, the child monarch of Bhourgbon, she proceeded to go to the other extreme and sing the somewhat tarnished praises of wily old King Béri of Eildres; a fellow who, if not exactly a paragon of moral rectitude, at least had the good sense and saintly forbearance to let others go to the fourteen levels of hell in the kingdom of ice and shade in their own way; letting them suffer the consequences of their recreation of choice.

168

When, in the afterlife, the courtesan from Bhel stood erect on her own two feet before Wihvir Lord of Hálsian, the commander and corruptor of spirits, she would have no apology to make. Let the grim god of damnation make his judgements, she would not protest. Let each fool's soul find its self-destruction in the folly that suits its own taste; that was Maev's philosophy.

Turning a slow bend around a motionless pond encircled by willows they saw up ahead of them a squat, untidy figure in a sack-cloth habiliment sitting with his back to the thick trunk of a roadside tree. As they hove into view the seated man snatched up a crumhorn and blew upon it with some skill. At the same time he stretched forth his left leg to display the misshapen lump where the shin bone had been broken over the ankle. It had set in that position, leaving the foot twisted and the man crippled. He was both beggar and musician but, as a performer in want of a charitable audience, he had chosen a singularly empty stretch of road on which to seek alms. A busy city boulevard might have served his turn better.

Ealdræd would hardly have deigned to notice so lowly an itinerant minstrel but for one feature that caught his eye and his curiosity as they drew within thirty yards of the humble petitioner; the man was wearing a mantle of Gathkaree design. His tunic and cloak were unremarkable but Ealdræd hadn't seen a fringed Gathkaree turban-mantle for many a long year. At twenty yards a second look and a closer inspection showed him that the darkness of the fellow's complexion was not caused by the deep shade of the tree. He was a Negro.

The keen vision of Maev de Lederwyrhta had noticed this also. With a tongue as sharp as her eyesight she voiced her amusement.

"Here is one who has travelled in vagrancy as far as you have Aenglian, though you might claim with some justice to have prospered better with your spear than he has with the mournful instrument upon which he plays."

The light touch of laughter in her comment derived from the mildly sarcastic tone that she used too often. Ealdræd had a fighting man's intolerance of anything remotely disrespectful, which was perhaps her particular reason for leavening her speech with a hint of mockery, to prompt a response. In this instance any reply he might have made was cut short by the startled chirp of surprised excitement from the young woman at the reins.

Mistress Bryony, her attention directed toward the tramp not by his music but by her lady having spoken about him, gaped in unself-conscious inquisitive marvel at the oddity. She had never seen a black man before in her life. So rare a phenomenon was an astonishment and a fascination. She stared like a child at a festival fair.

Ealdræd had not yet returned the javelin he was holding to its saddle sheath, after having taken the weapon in hand whilst they passed a wagon travelling south a few minutes earlier. Even so, the presence of the length of ash in his fist was not accompanied by his usual wariness, for the cripple provoked no suspicion of danger. The creature was a novelty and that would surely be an advantage in his trade, for folk would be more likely to pay to see a Gathkaree with a crumhorn than some common-or-garden local. But he prompted no other thought in the wily old veteran's head than the sardonic idea that the black would not be walking all the way home on that twisted leg.

Astride the mighty Hengustir, Ealdræd had been between the women and the seated man but when the carriage came alongside the exotic rarity Mistress Bryony pulled back on the reins and stopped the carriage. Hengustir's steady, stately step took the horseman a few yards beyond the tree and Maev de Lederwyrhta was just about to reproach her youthful lady-in-waiting for such unsophisticated gawping when the minstrel ceased his melody, placed the crumhorn on the ground beside him and picked up a sinister contraption which Ealdræd had only seen once before, and that very recently in the hand of his noble lordship the Eorl Atheldun of the Wehnbrian Marches. It was a small bow held horizontally with a solid iron arrow strung in place to be fired by a metal trigger built into the wood of the handle. Ealdræd, with a professional's interest in weaponry had asked the Eorl the name of this infernal device and had been told that the mechanism was called a crossbow.

Ealdræd shouted one word of warning to the women: "Assassin!"

The thrum and slap of the release of the arrow was unnaturally loud in their ears as sudden fear heightened their senses with an injection of adrenalin. The iron bolt ripped right through the flounce of Maev de Lederwyrhta's skirts and sheared a gash out of her corsetry but did not penetrate her body. Mistress Bryony was saved by the fact that she had been leaning forward to gaze at the beggar.

The narrow iron bolt of an arrow rasped right between the two women like a murderous insect.

Ealdræd, caught off-balance with his enemy behind and to the left of his position, had to twist hard in the saddle and launch his javelin right-handed over his left shoulder. In the same motion he hoisted his right leg over Hengustir's head to roll off the horse to his left, already reaching for the broad-bladed knife at his belt. He barked a second warning to the women he was guarding but his two charges had sense enough to already be lying flat as low down as they could get in their small carriage.

Ealdræd's javelin, hurled blind toward an uncertain target, had embedded itself in the bark of the tree behind the assassin. Both had failed with their missile attacks. The braided soldier moved swiftly down upon his opponent.

To a wagering gentleman it would have appeared to be no contest. The Gathkaree should by rights have been a dead man. He was a cripple facing a mercenary skilled in the arts of war. But had the man been no more than a disabled beggar he would not have accepted a commission as an assassin. Favouring his good leg but standing on both feet, the Gathkaree rose, brandishing two small but lethal hand axes; an identical pair, with twenty inch shafts and double-headed blades in quarter-inch iron. His ankle may have been an unsightly mess of badly fused bone but it still served him as a sturdy prop by which to meet the world standing upright and ready to kill to earn his bread.

The assassin swung the two axes simultaneously in rhythmic scything arcs. It created an impenetrable barrier of moving razor-sharp iron in front of him. Once or twice the blades glanced off each other, striking sparks. This would normally have determined Ealdræd's tactics for him. Rather than attempting to get passed that whirlwind of axe-blades he would await his enemy's rush and rely upon a counter-blow. But in this case there was little chance of a rush, for his opponent had a game leg. Upon realising this, the Aenglian mentally complimented the Gathkaree for having found a style of fighting to suit his disability and largely negate what should have been a serious disadvantage.

The fight began, because of this, in some degree of stalemate. The two men slowly circled around, the assassin limping heavily but not so as to impede his defensive strategy. However, Ealdræd was circling with a purpose. When the tree was beside him he dodged swiftly to his left and plucked the javelin from the wood. The slicing axe-head that instantly sought his flesh cleaved through empty air.

Now armed with his knife in his right hand and the javelin held for thrusting in his left hand, he had the means to take the initiative. He jabbed at the man's hands with the spearhead point of the forty inch javelin with the intention of stabbing him sufficiently to make him to drop one of his weapons. The assassin's twin axes continued to maintain their defensive cross-body rotations; impassable upon pain of death. Eventually he must tire, and if Ealdræd managed to stab into one of his wrists, the tide of battle would turn in the Aenglian's favour. But it was not a foregone conclusion. There was plenty of time for either man to make a mistake in this duel between seasoned warriors.

Or so it seemed. But the Gathkaree had already made a fatal mistake; it would cost him his life. He had assumed that only the bodyguard presented any threat. He had discounted Maev de Lederwyrhta on the grounds that she was only the rich woman that he had been hired to kill. Like so many before him, he had not appreciated the quality of the Lady Maev and would get no second chance.

The carriage contained several bags, most of which contained clothing of various sorts. But not all. Once the two men had engaged in combat and their attention was fully taken up with the mortal adversary in front of them, Maev had been free to take from a bag at her feet a wooden box which she opened. From within she very carefully took a transparent sphere made from an Ahkrani preparation of sand called 'glass'. Inside this round ball of thin, brittle glass was a colourless liquid.

Taking her time to aim as precisely as she could, the Bhelenese courtesan, a woman of arcane knowledge and deep guile, known to the world as a scandalous witch, waited until the assassin turned his back to her. Putting no strength into the action, accuracy being her primary concern, she threw the sphere at him. It landed smack in the middle of the target. The impact broke the fragile glass and the liquid splattered all across his back. Almost instantaneously smoke or steam or some freakish combination of the two began pouring off him and as the liquid penetrated his sack-cloth tunic he started to scream.

Exploiting whatever this was, Ealdræd struck forward with the javelin and was rewarded with the satisfaction of seeing the ash drive right through the man's forearm, causing him to drop the hatchet in that hand. Despite his pain, with his remaining axe the Gathkaree cut right through the middle of the javelin, robbing Ealdræd of that weapon. Not that there was any saving the assassin now. Before he could raise the axe to strike again, the Aenglian had lunged inside the man's defence and plunged his knife deep into his combatant's belly.

With a solid piece of ash through his arm, a back burning with the blistering fire caused by the potion that Maev de Lederwyrhta had unleashed with her demonic acid, and a large knife in his guts, the Gathkaree collapsed to the ground dying. But he was not yet dead. The Aenglian mercenary took hold of the remains of his javelin and tore it loose from its prison of ripped meat. He set the iron point of the broken javelin against the man's throat.

"From the Marches?" demanded Ealdræd.

The Gathkaree said not a word but the answer was in his eyes. No one could conceivably have mistaken the fellow for a Wehnbrian but the country of this assassin's current employer was not seriously in doubt. There was a certain aristocrat just a week's ride south who would dance at the news of the deaths of Maev de Lederwyrhta and Ealdræd of the Pæga.

Ealdræd nodded, as if in unspoken acknowledgement of something, and forced the spearhead of the broken javelin right through the villain's throat. It burst through at the rear in a grisly siphon of blood.

Hunched down over his defeated adversary the Aenglian twisted round to look up at Maev de Lederwyrhta, still seated in her carriage, her poise almost unperturbed but for the tiny fact that she held on to the side of the vehicle with a hand that showed its knuckles white.

"The Eorl's rascal," deduced the veteran, "sent on a fast horse to overtake us and lay in wait. The woodland on either side of the road is open enough for a horse and rider to pass through easily to get ahead of us. His lordship's word to us that we were free to go seems to have been nothing more than a ploy for him to kill us without spilling blood on his own doorstep."

As if in afterthought he added: "A timely intervention, I thank you."

The woman smiled amiably but briefly at this recognition. Gratitude was unnecessary between comrades. Instead the lady looked strangely at the corpse on the ground.

"A lame assassin," she observed dryly. "I would not have given the Eorl Atheldun credit for such wit; he is not normally so creative in his thinking."

"If there were any originality in the method, mademoiselle" replied Ealdræd, as if protective of his brother mercenary's reputation, "the credit would be due to the assassin, not his Lordship. I do not believe the Eorl to have ever had an original thought in his life. This Gathkaree fellow was an assassin before he was a cripple. Having injured himself he did not feel the need for a change of trade."

The Bhelenese angled her head tartly on one side and concurred: "Perchance I do give his numbskull lordship rather more credit than is plausible; cunning is far from his forte."

"And such cunning as there was has not prevented the assassin's death whilst we three still live," muttered the Aenglian half to himself.

"One supposes," said Maev in an overly loud and decidedly acerbic tone to draw attention to Ealdræd's low muttering, "that the poor lamb was unaware of just what a slayer of dragons he was about to meet in battle."

The comically sour expression on Ealdræd's weather-beaten face as he looked up at her doubled and trumped her sarcasm. Then, with more sincerity, he said: "It was mercenary justice, and no better or worse than the bastard deserved."

Maev de Lederwyrhta nodded to herself, solemn now. In a voice devoid of any trace of humour she spoke aloud the names of those whom, she knew, had sentenced her to death:

"Eorl Aykin of Chestbury; Eorl Caridian of Shrewford; Eorl Atheldun of the Marches; murderers all. You, friend Ealdræd, have had your mercenary retribution upon their agent and I do thank you for it. Moreover, I swear by every tooth in my head that before I die I shall have my own justice upon those three gentlemen who set the assassin upon us."

Ealdræd grunted his approval of her bloodthirsty sentiments. Then the dark mood that had settled upon the lady's bewitching loveliness passed away and her jesting drollery returned.

"You have murdered your master's servant and frustrated his plans for my despatch," scolded Maev de Lederwyrhta playfully. "You had best take care if ever you return to the Marches."

"Mademoiselle," said Ealdræd firmly and with some warmth, "I have told you before that the Eorl Atheldun is no master of mine, and I have little patience on the subject."

"I apologise," said Maev de Lederwyrhta quickly and quietly. A moment later it was something of a shock to her to realise what she had done. The last time she had apologised to any man she had been seventeen years old and he had been the sovereign ruler of the country of her birth. Why did she now apologise to this elderly spearman of no social status from the barbarian forests of distant Aenglia? Not from fear, certainly. Nor from need, nor even from gratitude. She gave him respect because respect was due. It was an extraordinary feeling for Maev de Lederwyrhta in her wide experience of conducting business with men. Yet somehow she found that she did not resent it overmuch.

There were, besides, matters of their continued survival to be attended to. That the Eorl's dishonourable and foresworn hand had been revealed in this way required a re-evaluation of their position and the best way to proceed.

"Atheldun will not be such a fool as to rely upon a single assassin to exact his lordly revenge," mused Maev de Lederwyrhta. "He will not, as the Bhourgbon peasants say, keep all his hens in one coup. He will have set in play more than one method for our destruction."

"One thing is certain," agreed Ealdræd, "he will have sent emissaries into Heurtslin to warn of your coming and rouse the country against you."

She knew that he spoke sooth and, again, a shadow crossed over her sublime face. She whispered softly under her breath:

"Is there nowhere that a woman of the boudoir with a fancy for politics can live in safety?"

Ealdræd did not catch her comment. He simply stated the obvious: "From this point on, mademoiselle, you must not play the lady."

"Yes, yes," said Maev, who knew it as well as he did. "Bryony, my dear," she said turning to her lady-in-waiting, "I fear I must impose upon you for your least becoming cloak."

She borrowed from her lady-in-waiting a very plain and all-concealing hooded cloak which covered her entirely from her head to her curly-toed shoes. It was a garment that Mistress Bryony had included in her travelling wardrobe to be worn only in the most inclement of weather. She had imagined herself in the midst of storms at sea and had brought this undeniably unflattering cloak as protection against the tempest.

In the moment that the enticing, self-possessed courtesan threw on this shroud, Ealdræd instantly understood her preference for grandiose display. The cloak turned her into a small, insignificant figure that few would take any account of unless they happened to notice the dazzlingly fierce intelligence in her exquisitely expressive blue eyes. Even Mistress Bryony, who had never seen her lady in so drab an item of apparel before, seemed to appreciate the radical difference it made. The younger woman appeared crestfallen at the sight her mistress so reduced in the force of her splendour. In terms that Ealdræd could identify with, Maev de Lederwyrhta was a warrior stripped of her weapons; a skilled combatant deprived of her select armoury, and left with nothing but her natural attributes for personal defence. Of course, in the case of Maev de Lederwyrhta, these natural attributes were still very formidable. And she entirely grasped the imperative necessity for disguise; that she most of all must camouflage herself. What mattered urgently at present was to reach a port on the northern coast of Heurtslin and for that, with the Eorl's agents abroad, she must be inconspicuous.

There was less need for disguise where Ealdræd was concerned. Mistress Bryony was again prevailed upon to unplait the braids of his hair and beard so that he might be less obviously Aenglian. The first time she had performed this service for him had been back in Amsburgh and on that occasion the embarrassment of the soldier's physical proximity had made her squirm. But things had changed a good deal since then, as the lover's welts on her milk white bottom gave testimony, so that this time she found it a pleasure to serve. She decided that she preferred him with his mane of hair untied.

176

With this amendment to his appearance done, Ealdræd's own rough cloak and leather mantle made him look like nothing more than what he truly was, an old soldier looking to earn a crust and a flagon of ale, and the world was full of those.

*   *   *

As they crossed the border into the territory of the Heurtslin, the lady-in-waiting and the man on the huge roan horse were receiving a Bhelenese courtesan's assorted political insights into recent local history. It was, as before, a salty tale. As the trio made their discreet and unnoticed way through scenery that was now decorated with silver birch and pine trees rather that the Wehnbrian oak and willow that had been their constant landscape for the previous two weeks, the mademoiselle's lovely intonation lectured melodically.

The Heurtslin as a people, explained Maev, were hardy but ugly. Strong workers, capable craftsmen, and tenacious fighters, but as ugly as a cow's arse in a heat-wave. Their celebrated monarch, King Håkon, was a silver-haired gout-ridden man of fifty who was a martyr to the backache. The third of his nine wives had been a Vespaan Baroness exchanged in military spoils, a famous beauty called Blanchefleur. They were popularly known outside their native countries as 'the pearl in the oyster' and it was the only time that fashionable gentlefolk had noticed the existence of King Håkon or his realm. In his youth he had carved out several minor victories against half-hearted invasions and incursions by the army of the Fiefdom of Vespaan, and had made himself something of a thorn in the flesh of the father of the current feudal liege lord of the Fiefdom, Count Gustave du Sanhk. Perchance this was the reason why Count Gustave was more inclined to aggression through three-faced diplomacy than through open hostilities under a banner in the field, which had left the three hundred miles of the border between Heurtslin and Vespaan in peace and quiet for some years.

From this she digressed into a treatise on the peculiar forms of madness which afflicted the Heurtslin tribes of the borderlands who lived under the shadow of the immeasurably tall silver-barked trees that flourished in such numbers in those impenetrably thick forests that they permanently shrouded the ground below in complete darkness. Maev even had a word or two to say about the etymology of the word 'loch', meaning lake, which featured in no other language but that of the Heurtslin and their habit of giving all lochs female names, a practice which Maev held to be highly suspicious. But the subject which most occupied the mind of the mademoiselle was the alleged story, which she could not swear to be true, that King Håkon's eighth wife had secretly been a boy.

At Ealdræd's insistence they avoided entering the capital city, Skælig, despite its lying directly in the path of the Archer's Furrow. Indeed, they had to take various country byways to get around it for in that part of the world all roads lead to Skælig. But for them it held only the threat of exposure and capture so they pressed on, gaining confidence with every mile, to the port of Picgowan on the northern coastline.

Picgowan was a major port, being coastal and yet able to provide sheltered harbouring because it was located just inside the mouth of the Aberteth river, a spacious and prosperous waterway with numerous quays and landing places along its length for some miles inland. With such a diversity of shipping, there was an excellent chance that an anonymous passenger or two could pick up a vessel bound for Bhel without delay.

With their arrival at the sea, the Aenglian mercenary had made good the mission entrusted to him by Eádgar Aeðlric and the perturbation induced by this thought was clouding the blissful symmetry of Mistress Bryony's elegant face. She made so bold as to raise the issue.

"Shall you now return south?" she asked of her lover.

"No," grunted the Aenglian, "I think I shall keep to my duty as Bailey Ward yet awhile."

It was transparent in Bryony's air of angelic confusion that she had not the least idea of what a Bailey Ward might be.

". . . Someone who occupies the position of bailiff and watchman," Ealdræd explained, "as I do to you and your lady. I must escort you to your deportation but ensure your safety also".

"But you have completed that task," said Bryony tentatively, hoping for a further admission.

"Then let us say that I have never laid my eyes upon the Grand Duchy of Bhel and choose to do so, now that there is nothing between it and myself but a short ride in a sailor's jolly-boat."

The glittering luminosity of Mistress Bryony's smile put the sun to shame. "I have never seen the Grand Duchy before either," she said happily. Then her sweet face fell. "But I fear the boat ride will be far from jolly!"

Since the Grand Duchy was a place that nobody from the Ehngle nations was at all likely to visit except for those engaged in trade, the three fugitives needed to avail themselves of a persuasive cover story or an idiot ship's captain. They contrived a little of each. It was decided that since Mistress Bryony was of Sæxyn origins, a fact of which Ealdræd had been unaware previously although it explained her flaxen hair, they would masquerade as a Sæxyn goodwife and her older widowed sister travelling to Bhel in order to marry the widow to a merchant with whom their family had a business acquaintance. Ealdræd, still with his dark hair and beard unbraided, was to play the family servant acting as escort and protector.

The pose was not wholly convincing, but that seemed to matter far less than the jingling of their gold when they bought passage on a ship whose captain was a guttural, inarticulate Heurtslin bigot, spitting at every fifth word, speaking in an accent that sounded like he was clearing the phlegm from his throat, and expressing his detestation of anyone and everyone from outside of his own country with every sentence he uttered.

His name, as he gave it, was Captain Ròidh, and it was surely on account of his flaming red hair that he had acquired his name, if not his captaincy. The latter was probably down to the volatility of his temper and the free way he had with his fists towards those unfortunate enough to find themselves under his command. His first mate and chief victim was a dullard called Sionn whose personality and demeanour managed to combine the jackal with the sucking pig but had nothing of the fox suggested by his name.

The negotiations for passage were conducted with the captain in the evening dusk at quayside. With the price agreed, it was arranged also that the three would spend the night on board so that there need be no delay in catching the morning tide at dawn. Captain Ròidh repeatedly referred to them as 'Scamian-Sæx', which implied the shamefulness of their origins and was, in a offhand way, a considerable insult. Had the brute spoken in his manner of his Aenglian ethnicity Ealdræd would certainly have taken offence and sliced a few pennyweights of blubber out of the captain's excess of corpulence, but since it was only a fictional Sæxyn ethnicity that was being disparaged Ealdræd was content to let the comment pass.

The ship that was to take them passed the Fiefdom of Vespaan and the realm of Guillaime was a cog, a flat bottomed clinker that did not have a keel; it was powered by a strong central square-rigged sail and guided, after a fashion, by a system of stern rudder, side rudder, and quarter rudder. Like all of its clumsy, unwieldy kind, this cog was high-sided and heavy in the timbers. Primarily an open cargo vessel, the 'castle' in the stern none-the-less provided a measure of protection in the event of a naval battle. Warfare at sea was largely an affair of archery, with fire arrows being the weapon of choice. Marine soldiers sometimes used small catapults also, firing bundles of loose lead balls or alternatively launching a single lump of lead whose weight could put a sizeable hole in the deck of an enemy ship if it landed cleanly. This particular cog was named the Port Casket, doubtless after one of its more lucrative cargos. But it wasn't so bad an old tub as it at first appeared, for not only had it a stoutly carpentered castle large enough to house two dozen men, in addition it had a raised deck in both the bow and the stern, affording ocean views from above deck and shelter from the elements when below deck. The captain had offered the space below the bow deck to the enchanting widow and her sister for their personal occupancy during this voyage; an offer which the widow had graciously accepted.

The captain asked, with a failed attempt at rakishness, what so beauteous a lady's name might be. With an almost suicidal bravado the mademoiselle answered him that she was called Maev. It was not an accidental blunder on her part, merely a measure of her contempt for the fool that she casually thrust this clue to her real identity under his very nose. The captain gave no sign of the name having any particular significance for him and merely observed, with a certain lusty relish, that her name in Heurtslin would be Meabh which meant 'intoxicating'. The widow bestowed upon him one of her more alluring smiles, for she rather liked the observation, after which the captain was her adoring slave.

Ordinarily, when in port, smaller vessels and the distinctive Heurtslin galleys anchored in the shallower waters of the harbour near the quays but the ocean-going ships stayed out in the slightly deeper waters offshore. One advantage enjoyed by Picgowan was that it was a deep water port, so the larger vessels could anchor closer to the shore. Even so, Ealdræd's party had to be rowed out to their cog on a ferry-raft. Mistress Bryony, who had never had occasion to learn how to swim, had an expression of morbid despair on her face which comically declared that she had already given up her soul into the keeping of the gods.

The three passengers and their animals were hauled on board ship one at a time by a rope-harness and tackle. It took more rope and a lot more sailors to pull on them when it was Hengurtir's turn to be hauled up. The fancy carriage in which the women had travelled up from Wehnbria they had sold in Picgowan. They would purchase another upon their arrival in Oosted, the city that was the chief harbour of Bhel.

Although it was full dark by the time they settled their few belongings under the raised deck in the bow, even at night the port gave the impression of bustling with shipping. A larger vessel, a hulk with its great keel carved from a single massive log that had cost the life of a forest giant in its construction, was lying at anchor nearby, with lanterns flickering dully fore and aft. Strange voices called out to one another across the deck of the hulk in the darkness, as they did from the Heurtslin galley on the starboard side. Sitting low in the water and without mast or sails, a galley like this one was powered solely by the aching backs and cracked muscles of the slaves who rowed at oar. Galleys never travelled out of sight of land if their captain had any sense. They were coastal craft and had been designed originally for use on the three enormous lochs known as the three sisters, Mòr, Mòrag, and Mòruireall, in the west of Heurtslin. But since Heurtslin had a northern coastline that ran the full width of the country, the galleys saw a deal of service as cargo transport between east and west.

In contrast, there was a smart carrack anchored leeward of the Port Casket. Only the seafarers of the Canbrai Isles had mastered the construction of the carrack, with its three separate masts, each carrying a sail of its own, providing the Canbrai carrack with a speed unknown to the older patterns of vessel such as the cog and the hulk. Captains of the latter could only gaze with wonder and envy when the men of Canbrai sailed into port with their high-castled rounded sterns and a forecastle toward the bow. Though square rigged on the foremast, they were most often lateen rigged on the mizzenmast, and the hull would hum like a cat purring when rigged with full sail. They were the kings of the sea and could take in their wake the white water of the Mariner's Cauldron, although the chop and splutter of that fateful place were rough enough to sink any other craft at sea. In truth, the carrack was the only genuinely ocean-voyaging ship yet built. Ealdræd could have wished that their journey to Bhel would be by carrack rather than by cob.

With the glimmering light of dawn spreading like oil over the surface of the ocean, the Port Casket hauled up the anchor and put on more sail. It was time to depart, though at first the matter was in some doubt. For a laden merchantman inadequately crewed, getting the cog out of port was proving to be something of a struggle against the unfavourable wind. Ealdræd hoped that they wouldn't end up being trapped in Picgowan for days until the prevailing winds turned, as happened not infrequently. With its square cut stern and its single mast, the Port Casket was a cursed beast of a ship when sailing into the wind, covering almost the full width of the harbour mouth each time it tacked to and fro, but luckily they broke free of the harbour and headed out into easier sailing.

They faced a thousand miles at sea in a 60 foot cog which had an average speed of around 5 knots in moderate weather, in the absence of adversity. Smaller ships sailed more slowly still. Fortunately, apart form the diversion to go around the Cauldron, their captain would be certain to hug the shoreline for the entire trip from Picgowan to Bhel so, if the watchmen stayed awake at night, at least the ship would not go astray during the hours of darkness and time be lost in recovering their course. But even if they weren't delayed by weather, or driven out to sea or becalmed or drowned in the Mariner's Cauldron, the voyage would likely take them over two weeks in perfect conditions. The real journey time could be expected to be anywhere from three to four weeks.

It felt like four years to poor Bryony who quickly proved to be the worst sailor afloat. Her seasickness was so severe that she set up an incessant soft moaning which only quietened when her mistress would whisper in impatience "There, there, Bryony dear, do try to bear up bravely, my dear." After which the nausea-racked lady-in-waiting would set her petite jaw in firm resolve for an hour or so, until the awfulness of the pitching and tossing and plunging and rolling made stoicism too harsh a trial.

It was, by anyone's standards, a wretchedly uncomfortable voyage. The slate grey waves were malevolent in their battering of the graceless ship which seemed to force its way through the water rather than float upon its surface. It was a war between the artifice of the shipwright and the carpenter against the elemental intransigence of an aquatic environment in which humanity did not belong.

The mademoiselle herself was far from happy with her circumstances, for she was a woman who enjoyed the finer things in life and her accommodation was of the sparest and most frugal, but she was also a woman who could endure what had to be endured, as the torturers in the dungeons of the Eorl Atheldun could testify. She could suffer an unpleasant journey without flinching. Besides, every day spent on board this tub put her closer to her native Bhel, perhaps the only place in the world that she could breathe freely now, which left her disinclined to complain about the vehicle that was taking her thither.

One thing that she and her pretty servant did not have to worry about was fending off any untoward attention from the crew. For reasons unknown to themselves, every man jack on board was unaccountably afraid of the Sæxyn widow, although they had no earthly cause to be for they had not the least suspicion of who she really was. Even the boorish captain, who paid her his occasional sycophantic attentions, seemed cowed in her presence. There was something inside Maev de Lederwyrhta that intimidated the lower orders, that had nothing to do with her beauty or her jewellery or her fine flaunted bosom. She had a quality that made them not wish to encroach upon her. It was an uncanny and a marvellous thing.

Only once did a crewman, other than the ship's boy who brought them their food, even approach the passengers and that was on the second night. The gossip and boasting below decks on the subject of the ladies had caused one bold soul to saunter over in the middle-watch, not long after midnight, to win favour by playing the hero with reassurances as to the protection he would offer as their champion should they need it. Seamus, his name was, and he held the position of the boatswain's lackey; a right brownnoser who believed himself to have the gift of the gab. From his post on the forecastle he had noticed the widow prowling wakefully in the bow and had left his duties to steal a word or two with her in the concealing darkness. But no sooner had he swaggered alongside her, tugged his greasy forelock, and grinned an amiable howdy-do when he caught sight of the supercilious austerity on her chiselled features. She looked at him as she might have looked at a cabbage worm wriggling on her dinner plate and, finding himself bereft of words for the moment, he stood mute with his jaunty smile slowly draining from his face. Then there was a flash of something to his left which he realised with a jolt was the glint of moonlight on the polished iron of the blade of her greybeard attendant's long knife as the old man rose from his bed with the younger woman to investigate the intrusion. This was more than enough for Seamus to beat a hasty retreat, muttering apologies, back to the forecastle to spend the rest of the middle-watch rehearsing the lies he would tell his shipmates in the morning. All things considered, the worst threat presented by the crew was the stink of their unwashed bodies that occasionally wafted up from their living quarters below.

With the female members of his party not exactly at their best or welcoming company, what with Maev's nursemaiding of the ailing Bryony making both women a little temperamental, Ealdræd spent the majority of his days on the Port Casket leaning against the wooden rail of the upper deck watching the distant coastline slowly, slowly pass by in the relentless grey mist. Hengustir was stabled above decks nearby and it helped the horse to remain settled and calm if he could see his master close by. The remarkable animal coped with the unnatural motion of the ship amazingly well, given his limited previous experience of a long voyage. The coal-black mare was more skittish.

If his days had nothing but a hard rail to lean on, he spent his nights curled up soothingly with Mistress Bryony, which was the only other thing that could silence her plaintive moans of distress over her ill-health. She became increasingly voracious for sexual pleasure as the voyage went on, losing herself in the intensity of her recurring orgasm. The same was true of her attitude toward the whippings she received during sex-play. She came to beg for the concentrated passion of the experience, and sometimes would faint in the midst of the frantic rutting that followed it, overpowered by her own physical sensations. She escaped into it.

It was the first time that Maev de Lederwyrhta, who slept just a few yards further along deck from them, had realised that a vigorous fucking could be a cure for seasickness. She contemplated drolly that perchance it had something to do with co-ordinated rhythm.

The Port Casket was soon alongside the flat, dull shores of the Fiefdom of Vespaan which, unlike most of the northern coastline of the continent, had little in the way of contour and inlets. For mile after mile the bland shale beaches stretched in an unbroken line.

The prevailing currents in the Bay of Weáspell through which they were journeying washed the Vespaan shore like a lathe shaving a piece of wood. All the outcrops and small offshore islands had been washed away over the millennia. This consistency of appearance added to the interminable intuition that Vespaan was a country that went on and on forever.

The oddly named Bay of Weáspell, meaning the Bay of Tidings of Woe, had not received its name in a comical spirit as a play upon words. It had earned its appellation from generations of exploratory ships having set forth into the vast northern sea never to return. Not one of the brave souls who had explored for land in that direction had ever found it. Nothing was heard of them again in their home ports, and so the bay had only tidings of woe. It was for this reason also that the sea itself was known simply as The Empty Sea, for as far as anyone knew there was nothing in it.

Eventually the shale beaches a league from the Port Casket became a rockier and more broken landscape. When from the starboard rail of the ship Ealdræd could see the distant icy tips of the Cordennes Mountains he knew that they had reached the short northern coast of the Kingdom of Guillaime. This meant that they would soon have to put out to sea to circle round the Mariner's Cauldron. The most dangerous part of the voyage was about to start.

From their current position, they would be only a few days sailing from the west coast of Bhel if the waters ahead of them were calm. But there were no ports in the west of Bhel, no docks and quays for ocean-going ships, only landing bays for small fishing craft that never ventured further than a mile from shore at the utmost. No one ever sailed directly across the Mariners Cauldron to make landfall on the west coast. Sailing around it was dicey enough. There was a restive feeling of apprehension amongst the crew which, in the mysterious way of these things, somehow communicated itself to Hengustir. For the first and only time he became agitated in his shipboard stable. Ealdræd remained close by him at the rail and watched the dull green water around the hull of the ship change its nature.

The Mariners Cauldron covered many leagues of open water where the strong south-western currents from the far north met the backwash of convoluted currents that had looped round inside the Bay of Weáspell, so that these returning streams within the sea broke up against the fresh waters on their way south-west. It was said by those wise in the mariner's arts that the sea-bed thereabouts was unusually undulant, having once been a part of the irregular chain of mountains that swept from the Heights of Turghol, through the Cordennes, as far west as the wizard-infested mountains of Bvanwey. These once-upon-a-time mountains of long ago had since sunk beneath the sea but their underwater influence upon the tides combined with the natural contrariness of the sea in that region to create multitudinous swirling whirlpools and perilously crashing cross-currents that made the whole area virtually death to enter. The additional complication and contrary hazard, of course, was that in trying to ensure that they kept clear of the Cauldron ships would sometimes venture too far away from land and become lost in the Empty Sea. For some in the crew, this was a more fearful prospect than that of being dashed to pieces in the Cauldron.

From the soaked deck of the Port Casket Ealdræd watched the sea appear to boil and bubble with the internal conflicts below the waves. Great plumes of spray reared up to smash against the hull and flail over the ship. Captain Ròidh may have been pig-swill but it transpired that he knew his business, or his navigator did. One or the other was demonstrating consummate naval skill in skirting the very edge of the Cauldron so as to stray no further from shore than was absolutely necessary and yet keep far enough away from the peril to avoid any risk of being sucked into it.

The Aenglian was joined at the rail by his two companions. Mistress Bryony was white as a ghost before she ever saw the state of the sea around them, and she shuddered when she did see it. But it was a shudder of revulsion rather than of fright. As with the truly, appallingly seasick, she had ceased to fear death. Maev de Lederwyrhta had one protective arm around Bryony's thin shoulders but the courtesan's abstracted gaze went far out over the waves in the direction of her native soil. She was almost home now, but what would await her there?

Although the Bhelenese woman was still no more than twenty-seven or twenty-eight years old, despite her colourful history, as she stood there, so indomitable in the mist and spray, she struck Ealdræd as being indestructible and imperishable, as if she must survive in perpetuity. But he knew that it was very far from being so. If she did not find an adequate political power-base in the Grand Duchy within the next few months, it was improbable that she would ever reach her thirtieth birthday. Then again, if there was one thing to which the

Aenglian mercenary would swear in blood, it was that only a headless fool would presume to underestimate the unique and redoubtable Maev de Lederwyrhta.

Like so many things in life, the Mariner's Cauldron turned out to be a bit of an anti-climax. Oh, it was deadly enough, there was no doubt about that, but the gallant little cog, the Port Casket, battled its way through a tight crescent around the sailor's bane over the course of the next four days and nights, and then they were beyond its clutches and sailing freely passed the numerous small islands that peppered the north shore of the Grand Duchy of Bhel and Maev de Lederwyrhta was able to look reflectively upon the land of her girlhood from the bow deck. Three days more and they found themselves making landfall, safe and sound, at the sprawling trading port of the maritime city of Oosted.

*   *   *

The Grand Duchy had a well-deserved reputation for its debauched and grossly abandoned ruling caste. The nobility of Bhel were a byword for wanton sexual defilement and warped perversions of the most obscene kind. In the countries of the west one of the most ubiquitous and widely enjoyed stories about Maev de Lederwyrhta herself was that she had first come to social prominence as the teenage masochistic lover of the sadistic Grand Duchess Griselde, who was over sixty years old even then. Unlike so many of the tales told of the Lady Maev, this one was perfectly true. Certainly, the depraved sexual profligacy of the court of the Grand Duke Belaric was the most damnable and deviant to be found anywhere except those of the Queens of Gathkar.

This disgraceful state of affairs was actually of some political significance. The Grand Duchy of Bhel was a semi-autonomous state to the north of Guillaime and Eildres. Although it was nominally a part of the Geulten world, its geographic location ensured that it was effectively an island. It was sealed off from the other Geulten lands to the south by the gigantic natural barrier of the Cordennes Mountains; an immense barricade of rock and ice. To the east were the quicksand bogs and marshlands of the Marécage; to the west were the whirlpools and treacherous tides of the Cauldron. Protected from invasion by these various adversities which had been provided by a bountiful and felicitous nature the Grand Duke

187

Belaric ruled his seemingly impregnable realm with the power of an anointed king to which he had no right.

The true-born kings who wore the three crowns of the Geulten Alliance suffered this offence to their majestic dignity solely because it would have cost far too much in gold and ordnance to march an army over the frozen peaks of the Cordennes or through the waist deep bogs of the Marécage in order to cut the insolent Grand Duke's head from his shoulders. The bad taste of this pragmatism was sweetened slightly by the fact that the dissolute Bhelenese aristocracy were so deplorably degenerate that they offered no threat to anyone but their own peasant class for whom syphilis had become the most endemic of all diseases; a fate imposed upon them by their licentious masters and mistresses. The Grand Duke Belaric was popularly believed to take no interest in anything but the breeding of lapdogs and it was due to this lordly negligence and crushing diffidence toward all matters of importance that it was politically acceptable for the three crowns to ignore Bhel. But that was not to say that they would not bestir themselves to vent their royal spleens upon the miscreant duchy, if the provocation became intolerable.

Ealdræd's first impression of Oosted was very favourable. It was an exciting place, with a population of over fifteen thousand spread out around the great horseshoe shaped bay that was an ideal haven for sea-traffic. Oosted enjoyed the kind of prosperity that only international commerce can generate, and only then when a city is pivotal in the process of trade. The peculiar geography of Bhel meant that there was no commercial traffic to the west, south, or east. All of the Grand Duchy's dealings with the outside world were conducted through its heavily fortified northern ports and the greatest of these by far was Oosted. It reeked of affluence for it was rich in its possessions, rich in its variety, and rich in its desire to provide all comforts to a weary traveller with the coin to pay.

Ealdræd had no opportunity to indulge any such comforts. After the Sæxyn goodwife, her widowed sister, and their tall sinister servant with the blue-roan warhorse disembarked from the Port Casket the threesome went swiftly to a country cottage en pension in a rural suburb of the city. Maev de Lederwyrhta had planned to look up an old friend who lived there but upon their arrival they found that the old friend was absent and another tenant was in residence. He was there for the express purpose of awaiting the arrival of Maev de Lederwyrhta. Her connection with the owner of the cottage was known and it had been correctly guessed that Maev would make for this hideaway as a place of immediate refuge.

The gentleman temporarily domiciled there was no less august a personage than the Baron Édouard á Gascon; a minor Baron, truth to tell, but he was there as a representative of the Grand Duke Belaric and his mother the Grand Duchess Griselde. It was the latter who was the real power in the nation, although she was now over seventy years of age, and it was she who through her intricate network of spies throughout the Geulten Alliance had received word of Maev de Lederwyrhta's impending return.

The Baron was a young man, no older than his early twenties, Ealdræd judged, but badly marked by a skin disease that marred his looks. Maybe that was why he had taken an interest in politics at so young an age when all his contemporaries were out sporting and ruining themselves with excess and poxy whores. He was not alone in the pension; he had what he described as his two 'gentlemen associates' with him, though these were self-evidently not gentlemen by any acknowledged definition of the word. They were Valéry and Séverin, both from burly peasant stock, both as eager as dogs to perform their master's bidding, and as ripe a pair of callous cut-throats as could be found at bargain prices.

Mistress Bryony was invited to take a stroll in the delightful cottage garden whilst the Baron had words of state with the Lady Maev. Understanding her place in matters of politics, Bryony obediently left the room but when Ealdræd moved to leave with her the Baron motioned for him to stay. Puzzled but not reluctant, the veteran mercenary took a seat by the window where he might keep a watch on the road approaching the house during the conversation that was to follow. Valéry and Séverin were, it need hardly be said, surplus to requirement, and so they went out the same way as Bryony, in the direction of the garden to the rear.

The Baron Édouard á Gascon spent some little time in getting to the point. He went through a tedious rigmarole of welcome to the courtesan, with many salutations of greeting from what he referred to as the 'royal family'. Maev de Lederwyrhta was accustomed to such verbiage but Ealdræd was growing visibly impatient by the time the young aristocrat finally got to the heart of the matter, especially given that the Bhelenese dialect of the Geulten language was making it difficult for the Aenglian to follow his host's rather flowery phrase-making.

"Her highness the Grand Duchess Griselde and his majesty the Grand Duke Belaric are content for you to take your place within the entourage of the select once again," the Baron informed her, "indeed, they are eager to learn all that you know and have learned of the royal courts of the world through which you have made your way in your . . . own inimitable fashion," the disfigured face smiled ingratiatingly, "but naturally they must ensure that those foreign powers who are ill-disposed toward you do not use your presence in Bhel as an excuse to take hostile action against the Grand Duchy. There are such things as trade embargos and import taxation; we are a small nation and vulnerable in our reliance upon foreign commerce . . ."

"Just so, Monsieur le Baron, I do understand," chimed in Maev de Lederwyrhta, hoping to egg him on at greater speed. The Baron took the hint and said what he had come here to say:

"Your future involvement in state politics must be covert, and the best means to ensure this is to make it appear that upon your arrival you were, shall we say, removed from the scene by their majesties. The ambassadors for Bhourgbon, Guillaime and Eildres are all frankly adamant that you must be killed. They positively insist upon your death. This is not at all the wish of the Grand Duke and Duchess, therefore we must arrange for a . . . substitute to take your place, so that you are left free to be welcomed into the bosom of the court once more, to act for their majesties in the future as you have done so ably in the past."

"I am aware that with my detailed knowledge of the power-relations inside the courts of the continental crowned heads I am an extremely valuable commodity to their majesties, Baron," said Maev de Lederwyrhta dryly, "but I am not sure I follow you in this matter of a substitute?"

The fellow looked a little chagrined and then said:

"In order that it can be claimed that the notorious Maev de Lederwyrhta has been executed the instant her foot touched Bhelenese soil, I must, on the orders of their royal highnesses, supply a fresh corpse to play the part of your deceased self, so to speak. Witnesses will have to be produced to attest to the fact that this is indeed the body of the woman who was brought here upon the Port Casket. We already have the odious captain of that ship

190

under lock and key so that he may swear by his barbarous Heurtslin gods that the dead woman was his passenger. Wishing to attend to the matter with the minimum of fuss, I have taken it upon myself to have your lady-in-waiting perform this function for us. Whom else could we choose, when you really come to think about it?" he asked blandly.

There was a long moment's silence as Maev de Lederwyrhta and her companion Ealdræd of the Pæga tried to work out whether this was some lordly joke or whether the man was serious. Then in a growling tone redolent with feral menace Ealdræd gave the man his personal vow that the girl's death would be the Baron's own death. Édouard á Gascon, somewhat nonplussed by this totally unexpected reaction, groped for words until Maev de Lederwyrhta stated with a flat finality "The plan you outline is entirely unacceptable, Monsieur le Baron, and I beg that you will not mention it again."

Édouard sat perplexed, having had the floor taken out from under his feet. He was genuinely bewildered by the eccentric reluctance these two people had to pursue what was plainly the correct course of action. Nor could he quite see what there was to be done about it now. At this point the Baron's two gentlemen associates, Valéry and Séverin, returned. With a reckless disregard for discretion, they had no sooner closed the door behind them than Valéry grinned at his master and reported with some gratification that "The bitch is dead, my lord".

There was an unearthly roaring scream that filled the room like the manifestation of a banshee. None there recognised the piercing, eerie noise as human until in the next second the thing which had but a moment before been a man, a cynical mercenary soldier, a callous veteran of a lifetime of military encounters, an unfeeling survivor of a thousand battles, leapt like a pain-crazed wounded animal upon the Baron of Gascon and, with muscular fingers finding the first available target, gouged out the nobleman's right eye. Édouard, reeling back shrieking in abject terror, tumbled messily over a table and on to the floor. The ferociously bestial thing that had attacked him bellowed incoherently like a bull and cast the orb aside.

In defence of his liege lord, Séverin threw himself at the Aenglian's broad back, dagger poised for the killing blow but the big man, still wailing like damnation's chorus, spun round with such breathless speed that he had seized Séverin's extended arm at the wrist and shoulder before the murderer knew what was happening. The snarling brute then placed a knee against the elbow of the extended arm and pulled back on the wrist and shoulder. The elbow, bent the wrong way, cracked sickeningly, and the arm became limp. The enraged Aenglian, deranged to the point of savagery, had still not drawn his own weapon; his mindless fury leading him to attack bare-handed. But now he snatched the dagger from Séverin's nerveless fist and brought it down with such piledriving force that he buried it up to the very hilt in the man's chest. Séverin was dead before he hit the floor.

Maev de Lederwyrhta, stunned at the sudden fantastic barbarity that had been unleashed in the room, staggered back against the wall, whilst Valéry, unable to comprehend the situation and ghostly pale with numb dread, stumbled desperately for the door. The inhuman monster overtook him before he reached it and, crashing into him from behind, took hold of Valéry's head and smashed it hideously into the heavy round iron door handle. The wet sound of the impact filled the room but a second later there was another impact against the handle, repeated over and over and again, until the count was five, ten, fifteen. When the incensed and lunatic Aenglian finally dropped the bloody mass of pulp to the wooden floorboards after the twentieth collision of bone and iron, the whole of the front of the skull had been hammered concave. Valéry had died after the seventh blow but the creature of vengeance had been literally unable to stop pounding it into the door.

This seething ogre now turned to stalk toward the Baron, who was on his knees in utter disorientation clutching at his empty eye-socket. Maev de Lederwyrhta, the only person in the room of death who still retained her faculties, was thinking that the Baron's death would be disadvantageous to her for he was, it should be remembered, the Grand Duke's emissary, and although Bryony's death was bitterly tragic and heartbreaking it could not be undone, and peace still had to be made with the royal court, and she would have spoken to calm the Aenglian except that she then caught sight of his face. The vehement distortion of wrath made him almost unrecognisable as the man that she had thought she had come to know in the last several weeks, and she realised upon the instant that there was nothing she could say or do that could save the life of the Baron Édouard á Gascon.

192

The powerful muscles of the mercenary's bare arms rippled in anticipation of what was to come. Holding the back of the man's head in one hand, with the fingers of his other hand he speared out the second eye. The high-pitched screeching increased as the blind nobleman involuntarily pissed himself. But the Aenglian had not let go of the back of the man's head. He stood over the Baron, cupped his other hand under the weak chin and slowly pushed the head backwards until the vertebrae of the neck were bent to their absolute limit. And then he continued to push. There was a gruesome grinding noise of bone fracturing and a sibilant rasping rattle from the dying man's contorted throat. He could feel his own death as it was happening to him; feel it and understand what it was. The distressed woman who was watching him die could feel it, too, just from watching. The audible crack of the Baron's spine snapping as his neck was broken was almost a relief to Maev de Lederwyrhta. There is no knowing what it was to the Baron of Gascon.

With all his enemies dead and with there being no one left to kill, the unhinged Aenglian took a few steps toward the window and then sank down upon the floor panting and stricken with despair. His surging grief pulsated through his crumpled body like a physical pain and finally he fell silent. Amidst the butchered remains of those who had murdered his Bryony he wept the glacial stones of an old man's tears.

The Lady Maev made no sound or movement. She did not dare to approach him for ten minutes, but just left him where he was. His blood would not cool all at once. Eventually his breathing sounded more controlled and she walked carefully over to him, knelt down beside him, and placed a soft, cool hand upon his shoulder. She said, gently:

"Mercenary justice, my friend?"

The old man, slumped in a heap on the floor, felt the caress of her palm and the gentleness of her voice. He raised his head and Maev de Lederwyrhta saw that sanity had returned. He stared achingly at her for several long seconds and then replied:

"Mademoiselle, it is the only justice I have at my disposal."

Chapter 5

Daughter of the Steppes

The mists were so thick and noxious that vision was limited to a few yards at best. The wet foliage, limp with moisture, was washed with the sluggishly wafting condensation. It was mid-morning, yet the sky had the feel of twilight. The ground underfoot was so irregular and uncertain that Hengustir, the massive ghostly blue-roan warhorse shied from time to time, testing the ground with a tentative hoof before continuing on. The huge grey shape of the horse with the tall, cloaked rider astride him, slid through the wreaths of mist like an equine spectre. Ealdræd of the Pæga, a clan of the Aenglians, was making the dangerous journey through the marshlands of the Marécage.

He was coming to the end of the worst of it now, the gaseous stretch of bog in the centre of that narrow strip of Eildres which, being of no earthly use to anyone whatever, had been left deserted by humanity since time began. The damp fog, though not actually poisonous enough to be lethal, was sufficiently toxic to be harmful to the lungs if a person spent any length of time in these parts. Ealdræd had no intension of dallying a minute longer that necessity demanded. The mildewed stench of sodden and rotting vegetation was all the reason he needed to pass through this unpleasant and injurious country with as much speed as the difficult conditions would permit.

He was a week and a half into his discreet departure from Bhel, exercising much the better part of valour in absenting himself. On the evening of his very first day in the Grand Duchy a cruelly provoked Ealdræd had murdered a Baron, albeit a minor one, the Baron Édouard á Gascon, who carried the Grand Duke's seal and was conducting government business. This had left the Aenglian with little option but to depart from Bhel as swiftly as he had entered it without time for a backward glance.

This inevitably meant that Ealdræd and the woman who had become his friend, the internationally notorious Maev de Lederwyrhta, needs must part company forever. They had done so amicably; indeed, with a certain restrained affection. The two had travelled together as comrades in a rough and ready mutual respect, so that it was no small thing for the veteran mercenary and the courtesan to part, and it was a true measure of her fidelity to him that she had made no attempt to betray his direction of flight to the authorities after his exodus and thereby advance her own position with the Grand Duke; which she would most certainly have done had he been anyone else.

The Bhelenese authorities had perfectly reasonably assumed that the fugitive would attempt to take ship once again to return to Heurtslin and so find safety in the Ehngle peninsula. Where else would one of the Ehngle folk bolt to but the nearest of their own lands? Those same authorities, on the strident orders of their Grand Duke and Duchess, had made the ports of the northern shore as tight with security as was humanly possible. The iron blades of the Bhelenese soldiery bristled openly at docks and quayside. For a man alone it would have been a desperate gamble to attempt a ship of any sort, but for a man with a horse as distinctive as a blue-roan war-charger it was suicide. With Hengustir, Ealdræd was extremely conspicuous, so much so that he had not the slightest chance of getting himself and his animal on board a ship that was large enough to navigate around the Mariners Cauldron and so make passage to Heurtslin. The only vessel he might get would be a small fishing boat but none such would dare to risk the Cauldron. He needed a ship not a boat.

But the Aenglian would not give up his horse. This left him with only one option; that of doing the unexpected. Instead of heading homeward, he had decided to strike out in the opposite direction. Ealdræd had set his nose for the east into the Geulten kingdom of Eildres, which was no more than one hundred leagues wide this far to the north, in hope of passing between the bogs and marshlands of the Marécage and the frozen rock of the Cordennes. If Ealdræd could cross the narrow strip of Geulten territory and enter the racially Khevnic country known only as the Torvig Steppes he would be alone and friendless in a world full of predators but at least he would no longer be a hunted man.

He had been on horseback continuously for the last eleven days in the hours betwixt dawn and dusk. In the first few days he had ridden the one hundred and twenty miles from the great sea port of Oosted in the Grand Duchy all the way to the national border with Eildres. During this time he had made an excellent pace, with the cantering stride of the mighty Hengustir eating up the Bhelenese countryside at a rate of forty miles a day. He could hardly go wrong in his route.

He had merely to keep the enormous ice-peaked mountains of the Cordennes always on his right to be sure that his course was eastward.

Heading directly on he had covered as many miles again into the country of his ethnic enemies, the Eildres, and was now but forty leagues from the great emptiness of the Torvig Steppes where the vengeful Grand Duke's militia would be unlikely to follow. But the last few days had been a story not of striding through the miles but rather one of slowly trudging along at a comparative snail's pace.

The Marécage was a region of swamp and marsh that contained the deadly sucking mud in which a man and horse might drown if the steed misplaced his footing. Yet Ealdræd knew that when he finally emerged from the constant fogs of this accursed land he would see ahead of him, looming like giants on the horizon, the Heights of Turghol; an extension of the same chain of mountains of which the Cordennes formed so significant a part, but the Heights were outside of Geulten sovereignty. Between them and the Cordennes was the mountain pass of the Col du Selle, and it was thence that Ealdræd would make his way. He had never been through these realms before but he had received from Maev de Lederwyrhta a well-crafted map which enabled him to make a fair judgement as to bearing and distance.

First, the mists cleared and he found himself in open country, lightly wooded and increasingly rocky as Hengustir climbed steadily up a shallow but continuous gradient that lasted for many miles. Second, the air grew sharp, signalling that they had achieved altitude and were still climbing. This high up you could feel the cold in your lungs as the air went down but Ealdræd didn't mind that; he welcomed it after the choking haze of the marshland fog.

The days spent on this section of the journey were strenuous for the horse but otherwise quiet. Fortunately they would not need to climb above the timber line, which meant that Ealdræd had wood to make a fire each night, and it was still too early for snow. Indeed, the weather was fair, but notwithstanding the bright sunshine the Aenglian wore both his cloak and mantle over his tunic and wrapped the heavy wool of his cloak tight around him when the wind blew. As they continued upwards he took to spreading his own sleeping blanket across Hengustir's back in an attempt to keep the chill out of the animal's muscles. But, truth be told, the horse was faring noticeably better than his master. The old wound in Ealdræd's calf was proving troublesome again, as it always did in the cold weather, Buldr's curse upon it, and the ache that sometimes afflicted his joints was also making its presence felt. Injuries and ailments of this sort were inevitable in a mercenary's life if he lived to the Aenglian's age and the only cure was to die in your youth.

But there was no one to complain to except the gods and they had never been known to care a tinker's toss for the doings and sufferings of men. All born of this earth came forth out of the Well of Mægen and at their deaths all must surrender to Wihvir Lord of Hálsian, the commander and corruptor of spirits, but from birth to death there was little to be gained, in Ealdræd's opinion, from being over-fussed with god-worship. They were not disposed to grant favours. So the veteran kept his temper and tried to borrow for his soul a little of the calm placidity of his surroundings. He sang a little to his horse for company. It was a very coarse song about a syphilitic whore who married an old Merthyan widower and all his four sons died of the pox though the old man never fell ill at all. Ealdræd's Aenglian accent became more pronounced when he sang and it was his fond belief that Hengustir enjoyed the vulgar songs the most.

After so long an ascent, when they finally stood upon the clear, clean skyline of the summit of the saddle-shaped pass of the Col du Selle Ealdræd paused to take in the grandeur of the panorama that greeted his senses on all sides. His eyes soaked up the startlingly blue and cloudless sky, his skin absorbed the contrast of warm sun and cold wind, and his palate could almost taste the purity of the thin but sublimely fresh air. With the high mountains on either side of him to east and west, the Col du Selle was like a gigantic gateway carved in the rock by whatever gods plagued and burdened this land as their one act of mercy toward a sorely beset humanity.

Gazing back down the natural path of scrub grass and flint that the steadfast Hengustir had patiently ascended to scale this pass between the Cordennes and the Turghol, the Aenglian was surprised to notice another figure upon the mountainside, perhaps a mile below. This person's horse was making tough-going of the terrain and Ealdræd's instant judgement was that the rider had not been permitting his animal sufficient pauses for rest and feeding. Unwise; in fact foolhardy, in the mercenary's experienced opinion.

The veteran spearman's keen eyes, undimmed by his more than forty years, could make out the figure as a soldier as it approached to within a half mile, and when it was within a few hundred yards he could see the fellow in detail. It was a lancer of the Grand Duke's personal Guard, in the olive-green hose and curled-toe boots of that uniformed regiment; his close-fitting sleeveless jerkin cut from buff-coloured leather was worn over a cambric shirt. His costume was topped off by a wide, flat Tellerbarret beret from which the feather had long since been lost, set at an angle on his head like a round platter made of brown moleskin.

Of course, Ealdræd knew too little of the Bhelenese military to be able to identify any particular dress but the mere fact that the man wore a uniform marked him out as a member of the urbane and cultured roll of honour. Only those whose soldiering was performed for the wealthiest of the social elite had a recognisable set of liveried colours to wear. This solitary fellow was one such. He might more properly be found running errands for his superiors on the general staff or currying favour with the aristocracy. What he was doing out in the barren wilds of the Col du Selle with his pretty clothes caked in mud was a puzzlement.

But for the filthy condition he was in after his struggle through the Marécage it would have been plain from his apparel that he was something of a dandy, with his long side-whiskers but no beard, in the Bhelenese courtly style. Had Ealdræd been aware of such matters he might have thought that here was an aspiring lad with his eye on a promising future with the military toadies who bow and scrape their way into an advantageous marriage. His name was Under-Captain of Lancers, Estragon Bailé, in the Grand Duke Belaric's Household Guard, but Ealdræd was not destined to make the fellow's acquaintance for long enough to enquire into his rank and career ambitions.

Estragon Bailé had just spent the most torturous week of his life commanding a small troop of Bhelenese volunteers through the shifting and perfidious marshes in pursuit of one solitary foreign murderer whose barbarous name had been proclaimed by the orders of the day to be 'Aledred of Aenglia'. Estragon knew enough of geography to know that the country mentioned was a nation of the Ehngle and about as far west as human habitation extended before dropping off the edge of the continent into the sea. How such a savage had found his way to the Grand Duchy for the express purpose of butchering the Baron of Gascon, a mere Under-Captain of Lancers could not be expected to fathom, but one thing Estragon did know for certain sure was that when he eventually caught up with this Ehngle assassin he would carve the regimental coat of arms into the stinking Aenglian cur's backside.

The intemperance of his feelings in the matter had considerable justification. This loyal soldier of the Grand Duke was the only survivor of a small troop of Bhelenese guard who, almost as an after-thought, had been sent eastward whilst everyone else was watching the northern ports. The Grand Duke Belaric and his mother the Grand Duchess Griselde were a wily and a scheming pair. Although certain that their quarry must seek a ship, they had yet the cunning to send one force of men eastward, just in case. This band of peacetime soldiers, unused to the rigours of real soldiering, had not taken long to fall foul of the treacherous Marécage. Pushing onward recklessly in the haste of their pursuit, three had been devoured by the wet ground, pulled under screaming and beseeching their comrades for succour. None had been forthcoming. Two more of the troop had simply disappeared into the mists and had in all probability wandered hopelessly astray. Perhaps they might find their way out of the all-concealing vapours or perhaps they might not.

They could meander off to hell for all Estragon Bailé cared. He, the only man remaining, as the officer in charge of the other five, cared solely for the threat this posed to his reputation as an officer. If he were to capture or kill the fugitive, he would be a made man. But he had no stomach for the thought of returning to his lordship reporting total failure and the loss of every man under his command. He had placed all his hopes in the signs of fresh hoof-prints he had found in several places through the interminable bogs. Perchance the killer had travelled this way, for who else would ride through such a waterlogged quagmire? And so Estragon Bailé had pressed on, coughing on the grey miasma and braving the imminent terrors of submergence. For his courage he had been rewarded; upon reaching the base of the Col du Selle he had finally caught sight of the game he had been chasing.

His mount was fatigued but Estragon urged the creature on, fearful lest his prize should escape at the last, but then he saw that the rider ahead had stopped on the very summit of the saddle of the pass. In Estragon's reckoning the dullard must also have seen him and yet the fool remained sitting there on his monster of a horse as if he didn't realise that an officer of the Duke's own personal Guard was on his trail. Estragon Bailé resolved to wound the simpleton painfully with a skillful turn of his lance to punish the swine for having led him such a merry dance, and then walk the oaf back to Bhel for a judicious and overdue crucifixion. If the barbarian gave any show of resistance, Estragon would simply skewer him lancer-style and carry the carcass back draped over its own horse.

When he could see the Aenglian more closely, so distinctive with his braided beard, the Bhelenese officer gave a great shout of recognition and success, and began urging his horse onward at the canter, trying to raise a gallop. The silent spearman had not moved, and even in the face of this assault he remained where he was, looking down impassively at what had revealed itself to be a hostile pursuer, albeit a forlorn and bedraggled remnant of the hunting party that it must once have been. Ealdræd assessed his foe, an impetuous man on a tired-looking black gelding, and was not impressed. The mercenary's martial brain noted the significant factors; armed with an eight foot lance; carries the lance left-handed; gelding struggling to maintain the gallop because its over-confident master hadn't the sense to know not to attack uphill on a tired mount. Ealdræd determined his tactics in the few seconds it took him to sum up his enemy.

He shifted his spear into the lance position in his right hand and set Hengustir to the gallop straight at the other rider, taking advantage of charging downhill. Hengustir could boast over 2,000 lbs of muscle and bone, being barrel-chested and thick in the shanks, and the power of the weight of the horse multiplied by its momentum would be doubled by the force of gravity on so steep a gradient. The lancer, realising that his man wanted to make a fight of it, dug his spurs into the flanks of his own lacklustre mount and urged it up the hill at its best speed. Estragon Bailé had never before fought with a foreigner but he was confident that a savage with a spear would hardly have a chance against a trained lancer in the joust.

Against a left-handed opponent Ealdræd's usual strategy in the joust was to seek to get his spear inside the opponent's weapon to deflect it away; that would serve very nicely today for with the steep hillside working in his favour, the rest he could leave to his huge blue-roan warhorse.

Clods of earth were thrown up as the two animals thundered towards each other, the men crouched upon their backs leaning forward high in the stirrups with hunched shoulders and muscles tensed. The eight foot lance had twelve inches greater reach over Ealdræd's seven foot spear, but this advantage was negated by the lancer holding his weapon tucked under the armpit clamped tight by the elbow, whereas the Aenglian's looser style permitted him to extend his point more in an elongated jab than a short thrust. The lancer was trying to pick a line of attack that would take him smoothly wide and to the right of his oncoming adversary to make space for his left-handed strike, forcing the antagonist to make their right-handed thrust over the top of their own horse's neck. It was a technique that the left-hander had employed to unsettle many an opponent when tilting in the lists at his lordship's joust. But the Aenglian was wheeling his charger very slightly to avoid getting on the wrong side. Yet neither was he taking his own line of charge to the other side. Instead the two irresistible forces careened head-on with the last few yards between them vanishing at blinding speed under their combined velocity.

At the last second, suddenly understanding that the Aenglian actually intended a collision, Estragon Bailé tried to improvise a thrust with his lance over the head of his mount. The Ehngle mercenary's totally unorthodox approach had made a hidebound nonsense of the etiquette of the joust. Estragon's hasty stab went high and Ealdræd's deft parry with his spear took both weapons out of the equation as the two horses crashed deafeningly into one another, breast to breast, with an impact like the end of the world. The lighter gelding was swept up and knocked right over on to its back, screaming its panic, its rider thrown clear out of the saddle. Brought to a stop by the tremendous bone-crunching wallop, Hengustir reared up on to his hind legs, neighing his triumph like the king of all horseflesh, and brought the hooves of his forelegs smashing down upon the sprawling gelding, one iron shod foot catching the other horse in its sinewy neck.

But it was the man that Ealdræd must despatch. As the Bhelenese officer rolled on the ground, tumbling and disoriented, Ealdræd jerked Hengustir aside from his fallen foe and put him to the lunge toward the Lancer of the Guard who, having groggily regained his feet, made the suicidal mistake of turning to recover his lance. He was four yards away but Hengustir covered the distance in one leap. Ealdræd's spearpoint caught the man dead centre between the shoulder blades and its eighteen inches of polished, razor-edged metal ripped through the torso and burst out the chest of the prettily uniformed but sadly inexperienced Estragon Bailé.

*   *   *

There was nothing to signal the border between Eildres and the land generally referred to as the Torvig Steppes. It did not have any name attributable to a nation-state since the people were largely nomadic and unworthy of the status of geographical nationhood. The steppes were too wind-swept and dusty to be of much use as arable land; the soil was poor and hard enough to break a plough. Consequently, nobody had ever really bothered to claim it as a nation. It was merely a part of that great, some said infinite, expanse of open country populated by the foul-smelling and warlike tribes of the Torvig.

Ealdræd arrived in this new land in remarkably good condition for one who had been on the road for so long. He had scarcely stopped in his travels, by horse and by ship, since he had left Amsburgh in faraway Wehnbria, and that, by his rough reckoning, was getting on for three thousand miles back. But then he had spent most of his life in transit from somewhere to somewhere else, and he knew every trick to make the journeying easier, both for himself and more importantly for his horse.

He had lost one of his javelins in combat on the road out of Wehnbria but he now had two horses, having brought the dead lancer's black gelding along, and despite the wound that Hengustir had inflicted to its neck, it was already looking a deal healthier for Ealdræd's sensible pace and his habit of stopping to let the animals feed whenever there was suitable grassland. It was also Ealdræd's regular practice, as it was for all the cavalrymen of Aenglia, to dig up edible roots and vegetables if he spied them growing nearby to provide man and horse with a more nourishing ballast than cheese wheybread for the man and grass or foliage for the horse. So far from home, Ealdræd was entirely ignorant of what the steppes might be like other than the conventional talk of their utter desolation, so he was keen to feed his animals as much as possible while the chance was available to him. He even managed to collect a bagful of edible roots and grasses which the gelding carried in place of a rider, along with, Buldr be praised, a recently filled pair of water sacks. His remaining javelin and his spear were sheathed on Hengustir's saddle and Ealdræd's mail shirt, worn over a gambeson tunic, was still free of rust despite the wetness of the Marécage. The twenty-inch broad-bladed knife that Ealdræd wore at his belt was always a reassurance and the four-plate iron pot basin helmet concealed under his leather mantle was a valuable supplement to his mail. The old veteran was still in control of his own destiny, as far as any man was, and all things considered, went his way in relative ease and ready to meet with whatever his road had in store for him.

To the north loomed the Heights of Turghol where the mountain-dwelling Torvig goat-herds killed one another over the bartering of their fetid cheese. There was nothing in those peaks and plateaus for Ealdræd and he kept a straight course eastward. Not wishing to remain too close to the Eildres border, he chose caution over comfort and rode several days into the steppes, with the idea of being well clear of Geulten land before he turned southward toward the civilized kingdom of Piccoli.

Ahead lay the Tundra, a treeless plain over which blew an incessant, relentlessly dry wind that could flay the skin off you if you didn't take care. Ealdræd tugged the heavy wool weave of his cloak up a fraction to cover the lower half of his face. His primary concern was for the horses, and more specifically for Hengustir. There was no means by which he could protect the animals as well as he would like. But they were creatures of stamina and internal fortitude as they had proven already and the gusting breeze was not so bad as yet.

To Ealdræd the topography that confronted him was simply a deserted, monotonous, ugly wasteland with inadequate forage and a conspicuous lack of solace or good cheer. But to those who lived here this was the country of the multitudinous Khevnic tribes, the most significant of whose various ethnic groups included the Tartari, the Tsurbac and the Czechu, all of whom were proud in their cultural autonomy, therefore intrinsically hostile to one another, therefore constantly at war. The peoples of the Torvig Steppes were as uncongenial as the landscape they lived in.

All the Khevnic tribes were nomadic because there was no reason for them to stay in any one place for any length of time. The grey-brown Tundra soil was frozen throughout the winter, parched throughout the summer, and useless hard clay all the year round that could break a spade in the hands of anyone with the idiocy to dig. It lacked just about everything required for successful agriculture. Even natural vegetation was fairly sparse, with long stretches of barren ground and extensive areas of mosses and lichens; dwarf trees, and dry shrub. There was little in the way of woodland and what there was barely managed to rear up from the inhospitable ground, stunted and twisted. Animal life was poor, too, apart from half-starved wolves, some wild boar, and the ubiquitous goats which were shepherded by the indigenous population for milk and meat. These recalcitrant goats were one of the few species of creature that was hardy enough to survive in this part of the world and mobile enough to accord with a nomadic lifestyle.

Another domesticated species of whom this was true, and one even more beloved in the lives of the local tribesmen, was the shaggy, stout Khevnic horse. Built for endurance in extremes of weather conditions, it was none the less surprisingly swift on its short legs. It was a durable riding horse, wearing the distinctive raised Torvig saddle that had a pommel behind as well as in front, and it was a good carriage horse as well, pulling the wagons of the caravans that criss-crossed the plain. It had to thrive in a harsh climate on a meagre food supply, covering huge distances generally unshod, and prey to attacks by hunger-frenzied wolf packs. Its stamina could, at times, be remarkable.

The dozens of ethnic peoples that populated the Torvig came together over one thing only; their equine and equestrian culture. This, naturally, was a subject of competition between them that had frequently been a cause for dispute. But then everything in life seemed to be a legitimate cause for violent conflict on the steppes, nowhere more so than the Tundra.

There were said to be innumerable breeds of the Khevnic horse but for the short time that Ealdræd was to be their country every horse he saw looked identical to every other. Never the less, the fighting men of the Tartari, the Tsurbac and the Czechu would dispute the superiority of one breed over another and seek to prove their words in competition, and to prove the superiority of their own horsemanship, too, which might sometimes settle the matter to the satisfaction of some but absolutely never to the satisfaction of all. Deaths were common at Khevnic horse races but mostly they occurred off the actual race course.

All warfare on the steppes was conducted exclusively in cavalry engagements. The warriors of the Tundra fought on horseback, as they did everything else on horseback from the age of about four. On the battlefield the Khevnic horse was a fast-moving vehicle for men who fought singly, not in rows and lines or regular formations. Warfare on the steppes was a matter of several hundred men and horses careering around in a disorderly melee and nobody the wiser as to whom the victors were until the women counted the number of dead husbands afterwards.

The rider from Aenglia, still in the shadow of the Heights of Turghol, drew rein upon his horse and squinted into the expanse of low valley in front of him; not a real valley, more a shallow depression a league wide with a scattering of spruce trees and a small covert of fir and pine in the centre. A furling or so in front of him stood a man, a woman, and a dog. The dip in the earth had been just deep enough for them to be out of sight until he came level with the edge of the valley.

Ealdræd slipped his javelin out of its saddle sheath at the sight of strangers and rode on. The threesome held their position but only the dog gave the impression of being prepared to stand up for itself. The newcomer to this alien land appraised these people of the steppes as his horse walked steadily toward them.

He needn't have bothered to arm himself. The family group were a picture of docility. They barely dared to look at him. In the west Ealdræd was considered a tall man, being some inches over two yards in height. This man was around twelve inches shorter. It subsequently transpired that, although the average Khevnic male was as robust as a brace of oxen and so strong that a blacksmith could use him to hammer iron, he was a comparatively short example of manhood, with an average height of about five and a half feet. To the Khevnic who now stared sullenly up at the strange foreign rider, Ealdræd was freakishly big. Seated upon his majestic warhorse that stood seventeen hands high, the outlander had the intimidating aspect of a giant. The Khevnic could not be sure if this was a man of flesh and blood or not, for all Khevnic horses were brown or black and this monster was a blue-grey colour and twice the size of any normal mount. The Khevnic kept his head deferentially lowered, reluctant to meet the outlander's gaze.

The man of the steppes was probably not more than thirty but with a skin beaten into leather by the winds, he was sufficiently prune-like to pass for fifty. Ealdræd greeted the man with a salutation in the Geulten tongue. Eildres was merely a few days ride away and it seemed reasonable to suppose that the language would be familiar here. Not a flicker passed over the nomad's cowhide face. Ealdræd did not bother to try to communicate in his own language, the speech of the Ehngle peoples, for if the fellow understood nothing of Geulten, not even a simple greeting, then he most certainly would recognise not one word of Ehngleish.

In the west of the continent there was a bifurcation of culture into the Ehngle nations of the peninsula, all of whom spoke some variation of the Ehngle language, and the Geulten nations, all of whom spoke some dialect of the Geulten tongue. Consequently, across twelve countries only two languages were spoken, and if the convoluted diversity of accents made conversation difficult at times, it was at least possible to converse. Like a great many westerners whose trade as a man-at-arms or as a merchant brought them into contact with folk from faraway places, Ealdræd was bi-lingual in Ehngleish and Geulten. But he began to suspect that amongst the Khevnic tribes of Torvig he could anticipate finding no one who spoke either of these languages and, needless to say, the Khevnic tongues were gibberish to him.

The defeated and stooping female who stood next to the man was obviously a slave or a servant or a wife. There was likely little difference in the status of all three in such a place as this. She had that facial expression of permanent emptiness; devoid of anything but patience. It was the visage of someone for whom life had utterly and irredeemably failed. Suffering had been heaped upon suffering, indignity and humiliation had filled the days and nights for long enough that nothing but these degradations could be remembered. Whereupon the features lose their individuality and their animation and collapse into a blank mask, as featureless as the Tundra itself. It was the expression of those forced into slavery and then forgotten there, the whole world over.

The dog was a Gortzi, the breed known as the 'steppes hound'. A little over two feet high, its dumpy body solidly built under its short hair. Its head was long, the skull broad with a pointed muzzle. Thin, tapering ears lay back on its head to leave unobstructed the clear vision of its big, dark eyes. Their tempers were legendary. It was sometimes said that no true-bred Gortzi had ever made a friend of a human. It may have been true. Certainly, they made tremendously efficient guard dogs for they would bark and snarl and bite at anyone who came near. Tie one to a peg driven into the ground in front of your tent and you would have a very audible warning if anyone approached your tent. There was always a dog or two guarding the outskirts of any encampment on the Tundra. Ealdræd had never met this breed of dog before but he was of the opinion that the dog was the only one of the three who still retained any pride or self-respect. It yapped and yowled ferociously at him as he rode by.

This Khevnic couple would not be alone; where there were two there was a community to which they belonged. These would be stragglers. And there it was, strung out in the valley, a long caravan of horsemen, wagons, and footsore pedestrians making its nonchalant progress slowly across the wind-swept vale. Ealdræd gave some thought to whether he should approach this band of nomads at all, and if so, then whether to approach with weapons in hand or with them sheathed. At that moment a startled cry of alarm went up from one of the men riding guard on the column and three riders peeled off to come charging over the plain to where the Pæga spearman awaited them with spear in hand and his jaw set firm.

They drove their horses hard until the last fifty yards when they abruptly hauled back on the reins to bring their mounts to a halt in a swirling cloud of dust. Ealdræd sat alert to any move on their part as the dust cloud swept over him. No move came. They had taken up positions to the front and each side of him but showed no sign of instigating an attack. He could tell that they were eying his second horse, the black gelding, for this was a temptation to such lifelong horse-stealers, but they resisted the urge.

The hungry, predatory faces of the Khevnic riders, homogeneous in their high-cheekbones black irises and drooping moustaches, all but licked their lips with hyena relish. Their livery of goatskin jackets and fur-fringed pantaloon was bedecked with a fairly extensive armoury of sharpened ironmongery, especially a distinctive crescent short sword that each man carried slung across his back. Yet with odds of three against one they still hesitated to take the initiative. Ealdræd thought back to that poor clown of a Bhelenese officer who had charged him uphill in joust against a horse twice the weight of his own, and the Aenglian couldn't decide which he despised the more: the arrogant, over-confident Bhelenese or these cowardly poltroons of Khevnics.

A forth rider came cantering up and something in the pompous self-importance of the man told Ealdræd that this fellow was the chief of this nomadic band; his moustaches were puffed a little more splendidly, his goatskin more ornate; his eyes a shade blacker. He guided his animal to a point a little to the fore of his warriors and halted there. He looked the intruder up and down and the bristling ferocity of his manner was a certain indication of his fear. Only the truly frightened make such a parade of their dauntless valour. He reminded Ealdræd of the Gortzi dog but without the sincerity.

He declared boldly to this trespasser of evil aspect on the gargantuan devil horse, that his name was Borislav Vsevolod. He did not admit that it was one he had taken for himself. But now that he was chief nobody ever dared call him by any other name. Whatever his given name might have been he was now Borislav Vsevolod to the death. It was more than a name, it was a title, and it was a political manifesto; *bor* for 'battle' and *slav* for 'glory' meaning 'glory in battle' combined with *vse* for 'all' and *volod* for 'rule' meaning 'to rule all'. His destiny was that through glory in battle he would come to rule all. Or, at least, so he believed.

Ealdræd, having not one word of the language, knew nothing of this, of course. But he knew a worthless bastard when he saw one. The chief wore a *czapka*, the round fur hat that proliferated amongst those of the Khevnic who could afford it. The rest wore the peasants' thick cotton cap or went bare-headed. His under-tunic was a *sorochka*, a simple shirt without fastening, worn beneath the knee-length *kievan* tunic in a thick woven fabric designed to keep out the wind rather than to display any elegance or sartorial charm. His curly beard was dense and blue-black and just as bushy as his brows. He was 300lb of muscle and blubber and if he had killed more people, or had more people killed, that he had eaten hot goulash, it was not because he was on a vegetarian diet.

He roared that this was the territory of the Czechu tribe; that there were a hundred Czechu caravans on the Tundra and the caravan of Borislav Vsevolod was the finest of them all. He demanded to know why Ealdræd was in Czechu lands and then he offered fifteen dracha for the black gelding, which was approximately a third of the going price. Borislav Vsevolod, in the manner of indigenous people everywhere, assumed that foreigners were ignorant of all civilized practices and customs, and thus were sheep to be shorn. As the hillmen of Turghol said, if goats were not born to be milked, the gods would not have given them teats. The Czechu word for foreigner was *ziedmol*, which was also their word for shit.

Ealdræd disregarded the nomad's ostentatious and incomprehensible jibber-jabber. He took his spear in one hand and his purse of coin in the other. Tapping himself on the chest, he shook the spear, then rattled the bag of money. A glint of understanding came into the eyes of the bandit chief: this man was a mercenary; a fighting man for sale. The hairy lord of the plains grinned like a priest receiving charity. It was a sign of affluence and power when a tribal head could boast of having soldiers who fought

208

for wages in his war band, and that the mercenary should be a giant *ziedmol* with a beard like snakes riding a horse that anyone could see at a glance had been born in the ice of hell, well, that would be prestige indeed.

Borislav Vsevolod made gesticulations of eating, drinking and talking, and the Aenglian understood that he had been invited to parley over his terms of hire. He nodded and this motion was greeted by rapacious smiles from the four horsemen. The body language of gesture, at least, was universal. Ealdræd accompanied them warily as they returned to their column of march. Borislav Vsevolod talked loudly all the way, with much waving of his hands and sweeping of his arms, but for the most part addressing himself to the four winds and to the tundra that lay around them. Certainly his men seemed to take it for granted that he was talking to himself for they ignored him and the Aenglian followed their example.

The Czechu caravan was in the process of picking out a place to settle for the night and Ealdræd rode alongside it for the last few miles before they found a likely spot. The community over which Borislav Vsevolod ruled like the petty tyrant that he was, gave Ealdræd small cause for concern. Women were in the majority, downtrodden drudges like the one he had seen earlier, and such men as he saw were of the same character as the weaklings who had ridden out to meet him. There were a number of slaves amongst the rabble, of course, but feeble specimens for the most part. All but one.

For amongst the convoy of miscellaneous riff-raff was a slave whose circumstances appeared bitter indeed, but whose deportment caught the mercenary's notice. His attention was drawn by the weird slanting of her eyes. He had never seen oriental eyelids before and it intrigued him. It was not a deformity, he was sure, for all its outlandishness. It did not detract from the essential beauty of her delicate features but lent them a cryptic quality. At first glance she looked very young but at second glance her physical maturity was apparent for she was half naked in a thin cotton chemise that was ripped so ragged that much of her sorely bruised and whip-welted flesh was displayed through it. It was no more than tatters at the back where the incessant application of the whip over time had shredded the cotton to mere threads all the way from shoulders to buttocks. The chemise had originally extended to the knee but at the front it had been badly torn by many hands, as if they were in a hurry to get at her body, until her breasts and thighs were scarcely

209

concealed by it at all. Ealdræd judged her to be about nineteen years of age. No child ever had contours like that.

Around her neck was a thick wooden yoke in an oval shape that was weighty enough to make her stagger in her weakened condition. The scissor-hinged wood locked around her neck but also imprisoned her hands on either side, so that she must keep her hands shoulder high all the time. Her arms and shoulders would naturally tire quickly, after which their weight would be added to the burden upon her neck, dragging her down. Barefoot and splattered with mud, she stumbled forward repeatedly trying to lift her head up so as to walk with her chin raised.

Her crow-black hair was plastered to her head with sweat and the dirt and grime that encrusted her petite round face had been smeared by the residue of the many rivers of tears that had dried upon her cheeks, and yet upon that diminutive countenance was etched an expression of such belligerent, stubborn resolve that Ealdræd immediately warmed to the girl. It marked her out from amongst the cattle of the other slaves as a person of character. Her eyes may have betrayed her with their watering but her heart and her will were firm. A person of profoundly obstinate and aggressive temperament, in chains and under the lash she was yet unconquered.

Ealdræd grinned at her mulish antipathy. He liked a fighter and this little miss in her wretched humiliation had an obdurate tenacity and a dignified hostility toward all and sundry that earned his respect. But the set-in-stone impassivity of the face could not belie the exhaustion of the limbs. She could scarcely drag herself along and only the occasional crack of a long flail across her back kept her in motion. When the caravan reached their sheltering place for the night, the girl dropped where she stood and was ignored by everyone around her. One or two of the scampering children enjoyed some sport with her, kicking her and pelting her with goat manure as she lay in the dust. Their childish giggles were festive.

The veteran found himself frustrated at having no means by which to learn her story. His inability to communicate in anything but the most basic terms with this Torvig vermin denied him the satisfaction of his curiosity about the odd, splendidly defiant, slant-eyed girl. Still, there was nothing to be done about it and he dismissed the woman from his mind.

She was actually of the far-flung land of the Menghis and had been taken captive by Khevnic raiders who had butchered her family and carried her away westward to the Torvig Steppes, using her as a beast of burden and pleasure slave. After several months of the harshest conceivable treatment at the sadistic whims of these depraved and debauched villains, she had been sold to the Czechu, just a few weeks since, when they were at the easternmost extreme of their cycle of travel. The Czechu had been on the point of turning back to their fatherland on the Tundra and when they did so they brought their newly purchased Menghis slave along with them. As a result, since her first capture she had been forced to travel further from her native territory that Ealdræd had travelled from his. Unable, as well as unwilling, to even converse with her captors, she was absolutely abandoned to her fate in an alien land.

That this could be done successfully to a Menghis woman, and to very many others of her countrywomen beside her, was proof positive that the great Menghis Empire of a millennia past was in terminal decline. Its glory days of former generations were long gone. In the present century it was the Khevnic nomads who were on the rise and these were years of trial for the Menghis.

Her name was Eiji. As the offspring of two ethnically Menghis parents she was a true-born daughter of the steppes. In the west people spoke of the Torvig Steppes as being a vast, impenetrable, endless void but to those who lived further east the Tundra was a minor region of a much larger land mass. The Menghis were a widespread nation of pony riders and they had once had an empire in the Far East that had extended a thousand leagues in all directions from its centre. The Menghis Empire had once covered an unimaginable vastness, and their country was still thought of as the land of the Great Steppes.

The Menghis were a people of which Ealdræd, of course, was totally unaware. He had never heard of them, and would not be enlightened by the Czechu since there was no one here who could speak to him of them. Their lands lay beyond the continent that was the known world of the realms familiar to Ealdræd. As an Aenglian he had never even heard the names of such impossibly distant places as had previously bounded the experience of the girl Eiji, let alone had occasion to discover anything of their ways. To those of his clan of the Pæga who had settled for lives in the villages of their ancestors, where Ealdræd now stood on the Torvig Steppes might as well have been the moon. That there could be places in the world still more remote than this from the forests of Aenglia would have made no sense to them. Such ideas could not have been believed. After all, the earth must have some end to it.

The mercenary was invited to break bread with Borislav Vsevolod and his senior men that evening and so he waited with his horses, being stared at by apprehensive children, whilst the caravan erected their tents and built their fires and stabled their animals and generally busied themselves with the construction of a village that would exist upon the steppes for one night only. He could not help but observe the Menghis girl in the wooden yoke being cursed and beaten by a harridan with a necklace of sparkly beads that in a society like this would probably be thought more valuable than the slave who was being chastised.

She was Lyudmilla, incestuous sister of Borislav Vsevolod and the despotic matriarch of the tribe. She was the worst of this nightmare of relentless brutality where Eiji was concerned. No slave lived more than two months under the heel of Lyudmilla and most lasted less than half that. It was a tribute to Eiji's resilience and her capacity to endure extraordinary quantities of pain that she was still so healthy and free from broken bones after five weeks of being driven by Lyudmilla's whip. For so slight and delicate-looking a young woman, the Menghis girl was deceptively tough.

As Ealdræd watched with a cynical detachment, the broad-shouldered, raw-boned Lyudmilla stomped over to where the exhausted Menghis lay sprawled in the dirt and set about her with a donkey-whip. The girl in the shredded chemise started to crawl toward a small tent that had been pegged out nearby. Apparently the slave knew that this was where Lyudmilla wanted her to be. Even from fifty yards away Ealdræd could hear the girl snarling and hissing at Lyudmilla in what he assumed must be her own language. Amongst the choicer phrases from what the Menghis was saying was "you malodorous spewings of a comfort-woman's cunt!" but because she spoke only Menghali and her captors spoke only Czechu, Lyudmilla could not know what atrociously obscene abuse Eiji was hurling at her. But she could guess, and the donkey whip rose and fell with real venom as the Czechu matriarch flogged her slave in pitiless fury.

Eiji scrambled into her tent on her elbows and knees, the slave collar causing her to crawl clumsily, whereupon Lyudmilla returned to other matters. The Aenglian mercenary, new as he was to the customs of the Khevnic tribes thought that he could tell, all the same, what the little tent was for. The Menghis girl was being kept as a rape-slave. Every night after the caravan settled and raised their canopies, she would be visited by any man who wanted to use her. They would find a lithe-limbed young woman with some spirit in her like the Menghis slave greatly preferable to their dull, lumpen drabs of wives. In a community of this size, she would probably be forced to serve forty of fifty visitors a night.

*   *   *

Negotiations as to his wages for mercenary duty had taken only the first ten minutes of dinner. Borislav Vsevolod knew that he would not pay whatever he promised this *ziedmol;* he wanted merely that his brother nomad chiefs should hear of Ealdræd's presence amongst the Czechu and so realise what a power in the land was the leader of such a caravan. At the same time, the Aenglian had no intention of placing his spear in the service of this Torvig trash, he would agree terms solely in order to spend a few days eating well and then he would continue on his route south. With neither man meaning anything they mimed to one another, Borislav offered a higher wage than he ever would have otherwise, and Ealdræd accepted without haggling.

Then they hunkered down to serious feeding and to his surprise Ealdræd found the goulash gratifyingly tasty. The meat was goat, of course, but well-seasoned and soaked in a rich gravy. The alcohol, however, was a disappointment. The favourite tipple of the Czechu was an aniseed liqueur mixed with goat's milk called *rakija-molako* that was not particularly palatable to a westerner because of the liqueur's high sugar content. Ealdræd, a man of his people, enjoyed good bitter beer and wood-cask ale. All other drinks were piss in comparison. But he was two thousand miles as the crow flies from the nearest flagon of nut-brown ale and needs must when there was nothing else.

During the meal the new recruit met the chief's senior men. Ealdræd took note of only two, dismissing the rest as negligible. The first was Yevgeny. With his scraggy beard and flea-riddled goatskin coat, he was the very image of the goat-herder's son made good. A dependable and resourceful second-in-command, through cut-throat malevolence and a delight in malicious humour, he had risen to the

213

exalted rank of chief lieutenant. His father would have been intensely proud of so fine a son, if Yevgeny hadn't ripped his father's belly open with a knife in a quarrel when the boy was sixteen so that death had intervened between a father and his pride. The second was Sergej, an ogre so wide across the back that he took a double place in the dinner circle. He had a livid scar that started at the crown of his head and ran down to his chin. It was perhaps the most impressive scar Ealdræd had ever seen, and he speculated that much of Sergej's fearsome reputation amongst his peers depended upon it. His fellow nomads would assume that a man with such a scar must be a slayer of wild boar with his teeth.

They were all sat in a circle in the outer compartment of the chief's pavilion tent. It was a dull evening in that his hosts all got drunk as quickly as possible. In conformity with local custom, Ealdræd joined them in their distasteful quest for alcoholic stupefaction. The aniseed was repeating upon him by mid-evening and he slowed his guzzling. Drunken bodies began falling into their empty goulash bowls and when all but a few were comatose Borislav Vsevolod reared up onto his feet unsteadily and gestured to the Aenglian to follow him. Ealdræd did so and the two entered the interior apartment of Borislav's tent. Lyudmilla was inside, naked but for a shift, but her brother cuffed and buffeted her out, growling incoherences that were presumably orders for her to sleep in her own lodging tonight.

He produced another gourd of *rakija-molako*, tapped a finger against his nose and winked to signal that this was the good stuff; the special reserve. Ealdræd acknowledged the compliment and sat upon a cushion next to his host determined to do justice to this bottle since he was being especially favoured. In the event, the Czechu poured twice the amount into his own boar's tusk cup than he gave to his guest. No one, in the habitation of Borislav Vsevolod, was that especially favoured.

The veteran mercenary began to get bored, and that invariably made him melancholic. The gloom of the Pæga forest hung upon him when in this mood and his manner became surly. Still the two men drank. Borislav Vsevolod leaned over blearily, pushing his hot, sweaty face in close to Ealdræd's own, almost nose to nose, grinned like the cheerful murdering rapist that he was and belched hugely. The stink of it was foul.

What Ealdræd could not know was that in Czechu culture this was a friendly gesture of mutual well-being after a hearty meal and ample quantities of strong alcohol shared between men of respect. What Borislav Vsevolod could not know was that in Aenglian culture to aim your flatulence toward a person was a gross insult, implying their equivalence with the content of your bowels. In the civil wars between the Pæga, the Wódnis, the Wotton, the Glæd and the Wreocan, the clans of Ealdræd's own people, during the preamble to battle warriors would often dismount, turn their backs upon the enemy, bend over, spread their legs and their arse-cheeks, and fart stentoriously toward the assembled fighting men of the rival clan. So Borislav's gratuitous belch into Ealdræd's very beard was like spitting in his beer.

Without a full awareness of what he was doing, the Aenglian drew back a brawny fist and smashed it into the vile belcher's mouth, loosening a tooth and splitting the lips to spill blood. Borislav Vsevolod sat immobile and stared in silent disbelief, as if uncertain as to what had happened, then seemed to collect himself and recognise the affront, the slight to his dignity entailed in what had been done to him in his own tent, under his own canopy. Like some bristling bear he clambered awkwardly to his feet, raised both arms above his head, and roared in drink-sodden rage. Poltroon he may have been but his inebriation had caused him to forget this in the emotion of the moment. In the confusion of his mental disorder, one maudlin sentiment overcame all other feelings; the indignity of the insult.

Ealdræd was still seated, his mind swimming in aniseed liqueur, not entirely clear on the course of events either. So when Borislav reached down and grabbed his guest with both hairy hands by the neck and started trying to throttle him, Ealdræd reacted impulsively by punching an uppercut between the man's legs into his genitals. He connected solidly but it wasn't enough to force the 300lb Czechu bandit chief to release his strangulating grip upon Ealdræd's windpipe. Irate now, Ealdræd struggled to his feet in the grasp of the drunkard and wrestled to get free.

Neither man was armed, for they were dining together in friendship, but Ealdræd managed to lash out sideways with an elbow that sunk deep into the eye socket of his host, and in the shock of his eyeball popping the fellow's hands finally let go of Ealdræd's throat. The Aenglian stepped inside Borislav's outspread arms and drove a fist into his face with all the weight of his body behind it. The nose burst open and the man was hurled backwards over his chair cushion and, knocked into a heap, he hit the ground like a thunder of trumpets and lay still. He was not dead, merely unconscious, partly with drink and partly from the blow.

A small voice of reason chimed in the Aenglian's head, telling him that perhaps he had done a foolish thing. Czechu bandit chiefs were sure to be the type to frown upon being thumped insensible by their guests, especially foreign ones. Half brain-addled from the *rakija-molako* he had been quaffing all evening, Ealdræd had reacted without thinking. But now sobriety was rapidly returning to him along with his highly-developed sense of self-preservation and his mind started to clear as he thought earnestly on the subject of what now to do for the best. He could not gamble upon Borislav being too drunk to remember the incident when he awoke because the man would doubtless drink himself into a stupor every night and his constitution would be used to it. There was no question of an apology since that would be acceptable to neither of them. Which left only the option of killing Borislav Vsevolod while he slept and riding away while it was still dark in the hope that when the Czechu discovered him in the morning they would be leaderless and this would delay any pursuit sufficiently for Ealdræd to have disappeared from the scene before they roused themselves into good order. And vanish he must because, though cowards they may be, he could not possibly defeat the fighting force of the whole tribe if they laid hands upon him.

He swore softly to himself at the habit he was developing of having to flee countries into which he had just arrived on account of his having murdered some important politician. But it was clearly the safest course of action. Besides, he had not liked Borislav Vsevolod personally and was now decidedly ill-disposed towards him for having brought down upon Ealdræd an entirely superfluous aggravation with his boorish Czechu table manners.

But if he were to be taking to the road again he might just as well take a portion of the excellent goulash with him. It might turn out to be the only thing of value that he would find in the Khevnic Tundra. Finding an empty three-quart jar with a cork stopper, he filled it with the nourishing stew. Six pints of the flavoursome concoction should serve as sustenance for several days' ride. Before taking to horse, there remained only the necessary removal of Borislav Vsevolod from this life.

The Aenglian peeked into the outer compartment of the pavilion. All was stillness and silence except for the general muted cacophony of snoring. Even Yevgeny and Sergej were sound asleep. Ealdræd noticed that, unlike the other diners, Yevgeny carried an exquisitely curved Boyarin knife on his belt. This suggested a possible stratagem. The wily veteran tiptoed over to the sleeping Czechu and, with pickpocket dexterity, slid the eleven inch blade out of its well-oiled sheath. Then he crept back into Borislav's personal chamber.

Ealdræd had decided to use the Boyarin to despatch the inconvenient Borislav in the hope that it might look like Yevgeny had committed the murder; perhaps in a bid for power. To his knowledge, only Lyudmilla had seen him enter the chief's inner apartment, and any useful misunderstanding he might cause with his choice of weapon was certainly worth trying. He leaned over the inanimate bandit chief, placed the point of the knife precisely against the expansive chest, thrust down forcefully with both hands, and buried its point deep in the man's heart. Borislav Vsevolod didn't even wake up. Gore ran in tiny rivers and began to collect in a pool around the corpse.

Half a minute later Ealdræd was already outside and leading his horses quietly over to the perimeter. He confidently expected to find no guards and his low opinion of Czechu security was proved correct. With no other caravan's around for many leagues, the men assigned to guard duty had simply deserted their posts and slunk off to their beds.

He was on the very point of swinging up onto Hengustir when he noticed that the camp was not entirely at rest. There was a man leaving the rape-slave's tent and another, the final man apparently, entering it. That poor fellow had endured a long cold wait behind his more assertive brethren. Finally it was his turn. No doubt he would give the slant-eyed doxy hell to punish her for his being her last visitor of the night.

A spirit of mischief stole upon the Aenglian. What he had seen of these Torvig brutes he had viewed with revulsion and if he must now sacrifice a night's sleep and ride hard all day tomorrow because of their abusive chieftain, he was of a mind to spit upon their bogus honour as he took his leave. What better way than to take with him their exotic communal strumpet. He walked his two horses over to the pitiful little love pavilion of the steppes.

As he looked into the miniature tent, just large enough for its purpose, he saw the Czechu between the young thighs of the Menghis girl. Her legs were draped over his shoulders so that the soles of her feet were almost touching the roof of the meagre canopy. The wooden yoke had been removed but her wrists were chained behind her head to an iron peg staked into the bare clay earth. The gleam of moonlit filtered in and cast its pale glow upon the countenance of the rape-slave. It was impassive, as if the girl were emotionally detached from the powerful thrusts of her visitor's erect phallus shafting frenziedly inside her. He was approaching ejaculation and as he fucked her he spat on her to show his contempt. Yet the impassivity of the girl did not flicker as the saliva splashed on her forehead and it seemed to Ealdræd that even in the half-light he could discern an intractable defiance in her eyes. Only the body had been surrendered, having no choice in the matter, not the spirit.

She took it for granted that the silhouette framed in the moonlight was just another of those she must service sexually, for no one came here for any other object. As each enthusiastic rapist in turn spewed the wet contents of his bollock sack into her, the shadowy outline of the next in line would materialise and hover expectantly at his shoulder as the queue of fervent fornicators passed through her by the dozen. The girl continued to stare up at the sagging canvas of the tent paying no heed to the squatting figure in the narrow entranceway as the panting Czechu on top of her shuddered in spasm with a groan of fulfilment.

But when the new arrival's left hand closed over the rutting rapist's mouth and a massive knife reached round the neck of the suddenly interrupted paramour and slashed his throat in a hideous eight inch gash, the blood spraying all over the girl underneath him, her beautiful oriental eyes opened wide in genuine astonishment. Then she smiled. It was fleeting and it was grim but it was unquestionably a smile.

She lay limp as Ealdræd dragged the carcass off her and she remained so as he pulled the iron peg from the ground by sheer brute force, unwinding the chain from her bruised wrists. He shuffled back out of the low tent, giving her a slap on the thigh in passing as if to encourage her to look lively and get her shapely form in motion. Then the bizarre foreigner in the eccentrically braided hair and beard turned and beckoned to her to follow.

218

The Menghis girl was at the very end of her long eternity of a day. When the men finished with her for the night she would have a few hours of sleep before the whole cycle of agony started all over again from the beginning. But tonight there was to be no sleep. Somehow she must stir herself. Whatever this white-skinned devil had in mind, it was some sort of opportunity to flee. She squirmed out from under the canopy, staggered up onto her bare feet, swayed and almost fell, then she followed; she followed without question, not knowing who he was, what was happening, or where he was taking her, but caring only that he was setting her upon his spare horse for what was obviously her sole chance to escape the Czechu. With the support of his arm, she hauled herself up onto the gelding's back, though it cost her the last of her strength, and lay forward across its neck, her fingers tightly entwined in its mane, her thighs gripping its flanks, unable to sit upright but clinging on by sheer will alone. A fatal weariness sought to overwhelm her with sleep but the mulish obstinacy of the prideful Menghis soul would not be defeated by it. She would fight until death claimed her.

Ealdræd took to the saddle upon Hengustir, stroking him to keep him quiet, and holding the reins of the black to keep the gelding at his side, he took them silently out beyond the perimeter. On horseback again, the Aenglian already felt good about his decision to quit the camp. He did not belong amongst such folk. Having gotten himself quite out of place by his wanderings, he would now set about returning to civilization. Aside from Eildres, which it might not be safe for him to ride through, the nearest civilized country to the Torvig Steppes was Piccoli to the south. Since that had been his intended destination when he crossed into the Tundra, he would make his way there at a sprightly pace and put the sorry episode of his encounter with the Khevnic nations behind him. With the moon for guidance, he headed for what he hoped would be the richer plunder of Piccoli.

*   *   *

Forty eight hours later they were a hundred miles from the settlement and relaxing amidst a clump of spruce trees. They had spent forty of those forty eight hours in the saddle at a consistently brisk pace to stay ahead of capture by the vengeful Czechu who must surely be at their heels, no doubt swearing to bring back the

219

foreign murderer's head and testicles as a gift for Lyudmilla. The horses were showing distinct signs of weakening at the knees. In fact, the animals were incapable of continuing any further without relief. They had done splendidly to have borne up under the strain for as long as they had. The Aenglian was at a loss to explain how the Menghis girl had managed it. She had been prostrate with fatigue when they had set out, having endured five weeks of floggings in the wooden yoke, not to mention her other labours after dark.

Throughout the first night as they rode he had expected any moment to hear the sound behind him of the violent thump of her slender body hitting the ground as she fell off her horse and yet when the pale sun had arisen the next morning there she was, still in place like a flea on horsehide. When he had stopped for a short rest and offered her some of Borislav Vsevolod's cold goulash she had looked at him with the eyes of a feral beast, barely human, but as he poured the stew into her mouth she had swallowed greedily like a calf at its mother's teat.

Sadly for the girl there had been no luxury of time to waste and he had permitted them only a brief respite, exposed as they were on open ground and visible for a mile around. Besides, the winds were harsh here and the cold would get into the horses hot muscles and give them cramps. The effects of the chilling wind upon the Menghis, naked but for the ragged remnants of her torn chemise, he could easily guess. She must be frozen to the bone. But Ealdræd had hoisted her back on to the gelding and as he did so he had noticed how her body moulded itself to the shape of the horse's back, her unresponsive fingers somehow finding and gripping the mane again though they were still numb from the freezing night just passed. The Aenglian shook his braided head from side to side in frank admiration. Tenacious bitch.

All the next day they had ridden. When he allowed them to stop for more goulash and a few hours sleep the following night, her physical condition had convinced him that she would be dead before they reached safety and for the subsequent ride, setting off again before dawn, he had tied her to the saddle with rope. Yet somehow the vitality of life continued to burn inside her and when, at the onset of the evening of their third night, he was forced to take a longer rest amongst the spruce trees in order to save the horses, he found that she was breathing regularly and deeply while she slept and he judged that her prospects were good, for the worst was over.

220

Hereafter they could travel at a more leisurely pace. She was in a pitiable state of wretchedness, having overtaxed her strength far beyond exhaustion, but her commendable grit and tenacity had kept her alive. The girl must have the constitution of a Merthyan donkey and the doggedness of a Heurtslin rat-terrier.

His respect for such courage and his high regard for so incredible a feat of will power had affected his reading of the situation. His original motivation for stealing the girl had been spite against the Czechu. They were a callously malicious people and he had responded in kind. But now he wished to keep the girl out of their clutches for her own sake. He was convinced that if they were following his track then they would trouble him before dawn or not at all. It was not the way of nomads to stray too far from their caravan. If they found him now they would have drifted a hundred miles from their livestock and their women and their baggage train. They would not deviate from their normal business to any greater extent than that. Had he chosen to push on through the night he would have assuredly avoided their catching up, but the animals were quite badly blown and if he made them run through the night the black might well collapse and even Hengustir could suffer injury. He was not about to sacrifice his horseflesh. So he would hide behind the spruce and await developments. If nothing had occurred by dawn, they would soon be moving south again and with much less haste.

It seemed that things would turn out that way. The stallion and the gelding had both visibly improved by sunrise and the Menghis was more awake and aware of her circumstances than at any time in their journey thus far. He actually had her in the saddle and his gear stowed in his bag when he saw the puffs of dust in the distance. The girl had seen it too. Strong emotion registered on her habitually stoical features but such a complex conflation of diverse passions one atop the other that it was impossible to read. The Aenglian's wry grin was his only acknowledgement that battle must be enjoined.

There were five Czechu cavalry trotting straight towards him. He would have been prepared to wager that their number had been greater when they left camp but that some of the stalwart heroes had already turned back. Those that were still coming on must have been riding all night and he flirted with the idea of galloping away and making a run for it, his horses now being fresher than theirs. But they were already close enough for him to recognise Sergej and Yevgeny amongst their number. So instead he motioned to the girl to ride ahead while he stayed behind to shed some Khevnic blood.

She kicked her heels into the gelding's flanks and the animal jogged forward but no sooner had Ealdræd set off to confront the Czechu than she halted the black and turned to watch what transpired. Her dark enigmatic eyes, almost as black as her horse's coat, were unfathomable.

As the Aenglian took the shortest course to meet the five men he noticed that they were not putting their steeds to the gallop to run him down and he remembered the hesitation of the three nomads who had met him when he first came across their caravan. Poltroons all. Ealdræd could feel the power of Hengustir beneath him, his strength recovered by the night's rest, and the braided mercenary grunted the command for the gallop. The mighty roan surged up and forward joyously and charged with his eyes alight and his sensitive nose quivering with the scent of combat. The pounding of his hooves was the timpani of battle and Hengustir's warlike soul sang to its drum beat.

There was consternation amongst the Khevnic warriors who had assumed they were chasing a slave and a *ziedmol* thief whose only concern would be to run for their lives. When the terrifying prospect of the spearman on the demon horse came charging for them, their pace slowed still further, each hoping that another would take the lead. In this way, they had lost their momentum when Ealdræd drove the roan into the half-hearted defence of the first Czechu. The man's wild sabre swing was so inaccurate that the veteran didn't bother to block or avoid it but countered immediately with a lunging thrust of his seven foot spear. It hit the target in the midriff and stuck. As the Aenglian rode right by he pulled the spearhead out and the impetus knocked the man out of the saddle to drop heavily to the hard clay of the Tundra Steppes. If he was not yet dead, it would not take long.

Seizing this as his moment, Sergej spurred his charger in at Ealdræd's back. As the mercenary managed to half turn his mount, Sergej whirled a chain flail with a spiked ball on the end of it around his head with the eager desire to kill. As he swung in close for the barbs of the spinning ball to impact upon the back of the damnable *ziedmol's* head, the spear struck out, not at the man but to parry the chain, which then wrapped itself around the ash stock of the spear. The veteran snatched the deadly flail from out of the startled Czechu's hand and in the same movement pivoted the spear around into the low lance position, as Hengustir circled on the spot, the enormous stallion changing direction with the grace of a dancer.

With the chain flail still snared on the spear, its point found the nomad's side, unprotected by the breastplate he was wearing. The lethal iron spearhead sank in with a hideous squelching sound.

The other three Czechu saw their fearsome Sergej of the terrible scar crash brutally to the rocky ground like a sack of grain and they realised the impossibility and futility of a conflict fought against the diabolical. This was not a man but an evil spirit conjured from amongst the unquiet souls.

Yevgeny, who was the new chief, called out a frantic guttural command to retreat, not wishing to waste his men on a fight no mortal man could win, and the band rode off with all the speed that the short legs of their Khevnic horses could muster. Ealdræd made no attempt to follow. Their lives meant nothing to him, therefore their deaths meant nothing to him either. The skirmish had lasted less than a minute.

When he found the Menghis girl waiting for him by the cluster of spruce, he was no longer sure if he was surprised or not. That she had not done the manifestly sensible thing and bolted for her life was just more evidence that here was a person of real mettle. As he trotted the roan in alongside her that very brief smile flashed again for just long enough to register. It changed her whole appearance for the fraction of a second it lasted before it was replaced by her usual stoical impassivity.

They continued their voyage south without comment. The girl seemed willing to ride in any direction that took her further away from those who had enslaved her. Ealdræd let the horses walk for there was no hurry now. Taking it steady they were at least a week from the border. As Ealdræd and Eiji progressed into the lower Tundra the environment began slowly to change in character. The dry winds gave way to a less desolate climate with occasional areas of small forest with the spruce and fir in comparative abundance after their time spent on the plains. There was moisture in the air and richer soil underfoot. They stopped frequently now to make up for their previous exertions.

They found a shady pool at which they finished off the last of the goulash, leaving them with nothing but the cheese whey-bread that Ealdræd always carried in his saddlebag. When Ealdræd washed himself in the pool, Eiji did likewise, which improved her appearance very considerably. She still had no garment other then her shredded chemise but at least the layers of dirt had gone. He had only seen her caked in mud up to this time. No words passed between them for they had no language in common, but the silence was not uncomfortable. Her manner was mutely accepting of her circumstances. Eiji's sufferings in slavery had been grotesquely appalling and she would doubtless carry the scars upon her mind for many years to come, perhaps for the rest of her life, yet already Ealdræd thought that he could discern outward signs of the girl recovering her self-possession. He had been right about her spirited disposition; she was a hardy and resilient soul.

With their increasing proximity to the Piccoli border things continued to improve. The scenery around them was becoming kinder the further south they travelled. Now there were birch trees and the larch became almost commonplace. There still wasn't any land that had been cleared for agriculture, but the timber showed that it could be if anyone cared to do the work of clearing it. Besides wolves and elk, of which Ealdræd had seen plentiful signs for quite a while, there were also traces of bear, squirrel, and fox. Coniferous forest gave way to deciduous forest, with oak and elm trees that reminded the Aenglian of home. What had been discrete colonies of woodland had imperceptibly thickened into a genuinely verdant sweep of timberland; so much so that they had to pick their path through woods that were thick enough to have no recognisable pathway. On the steppes they had ridden a road that was open space hundreds of miles wide on all sides but as they meandered through the north of Piccoli Ealdræd had to guide Hengustir carefully in order to hold fast to their route.

Eiji was staring in gaping wonder at much of this. She had never imagined countryside of this sort. There were forested areas of Menghis amongst the vistas of its limitless seas of grasslands but as the panorama of the Tundra gradually metamorphosed into the undulating hills and dales of the vineyard region of Piccoli, her expression of amazement began to undermine her customary inscrutable truculence. She found herself looking everywhere at once. Kestrels wheeled overhead in a warm sky, once she spotted antelope skittering through the trees to temp any archer, and fat partridge hid in the undergrowth awaiting somebody's cooking pot. The latter was occupying the thoughts of the Aenglian, too, and making his belly rumble with hunger for something more satisfying than whey-bread.

He tied the horses in a copse but, uncertain of the girl now that she was so much recovered, he took her with him into the forest. Lacking a bow, he hunted with his javelin. It is no small thing to bring down a bird in flight with a javelin, even a bird as low-flying and ungainly as a partridge, but he killed the second one they flushed from cover and as they walked back to the horses he plucked the bird, scattering feathers behind them.

She watched him as he gathered wood together and arranged a tidy fire. He impaled the partridge on a stick and sitting by the fire he began to roast it. The Menghis squatted down beside him on her haunches, as supple as a child, and slowly took the stick from his hand. Considering this something of a breakthrough in personal relations he permitted her to take it, along with the role of chef.

Her cooking was unsophisticated but effective, much like his own. When the meal was ready she handed the stick back to him so that he might eat first. He tore off a large piece of the bird and tossed it over to her. She ate it the way a swarm of locusts eats a field of barley. She would have eaten the bones had they been a little softer. For more than a month the Czechu had kept her alive on one cup of *bouleon*, a watery vegetable soup, per day and now that she was getting tastier fare she was making the most of it. The Aenglian watched her devour the sizeable hunk of partridge, getting grease all over her cute face in the process, and the entertainment of it gave him considerable pleasure.

Then, whilst Ealdræd sank his strong teeth into the hot meat of his own dinner, the girl wiped her mouth on a fold of what was left of her bedraggled chemise and walked over to the horses. With both horses unattended, Ealdræd's ears were alert for the sound of her apple-cheeked backside slapping down into the saddle, should she attempt to steal the horses and ride off. Her behaviour had been impeccable up to now but it was when she was fed and feeling strong again that a dash for freedom was most probable. Ealdræd was not sure how he would react if she did run away. If she laid a hand on Hengustir, the stallion would know enough to toss her aside. But if she took only the gelding . . . .

He had not stolen her for himself but to score off the Czechu, and he had not kept her for himself but for her own sake, having been impressed by her fortitude. He did not need the gelding particularly and would not begrudge its loss, not in a good cause.

Eiji took the blanket from the rolled up bedroll, looked around for a suitable piece of ground, spotted one that she considered adequate, and strolled over to lay out the blanket carefully on a patch of soft grass. She pulled off her rag of a chemise and arranged herself decorously on the blanket. She assumed that the man would expect the reward of her body as payment for his service to her. After her long ordeal of imprisonment by the Czechu she could see men in no other light than as sexual predators. At least this tall foreign soldier was a true champion who had fought for her and slaughtered her enemies. Had she been back home in Menghis, in accordance with the custom of her people, she would have considered him entitled to her body. She glanced over at him but he was still squatting by the fire eating his meal. He seemed in no hurry, almost as if he were content where he was. She rested her eyes while she waited for him. The bed was comfortable beneath her and the food was warm in her belly. Twenty seconds later the little Menghis woman was snoring like a cart-horse.

Chapter 6

A Tower in Piccoli

In the voluble and bellicose crowd that elbowed its way around the main square of the market town of Pestoia in the wine-growing regions of northern Piccoli there were two figures amongst the pageant of domesticity and routine who palpably did not belong. Either of them alone would have turned heads in the midst of the local population but both of them together really caused something of a stir.

The first of them, and leading the way, was a big man of robust physique who displayed some sign of age in the weather-beaten texture of his skin and its innumerable scars. He wore his long hair and beard plaited into braids; something not normally seen outside of his native Aenglia and therefore invariably a cause of anxiety to the communities through which he travelled. Those who *looked* different therefore *were* different, and what was different was usually feared or ridiculed. But this was a man folk were unlikely to set to the sport of mockery.

He wore no cloak for the weather was warm. His hooded mantle had been pulled back off his head to reveal a simple four-plate iron pot basin helmet. He was otherwise attired in a plain sleeveless gambeson tunic, stiff with the dust of the road, and cross-gartered leggings, worn through at the heels. His arms and thighs were naked and exposed an exceptional level of muscular development from years of daily weapons training and a lifetime spent on horseback.

He was a stranger of dangerous bearing, two things that were seldom welcome anywhere in the world. Added to which, the horse he led by its bridle was so appallingly spectral in its appearance that its status as a creature of this earth might be in some doubt. The brawny, barrel-chested warhorse weighed over 2,000 lbs and dwarfed most other horses. But it was not merely his size; it was the colouring of the animal which fired the imaginations of all who saw him. His ghostly grey-white hair visibly tinged with an indigo blue except for the black feathering of its fetlocks and the peppering of black in his mane. Such horses were largely unknown this far to the east of the continent and were likely to be mistaken for reincarnated souls or witches' pet familiars and so be viewed as harbingers of ill-luck. The brass rings and terrets of its harness jingled in time with the great brute's ponderous step. In a hanging saddle-sheath was slung a seven foot spear of seasoned ash crowned by a spearhead that was eighteen inches of razor iron. Below this a second sheath contained a throwing javelin. Over the pommel of the saddle hung a small circular shield, a buckler made of teak and reinforced with iron. No one in all the riotous assembly of shoppers and merchants that filled the town square of Pestoia would have recognised it as such but this style of buckler identified its owner as an Aenglian; a country too far distant to the west for its customs and habits to be known in these parts.

The second person in the party was as different from the first as she was different from the Piccolians. She was a true daughter of the steppes from the once-great, now sadly declined nation of the Menghis. Formerly the Menghis had ruled an empire which had beggared all others in the history of the lands of the open plains that lay three thousand miles hence toward the rising sun. But unlike the man she walked behind, aside from the exotic slanting of her eyes there was nothing about her to identify the girl's country of origin for when she had been abducted from it by the Khevnic raiders who had slaughtered her kin and carried her away westward to their own homeland, she had been permitted to bring nothing with her not even her clothes. The Khevnics had used her as a beast of burden by day and a sex-slave by night, before eventually selling her to a Czechu caravan, where she had been treated still more harshly. The suffering she endured under the Czechu would certainly have caused her death had not fate intervened in its own whimsical way.

She also led a horse by the reins, in her case a black gelding. It had once belonged to an Under-Captain of Lancers in the Household Guard of the Grand Duchy of Bhel, and it still bore his saddle. She had been its rider since meeting Ealdræd less than a month before. As she walked she contrived to position herself immediately behind the tall man. Her only form of clothing was a chemise that was so riddled with holes it hardly held together at all. In truth, it was shredded so badly that her beautifully contoured naked flesh was scarcely concealed. The thin cotton of the chemise had been crudely sewn in places but this did little to alter its basic condition for it was no more than threads at the back and so much of the cloth had been torn away from the front that the majority of her remarkable figure was disclosed in all its youthful splendour. This exposure, of course, was in no sense unusual; wherever a person was in the world the same social convention always prevailed that the higher a person's rank, the more many-layered and voluminous was their costume, whereas the lower a person's rank the more paltry and derisory was their apparel. Slaves frequently went naked. Here in Piccoli the uniform of the slave class was generally a tabard made from any old pieces of leftover sack-cloth stitched into a long rectangle of sacking with a hole cut for the head so that the rough strip of material hung down from shoulders to thighs at the front and back but which were not even tied at the sides. Nobody would affect any surprise at this girl's lack of proper clothing; it would automatically be assumed to be nothing more than an indication of her very low social standing.

The Menghis girl was carrying a string bag containing the food that the man had just bought: two loaves of bread, a cold roasted chicken, a 6lb wedge of cheese, a jar of pickled onions, and an amphora of the local wine, as well as two bags of apples for the horses. Thus far had Ealdræd taken care of the necessities of life, but he also had in mind a purchase of another sort. He saw ahead of him one row of shop-fronts that were swathed in brightly coloured fabrics rolled in bales and garments of all descriptions, and he strode off toward it with Eiji and the horses following closely. The sea of bodies parted before them as they walked. The daunting man, the mysterious girl, and most of all the chillingly ethereal roan horse were nothing that any sensible person would wish to entangle themselves with and so the populace of the town were reluctant to draw too close to them. As a result, the two aliens with their terrifying beast were the only three in the whole of Pestoia not to be pushed and jostled on market day. The perfectly ordinary black gelding at the rear of their party found its hind-quarters being bumped and barged considerably as the sea of bodies closed behind them as they passed.

The Piccolians as a nation were a confusing mixture of the garrulous and the sulky, the charming and the quarrelsome; their national character was charismatic, yet irksome. A pretty people, olive-skinned and curly haired, they prized highly those conceits which enhanced and were pleasing to their individual vanity. Both sexes were as proud as peacocks and as pretentious as clergymen. At the same time they had a self-sacrificing loyalty to family and to relatives of any kind that was homicidal. This was a land of feud and vendetta. It had that in common, at least, with Ealdræd's native Aenglia where the clans fought continuously, none more so that his own tribe of the Pæga. But in Piccoli dispute and narcissism were reciprocal passions. Their narcissism gave rise to much disputation and the competitive nature of disputation fuelled their narcissism. Boys grew up fired by the romantic desire to avenge an assassinated father; girls could expect to be murdered for fraternising with a young man from an enemy family; mothers grieved copiously for their sacrificed children yet continued to raise all their progeny to hold as sacred the very same beliefs by which their martyred siblings had died. There was honour and there was life, and the latter placed a poor second to the former.

It was the principal mark of Piccolian manhood to be very sexually forward with women and despite the formidable aspect of the horse and man who accompanied her, Eiji received many lasciviously meaningful glares and ribald comments as they traversed the busy market square. The delicately lovely oriental was semi-nude in her tattered chemise and there was no mistaking the brazenly erotic appeal of the body within the threadbare yarn.

However, their unspoken advances availed them nothing for her natural temperament was ferociously aggressive toward everyone except the man with whom she was travelling, and her verbal abusiveness in the direction of any Piccolian who so much as looked at her twice was glorious to witness. Because she spoke only Menghali the targets of her vitriol had no understanding of what atrociously filthy names she was calling them, but the savagery of her snarling demeanour made the intent of her words transparent enough.

"Put your repulsive face away, you grinning cow's arse!" she hissed scathingly at one young buck who fancied he might ingratiate himself with a lecherous smile. The buck departed scowling at her outburst of indecipherable gibberish.

"Eat my shit you perverted cockless fellatio-boy!" she snarled with caustic dismissal at the inquisitively raised eyebrow of an elegant, androgynous dandy, who scuttled off damning her for a primitive yellow skinned ape in the ripest Piccolian slang.

Apparently she was a prickly, half-savage concubine with no knowledge of the refinements of polite conduct appropriate to a gentleman of cultured deportment. But for all the sharpness of her barbed tongue with the Piccolians, she displayed a very submissive attitude toward her tall companion. Respectful deference was written all over her where he was concerned and her obedience to any little command from him was instantaneous. The culture in which she had been raised made this the only proper stance for her to take because, at a time when they had not known one another or had even met before, this man had rescued her from the murderous oppression of the Czechu on the Torvig Steppes and had subsequently fought for her on the Tundra against five cowardly Czechu who had pursued the fugitive pair to reclaim their property. Two of the poltroons he had despatched to the pit of all souls before the remaining three had fled before him. After that he had fed her, and all this without having demanded any payment from the pleasures of her body. So she had given him her body freely, and her admiration too. This consensual surrender was motivated by something more than the obligation of duty, compelling though that was; it was inspired by esteem.

At first she had called Ealdræd "hoëh-hexep" but at his evident lack of understanding of a language which to him sounded like the girl was clearing her throat, she had switched to the equivalent word in the only foreign language she knew anything of at all: Uzbeghi, the country that was a neighbour and victim to the imperial hordes of the Menghis. Naturally, Ealdræd had never heard of Uzbegh and had no conception of what lands might lay in the vicinity of Menghis, since he had never heard of Menghis either. Eiji did not speak the Uzbeghi language beyond a vocabulary of a very few words, but she knew of one Uzbeghi word that seemed suitable. She used this word in speaking with Ealdræd in the belief that since it was a foreign word and he was a foreigner, he must surely understand it. It puzzled her greatly that he did not appear to register any comprehension of this word either. She called him "Effendi" which meant 'master'. Of course, in Uzbeghi the word also meant 'husband'.

The daughters of the steppes are bitterly harsh in their acerbic treatment of any man who fails in the masculinity that they require of him, but they are devoted to those men who excel in the manly arts. The type of urbane civility and practiced sophistication favoured by the Piccolian male would earn no such devotion from the women of Menghis. This was made manifest in every sneer and frown that passed across Eiji's otherwise attractive, if sullen, features when she took notice of any of the locals selling their wares in the thriving market town of Pestoia. Even the pedantically combative sales technique of the argumentative stallholders who called out to her Effendi to come and examine their merchandise was confounded by the aggressively pugnacious stare they received in return from the small but lithe oriental girl. In her the Pestoialini had met their match in the exercising of intractable confrontational belligerence.

Ealdræd strolled up to the row of stalls filled with textiles and tailoring. He stopped at a costumiers and, perusing uncertainly, held up for scrutiny a lemon silk garment of which he could make neither head nor tail; whether it was for a woman or a man, whether it were shirt or pantaloons, he could not tell. But then, the Pestoialini themselves were dressed as if to disguise their gender. It was the norm.

"Come, come, outlander fellow!" barked an oily and rather supercilious voice a few yards away, "Come and see what wonders there are to be purchased at the House of Guido!"

His 'house' was, in fact a large trestle table like all the other retailers in the square but the affectation was typical. As the Aenglian shifted over to inspect his goods, a row broke out between Guido and the market trader whose lemon silk Ealdræd had been handling a moment before. The poaching of customers was a fighting offence. By the time that Guido had sworn and cuffed his neighbour into an ill-tempered, grudging pacification and returned his attention to the stranger whom Guido judged to be some boorish breed of westerner, the customer was scratching his braided beard in confusion.

"And how much was you lordship thinking of spending?" enquired Guido, not quite keeping the sarcasm out of his tone. Taking note of the fellow's bare arms and thighs he added: "You wish a silken blouse woven by the alluring handmaidens of Tehlitz perhaps? Or the finest spun woollen breeches from Eildres surely, dyed and embroidered to be worthy of a nobleman and so very reasonably priced?" But then the rippling muscularity of those arms intruded itself upon his consciousness and he caught his next crude satire between his teeth. Moderating the irony implicit in his manner, he concluded with a cautious "How may I serve you, sir?" But, in any case, it transpired that all his saucy rhetoric had been wasted.

"Do you speak Geulten?" asked the customer. He spoke it in the style of the Bhourgbonese although he did not look to Guido like he hailed from Bhourgbon or anywhere else in its vicinity.

"But naturally, sir" replied the Pestoialini who, like most who lived in a country neighbouring the three crowns of the Geulten Alliance, had a smattering of the language.

Saying nothing further in response, the Aenglian jerked a calloused thumb towards the Menghis scarecrow standing behind him. The girl seemed to come awake in that moment and stepped forward, realising that something was to be bought for *her* not him.

Guido winked flamboyantly at Ealdræd, gestured amiably with his head towards Eiji in her rags and said:

"Your servant . . ."

"Companion," corrected Ealdræd.

Guido was somewhat taken aback as he sought to understand this bizarre assertion, and then gave up the unequal task. The slant-eyed fancy was both female and foreign; oriental by god. What else could she be but slave or servant? Here she was, semi-naked and quite properly walking in his shadow and carrying his baggage for him. Guido had been magnanimous in referring to her by the title of servant. This braided fellow's eccentric whim of insisting upon her being accorded the status of companion was beyond all comprehension and Guido would have none of the attempt. Putting the whole sorry muddle down to the intrinsic half-baked lunacy of all western savages, he instead took care of business.

The discussion was not easy, largely because Ealdræd spoke Geulten not only in the Bhourgbon dialect but with an Aenglian accent, whereas Guido had a strongly Piccolian accented Geulten from the Eildressian dialect. Still they managed to bargain sufficiently for Ealdræd to buy two items. Eiji, of course, remained in complete ignorance of all that they said in their unintelligible barbarian language and stayed interested but aloof apart from a softly muttered "Venal pimp!" in judgement of Guido when he ogled her a little too bawdily.

Ealdræd wanted something to replace Eiji's chemise and selected a Tehlitz smock; a fairly capacious linen shirt with laces down the front to open the garment at the neck and chest. They came in a variety of colours and the Aenglian held out three and grunted for her to choose. Her hand touched the smock that was a livid green, for she preferred bright colours and green was lucky in Menghis superstition. The big man took out a purse surprisingly weighty with coin and paid for the smock, handed it the girl who immediately squeezed between Ealdræd and his huge blue-roan horse where, only half-hidden from the eyes of all around her, she slipped out of her scrap of a chemise and threw on the green smock. The sleeves were baggy and the soft folds of linen covered her quite far enough below the waist for modesty.

She looked up at her man for approval and he grinned. Eiji was conscious of the fact that by leaving the lacings open at the chest she was displaying a considerable quantity of cleavage and his grin made no secret of his being conscious of this too. Both the woman and the man were satisfied. A Tehlitz smock was generally worn with breeches but Ealdræd thought the smock alone would be enough for his diminutive, if amply proportioned, companion. If anything her compact body was rather lost in all that linen; the smock fell loose and shapeless. She would need a girdle, to be worn outside her smock like a wide belt.

This was more of a problem since her waist was so tiny Guido was put to his utmost to find any corsetry that would fit her. In the end he produced one that, when reduced to its tightest setting, was a very snug fit. In order to establish this he had to try it on her and when his hands inadvertently touched her whilst adjusting the suede girdle, the careless draper was made the subject of some more of Eiji's coarsely abusive contumely. Had he known exactly what she was saying, blood would have been shed in violence. But as things were, his mind was focused upon the heaviness of the intimidating mercenary's purse. With all his skill in commerce Guido enticed the customer into a previously unfelt desire for a matching doublet and breeks in glossy black leather. Guido swore by his mother's liver that the leather was as supple as if the calf were still alive and as hard-wearing as horseshoes. Ealdræd's habitual garb was a less than fresh-smelling gambeson tunic padded in Hessian which served as both tunic and support under his mail shirt. But in these warmer climes a change of apparel might allow for greater comfort. The close-fitting jacket with the narrow breeches that tied below the knee were a major improvement upon what he was currently wearing. He even seemed to feel a very slight nudge at his hip from Eiji's encouraging hand. Guido offered him a competitive price, reluctantly of course, but with these tight-fisted barbarians you had to bend over backwards for a sale.

With his new clothing tucked under his arm Ealdræd was ready to bid farewell to the market but Eiji's attention had been drawn to a nearby stall. She had spotted a pair of ewe-leather men's boots and set her heart upon them. There was nothing of the feminine about them but she thought them the most handsome pair of boots she had seen anywhere since she had left the pony-trail grasslands of Menghis where the art of the cobbler is unrivalled. She wanted those boots. She tugged meekly at her man's left forearm and when he turned she indicated the boots, caressing the leather with her free hand. Then she gazed up into his eyes and smiled endearingly. It was the first time since they had met that she had attempted to play the coquette with him, and she did so now with an adolescent sauciness that was potently persuasive. There was a forthright frankness to Eiji's idea of flirtation that would have aroused the castrated and raised the dead. The salaciously obscene promise of unconditional concupiscence in her seductive black eyes would have tempted Wihvir the Lord of Hálsian himself.

Fortunately, the boots were made in boy's sizes as well as men's so a small enough pair was available. And, having been so free with his coin up to now, Ealdræd thought upon the holes in his doeskin leggings and resolved that he may as well have a pair of boots for himself to go with his new breeks. He bought a sturdy pair of bucket-top riding boots for his own feet and the ewe-leather for the adoringly supplicate and grateful Eiji, who had previously gone barefoot.

She wore her new boots Menghis-style, without any strapping to tie them around the calves; consequently, the soft leather sagged down around her ankles in slack folds. But this was the fashion in Menghis and Eiji was delighted with them. She took more pride in them than in anything else he bought her that afternoon except for her falcon-headed saw-toothed dagger. With a professional soldier's love of weaponry, Ealdræd had dallied at the ironmongers where, feeling fairly sure that she would not attempt to cut his throat in his sleep, he had bought Eiji an iron-handled Murgl dagger with a pommel on the hilt in the shape of a bird's head. The nomads of the Murgl territories prized their hunting birds of prey and would often decorate their armaments with depictions of falcons. The double-sided seven inch blade of the knife had a serrated lower edge and a straight upper edge, with a stiletto point. It was an evil-looking thing of great beauty. Eiji was enchanted with it. It was sheathed in a functional but ornamental engraved wooden scabbard that attached by a hook-ring to her girdle.

The Aenglian wanted the girl to have the means to protect herself since her flaunted sexual desirability and her volatile disposition made her a persistent lure for trouble. He could not keep his eye on her all the time and there might be occasions when he would need her to run errands for him and suchlike. He would have fewer concerns for her if she had a dagger readily to hand. With so incendiary a woman, let the rest of the world beware. This bestowal of weaponry, of even so small a blade, was symbolically significant. Eiji was deeply impressed with the status that this implied she had with him. The merchant Guido might not know the difference between a servant and a companion but the Menghis understood that by providing her with a weapon the Aenglian was acknowledging her as a comrade-in-arms.

He rented a room in a small house at the back of a stable for their stay in Pestoia. They had been on the road a long time and much of it had been hard riding and Ealdræd intended to spend a few days and nights in town to indulge themselves on the fleshpots of civilization for a while. He was well-provisioned financially since he had earned a purse of gold and another of silver whilst in Wehnbria and, despite the enormity of the distance he had travelled since, there had been few opportunities to spend money in any quantity. In which case, Pestoia could be the providential recipient of the first of his bounty.

He had chosen the room partly for its proximity to the stable so that he could be near his mighty warhorse, Hengustir, whom he had named after the fabled charger of the legendary giant Ffydon in the age of the Leviathans before the Well of Mægen first gave birth to all the races of humanity. The stableman seemed a reliable sort but the Aenglian was not one to take chances on things that really mattered like the care and safety of his horseflesh and was reassured by being only a dozen steps from where the roan and Elji's black gelding were both stabled. His second reason for choosing this dwelling was to avoid taking a room in a tavern. He would normally have done so but a man who bides in a tavern in company with an attractive woman is just asking for a sword-stroke in the back from any one of the many other men there who might think her worth killing for.

The house also afforded them plenty of privacy. This was an advantage because Ealdræd always enjoyed plenty of flagellation in his sex-play, finding a woman's sexual responses greatly heightened by the infliction of a few dozen welts on her backside, and Eiji submitted to a whipping as naturally as breathing. That same viciously scornful vixen whose fury was limitless when unruly hands were laid upon her by anyone else, acquiesced willingly and stoically to a flogging for the erotic gratification of her man. More than that, she expected her lover to savour the exquisite relish of her writhing under his whip in the bed of their lovemaking for she was a daughter of the steppes, where such pleasures are taken for granted. So the discretion of a private house was useful given the amount of noise they made.

*   *   *

The next morning they slept late. Eiji was curled up over Ealdræd's lean torso as if its slabs of muscle were the most comfortable of feather pillows. The previous evening they had eaten all the food that they had bought and drunk the whole amphora of wine. One of the many traits that the two bedfellows shared was their tendency to consume any available pleasure to the final morsel. Both of them, more than once in the past, had been hungry till their ribs ached. Starvation is a hard taskmaster and teaches his lessons well. Neither of them had a personality inclined to deferring their gratifications for the morrow. In a hostile life, each day they awoke might see them dead before sunset so if there were good things to eat they chomped them down and if there was drink in the cup they drained it.

When, some hours after dawn, they emerged blearily from their womb of sensual contentment the only breakfast to be had was out of doors. They adorned themselves in their splendid new raiment, the Aenglian finding that the leather doublet and breeks fitted his large frame passably well but for an undue tightness in the shoulders and sleeves, and sidled off to find a tavern that was serving food. Eiji, whose rosy red rump had wriggled under a dozen painful kisses of the whip for each of her orgasms, was feeling as famished as a winter wolf and just about ready to devour alive the first brace of oxen that happened to cross her path.

The town was full of bustle and sound, Pestoia being the kind of place where mornings and evenings were lively because several hours were lost to the siesta every afternoon except market day. The mismatched pair, a tall braided man of the west and a short

237

exotic woman of the east, walked free and easy down the streets, the girl a step behind to show due deference, and they soon found an open-air canteen serving meat dishes from a grill-oven which was producing aromas so delicious that they were not to be denied.

But just as Ealdræd was heading off on the route determined by his stomach Eiji was suddenly pulling on his arm. She was gesticulating excitedly in the direction of the passing traffic and tugging urgently on his wrist. Her cheekily insubordinate face was set in a pleading expression that he hadn't seen from her before and she had a sense of panic that was quite out of character. At a loss to explain this abrupt shift in her mood, he warily allowed himself to be pulled along behind her. She was jabbering away in her own tongue, which they both found exasperating, she because she was unable to reach him with it, he because it was so pointless, and they must have made a slightly comical sight as she coaxed and cajoled him down the road.

Then he saw what she had seen. A man dressed rather outlandishly in a kite hat and some form of fur-skin coat made of an animal hide that Ealdræd didn't recognise. The man had oriental eyes. Eiji was pointing a slender finger at him and saying "Menghis, Menghis" and then pointing at herself and saying "Menghis, Menghis" and the light of comprehension lit up the Aenglian's befuddled wits and he took her meaning and also the reason why she was so energized about it.

Having no language in common, Ealdræd knew nothing of Eiji and she knew nothing of him other than what they had witnessed with their own eyes during their time together. Ealdræd had liberated her from the rape-tent of the Czechu caravan without knowing anything about her, and she had fled with the freakishly braided giant foreigner because she was desperate to grab at any chance of escape. They had become unexpectedly intimate since then and yet in many ways they were still as foreign to one another as they were to everyone else in this country. But if this Menghis in the kite hat was in Piccoli on business, perchance he would speak Geulten. If so, then this was an opportunity for Ealdræd and Eiji to communicate in something more than grunts and gestures.

Ealdræd imposed calm upon his woman with a stern word. Once she realised that he, too, was aware of what was in her mind, she calmed down instantly. They approached the Menghis trader without rush so as not to alarm him, but he was one of the few folk in Pestoia unlikely to be alarmed by the curious improbability of finding two such contrasting characters in company with one another because he was a foreigner himself. Having spent twenty years of his fascinating life as a spice-trader his own travels had been extraordinarily extensive and there was almost no form of humanity that was strange to him.

His name was Naimun and with great good luck it turned out that was a sociable sort, as he needed to be if he wanted to make his profits and earn his livelihood by the exporting of spices, and when he had been subjected to an explanation of their wishes in both Geulten and Menghali he readily consented to offer them his services as a translator for the price of a large meal with plenty of Bhoulphari citrus wine. This suited them admirably since they had no desire to delay their own breakfast. Rather than return to the open-air canteen, the Menghis trader Naimun took them to a restaurant he knew called *La Trappola Per Topi*, a name which he did not bother to translate, that was discreet without being squalid in which the three of them settled down happily and proceeded to munch and guzzle their way through food enough for six whilst Ealdræd and Eiji badgered the good-natured Naimun for translations to their questions about each other.

For the first time Eiji heard the names of the Pæga and the Aenglia and the Ehngle, though her initial attempts at pronouncing them had the man whose identity was encapsulated in these words slapping his thighs with merriment. She flushed at this and demanded, through Naimun, to know which of these three Ealdræd was. His reply that he was all three, for his clan, the Pæga, were one of the tribes of Aenglia and the Aenglians were a part of the folk known as the Ehngle caused Eiji considerable exasperation until Naimun explained that it was much the same as her own kith of the Kajhin being of the community of Alijah who were one of the nations of the Menghis. She smiled broadly at this for it made Ealdræd's ethnic people sound almost civilized, being in parallel to the Kajhin of Alijah.

Now it was Ealdræd who tried to make his mouth conjure these new names of Kajhin and Alijah and Menghis, and it was Eiji, the very personification of a hypocritical minx, who screeched with mirth and shook with laughter at his flattened vowels and leaden consonants, hiding her face behind her bell of coal-black hair and giggling through her fingers. The Aenglian took it in good part, rumbling with chuckles himself and rolling his head from side to side in the belief that never would his tongue twist itself around such unfamiliar murmurings and throaty burblings.

Ealdræd had taught Eiji a few words of Geulten during their journey south because Geulten would obviously be more useful to her in Piccoli than would Ehngleish. And if she travelled with him further upon his journey, then all the lands that stood between him and home were under the sovereignties of the three crowns of the Geulten Alliance. Ehngleish would be of no help to her for the next four hundred leagues. Naimun was now able to make her understand that Geulten was not Ealdræd's own native language. It took Eiji some time to grasp this since she could not imagine that there could be more than one foreign language; there was the civilized language of the Menghis Empire and there were the barbarous utterances of foreigners. The Menghali word for foreigner was *ghazboutyr* meaning 'those who cannot speak properly'. When, through patient perseverance the spice-trader had finally convinced her that there were many different languages amongst the alien cultures, she asserted with her usual firmness that her desire was to learn whatever was Ealdræd's own language. She wished to speak with him, not with these other *ghazboutyr*.

So next she wanted to know who the Geulten were. When Ealdræd explained in translation that they were the national enemies of his own folk, she was at a loss to understand why it was that he spoke their language. Was it not disgraceful to learn the speech of your enemies? For all the months that she had been the prisoner of the Khevnics on the Torvig Steppes she had refused to learn a single word of their foul tongue. Ealdræd's answer was that perhaps this was why he moved freely through the lands of his enemies whilst she had marched in a wooden yoke under the slaver's whip through the land of her enemies. She mused upon this for a time and then let the question drop.

For three hours they gorged themselves and exchanged biographies, courtesy of the multilingual spice-merchant. Ealdræd and Eiji learned more about each other's backgrounds in those three hours than in the preceding three weeks, and as the talk went on they became more serious and they listened with strict attentiveness as the loquacious Naimun translated their tales.

She told him of her childhood on the steppes and the constant fighting of her kith against the incursions of the Khevnics whom once had been but serfs to the great Imperial Khans of the Menghis

Empire but who now exercised the upper hand, along with the Bera tribes of the wastelands who struck out of the north just as the Khevnics swooped across from the west. The Golden Kingdom was dying cut by cut as their former dominions reaped the harvest of ethnic revenge.

Eiji had been married at the age of twelve according to Alijah rites and customs, but this first husband had died in a Bera raid before his rituals of manhood that would sanction the newlyweds to share a nuptial bed. She had been betrothed again at sixteen but had scarcely done her conjugal duty to her husband before he too had been killed. It was as if the land of the Menghis were running out of men.

She told him that she had been eighteen when her family had been annihilated and she had been taken into the shame of slavery. For a year she had been dragged into the realms of the Torvig nations and would have killed herself many times over if only she had possessed the means. Then she had endured the final indignity of the Czechu vermin. She did not know what had become of her beloved Kajhin kith or if there were any Menghis men left alive to ride their swift ponies over the grasslands to bring screaming death to their cowardly enemies. She felt as if she had fallen out of the world she knew and into another; one that was an endless mystery to her.

He told her of the complex unity of the Ehngle; of how even though they had clearly defined territories of Aenglia, Merthya, Sæxyny, Heurtslin and Wehnbria, and even though these countries had long histories of conflict and warfare between them, none the less these distinct ethnicities were very similar; close enough to one another to come together in a time of crisis into the unanimity of the Ehngle people. At least, it had always been so in the past for, until recently, there had been little in the way of large scale immigration into Ehngle territories from outside. They had a host of tribal and cultural identities within themselves, yet all spoke one language, albeit in a dozen different accents, and the sense of their union within the peninsula of land that was their birthright remained strong, no matter what their internecine disputes. If ever this distinctive identity was lost or surrendered, a thousand years of Ehngle culture would be swept into the sea. But the sea had always been their ally up to now, being almost surrounded by the great western ocean.

He told her of his times as a mercenary soldier, selling his spear for the price of his next meal; that he was the oldest man he knew, being now over forty years of age, and how his store of experience since he had set off on his wanderings had lasted more than a score of years and was a tale that would likely take as long to tell. He had seen and done much that was worthy of the telling. He spoke of the men of fame that he had known and fought alongside, like Eádgar Aeðlric, the son of a wine cooper who'd had the title of Aeðlric or 'noble ruler' conferred upon him by those men who had served under him at the battle of Ásgautr a decade ago. And of those unknown men like Godric Dudley, cowherd and longbowman, who had saved a certain Aenglian's life in a skirmish thigh-deep in the River Coerflód with an arrow shot that not one man in a hundred could have achieved, but whose fame lived only in the heart and memory of Ealdræd of the Pæga, a weather-beaten, battle-scarred veteran of a thousand military encounters, large and small.

Eiji was keen to hear more of Ealdræd's many triumphs at force of arms but Naimun had another financial transaction to conduct that day and was forced to call the conversation to a close. However, to alleviate the expression of discontent that had sprung quickly to Eiji's cute and always animated countenance, he promised that he would return at the same time the next day if the meal was as ample and as appetising. And so it was agreed.

Having bid goodbye to his newfound friends the Menghis trader made his way hurriedly to his own dwelling and only moments later Naimun was in his carriage and rousing his horse to a good trot. He had three leagues to travel and three more to return before nightfall. The chance encounter with the Aenglian and the Menghis was a stroke of luck that he would swiftly capitalise upon. As a good man of business he would not let so fortuitous a commercial opportunity slip through his hands. He was on his way to the Visconte Gregori of the family Lasinni.

*   *   *

The Visconte Gregori Lasinni was so august a personage that it was unknown for him ever to be seen in the nearest town, Pestoia, although his residence was no more than a couple of hours away in the rural grandeur of what once had been the Lasinni estate. Long ago the Lasinni had been landlords to the whole countryside but these days there were none amongst the Pestoialini who were their tenants and the exalted name of this patrician family had passed out of the consciousness of many. This was hardly to be wondered at. So reclusive was the Visconte and his sister the Viscontessa, that they seldom left their ancestral home for any reason whatsoever. There were none within five hundred miles that the Lasinni family considered their social equals, and so none upon whom they might wish to pay a call or have as guests in their own abode. Moreover, it was well-known that persons of such aristocratic refinement and superior delicacy preferred the seclusion of the life of withdrawal.

There was a man His Excellency employed to speak of his behalf; the Visconte's official representative, a young man called Cagliol, who held the title of the Keeper of the Keys. This brisk and energetic Bhourgbonese had been an out-of-place under-steward of the noble house of Bhoul who had been invited to join the household of His Excellency the Visconte Gregori as a factotum. In truth, it was a far less splendid establishment than the one Cagliol had been used to in Bhourgbon, for the Lasinni were more affluent in their lineage than in their coffers, but at least it was a respectable position and, as far as Naimun was aware, Cagliol was the Visconte's most trusted of servants. He managed all matters of importance for the Visconte.

Cagliol had the comportment of a soldier and there was a vigorous dynamism in the man which suggested a personality given to acting first and thinking later. He was strikingly blonde, with flourishing moustaches and beard. Although he dressed in expensive tailoring for his duties within the Castle Lasinni, when he rode forth into the world outside its crenellated towers his regular clothing was more along the model of a captain of cavalry; riding boots and a tunic with a brigandine, a thick suede tabard with miniature steel plates riveted between two layers of leather. It was lightweight, at around 8lbs, and permitted flexibility of movement. It was designed to be worn with a mail shirt but more often was worn instead of one. It was far less prone to rust. His choice of attire lent strength to the impression that this was a man of military accomplishment.

It was no later than mid-afternoon when Naimun arrived at the castle of the Lasinni in his carriage and rang the great bell at the gate-cage. Naimun had been here twice before but on neither visit had he met the Visconte face to face. However, he had been told by Cagliol that the Visconte Gregori was always interested in persons of oriental or negro extraction who would not be missed when they disappeared. Naimun had not been informed as to why the Visconte wanted them, and had not the slightest idea. He did not need to be told, only to be paid. He had come to the castle of the Visconte today in order to sell the information of Eiji's presence in Pestoia.

Naimun had first been approached by Cagliol as an emissary from the Visconte precisely because the spice merchant was himself Menghis and had trade routes to the east. Naimun had been hoping to import a few slaves from Menghis to sell to the Visconte but Eiji's arrival had been something of a windfall. When Naimun rang the ancient bell which hung at the cage-gate several minutes passed before a single raggedy servant limped across the courtyard to open the gate. Naimun drove his carriage inside the high walls that surrounded the residence but did not dismount from his vehicle. He knew that he would not be welcome inside the house itself. Instead he waited. Eventually Cagliol came out to stand by Naimun's carriage to speak with him there. The factotum naturally handled all matters relating to the present form of business.

Naimun played his role as informer upon Eiji who, as a Menghis vagabond and stateless wanderer without rank or property, was absolutely made to order for the Visconte's needs so long as her western 'companion' could have his head cut off at the same time. In short order Naimun was hired by Cagliol on behalf of his Excellency the Visconte Gregori to steal the woman Eiji without delay. When the spice-trader confessed himself unable to handle the dangerous Aenglian mercenary without assistance, Cagliol drew his long poniard from its scabbard at his waist, examined its edge and found it satisfactory, then assured the merchant dispassionately that he would deal with the woman's barbarous Ehngle companion himself.

*   *   *

Ealdræd of the Pæga and Eiji of the Kajhin were preparing to say their farewells. Four days they had spent in Pestoia with their friend Naimun but now they must go their separate ways. On the second day that they had returned to *La Trappola Per Topi* to meet with Naimun he had told them the news. Civil war was brewing amongst the mixed-race bedouin of the Tehlitzim and the roads east might be blocked before autumn. Consequently, he must travel to Menghis for the sake of his trading in spice sooner than he had planned. In fact, he must leave immediately and, although he did not presume to intrude upon their relationship, he felt obliged for the friendship that he already felt toward them both to make the offer that should Eiji wish to travel with him to take up her place again amongst her own people, he would welcome her to his caravan. He would ask no fee, nor would he suggest any impropriety, for his heart had been touched by the story he had heard the day before of her travails and sufferings. He was a Menghis too, and what sort of man would he be to leave for home and not offer a fellow countrywoman a chance to find her kith once more?

Ealdræd and Eiji had both known from the moment that the offer was made that she must accept and go for this would be her only chance. The Aenglian would soon be moving west and if she stayed with him she would be increasing the distance between herself and her kith. Besides this, the trip to Menghis was not something she could realistically attempt alone; she must locate herself safely within a column of march, yet caravans did not pass often between Piccoli and the Menghis Steppes. It was a stroke of extraordinary good fortune for Eiji to have found Naimun just as he was to make one of his annual trips along his trade route. She must go, and she would go with Ealdræd's blessing for he would not keep her against her will. If she owed him her life, he released her from the obligation freely.

She burned with the desire to ask him to accompany her, but she knew with absolute certainty that it could not be. The Menghis grasslands were three thousand miles to the east; his own land of forests was two thousand miles to the west; if he were to travel to Menghis it would be forever. A man of his age would not return. He would be condemning himself to the fate that she wished to avoid for herself; permanent exile amongst alien cultures.

And so she did not ask. He must continue on toward his home, and she must take the opposite road toward hers. With an insight and wisdom beyond her years Eiji knew that everyone belongs in their own country; in the community from which they draw their sense of who they are. To wander abroad and see the peculiarities of other cultures was one thing but to live amongst them forever was quite another.

Ealdræd's equally unspoken feelings were exactly the same. Although his wanderings had taken him long and far throughout his adult life, he had always returned to Aenglia again and again. But never to the clan lands of the Pæga. For he too was an exile, not from his nation but from his tribe. When he had been no more than Eiji's age he had been banished and had never set foot upon Pæga territory since. That banishment had been the first cause of his roving and although he had returned home to Aenglia frequently, he had never once returned to the hearth of his home; that strip of land in the northwest of the country that was the dominion of the Pæga. He had not told her anything of this during their translated conversations with Naimun over the last four days, for he never told anyone of it. It was the one secret he had not shared with any comrade-in-arms, any lover, any friend, in two decades. It was the only thing in his life for which he felt shame, not for the cause of his eviction but for his acceptance of it. It meant, now, that his sympathies were all with his companion who might still, in her youth, sit by the hearth of her own kin.

Naimun's simple ploy to inveigle the girl away from her intimidating protector by pretending that he was returning to Menghis had worked so effortlessly that he told himself the trollop deserved what was coming to her for being so stupid. Naturally, he had expected a certain amount of resistance from the braided beast of an Aenglian *ghazboutyr* and he had been greatly relieved to find that the dotard was just a feeble-minded romantic. Perhaps the grandpa fancied himself in love with the cunning, mischievous wench. Well, if so, then he deserved the death that was coming to him.

The time for departure was set for the dawn of their fifth day in Pestoia, and it was a doleful Eiji who rode her black gelding to the habitation of the spice-merchant from the house she had been sharing with her Effendi for so short a time. Ealdræd rode with her. At the last minute he had decided to accompany the caravan for the first few nights of its journey before turning back. Neither of them had been happy with the thought of a sudden severance of their gladsome companionship, nor of any swift ending to their sexual enjoyment of one another. So Eiji's tent would resound to the orgasmic groans of her wet sensuality and the complementary percussion of the smack of leather on her flesh for the first stage of her long voyage at least. After that, she must make do with memories.

Standing at the window of his premises looking out into the street, Naimun's gratitude at the old mercenary's romanticism faded upon the instant that he saw the Aenglian on his enormous roan warhorse riding alongside the girl, clearly intending to escort her upon her

246

road. Why had the western oaf not kept his word and broken with the girl? Cagliol had not yet arrived. How was the soldier to be disposed of; must he fight the veteran himself? That would not do. Naimun was half a dozen years younger than the Pæga spearman but he did not deceive himself that he could best the older man in martial contest. Ealdræd was Naimun's physical superior without question. What to do?

The two would-be travellers tied their horses to a rail outside, there being no stable or yard. The window in the front wall had its shutter up for fresh air so they would be able to keep a watchful eye on the animals from inside. They entered without knocking but Ealdræd paused in the doorway to recite, in the manner of the society that raised him, "I honour the fetish of this house and seek its blessing while I bide here." The house had no fetish but that did not seem to matter to the Aenglian.

Naimun greeted them with a smile and invited them to his table for a repast before they went along to the barn where the merchant's caravan would be waiting for them, loaded with the manufactured ironmongery which, on the faraway steppes, he would trade for spice. His wagon master would be arriving soon and then they would away. In the meantime he would fetch sustenance.

He left the room and they sat at a table. Eiji put herself close enough to Ealdræd to rest her head upon his shoulder. But something was nagging at the Aenglian's sense of hazard. With an experienced soldier's instinct a small troubled voice in his mind was whispering to him that all was not as it should be; there was some contrary note in the situation. His eyes scanned the room but all was quiet, neat and tidy. It was peaceful. Nothing was disturbed. Surely he was at fault. The room was that of a fastidious man who kept everything in good order. No jeopardy threatened. The setting was positively homely.

And then the veteran's mind released the thought which had been gestating all this while. What was wrong was precisely the good order of the room. This man was supposedly on the point of a journey of several months, perhaps the best part of a year. Why had the room not been packed up? Did he propose to rent this house for the whole time he was so many leagues distant? Ridiculous. The house should be bare floorboards and devoid of its many little comforts. Instead it appeared as cosy and well-furnished as a nest of kittens.

Even as this thought struck him and Ealdræd began to rise to his feet, the door burst open and Cagliol came through it. He already had a curved sword naked in his fist and he wore a coat of mail over his brigandine and a coif of mail over his head. Seeing the braided man who was assuredly the one that he had come here to execute he made a rush for the Aenglian.

The blond Bhourgbonese was entirely unknown to Ealdræd but he wasted no time in wondering who the man might be, why he was here, or for what reason Naimun had betrayed them. His mind calculated the circumstances of the combat, nothing else. The blonde man was not so tall as himself but the sword gave him a serious advantage in reach; Ealdræd had only his twenty inch knife. Before this thought had fully cohered in his mind he had picked up the chair on which he had been sitting and reversed it in his hand for use as a shield.

The man was already upon him and the first stroke sliced down from above to be met by the solid teak of the well-constructed chair. The sword blade bit deep into the wood but the chair held. Having got underneath his enemy's attack, Ealdræd was close enough to counter with his knife. He made no assault upon the mail, knowing that his blade would not have the weight to pierce it. Instead he buried the knife into the fellow's unarmoured knee and heard the screech from above. With his momentum already driving forward from below Ealdræd shoulder-charged into the man's midriff knocking him backwards off his feet and propelling him hard against the far wall. The small house thundered to the sound of the impact.

Naimun came running in from the side holding aloft an immense butcher's cleaver. It was designed for the felling of bulls and Naimun had a similar intention at present. But the mercenary had seen him coming and stepped back at the last instant so that the cleaver cut empty air and the Menghis trader staggered right passed his target. Ealdræd grabbed the leading arm that held the cleaver and swung the clumsy merchant around in a circle, twisting the weapon out of his grasp and sending him crashing face-first into the table. There was the crack of bones breaking.

The blonde swordsman had recovered in the interim, wrenching the knife from his gruesomely wounded knee, gathering his courage, and taking a second hacking lunge at his cursedly nimble enemy. How could the old man be so fast? Certainly his speed of foot proved sufficient for him to sidestep the deadly arc of the scything three foot curved blade, and from there to kick into the blonde bastard's good leg to sweep it out from under him. Cagliol's wounded leg hadn't the strength to support him and the man did an ungainly splits until his good knee hit the ground to hold him up. On one knee with his injured leg stretched out uselessly, Cagliol was all but immobile as the Aenglian, from behind, kicked a foot powered by all the muscle of his horseman's thighs into his adversary's groin. Again the Bhourgbonese was propelled across the floor and this time, vomiting in a suffocating nausea of pain, he let go of his sword. It fell just inches from Naimun. He snatched it up and turned with terrified eyes upon this Ehngle monster whom even the doughty Cagliol could not kill.

Eiji sprinted a few paces and leapt on Naimun's back. The shock of it made him drop the sword again. Her falcon-headed Murgl dagger swept over his shoulder and struck into his chest but not deep enough to kill. The wily merchant had worn a leather jerkin under his flowing tunic and the tough cowhide was just thick enough to reduce the full force of her blow. He staggered about weaponless, trying to shake her off but she clung tenaciously, striking again and again with her blade but not able to finish him. His bellowing terror filled the room.

The Bhourgbonese was only half conscious and struggling to rise. Ealdræd called out to his comrade: "Eiji, do not kill him, we want him alive!" and then realised that she would not understand a word of what he'd said aside from her own name, and in the state of frenzy she was in, perhaps not even that. He must finish the blonde fellow at once before Eiji had silenced Naimun forever, leaving them no wiser as to the meaning of all this.

Picking up the curved sword, Ealdræd pulled on the mail coif, lifting the man's head and half dragging the coif loose. With the man's chin raised Ealdræd drew back the sword then swung it mightily in a wide low horizontal swipe that dug the sharp iron into Cagliol's neck, sliced right through the spinal cord, and cut his head very cleanly from off his shoulders. Only the mail coif stopped the blade, leaving Ealdræd holding the armour as the blonde head rolled forward on to the floor.

With that done Ealdræd hurried to where Naimun was crouched upon the ground, fending off the constant downward plunges of Eiji's saw-toothed dagger, using his unprotected arms to shield his vitals, to the terrible detriment of his arms. Blood splashed in every direction as the wretched spice-merchant pleaded for his life and for mercy. He had chosen the wrong woman for that.

Ealdræd caught her wrist as the knife plunged downwards again and she turned snarling until she saw who it was. Even in the fever of her bloodlust she had the sense to understand that there was something he wanted from her enemy. So she vented her spleen by hurling the filthiest tirade of verbal abuse at her cowering countryman as might be heard between here and the women's quarters of the Kajhin settlements of the Menghis Steppes.

If Naimun thought himself saved, he could not have been more wrong. Better for him if Eiji's dagger had found some vital spot and finished him quickly. Ealdræd had determined to discover the cause of Naimun's betrayal and there was only one way to do that; inflict excruciating pain upon him until he confessed. It was a method that neither Eiji nor Ealdræd had any scruples about, especially where treachery was concerned.

They cut the tunic and leather jerkin from the defenceless merchant with their knives and heaved his naked and trembling body on to the table. Ealdræd used the cords from the draperies to tie Naimun spread-eagled to each corner. He tied him tight. Then the implacable mercenary informed the quivering tradesman that only a complete account of this mystery could avail him an end to his sufferings. The veteran mercenary looked across at Eiji, who smiled like a devil and jumped up onto the table to stand menacingly over the helplessly exposed Naimun. Even before the torture began, he squealed his abject fear. In Geulten Ealdræd demanded to know:

"What is the name of the person who set you on to this? Who is the man I have just despatched? Where are our enemies to be found? What means all this?"

After each question Eiji stepped on Naimun's genitals, crushing his testicles underfoot, and hissing "Speak, you piss-drinking, spice-smelling traitor!" whilst Ealdræd repeatedly asked the hideously agonised man the same questions over again and kept him awake by pouring wine over the man's face from a handy bottle. It was passing strange that Naimun did not admit everything at once for he was not a particularly brave man. It was more that the shock of events had so disoriented his wits that he could not gather them sufficiently to formulate an answer. When he managed to recover the power of speech and divulge the name of his employer, the dam broke and he told all very rapidly. But Eiji saw no reason to cease her tormenting of his genitals all the while. Ealdræd watched her indulging herself for a time as he again repeated the questions that Naimun had already answered so as to make sure that Naimun had told all and told true.

When Ealdræd was satisfied that the man had not lied, he said to Eiji: "He is yours", signalling his meaning with a wave of his hand. Her eyes flashed bright as she grasped his intent and she replied with heat: "Thank you, Effendi" adding a Menghis blessing to the generous. Whereupon she killed the fevered and delirious Naimun by carving him from cock to ribs with her cherished Murgl dagger.

Ealdræd looked at her appraisingly and could tell that here was a woman ready to kill anyone who presented any danger or did any injury to him or to herself. It was something more than valour; it was a passion for personal dignity. Just as he would not bear an insult, nor would she. As he watched her spit upon the corpse he could see her pride in having fought and killed alongside her Effendi. The slightly cherubic face had a hint of self-congratulatory satisfaction to it. She expected him to be pleased with her. Ealdræd took her in his massive arms and gave her a long, lingering kiss.

They had been given the answers they wanted. Or some of them anyway. Naimun had not known all the details of his employer's purposes. But he had said enough. The Visconte Gregori of the Castle Lasinni, southeast of the city, had wanted the Menghis woman. They did wicked things at the castle; sorcery, hexcraft, child-sacrifice in blasphemous demon worship, unspeakable obscenities, Naimun did not know what. The dead Bhourgbonese had been the Visconte's trusted Keeper of the Keys. He must have known but he was dead.

Ealdræd berated himself for a mutton-head. He had kept the wrong man alive. By assuming that it must be the spice-trader who would know of the plot he had permitted himself to decapitate the man who actually knew all the answers. But there was nothing to be done about it now. It was time to leave the friendly little market town of Pestoia. He and his woman would leave together. They would not be parting company after all. Not yet.

The anger that boiled inside the mercenary demanded justice. His blood called to him for retribution. Eiji was beside herself with sustained rage. As the full import of what had taken place dawned upon her she reddened and cried tears of fury. She had been deceived in the matter of her return to Menghis. Now she would never see her home again. She had wept in remorse over having to leave Ealdræd when this had really never been anything more than a wicked lie told by Naimun. She had suffered heartache; she had been made foolish, and now she must face exile in the realms of the *ghazboutyr* for the rest of her life. She had become a displaced person, forever shorn of her roots in the soil of Menghis. Eiji seethed with righteous indignation and was hopping from one foot to the other in the intensity of her agitation.

Having missed his chance to force the dead Bhourgbonese to speak, Ealdræd sought to make some small amends by searching the carcass. He found treasure. Cagliol had not been given the title of Keeper of the Keys for nothing. They were literally in his possession; an immense iron ring of outsized keys. Access to the castle would present no difficulties. But what would they find inside? Some of these affluent aristocrats had private armies at their disposal. Ealdræd determined to take a look at this Castle Lasinni to see if the visiting of retribution upon the guilty were possible. If it were not, then he would just have to bite his lip and forego justice. One man and a woman against a castle full of troops was not a very advantageous prospect. There was no point in wasting their lives futilely. But if there were a realistic possibility of revenge, then he would have it and it would taste sweet; he would satisfy himself upon the person who had insulted him. Aye, and Eiji would follow him and satisfy herself, too. She had as much right as he to vengeance. Never let it be said that the spear-arm of Ealdræd of the Pæga had failed to be lifted in defence of the rights of a friend.

*   *   *

The land around the castle was poor and showed small sign of agriculture. There were some dried-up vineyards in the valley and some more on the hillside which displayed frail indications of cultivation. The wine cellars of the Visconte would likely have little of recent vintage. There were no peasants working in the fields and no suggestion of activity from within the walled estate as the two riders approached it. This Visconte Gregori Lasinni made a lacklustre showing as a landowner.

The so-called castle was no bigger than a large manorial residence. None the less, it did have a round tower rising three storeys high in each corner of its rectangular acreage, and an internal courtyard. The crenellated turrets of the four towers were entirely typical of Piccolian architecture; a style for which Piccoli was internationally famous. The towers did lend the place an aspect of ruling caste authority even in its currently rather dilapidated condition. Its pretensions to nobility were further articulated in the iron cage-gate before the courtyard doors, which were twelve feet of stout oak, imported from the shores of the Lac de Massif in Eildres. But despite this façade of grandeur, it still gave the impression of having been abandoned in time; lost in a vanished past; the residue and detritus of history. The closer Ealdræd rode toward his destination, the more confident he became. There would be no private army in a tumbledown relic like this.

Appearances were not deceiving. The title owned by the Visconte Lasinni was one which entirely lacked its former feudal dominions, the only land they still possessed being the declining vineyards around the castle itself. But the family did descend from an ancient feudal line and they were related to a whole pantheon of much wealthier and more powerful barons and counts around the country. The Visconte and his sister, the Viscontessa, were entitled to the formality of being addressed as "Your Excellency" but there was no one to address them thus except for their shrinking retinue of servants and these, leaving aside the dead Cagliol, numbered a grand total of five.

Ealdræd and Eiji rode openly up to the outer wall without being challenged. There was not even a single guard. Ealdræd found the correct key on the ring he had taken from Cagliol and unlocked the cage-gate. This device was designed as a means for taking hostile callers prisoner. Once inside the gate the cage could close upon the unwary. Ealdræd was far from being unwary but since there was no one stationed at the gate to work the mechanical contraption it hardly made any difference. The Aenglian and the Menghis entered the confined internal courtyard of the castle. It was empty.

They crossed over to the admittedly impressive main doors of the central building. Again they had to select a key and again there was no servant to confront them or bar their passage as they entered. The hall was vaulted and expansive, with a marble floor that must have cost a colossal fortune when the house was first built. Yet there was nothing inside but silence. It had all the dusty stillness of a mausoleum. Then Eiji froze at the slight sound of a muffled wailing from somewhere below. High-pitched and forlorn, it had sounded like a cat. But she did not believe it to be a cat.

Ealdræd noticed her disconcert and made a face to enquire what the matter was. She pointed down at the floor and then over to a door that looked likely to lead to the cellars. Ealdræd nodded and the two trespassers unlocked the door, passed through it, and descended a stairwell to the underground level. It was pitch dark below but at the extreme limit of the light from upstairs they could just see a torch in a brazier with a flint and tinder adjacent. Ealdræd lit the torch and they proceeded.

There was a restless shifting in the cellar in response to the approaching torch. The subterranean crypt was alive with something that rustled; something swarming; some form of small animals. Eiji felt the fear rising inside her chest, constricting her throat, and she had to fight hard to resist the desire to run back to the stairwell. Ealdræd thrust the torch forward to cast it's light further into the blackness.

Lit by the flickering gold flame were faces; dozens of small grubby yet luminously pale faces, full of misery. The cellar was teeming with children, foully begrimed and crawling with lice. Their bodies were afflicted with distortions of limb, their skins were scabby, and the vacancy of their expressions made them appear mindless. One cried out, though whether in alarm or appeal or for what other reason it was difficult to tell. At this, all the rest took up the cry and suddenly the clammy underground cell was loud with a mass howling that caused the hackles to rise on the necks of the two adults who had stumbled upon this inexplicable foulness.

Wanting no part of this, the intruders hastened back to the stairwell and almost ran up into the light and comparative sanity of the living quarters above. Its hollow silence seemed to mock them. Where were the residents of this uncanny house of imprisoned children? The two comrades moved quickly into an inner chamber, and then through that to an interior apartment. It was circular in design, from which Ealdræd deduced that they must be in one of the four towers of the castle. It was a scene from a madman's nightmare.

There was another child, but this one was about fifteen years of age, much older than those below and, in stark contrast to their filthy rags, he was dressed in extravagantly affluent style. The magnificence of his clothing was royal in its richness and luxury. And yet one glance was sufficient to tell that this superbly decorous boy was pathetically slow-witted; a dribbling cretin who quite obviously spent his days in the throne-like chair in which he sat being tended by two impatient attendants; an elderly married couple by the look of them. The way they hovered over him gave evidence that this was how they spent all their waking hours. At the moment the old woman held a bowel of broth under the seated juvenile's nose, ladling it into his gaping mouth with a large spoon.

This sad imbecile was, to judge from the audible comments of this servant, His Excellency Visconte Gregori Lasinni. For when serving him the soup the old woman was continually muttering archly under her breath: "Has Your Excellency spilt Your Excellency's soup down the front of Your Excellency's ruffled Langelais silk blouse? Well, let Your Excellency just sit there while old Roxana wipes Your Excellency with a wet cloth, there and there. And will Your Excellency swallow the next mouthful?"

The sheer undiluted hatred in every word was truly chilling to hear and yet it went ignored and unremarked by the old man nearby. The Visconte was the least aware of any. Her icy speech had the quality of habitual unthinking action, as if she always spoke thus. She and her husband were sorely tried. They had to feed the zombie in the chair and wipe his arse for him and change his breeches when he emptied his bladder incontinently. They did all these things every day, and they did them with a measure of cold contempt that only those in positions of such intimate care and nursing can ever achieve.

Ealdræd walked over to the two unpleasant menials and seized the man by the shoulder. The ancient retainer winced at the contact, his saucer eyes blinking slowly as his mind, unaccustomed to novelty, sought to come to terms with this enormous foreigner who had apparently just fallen out of the skies. Looking beyond the fearsome apparition for some sort of explanation he saw only a young woman with slanted eyelids and skin the colour of olive oil. His mouth opened but no sound came forth. His wife had turned from her patient and stared at Ealdræd in just the same way as her husband, and for the same reason. This could not be happening; it was impossible.

Ealdræd demanded to know if the drooling thing in the lordly apparel was indeed the Visconte Gregori. The man held in the mercenary's grip nodded his head hesitantly, whereupon the ogre in the braided beard demanded to know who ruled in this castle since it clearly wasn't this boy. Ealdræd had spoken, of course, in Geulten, having no Piccolian. Finding a whisper of his voice the elderly servant said in barely comprehensible Eildressian-accented Geulten that the Lady ruled here; the Visconte's older sibling, Her Excellency the Viscontessa Magdalena.

Ealdræd released his hold on the fellow's shoulder. The lackey staggered a moment and then joined his wife who had stepped behind the throne-like chair as if for protection. The Aenglian was musing aloud that if the real power in the castle lay with the lady, then she it was who had wanted Eiji for her own damnable purposes and she it was who had set her dog upon Ealdræd with the intent to kill. It was the Lady who must answer for her conduct.

As if summoned by his reflections, a woman walked into the room from the far door. Although quite tall and willowy in a bejewelled full-length blue silk dress that concealed her from her buttoned-up throat to the floor, there was a deformity to her spine that made her seem much shorter; it twisted and hunched her slender back. Her wimple was embroidered in a richly elegant design which included small jewels sewn into the lace. It was an act of extraordinary profligacy to have jewellery adorning so humble an item of clothing as a wimple in addition to those that decorated her gown. Even without such evidence Ealdræd realised that this must be Her Excellency the Viscontessa Magdalena. He summed her up in a moment with a mercenary's no-nonsense honesty: an imperiously regal, stiffly dignified, hook-nosed, crook-backed, in-bred, lingering remnant of an obsolete family.

What he could not tell from just looking was that Her Excellency the Viscontessa Magdalena was also a fanatical disciple of the alchemic arts. As she ambled into the room she had a roll of parchment in her hand and her attention was so compulsively occupied by it that she had halfway crossed the room before she became rudely aware of the intruders when the female servant called out plaintively: "Your Excellency!"

The haughty face had all expression wiped from it as her eyes lifted and took in the presence of bizarre interlopers trespassing upon the possessions of her family escutcheon in a way that had not been conceivable for three hundred years. She could make nothing of it by way of elucidation. Such things did not occur.

As if to add to the growing confusion, a small child totally blackened with dirt shuffled into the chamber, followed by several more petrified waifs. The rough sack-cloth tabards they wore were as smothered in muck as their emaciated bodies. They were looking for food. Not even their unrelenting fear was as strong as the endless insistent aching of their hunger. Ealdræd and Eiji had left the door at the top of the cellar stairwell open. In doing so they had released the feral pack of children from their dark captivity; children who were now, presumably, tottering all around the castle.

"How dare you?! You . . . you . . ." exclaimed the Viscontessa, slowly grasping that all this was real. This uncouth inferior swine was making free with the house of the Lasinni. It was unthinkable, yet it stood before her. The lady's vision was fixated on the braided hair and beard of the vulgar churl that had started to walk towards her. She dropped the parchment she had been carrying.

The scribblings upon the roll of paper would have meant nothing to the mercenary beyond the obvious fact that this was the magic of the runes; that bafflingly inexplicable secret knowledge of the necromancers who, by means of written symbols, were able to speak with each other even when they were not present in the same place. How the enchanted parchment could capture the voice of the necromancer was unknown to all but they. Ealdræd had always found this to be one of the most compelling instances of the dark arts. Had he observed the writing upon the paper it would have quickened his step as he approached her.

The parchment was one roll of an extensive library on a single subject: corporeal metamorphosis. This cloistered and solitary Viscontessa was a biological alchemist who bred people in the same way that others breed dogs. Her cellars were full of malformed children because she must have subjects upon whom to experiment. But, despite her many attempts at inducing physical transmutation through potion and conjurement, it was not alchemy which had perpetrated these deformities amongst her human specimens, it was merely the same range of causes which had afflicted the children of poverty since time began: untreated infantile illness, prolonged malnutrition, and unsanitary disease-ridden living conditions. To which Her Excellency the Viscontessa Magdalena had added perpetual confinement in the darkness of a damp cellar. Their ailments required no supernatural manufacture; extreme neglect was fully competent in perpetrating the infliction of sickness and mortality.

Not that the lady scorned adult material. On the contrary, the Viscontessa Magdalena was currently conducting experiments in racial characteristics to observe differences in their constitution and their reactions to her drugs. Thus was explained her desire for oriental specimens such as Eiji, although what she was most eager to lay her hands upon were the people of the black races. She was convinced that they must be closer to the animal and therefore more primal in their constitutional inheritance. This would increase their value for her life's work.

All of the impotent and worthless concoctions that the Viscontessa Magdalena brewed so assiduously were in pursuit of her obsessive belief that she could, by her alchemy, restructure human bodies to reflect the individual's social rank. It must surely be right and proper that the most aristocratic should also be the most physically and intellectually gifted. She had for some years been developing a theory of the 'primal progenitor', the original perfect ancestor, and believed that it was the waning of this element within her bloodline which had caused her own and her brother's deformities. She held that the begetting from primal ancestral roots must be replenished from generation to generation to avoid a thinning of the bloodstock. The Viscontessa Magdalena had an abhorrence of what she called 'mixed stock'. Rather than attributing to herself the misfortune of being too in-bred, she felt that somewhere in recent generations her line had been infected by some external malignity; that the stock of the primal progenitor had been corrupted by an alien bloodline. In short, she believed herself to be not quite in-bred enough.

Naturally, her own elite ancestral begetting was so fine as to be vulnerable to the least infection from the lower orders. Where another family might incorporate inferior stock into their line without visible diminishment, the biological inheritance of the Lasinni family could brook no such corruption. This was the reason for her all-consuming interest in the alchemic arts and their power to affect alterations to the physical and mental constitution. One day she would give birth to a daughter that was as flawless as the original ancestor; as unadulterated as the primal progenitor, and that child would take her place amongst the greatest in society. The Viscontessa Magdalena would acquire this power through her own superior intelligence and she would use it to make herself the princess that her forebears were, to bestow upon her own progeny that physical perfection which had been denied to the unhappy Viscontessa Magdalena, and above all to restore her family name to the glories that awaited them in the future.

Cagliol had not believed in any of this, of course, but as a man of good sense he had humoured her because for as long as she was happily poisoning her research specimens and her brother sat dribbling in his chair, Cagliol had been effectively in charge of the castle and he had lived in the grand style of a Visconte. He had cared not a twopenny damn for the creatures the Viscontessa subjected to her alchemic enquiries because, after all, they were socially inferior rubbish of no account and for the most part they had been born for the purpose. As he had seen it, they owed their very existence to the lady and would be guilty of a gross ingratitude if they were to resent the occupation in which she employed them and for which she had given them their lives.

But now the Keeper of the Keys lay with his head sundered from his body in the rented dwelling of a deceased Menghis spice-trader. These were the vagaries of life.

As Ealdræd closed in upon her with his knife unsheathed, Her Excellency the Viscontessa Magdalena understood that the barbarian horde had at last risen up against their betters. She raised her arms and proclaimed her credo into the aborigine face of the bestial primitive who had stormed the balustrades of her civilization with his irreligious heathenism and the keys to the door. Keys she had given to another because she was incapable of governing herself.

"Spawn of the inferior, thou art cattle compared to a prince of the blood!" she shrieked.

The tall man in the mantle, black leather doublet and breeks came on at a sprightly pace.

"The Lasinni were princes when your ancestors fought with animal bones and soiled . . . ."

Ealdræd drove his knife into her stomach and then ripped upwards, emulating to some extent the death wound that Eiji had delivered upon Naimun. The crook-backed countess, or whatever she was or believed herself to be, sank down with a dry rattle and was dead so swiftly it was as if the life inside her flesh had wanted to be rid of her. Or perhaps it was the twisted mind from which life had so promptly fled.

Eiji took a lead from her Effendi and scampered up to the old woman, giving her a lethal belly wound as if they were the fashion this season. Eiji had taken it for granted that the servants would defend their master to the death, and so they must be despatched to facilitate Eiji's slaying of the Visconte. She was mistaken in this but, being a woman of loyalty and moral values, she could have no conception of a society in which neither attendant would risk their own lives for the sake of their liege lord.

The elderly goodwife shrilled her unreadiness for life's end even as her innards spilled forth, and as his spouse died in front of his eyes, the husband ran for a concealed exit behind a tapestry. Eiji watched him deserting his master and his wife. She squinted in puzzlement. There was no making sense of the behaviour of the *ghazboutyr*. But let the deserter keep the air in his lungs; she was not here to be revenged upon servants. She turned to the cretinous youth in the chair.

His mental condition presented her with a moral dilemma. This was the man against whom she had sworn a blood vengeance, yet he was not a man and he was not capable of having made any hostile move against her. The sister had been guilty and the sister was dead. Eiji turned to Ealdræd as he returned to her side and she looked a question at him.

"There will be no one to feed him now," the mercenary remarked, shrugging his shoulders and nodding his snake-braided head.

Eiji nodded in reply. It was not in her nature to show mercy but in this case mercy would serve. It would settle the moral vexation. In a perfunctory manner she drew back her dagger and slashed His Excellency the Visconte Gregori Lasinni across the throat. The flesh sliced like butter and the fluid pedigree of his lineage sprayed like a fountain. For a dreadful second his misty eyes came startlingly into focus, as if a moment of rational cognition had been bestowed upon him at the end, and then he pitched forward and rolled on to the floor; the last of the Lasinni.

There was no hurry to leave, since there was nobody here who could threaten them harm, and it occurred to the Aenglian that despite the castle's state of decay, it would still be worth looting for booty. To communicate this thought to Eiji he took out his purse of coin, rattled it in front of her, and gestured to her to search by miming the actions of rummaging about. There must be valuables in a house like this. She bobbed her delightful head enthusiastically. She came from a people who took a righteous pride in plunder.

Eiji danced about from chamber to chamber knocking things over in the exuberance of her search for the Viscontessa's jewels. As she ferreted about she talked excitedly to herself in Menghali, recounting the events of the day and glorying in their triumphs. It was almost worth having been betrayed by Naimun to have enjoyed so complete a revenge. Honour meant more to her than baubles. Not that she lacked interest in decorative trinkets, but she had her priorities.

After a deal of hunting Ealdræd had found nothing but a handful of small gold coin, one plain gold ring, one sovereign ring, four bottles of claret and a cold roasted turkey. It was not the fortune for which he'd been hoping. The family Lasinni, for all their fine clothes and aristocratic airs, seemed to have been quite close to poverty by the time they met their end. But he could add the gold to his own purse of coin and he took comfort in the fact that he already had more than enough to buy passage on a ship back to the Ehngle peninsula, if he were able to reach the coast where a ship might be had. Any one of the Wehnbrian seaports, Ebb, Tarhampton, Moecre, or Hove were all no more than four or five weeks sailing from the coast of Gathkar or the Barony of Langelais. The latter being a Geulten nation, he thought that the Gathkaree harbour city of Phari might best serve as a point of departure; he had only to get there. But what of Eiji? Would she choose to cast herself still further into the lands of the *ghazboutyr?*

The girl in question reappeared as he was making his way back to the main doors at the front of the house. Her arms were full of silver-backed brushes and combs, bottles of perfume and various cosmetic subtleties that the grizzled veteran could not put any name to; the whole lot half-wrapped up in the blue silk dress that she had stripped from the Viscontessa's body. Eiji's grin was so wide that he thought her face would break.

They left all the doors and the cage-gate open on their way out. Hengustir and the black gelding were patiently testing the taste of the grass where Ealdræd and Eiji had tied them. They had been left undisturbed. There was nobody around in the land of the Lasinni to steal horses. With the bottles of claret, the roasted turkey, and a large bundle of the contents of milady's boudoir, it took a little while to position their newly acquired additional baggage so that it was balanced correctly on their animals' haunches. They hoisted themselves into the saddle and took their leave.

Behind them, in a room adjacent to the Viscontessa's private apartments, was a large woven tapestry from Eildres depicting a hunting scene. It covered most of an entire wall. The tapestry carefully concealed a locked iron door, the key to which was not to be found on Cagliol's ring of outsized keys. Only Magdalena herself had known the secret hiding place for the key to that door, which was the entrance to the strongroom of the ancient family Lasinni. It contained all those treasures which, even after they had been forced to sell their land, the Viscontessa had not been able to bring herself to part with, for these heirlooms were sacred to her. There was the Guillain lattice emerald necklace that her grandmother had long ago received from the hands of King Louis of Guillaime in person as a tribute to her beauty, the ruby hilt sword in its jewel-encrusted scabbard that her grandfather's grandfather had been awarded by Queen Constanza for his personal courage at the famous Battle of Tusco, and the exquisite brooch with a pink diamond set between two blue diamonds which legend said had originally been mined in the tribal lands of the Buntuu on the far side of the Mountains of God, not to mention a casket filled with four hundred and ten gold pieces, which was all that was left of the once great wealth of the Lasinni. Neither Ealdræd nor Eiji had entered the tapestry room. They had passed it by since it was empty apart from a few sticks of furniture and wasn't worth searching. So the contents of the hidden strongroom had remained unknown and untouched.

As the Aenglian and the Menghis rode off slowly toward the south the sun was beginning to set, bathing the low hills around them first in gold and then, as it set lower, in a deep lush red. They did not even notice the fire that had broken out in the noble residence they were leaving behind them. One of the waifs must have upset something in the kitchens. During the course of the setting of the sun, the glow of the burning castle competed against the soft glimmering of the oncoming twilight. The flames grew higher until the roof caved in and then the upper storey collapsed in an all-consuming inferno. Before darkness had fallen the normally deserted countryside around the Castle Lasinni was unaccountably full of half-starved children watching a grand old building being razed to the ground.

Chapter 7

The Matriarchs of Gathkar

When the late autumn wind blew hard from the east, rolling over the *Kanione Pluhurit*, the 'canyons of dust' in the impoverished dry plains of Tehlitz, it raised a column of sand a mile high which then spread itself westward to cloud the borderlands of Piccoli and Gathkar with a pestilential wind called the *rrjep lëkurën* or the 'flayer of skin'. The abrasive particles that swept through the air were like tiny specks of glass that would rasp across any exposed flesh to leave a painful rash upon the inflamed skin. No matter how tightly a traveller wrapped their cloak about themselves, the sand always seemed to find its way into every little crevice and crack to itch and irritate. It was worse still for any animals ridden through this infernal region because their unprotected hides would suffer great discomfort from the stinging blizzard of coarse sand. Anyone who knew the local climate avoided taking to the road at this time of year unless their business was pressing. Strangers had to take it as they found it.

Two riders had to their considerable relief passed out of the *rrjep lëkurën* that morning and were now progressing south in greater comfort, their horses walking steadily over the rocky ground in the dry heat. They had seen nothing but dust the day before and the return of the sun in a clear blue sky lifted their resilient spirits. They were both individuals who recovered quickly from life's many setbacks. Content for the moment to be free of the pestiferous 'flayer of skin', they rode at a nonchalant pace in companionable silence.

The first rider was mounted upon a huge ghost-grey blue-roan stallion of fearsome aspect but stately poise. He sat easy in the saddle, his upper body rolling in rhythm with Hengustir's undulating gait. He was Ealdræd of the Pæga, a clan of the Aenglians who were of the people of the Ehngle. The land of his birth was all of two thousand miles away in the distant west and he was on his way south in the hope of reaching a port on the coast of Gathkar and boarding ship to take him homeward once more.

Slightly behind him and to the left side, for he was her Effendi and he was right-handed, rode Eiji of the Kajhin of the community of Alijah who were one of the Menghis nations dwelling upon the Great Steppes. She was all of three thousand miles from the land of her birth but in the opposite direction to that of her Effendi. Unlike him she had no means by which to return home, for though she was a furious and tenacious fighter in her own right and had demonstrated her readiness to kill at the drop of a badly chosen word, she knew perfectly well that if she were to attempt to journey east alone through the vast open terrain of the Murgl and the Khevnic and the Uzbeghi she would most certainly find herself raped and enslaved before she had traversed the first one hundred leagues.

So, accepting the perversities of fate with a good grace, she had thrown in her lot with her Effendi and was now a stateless and displaced woman of nineteen, untimely ripped from the soil of Menghis and forever shorn of her roots. Although not reconciled to this loss of her homeland, she was young enough and had the necessary toughness of mind to cope pragmatically with a set of circumstances from which she could not extricate herself. Eiji's strong feelings for the man at her side had helped to make her acceptance of her expatriate status more palatable.

He had been a wandering mercenary for hire for longer than she had been alive and had seen as much of the world as any man without wings, yet it was his practice always to return to Aenglia when he felt himself straying too far from the hearth of his boyhood, for his ethnicity was strong within him and the novelty of exotic places paled after a time. So it was that he was making his way to the sea and a ship for the Ehngle peninsula, or as near to it as he could contrive. That the Menghis girl was content, lacking options, to journey along with him even though it took her west when her kindred lay in the east was perhaps explained in the word she had chosen by which to address him, Effendi, whose meaning might be translated as either 'master' or 'husband'. Or both.

The two dust-begrimed riders had reached the northern periphery of the Gathkar Queendoms, possibly the strangest place on earth; surely the most imprudent. It was a place where migratory and itinerant folk like themselves were often to be found because the government of Gathkar believed in open borders and made no effort to control or regulate who entered their sovereign territory. Consequently the queendoms were overrun with the worst criminal riff-raff and unruly scum of all their neighbouring kingdoms.

However, the dubious character of civil life under the Gathkar matriarchy led their neighbours to take stronger than usual measures to ensure that the borders were not open in both directions. All might pass into Gathkar but it was very much more difficult to move from Gathkar into any of the countries that surrounded it. Passage would not be so difficult for Ealdræd and Eiji because the braided white westerner and the slant-eyed oriental were so obviously not of Gathkaree nationality that they might safely be assumed not to be afflicted with the eccentric malady of self-negation that made the ailing queendoms so freakishly unnatural to the rest of the world. For who could be sure that the political disease of the Gathkarees was not contagious?

Ealdræd could hardly help but be aware of how Eiji, his companion, lover and devoted attendant, had frequent difficulties with foreigners. They brought the combative and pugnacious traits of her character to the fore. The Menghali word for all non-Menghis was *ghazboutyr* meaning 'those who cannot speak properly'. Notwithstanding his own foreignness to her, for she made him an exception, she tended to view all *ghazboutyr* as wilfully confusing and contrary-minded. For Eiji it was only the Menghis, who had once been the great imperial power of the immeasurable steppes, that lived in a civilized manner; those who lived differently were at best mistaken and at worst wilfully insulting. This tendency to consider the *ghazboutyr* to be people who were guilty of being unnecessarily awkward on purpose just to irritate her was a characteristic of her truculent personality that he foresaw might be a particular problem in the queendoms.

Eiji's culture was not one to tolerate women lording it over men. Whilst her habit of pouring the filthiest verbal abuse at most of the men she met was archly typical of Menghis women, this was not in any way a challenge to the male supremacism of the Menghis lifestyle. Rather the barbed tongues of Menghis womenfolk were intended to prompt and provoke highly masculine responses from their men to the mutual satisfaction of both sexes. Menghis girls used outrageously obscene swearing as a way to incite their men to prove their masculinity. Eiji was never abusive to Ealdræd because she had no doubts about him, especially when he was lashing her with a whip during sex. In her eyes, Ealdræd was all that a man should be, and her conduct toward him was therefore extremely respectful. Eiji's frequent taunts and slurs were invariably directed at men whom she felt had failed in their duty to be properly manly or who had encroached upon her prickly dignity.

This had happened quite a lot during their sojourn south through Piccoli and twice it had been unavoidable to settle the matter with iron. Once Ealdræd had found it necessary to put his spear in the belly of a very pretty teenage leader of a gang of similarly dandified youths whom Eiji had affronted by making hand gestures of eunuch castration toward them which unfortunately their leader had understood only too well. The second incident involved Eiji skewering with her much-prized dagger a pompous peacock of a Piccolian who had sought to slap her face after she had called him, in Menghali, a "cuntlicking poltroon of a widow's dildo" and he had comprehended her tone of voice if not the actual words.

What Eiji would make of the subservient Gathkaree men was all too predictable and Ealdræd had tried to prepare her for this uncomfortable experience by explaining that Gathkarees were under a kind of political spell in which the men had lost their manhood and lived by the matriarchal beliefs and values of their mystic religion. This level of communication between the Aenglian and his oriental companion was now possible, happily, for since their meeting with the merchant in Pestoia who had acted as translator for them, subsequently deceased by Eiji's hand, she had begun to learn Ehngleish from him so as to be able to communicate with her Effendi in his own language. But whilst she had gained command over a useful vocabulary of more than two hundred words, she had made less progress in her comprehension of why the stupid *ghazboutyr* behaved the way they did.

When Ealdræd had essayed the information that: "Gathkaree women rule men. Gathkaree men serve women."

Eiji had replied: "Effendi, why Gathkaree men not kill women?"

The astuteness of this response had stumped the veteran soldier for the moment as it was such a excellent question, very much to the point, and one for which he did not quite have an adequate answer. Even so, he tried.

"Gathkaree men worship woman god so serve women because they think women better than men, like god better than men."

But Eiji, not to be put off, had replied with her shrewd, no-nonsense Menghis reasoning: "Effendi, why Gathkaree men not kill women and worship man god?"

266

In the end she had more or less convinced him of the unassailable logic of her position and he had brought the discussion to a close by advising: "Gathkaree men mad. We keep away from." On this he found his sagacious bed-warmer in full agreement.

Ealdræd had visited the queendoms once before in his life, as a mercenary for the Ahkrani prophet-vizier in his war against the southern Gathkarees. There had been no profit in it for the Aenglian because the Ahkrani had poisoned the Gathkar army's water supply forcing a surrender from their priestess queen, who had not wished to oppose the invader even before her soldiers were decimated by poison.

At that time, more than a decade ago, incessant societal convolutions had convinced Ealdræd that Gathkar was a place barely able to hold itself together as a state due to its seemingly fatal internal contradictions. It had provided him with a good deal of comical bemusement, but it was an entertaining perplexity that was exceeded by his sheer astonishment that such a society had ever come into existence in the first place. He had found it safe to travel through the queendoms despite his evident maleness because his privileged social status as a non-Gathkaree, or 'honoured guest' as the matriarchy had instructed all foreigners should be called, took precedence over his political and cultural inferiority as a male. On his previous visit, short though it was, he had learned something of the history of this bewilderingly perverse place.

Long ago the original Gathkarees had been descendants of a wave of landless Geulten who had migrated eastward across the narrow strip of sea that extended inland and was known to the Geulten as *La Fossé* or 'the ditch'. Occupying the largely empty territory on the other side of the ditch they established themselves and built a nation-state where none had stood before. This was when the famous twin cities of Bhoul in Bhourgbon and Phari in Gathkar were erected in all their majesty to face each other across *La Fossé* as a testament to those who had constructed such architectural marvels.

The twin cities were conflated in the public mind in those glory days and referred to as Bhoulphari but in actual fact they had always been quite separate and distinct entities, not even belonging to the same country. Thus when Gathkar began its ill-advised road down to its current condition of shame and degradation, Bhoul had to watch helpless as its twin Phari, a once fabulous city deserving of respect, was slowly but pitifully reduced because of political incompetence and misrule. This did not happen all at once, yet the slide was always and ever downwards.

In the centuries that followed the founding of the Republic of Gathkar by its Geulten forefathers the negro tribesmen of the many Buntuu peoples, all of related ethnic tribes but with many different languages and allegiances, were brought into Gathkar as a source of cheap labour. Over time they settled and became an integral part of the Gathkar population. During this time there was a second mass immigration into Gathkar from the north east, with large numbers of mixed-race Tehlitzim travelling down to form colonies within all the Gathkar cities of any significant size. There were even substantial but transient communities of Khevnic-Murgl gypsies that routinely wandered in from the nomadic trails of the east. Since those days the Gathkar, Buntuu, Tehlitzim integration of cultures had amalgamated into a muddled and confusing social concoction that had undermined the integrity of the country to the point where the earlier sense of united Gathkaree nationhood had entirely fallen away.

Then it was, amidst a multi-racial fabrication of diverse and contradictory loyalties, that a revolutionary ideology had intervened to seize ascendancy amongst the ethnic Gathkarees; a religious faith based upon a sense of imperialist guilt for their Geulten ancestors appropriation of this territory in the past and of the masculine vices that were to blame for it. This emergent doctrine had established itself as a new ruling class; a theocracy that worshipped the lunar goddess Ertamis, the many-breasted, in the religion of *Mwanamke-mkuu* or 'Supreme Woman' in which the clergy were all female. The masculine vices of violence, militarism and xenophobic imperialism were cast aside. In their place the ideals of feminine sympathy and nurturance were exalted. With this revolution the former Republic of Gathkar was transformed into the Gathkar Queendoms.

Inside the labyrinthine temples where the intrusive tread of a male foot was unknown, the priestess cult of *Mwanamke-mkuu* venerated the deified female in adoration and reverence. They performed their prayers and rites wholly naked the better to reveal their femaleness before their celestial sister in heaven, their adulations following the natural order of the lunar cycle as written in the very structure of the cosmos and in the holy blood of their own sacred menstrual biology; a natural order from which the male was excluded.

For this reason the queendoms were not strictly speaking queendoms at all, since their rulers were high-priestesses not queens. But the name of queendoms had been coined by the good folk of Bhourgbon, the most powerful and influential country in the region, because it was the only word within the Geulten language that could in any way describe the extraordinary state of affairs of having a ruling caste exclusively of women presiding over a country in which the very concept of maleness was held in contempt. The name, at least outside of Gathkar itself, had stuck.

There were 33 high-priestesses of the faith scattered across Gathkar each of whom led a coven of 333 sister-priestesses. In addition to these there were many thousands of lay-sisters amongst the general population. Males were disqualified by their own biology from holding any kind of office or rank within the formal hierarchy of the theocracy of *Mwanamke-mkuu* other than as the very humblest and lowliest of lay acolytes; their inferior status ordained by Ertamis, the many-breasted, in accordance with mother nature.

The gendered bifurcation of the sexes that resulted, with its unquestioned belief in the superiority of the female in her intuitive emotionality and empathic sensitivity, had come to pervade every aspect of Gathkaree life. The inherent nurturance of the female was held to make her infinitely more suited to the grave responsibilities of the role of moral and political leadership; divinely gifting women with an ascendancy that pre-empted any need for masculine systems such as an evidence-based legal process. Any man accused of a crime by any woman was automatically guilty without trial, for it was axiomatic that no woman would ever tell a lie and that maleness was in all instances the surest sign of guilt. In daily life the most unfortunate aspects of maleness were kept in check by a few simple but necessary laws; no man was permitted to speak in the presence of a woman except by her explicit dispensation; no man had any claim upon his own children; no man had any right to defend himself, and so on.

The men of Gathkar had somehow convinced themselves of the rightness and justice of these gender relations and they sought to win favour with their betters by feminising themselves, whilst at the same time making continual public confession of their own bestial male vices and personal inadequacy. During Ealdræd's first visit to the queendoms he had seen many appalling examples of this feminisation; of men whose masculinity had been so degraded that nothing would induce them to exhibit any of the forbidden behaviour of being aggressive, combative, sexually predatory or, most sinful of all, patriotic. Ealdræd had been a younger man in those days and had been unable to restrain himself from expressing his disgust by boxing the ears of these abject compliant wretches who were so consumed by self-loathing. It was for this reason that he had tried to prepare Eiji for the full horror of it, lest she unsheathe her cherished falcon-headed dagger and slaughter half the male population of the country in her revulsion and repugnance at their effeminacy.

The rise to absolute dominance of *Mwanamke-mkuu* had given unprecedented totalitarian powers to the despotic matriarchs who were its priestesses. Not only had they divided their citizens by gender, they had further splintered the populace with their perversely self-directed ethnic prejudice, propagandized from the pulpits of the priestesses, by which the present generation descended from the original Gathkarees had come to believe that their historical imperialism made them morally inferior as a community to those whose heritage was identified with foreign cultures. This attitude toward ethnicity and race had ruptured their society into a disunity that must eventually prove fatal. Its effects were already apparent. The multi-racial character of Gathkaree society had bestowed upon some of its citizenry a light-brown skin colouring known locally with a great deal of pride as mulatto-muwallad. This, in addition to being physically attractive, might have been a beneficial social development had it been allowed to serve as a unifying and leveling influence. But, disastrously for the oppressed population, it had merely produced a deeper prejudice against those Gathkarees who retained the white skins of their Geulten ancestors, and so added to the burdens suffered by the descendents of the founding fathers.

As a result of all this, whilst Gathkar was nominally a federation of theocratic city-states under an authoritarian matriarchy, the reality was that their self-destructive political dogma and their military weakness had made them catastrophically vulnerable to conquest by their nearest neighbours. In particular, the Ahkrani had made significant incursions into Gathkar, colonising whole quarters of their cities. Like a swarm of locusts they had come, from as far south as Bayešić the inland sea in the southern portion of Ahkran minor. They did not colonise militarily, for it transpired that there was no need to, the borders being open. They merely arrived and imposed themselves upon a docile populace that had been taught to live on its knees in a permanent state of apology.

But not only had the rulers of Gathkar made no resistance to these incursions, on the contrary, they had been actively welcomed by the *Mwanamke-mkuu* matriarchy, who favoured the men of Ahkran over their own Gathkaree men in every respect. The ruling priestesses had ordered no military response to colonisation and, in any case, their emasculated soldiery lacked the will to offer resistance. To the matriarchs, a self-deluding surrender was a moral improvement to their country and one which they celebrated by adopting a new gown of office for the priestess class which was based upon the customary garb for women in Ahkran, a loose billowing garment called a *tevazu hapis* that enveloped the entire body except for the eyes and hands. In order that the priestesses could still display their femaleness to Ertamis, they redesigned the *tevazu hapis* to remove everything except the veil of the garment so that it covered their heads, apart from an eye-slit, and had a flowing train that splayed out behind them. In this way they could, from the neck down, remain appropriately nude before their lunar goddess. They also changed the material of which the *tevazu hapis* was made from plain black cotton to a transparent pink gossamer that was much more expensive, much more becoming, and therefore much more reverential to their deity.

In Ahkran the *tevazu hapis*, which translated as 'modesty prison', was a sign of the ownership of women by their men because it was intended to imply that the woman's body was the sole property of whatever man had authority over her so that she was to be visible to none but him. Yet in Gathkar, when the matriarchy began wearing their abbreviated version of the *tevazu hapis*, they somehow contrived to believe that this form of attire honoured women and lent greater distinction to them. This servility to Ahkrani influence had been forced upon them by their own religious doctrine because their values did not permit criticism of a foreign culture, so that it was their practice to embrace alien observances especially where the foreigners were forthright in demanding recognition of their customs. Indeed, so submissively acquiescent were the rulers of the queendoms toward non-Gathkarees that the female supremacism of their society had to some extent been undermined by this meek deference toward not only the Ahkrani but all foreigners, even those whose gender deviated from the divine femaleness of Ertamis, the lunar goddess.

*   *   *

Ealdræd had remained on the Piccolian side of the border for as long as possible so that it was only when he reached that realm's tiny coastline at the apex of *La Fossé* that he turned their horses south to ride down the eastern shoreline of the ditch, albeit a few miles inland. He was heading first for Phari, and if he could get no ship westward from there he would continue on to Porta Aberta. Nothing more than a fishing sloop would be needed to round the extension of land known as *Le Doigt* and make safe harbour on the coast of Langelais where some stronger vessel might transport him and his Menghis companion into the safer waters off the Ehngle coast.

The Aenglian mercenary had thought long and hard about making a dash across the south east of Bhourgbon to the sea-ports of the Barony of Langelais, thereby to avoid the queendoms altogether, but he had decided that the risk was unjustifiable. Ealdræd had heard no word about the latest political situation between his people of the Ehngle peninsula and their hereditary enemies the Geulten since the veteran soldier had left Wehnbria some months before as escort to the notorious Bhelenese courtesan Maev de Lederwyrhta at the behest of his general, Eádgar Aeðlric. At that time the Eorl Atheldun had just won a famous victory at the Battle of Proctors Wæl over the Geulten army under the Duke Etienne of Oénjil. So it seemed likely to Ealdræd that should any persons of Ehngle stock such as himself be discovered within the kingdoms of the Three Crowns of the Geulten Alliance at present, summary execution would surely follow, to say the least of it.

Although the Aenglian had passed himself off as a Geulten before and might well manage the passage across Bhourgbon were he alone, with a conspicuously oriental girl in tow he would stand out like a sore thumb. It might still be managed but it would be damnably perilous. The cavalry and whatever else remained of the coalition army of the Duchy of Oénjil would probably have retreated deep into Bhourgbon after their ignominious defeat at Proctors Wæl and for all Ealdræd knew the whole of Bhourgbon might since have become an armed camp in preparation for the inevitable renewal of hostilities next summer. The Aenglian would not abandon his admirable partner, who was both lover and comrade-in-arms to him, so instead he would resign himself to a ride down the coast to the Gathkar ports and from thence a fishing boat to the buccaneer harbour of Citadelle or perchance Forteresse in the Barony of Langelais. The realm of the 'sea-barons' was nominally a part of the Geulten Alliance but in practice it was so lawless a stronghold of villains and cut-throats that the writ of Geulten rule carried little weight there. A brief visit amongst the buccaneers was an acceptable hazard.

Their first night spent on the route south from the Piccolian border saw Ealdræd and Eiji camping on the edge of a Tehlitzim caravan encamped at a watering hole whose name they never knew. The merchants of Tehlitz used the northern reaches of Gathkar as a highway between their bartering posts with the Khevnic and Murgl nomads in the east and the rich mercantile port of Bhoul which had the whole of Bhourgbon behind it with which to trade. The pronounced Tehlitzim and Buntuu presence in Gathkar made it a friendly territory for them, and the Gathkaree attitude toward their 'honoured guests' meant that they could travel in comparative safety despite the turbulence of the ethnic conflict amongst the citizenry.

When the two outsiders approached the caravan, they came in slowly so as to make plain their lack of hostile intent. Figures emerged from amongst the pitched tents to look them over. The riders came to a halt before those bedouin who stood foremost and Ealdræd, speaking in Geulten, asked for permission to pitch his camp amongst them for the night. He needed to resupply his store of water and purchase such foodstuffs as might be available for sale at a reasonable price, especially grain or grasses for the animals. There was precious little natural supply of either in this barren territory.

As he spoke, Ealdræd glanced surreptitiously over the scene in front of him. The caravan appeared to be an amalgam of several smaller groups which had combined in convoy for mutual protection. It was not the caravan of a single extended family but rather a gaggle of unrelated merchants and traders from a number of the mixed races of the Tehlitzim. Most of them had the hook nose and sweeping brow of their eastern ancestry, dark eyed and swarthily handsome, with features which looked like they'd been chiselled out of rock. Some had the more open countenance and flatter features of their southern ancestry, their noses wider and their jawlines rounder. But all wore the headdress, elegantly flowing robes and soft leather boots of the desert dweller.

For their part, the Tehlitzim were wary but cautiously welcoming. These, after all, were men of commerce for whom every chance encounter was an opportunity for business, but they were also men of good sense who understood the perilous nature of the world.

The fellow sitting tall upon the blue-grey horse did not inspire confidence. He was obviously the type who earned his bread on the field of combat, it stood out a mile. Foreign, too. A man from the west and white-skinned despite his deep suntan. There was a seven foot ash spear and a four foot javelin hanging in his saddle-sheath and a small round shield hooked over the pommel. Equally alien was the way the horseman wore his long hair and beard plaited in braids. Like a tangle of thin rope it fell in a curtain to his shoulders, the beard reaching his chest, the hair showing distinct streaks of grey. Despite this, the veteran had a lithe fluidity to his movements that might more often be found in men twenty years his junior. He wore a close-fitting doublet with narrow breeches that tied below the knee, both stitched strong and secure in a durable black leather. At least they would have proved so on another man but closer inspection would have disclosed that the stitching was starting to split on the shoulder and arms of the doublet because it wasn't quite roomy enough to accommodate the muscularity of the soldier's upper body. His bucket-top riding boots still showed new having been bought, like the rest of his clothing, only recently in the town of Pestoia in the north of Piccoli. His weapons and bearing declared him a mercenary soldier but he was evidently unemployed at present. The Tehlitzim might have turned him away from their caravan had he been alone, but he had something in his possession which caused them to think again and permit him to share their camp fires for the night.

Alongside him, that possession sat astride a black gelding; an oriental girl with jet black hair cut in a bob to the neck. Her eyes were stoical yet spoke of an energetically defended sense of her own dignity. Her bright green Tehlitz smock was tucked into a constrictive leather girdle from which hung a falcon-headed serrated dagger in a cheap but skilfully engraved wooden scabbard. The smock had a latticework of laces down the front and was open sufficiently to display a healthy quantity of firm young cleavage in respect for her master's pleasure. The baggy linen garment normally covered her down to the thigh, as she wore it without breeches, but perched on her horse she was unselfconsciously revealing the full length of her athletic legs from the hip to the ewe-leather boots that she wore Menghis-style, without any strapping to tie them around the calves so that the soft leather sagged down around her ankles in slack folds.

274

If the old warrior was interested in trade, perhaps he had something better than coin to give in exchange. But the bedouin merchants said nothing of this, simply grunting their assent to these stray travellers to join their encampment. The Aenglian and the Menghis accepted gratefully, for they needed access to the watering hole quite badly, and it would be useful to bide a night with these gentlemen of the highway, unsoldierly tradesmen though they were, to reprovision. The Aenglian had no tent, only a bedroll which he shared with his woman, and the warmth of the fires would be welcome besides being handy for cooking their stew. The Menghis girl had introduced Ealdræd to a type of stew that she called *sijala-sija*, which literally meant boiled or stewed meat, and which tasted remarkably the same regardless of what source the meat came from, whether cattle, camel, sheep, goat, dog, or what have you. It served as an easily prepared all-purpose hot meal and they ate it often.

As Eiji crouched over her cooking pots at the fireside she was the object of a great deal of staring and considerable muttered gossip amongst the Tehlitzim women. These shrouded creatures did not care overmuch for her attire. Their men, on the other hand, eyed the girl as if it were *she* that they should like to have for dinner. Eiji gave them all her most sulky and disparaging facial expressions, which were positively artistic in their insolent contumely in a way that only the Menghis can achieve, but she refrained from indulging in any of her usual obscenely insulting verbal comments in deference to her Effendi's repeated admonitions to avoid unnecessary conflict and thereby reduce the amount of violent mayhem in their lives to an agreeable minimum.

The two outsiders filled themselves with stew and washed it all down with their last bottle of Piccolian wine, and then they settled down in comfort for their repose. Ealdræd had intended a short sleep and to be away early at the first light of dawn before the rest of the caravan emerged from their tents. But Eiji had ideas of her own.

She had not provided her Effendi with intimate comforts for the last few days of the preceding week because one of the several customs that the Aenglian and the Menghis cultures had in common was they did not engage in sex during the days of menstrual bleeding. The previous night would have seen her make up for the days prior but she was thwarted by the weather. In the midst of the wind called *rrjep lëkurën*, the flayer of skin, they'd had no choice but to huddle down to sleep wrapped around in a blanket to keep out the lacerating dust. With Ealdræd's leather doublet draped over his stallion's head to protect the beast's eyes and Eiji's linen smock doing likewise for her black gelding, they had slept sitting upright with the bedroll over their heads. Consequently, they'd had to forego sex yet again. But now that there were no further impediments Eiji was firmly resolved to provide her man with intimate comforts tonight, Tehlitz merchants or no Tehlitz merchants. In short, Eiji was feeling as randy as a stoat.

Moreover, the bafflingly unnatural things which Ealdræd had told her about the men of Gathkar had worried her far more than she had permitted him to notice. He had said that there was a political spell over the men in this monstrously aberrant country. The thought that perturbed her so seriously was that her Effendi was now inside the territory of this abnormal nation of masculine women and feminine men and Eiji wished to make certain that her own man was untainted and free from any contagion. She dreaded the thought that the foul disease perpetrated by the priestess cult might have infected him since they had crossed the Gathkar border.

So she laid out their blanket far enough away from the camp fires to bestow the privacy of shadow and no sooner had Ealdræd stretched himself out in comfort on the meagre bedroll than Eiji was squirming down beside him to loosen his breeches at the groin. It did not take her beguiling fingers, captivating lips, and clever tongue more than a moment to rouse her Effendi to the full performance of his manly duties. Neither of them wore anything in the nature of undergarments, of course, for they were not the sort of decadent sophisticates who are so ashamed of their bodies that they have to wear clothing underneath their clothing. With the artful Menghis practising her sensual arts in earnest they did not trouble to undress for matters swiftly became too urgent.

So adept was the skilful Eiji in her erotic enticements that even after her greybeard veteran had taken her vigorously from behind to her considerable satisfaction, emptying his seed into her like the onset of the monsoon, he hauled her over his lap for a firm spanking from his belt. This was a sure sign that he was far from finished with her. Already quite convinced that she need have no worries on the subject of his having been infected by Gathkaree effeminacy, she relaxed her mind and her flesh under the harsh repetition of the insistent whipping and let the sharp stinging pain of the belt burn into her in its very familiar, and on this occasion very reassuring, manner.

He had just flipped her over on to her back, the rocky ground smarting the fresh welts on her bottom through the thin barrier of the blanket, and he had just spread the supple girl's flexible legs to accommodate his muscular bulk between them, sinking into her with an erection that eased a sigh from her that was a blessing upon the gods for having made her a woman, when she looked over his brawny left shoulder and saw a grinning, swarthy, hook-nosed face smirking down at her. Over Ealdræd's right shoulder she saw a second face, turbaned and fork-bearded, and fully as evil-looking as his brother's, chuckling as he stepped forward toward the couple fucking at his feet, raising a lantern the better to see where to strike with his sword. Eiji cried out a warning.

If the Aenglian mercenary had outlived all the boys of his childhood, surviving his generation to reach the age of a true veteran, it was not only because of his fighting abilities with the spear and the knife. Having lived by the deaths of others, the issue resolved on the razor's edge of a blade in the blink of an eye, he was a man always ready to respond to threat. In the past he had been attacked whilst squatting in the undergrowth emptying his bowels, he had been assailed whilst pissing against a tree and whilst guzzling drunkenly in his cups. This present attack was in fact the second time in his life that he had been pounced upon by brigands whilst he was enthusiastically at his fornication.

Eiji's inarticulate yelp of alarm might have been a squeal of pleasure, given her eager appetite for cock, yet that sixth sense of self-preservation which had been a steadfast friend to the mercenary all his life, told him that death was but a fleeting instant from being thrust into his unprotected back. Without the least thought of looking to see where his enemies were, for a second spent craning his head around to assess the situation would likely prove fatal, he spun blindly to his left, taking Eiji with him gripping her to his chest, the pair of them rolling over and over into the shades of the night. Before the no longer grinning faces could cease their gawping at this unexpected turnabout, the girl had been tossed clear to one side and the man had sprung after her, following her into still darker shadow.

A filthy curse of vexation went up in the mongrel language of the Tehlitzim and curved swords flashed in the reflected lantern-light, flourished in anger. The brothers, Dëfrim and Afrim, had bethought themselves to sneak up upon the westerner with the barbarously braided beard and slay him from behind; thereafter to rape his woman for they had noticed the bounce of her breasts and the smooth skin of her bare legs as she had bent over amongst her cooking pots earlier that evening and had decided that she was worth killing for. If she gave them pleasure when they raped her, they would keep her for themselves. If she did not, they would sell her for a slave when they reached Bhoul. Anticipating no difficulty, neither had bothered to put on any armour or chainmail. They were dressed only in their loose cotton travelling habiliments.

But the murder had not gone to plan. The girl and her master had vanished into the night and the brothers must find the western swine in order to kill him. Carrying the lantern, Dëfrim rushed into the darkness in the direction that their quarry had disappeared swinging wildly with his sword. Afrim circled around in the hope that the white man, fleeing from the light of the lantern, might stumble out of the gloom right into him. Neither of the hunters called out, for they did not wish their fellows amongst the caravan to be involved in what was a private piece of business for the brothers alone. When Dëfrim met Afrim coming from the opposite direction he almost carved him up, assuming the dark shape in front of him to be the Aenglian. The pair of them sighed in annoyance. Their quarry had fled. Exasperated, they trudged back to where the mercenary's horses were tied. If they could not have the girl, they could at least steal the bastard's other possessions. But when they approached the horses they found the man they had been hunting for standing there awaiting them, clad in helmet and mail-shirt and with his seven foot ash spear levelled menacingly at their chests.

The brothers chuckled as before. This western savage was a fool or a madman. He was only one and they were two. Added to which, if they judged correctly from the strands of grey in his hair, he was their father's age. The man had no chance against them both.

Dëfrim placed the lantern on the ground and the fight began without any false bravado or wordplay. This was a matter of killing for the prize of the woman. Both Tehlitzim rushed at their antagonist together, launching themselves forward with murderous lunges. Their sword-blades swept in deadly arcs that, were they to make contact, would slice flesh and bone asunder. Yet they cut empty air. Though the brothers both struck quickly and continuously in an all-out attack they could neither reach their man nor cleave through his wooden weapon. Every blow was adroitly deflected with the eighteen inches of iron at the end of the mercenary's spear of good

Aenglian ash. The dizzily dancing spearhead seemed to be everywhere, not only parrying the frenzied assaults of two swords at once, but even attempting counter-strikes that came within a hair's breadth of cutting off the tip of a hooked nose or gouging out an eyeball.

Dëfrim and Afrim may have been accurate in their estimate of the veteran's age but they were quite mistaken in their assumption about its consequences. The greybeard's foot-speed far exceeded that of his younger opponents and his hand/eye coordination was sufficient to keep them both at bay. Scowling grimly, his braided hair flailing, he leapt in and out of their attempts to cut him down with the skill of a lifetime's experience. It was galling and frustrating for the younger men, who had predicted an easy victory. Dëfrim's impatience caused him to lunge with too much eagerness and in one motion the old soldier sidestepped and backslashed with his spear, grazing the bedouin's jaw. The man lurched back, adopting a defensive stance, and was only saved from further injury by Afrim's redoubled efforts keeping the Aenglian's blade fully occupied. But for all the Tehlitzim's wild cuts and thrusts he could get nowhere near the foreigner with the point or edge of his sword. The brothers roared and snarled but the mercenary fought in stoical silence. He had long ago achieved the secret that makes the most dangerous of foes; he had come to terms with the inevitability of his own death, with the absolutely inescapable certainty that one day he would die, and he did not concern himself as to whether it was today or tomorrow. He had already lived longer than a man in his position had any right to expect, so let these dogs of Tehlitzim come on and he would meet them with his spear in their teeth.

The noise of iron ringing upon iron would soon bring others to see what was happening. But, in a caravan comprised of various unrelated traders from amongst the mixed-races of the Tehlitzim, there was no guarantee that those others would side with Dëfrim and Afrim for it was the Tehlitz way to fight for family, not for national loyalty or for fellow countrymen to whom they were not related by blood. So the swordsmen pressed on, believing that they had the advantage anyway for surely the older man must tire first, facing two adversaries. It did not occur to them that their opponent was not alone; that the combat was actually two against two. As so often, the brothers who had set themselves to steal the westerner's woman had viewed the saucy slut merely as the object of their carnal desire; the trophy to be won. Once the fighting had started they gave no further thought to the troublesome bitch. This was another sorry mistake.

Eiji had removed her dagger and girdle before joining her Effendi in bed, hiding her knife in one of her boots, but now she scurried around amongst the horses to recover it. Yet before she had retrieved her own weapon a better option came to mind. She had noticed the javelin that still hung sheathed from the saddle of her master's horse. Her dark eyes gleamed malevolently as she slid the forty-eight inch short-spear free of its holster.

Eiji had never thrown a javelin and was far too intelligent to try it for the first time now. She did not propose to waste the weapon by throwing it without technique or expertise. She had seen Ealdræd use the javelin to bring down game and so she knew it to be a tool requiring years of training. Adapting it to her needs, she simply held it point-first in front of her in both white-knuckled fists and, being in the rear of her two enemies and entirely out of their line of sight, she made ready to charge with it at the back of the Tehlitzim filth closest to her. Eiji drew in a lungful of air and opened her mouth to shout livid curses at the man she was about to kill, but quickly snapped her lips shut again to choke back the words. Satisfying though her battlecry was, this was an occasion for stealth. Exercising her new-found ability to resist the desire to scream verbal abuse at those who had earned her wrath, she padded forward on surreptitious feet, any sound she made completely masked by the clanging of sword against spear. Then, when she was within half a dozen paces of the bedouin, Eiji charged, sprinting at him in venomous silence, affording her prey no warning. He was taken totally unawares and knew nothing of her presence behind him until the iron spike of her javelin ripped into his body and tore through his spine. By then it was far too late for him to repair his error.

As Afrim shrieked in his death-terror, Dëfrlm looked aside for a fraction of a second to see what had become of his brother. It was his final mistake, for it was suicidal. The Aenglian's spear leapt forward as if the thing were alive and thudded into the thick bone of Dëfrim's chest, the iron point split the bone cleanly, and under the tremendous impetus with which it had been thrust the spear-blade drove straight onward through vital bodily organs to perforate the torso all the way through. His eyes rolled up in their sockets. The corpse fell dead like a stone. A yard away, his brother, mortally wounded, was writhing in his death-agonies like a bleeding pig that had been incorrectly butchered. The body shuddered as its nervous system collapsed and crashed, quivered and twitched momentarily, then lay still.

The lovers, Ealdræd and Eiji, smiled in grim satisfaction at each other across the wrecked remains of their adversaries. He nodded his pleasure and approval at her performance and the Menghis, suffused with a justified self-esteem, pulled back her shoulders and lifted her chin high as if to promise ruination to those who would presume violence against herself and her Effendi. Without pause Ealdræd recovered his javelin from where his woman had left it in the backbone of her foe, then he rapidly scooped up those of his possessions that were not already stowed away amongst the baggage on his horse, all the while admonishing Eiji not to be slow in following his example. She was carrying both of the swords dropped by their defeated enemies and she was grinning from ear to ear with joy at these proofs of their triumph. Eiji loved weaponry of all kinds and delighted in these new additions to their armoury. Ealdræd would not have bothered with the swords himself, having no need of them while he still had his spear, but he did not begrudge her the spoils of war. Eiji stepped into her boots and buckled on her girdle and dagger, then sprang up onto her horse.

The rest of the bedouin caravan were all roused now, carrying torches from the camp-fire to investigate the noise of battle. Figures dressed in *ghutrah* headscarves and ankle-length *thobes* gathered together, watching the two strangers mount their horses and depart. They watched with hostility and menace on their fire-lit countenances. Ealdræd made no attempt to explain the skirmish, knowing that issues of justice and self-defence would be irrelevant in determining what reaction the other Tehlitzim might have to the butchering of their fellows.

In a thunder of hooves the riders sallied forth for pastures new and they were apparently free and clear when a volley of arrows, five or six shafts together, suddenly hummed out of the night behind them. Now that the remaining members of the caravan felt safe from the danger of counter-attack they had found their martial ardour. One of the hideous missiles buried its barbed point four inches deep into horseflesh. This parting shot had delivered a ugly wound to the rear flank of Eiji's black gelding, not mortal perhaps, but sufficient to drop the animal. Girl and horse went down hard. The girl was up on her feet in a flash but her animal was not. It lay on its side, bellowing and neighing in its distress.

281

They had no time to try to force the brute back up on to its feet. More arrows came shafting out of the blackness behind them, zipping through the air, and more would follow whilst they remained within distance of arrowshot. Disregarding the gelding, Ealdræd ordered Eiji up on to Hengustir in a tone of voice that had her leaping like a gazelle. She had to abandon the pack of dainty perfumes and toiletries that she had looted from the Castle Lasinni in Piccoli but she held tight to her two newly acquired swords. Eiji was a woman whose priorities were always clear. In a trice the mighty blue-roan was galloping forward, his courage stronger than his fear of missing his footing in the dark, and the three survivors could bid goodbye to, and damnation upon, their inhospitable hosts.

*   *   *

By the time that the sun rose next morning Ealdræd and Eiji were four leagues closer to Phari and confident that there was no pursuit to their rear. They had lost their second horse but Ealdræd's massive warhorse, Hengustir, whom he had named after the fabled charger of the legendary giant Ffydon in the time before the Well of Mægen gave birth to the human race, was so powerful that Eiji's diminutive weight on his haunches made little difference to him. The girl rode with her arms holding her man around his narrow waist and her head snuggled up against him.

The beckoning seduction of the aroma of the ocean was carried to them on a stiff sea-breeze. It was the first time that Eiji had been anywhere near a sea, and although the ditch was hardly much for the Aenglian to get excited about the smell of the salt intrigued the oriental and she kept sniffing the air in an affected manner as if to comment on the strangeness of this foreign shore where even the air smelt different.

After a while they passed through the small town of Bindje where the strangeness was more repellent and more disturbing. It took the form of a Gathkaree male pulling a cart of offal and dung. The job of removing animal waste to the cess pit in a handcart was a task so disgusting that it had been made a penalty for a certain level of criminal offence. Instead of the punishment of imprisonment or of being set in the public stocks for civic revenge, miscreants were made to perform a sentence of service to the community in the form of the most dishonourable and degrading municipal employments.

282

Under the matriarchal hierarchy of values imposed upon the faithful, these humiliations were believed to be the humane option. Men all over the country were consigned to this fate. This wretched creature in Bindje was one such. Around his neck was hung a placard which announced his crime: insulting language to our honoured guests. He had spoken to a foreigner in a way that they had deemed to be discourteous or offensive. It was the most commonplace of crimes these days; almost every Gathkaree male fell foul of it sooner or later.

Neither Ealdræd nor Eiji could read in any language so they could only guess at what the arcane scribbling on the placard might portend, but what struck them both most forcefully was that the fellow was not chained to his cart, nor was anyone supervising his grotesquely filthy work. He performed his allotted task of his own volition, and willingly applied himself in a genuine desire to atone for his sin, believing himself to be guilty as charged and fully deserving of the treatment that he was required to suffer. He felt his own shameful guilt so keenly that, enslaved beast of burden that he was, he was also his own jailer.

The banal yet unanswerable reason for the way that the men of Gathkar tolerated and endorsed their own oppression was that their religious faith required them to; they were sincere believers in the absolute rule of the lunar goddess of *Mwanamke-mkuu,* as translated to this earthly dimension by the priestesses of Ertamis, the many-breasted. As men it was a necessary act of faith to surrender themselves to a social order which treated them as deficient because they were deviant from the female. They did not resent this but merely wished to feminise themselves as completely as possible so as to draw closer to the sublime divinity inherent in the feminine.

Ealdræd had once been told that near the geographical centre of Gathkar was a large and inexplicably mysterious body of water called *Gjarin*, the salt lake. The word *Gjarin* meant 'tears' and the lake was said by political dissidents who did not believe in the doctrines of *Mwanamke-mkuu* to be the repository of all the salt tears shed by the men of Gathkar since their fall from grace. It had seemed to Ealdræd when he heard this dissidents' fable that the Gathkarees should have shed tears of blood but that if they must weep a lake of water then they should have been quick to drown their matriarchal rulers in it. But now that he had returned to this benighted country it was painfully obvious to him that the men of

Gathkar were far too steeped in the self-contempt that consumed their ideologically-conditioned souls ever to rise up against the women who ruled them with this nonsensical mysticism. The web of cultural constraints that bound the men made it psychologically impossible for such subjugated beasts to stand up and answer back, or slit the throats of their oppressors.

It became increasingly apparent to Ealdræd as he and his companion continued on their way south that the political nightmare which he had witnessed on his previous visit more than a decade ago had gotten a great deal worse in the years since. It was difficult to credit that devotion to a religious doctrine could possibly cause anyone to permit themselves to be used in the manner in which the men of Gathkar were treated. Their lives were far worse even than those of slaves for at least a slave can hate his oppressor and dream of freedom, whereas the men of Gathkar were required by their ideology to be complicit in their own humiliation; to endorse and approve their own disgrace.

At a tavern in a small seaside village Ealdræd came upon a Vespaan mercenary archer called Konradt who had become almost as displaced and far from home as the Aenglian was. The Vespaan, a beefy fair-haired fellow of about thirty with a deep scar that ran laterally across his forehead, had been in this part of the world for some time, plying his trade with his beautifully crafted recurve bow, 70 inches of laminated yew and hickory, the flexible wood kept polished and free from scratches although the archer himself was rather dusty and threadbare. The two men, both professional soldiers for hire, were natural comrades despite the hostility that existed between their ethnic nations, and they conversed in Geulten all evening over tankards of the weak Gathkaree ale which was all that the inns and hostelries hereabouts could offer, with Eiji taking no part in the conversation but curled up cosily like a cat on the tavern bench with her head resting in her Effendi's lap listening to the peculiar words and sounds of the Geulten language.

Konradt was actually travelling up from the south where he had been treasure-seeking in the lands of the Buntuu; the tribal kingdoms of negro peoples that extend beyond the cartography of map-makers into unknown jungles. Konradt had spent the past year in the tribal lands between the Bayešić sea and the unscalable range of mountains called the Oghli Barrier, the highest peaks in the world, the Mountains of God that no man had ever climbed. He said that there were tribal chiefs down there who had extraordinary wealth in gold body ornamentations and jewellery. Konradt claimed to have met one who had golden teeth; that the fellow had lost his natural teeth and so had them replaced by evenly moulded little blocks of gold of the appropriate size and shape. But for all his talk of treasure, Konradt did not appear too prosperous himself at present. He was heading back home to the Fiefdom of Vespaan.

Konradt found the Gathkaree attitude to foreigners like himself a great joke. He had benefited from it many-a-time, he freely confessed. As honoured guests in Gathkar the ruling caste of matriarchs had never presumed to impose upon foreigners the cripplingly oppressive laws than imprisoned the lives of Gathkaree males. Consequently, foreigners could largely commit crimes with impunity; a political situation which had created a thriving Buntuu and Tehlitzim criminal class, characteristically arrogant and swaggering and well-used to violating the locals pretty much as it took their fancy with no fear of retribution. The imperious Ahkrani, of course, were worse still. For this reason, although the matriarchy brought in harsher and harsher penalties for wrongdoers, these seldom applied in practice because those who were committing the crimes were exempt.

Ealdræd asked Konradt if he knew what had become of the Gathkaree Assassins Guild, for some months ago in Wehnbria the Aenglian had found himself in combat with one of these professional murderers and the man had impressed him as a dauntless and accomplished fighter. He could not have been more different from the grovelling creatures inhabiting the queendoms. Surely capable men proficient in the fighting arts did not still live here and succumb to this indignity?

No, he was told by Konradt, the Gathkaree Assassins Guild had been banished from the country by the high-priestesses for being an order devoted solely to the male arts of war. The assassin's guild could have disregarded the command had they so wished, for there were none in Gathkar who could have enforced it. As it transpired, the assassins declared that Gathkar was no longer a country worthy of them and that, far from being banished, they would enter a voluntary exile to pursue their honourable vocation in other places in the wide world that were more fitting domains for an assassin to reside.

So that, thought Ealdræd, was how a black assassin had fetched up in Wehnbria. He remembered how astonished Mistress Bryony had been to see a man with a black skin. Her pretty face had been a picture. But that set his thoughts in a sad direction and he brought his mind back to the seaside hostelry and his insipid flagon of ale and his impressively scarred interlocutor. The feelings that Mistress Bryony had stirred in him during their time together had made her abiding memory an affectionate one. Ealdræd stroked the unwashed, unbrushed hair of the half-dozing Menghis girl whose head rested in his lap. She murmured sleepily. He rested his hand on the warmth of her belly and she curled her knees up tighter to trap the hand there.

Konradt had been in the tavern swilling beer since the morning, several hours before Ealdræd's arrival, and even Gathkaree ale had its effect eventually. When the drowsily mumbling Vespaan archer was too much the worse for drink to be informative Ealdræd lifted Eiji in his arms without waking her and carried her out to the tavern's stable where they bedded down for the night alongside his faithful Hengustir. The roan was the only horse in the stable so there was plenty of room, and it meant that man and horse could guard each other in their sleeping vigilance. The straw-strewn accommodation was safe and quite comfortable, if a trifle malodorous. They slept undisturbed.

Konradt was still snoring like a ox with bronchitis slumped over the table in the tavern when the powerful blue-roan conveyed Ealdræd and Eiji out of the village at daybreak. There were similar little townships all along the coast. The mercenary's recent financial fortunes had been so favourable that he carried enough gold and silver in his saddlebags to buy half a dozen of these villages outright, but no one would have guessed at this hidden wealth had they seen him passing by. He was far too wily an old bird to invite robbery by making it known that he had anything worth stealing. It was problematic enough to forestall attempts by various bandits and lusty lads who fancied their chances at stealing Eiji. If they'd suspected that he also had gold and silver, he would've got no peace.

The temptation that his oriental companion presented to men of a rapine disposition was to prove an irritation once again upon their arrival in Phari. The place was in an advanced state of pillage and plunder. So fractured and divided a country as Gathkar was inevitably subject to repeated bouts of civil tumult, and the city of Phari was in a maelstrom of spontaneous bouts of riot and disorder as the two foreigners on their magnificent grey stallion crept into town as clandestinely as they could manage given that all three, man, woman, and horse, were distinctly unusual in their physical appearance. Several portions of the city were aflame as a result of Murgl and Ahkrani insurgence. The rioters had stopped just short of an armed uprising but the city had the pungent flavour of mutinous insurrection and the stink of charred flesh in the smoke from the burning buildings suggested the fate of at least some of those who had been caught up in the havoc of revolt.

Ealdræd had hoped to make it to the docks unnoticed by any of those merrily disobedient honoured guests who were cheerfully taking such liberties with their hosts' property. But to reach the quayside he had to pass through the harbour square and it was there that they came across a Gathkaree male in the public stocks being spat upon by a crowd of Ahkrani soldiers, all of them laughing like hyenas. The notice board on the stocks proclaimed his crime: causing offence to our honoured guests. With a chilling significance, it was written in Ahkrani, although Ealdræd's illiteracy meant that the significance was lost on him. The imprisoned creature in the stocks was continually apologising to his tormentors for having perpetrated so unforgivable an offence and repeatedly expressed his gratitude to them for helping him to do penance by spitting upon him. The speech that he recited was a formally prepared one handed down by the judge at his trial during sentencing as, in her learned opinion, it was an appropriate and important adjunct to his punishment. Confession was good for the soul. The jeering, spitting crowd of Ahkrani fighting men were only too pleased to assist the sycophantic Gathkaree to debase and defile himself in his utterly gratuitous remorse.

These military Ahkrani were very typical of their kind in costume and deportment. They wore the crimson and yellow-ochre turbans that were an identifying feature of Ahkrani, especially of their military; crimson and yellow-ochre being their national colours. Their tunics were the three-quarter length kaftan coats, made in silk for the officers and in cotton for the ordinary soldiers, buttoned down the front to the waist, with full and often embroidered sleeves. They favoured puffed out pantaloon breeches above the knee which were tucked smartly into puttee gaiters below the knee. The *shafra* knife, found on the belt of every Ahkrani male over the age of puberty, had a distinctive, down-curving double-edged blade that was between six and nine inches long and usually engraved with a family name or crest. The customary mode of barbering amongst the Ahkrani featured very long and drooping moustaches, frequently hanging lower than their chins, combined with much shorter, tufty beards. This, more than any other physical feature, set them apart from the clean-shaven Gathkaree locals, quite as much as did Ealdræd's own shoulder length braided hair and long braided beard.

Like many of their crimson and yellow-ochre kindred prowling the streets of Phari, these Ahkrani who were so amused by the indignities being heaped upon one of their hosts imprisoned in the stocks wore a splash of purple dye in their shrub-like beards which signified that they had completed the Ahkrani test of manly virtue, the trial of the *çorak atık*. This ordeal took its name from the desert that separated Ahkran Major from Ahkran Minor. Purple dye in a man's beard meant that he had crossed the *çorak atık* or 'barren waste' on foot. The distance was two hundred miles, north to south, if you kept to a direct line as the crow flies. Not that crows or any other birds flew over the *çorak atık*. There was nothing to eat in that scorched earth for nothing could live in the heat. A great many young Ahkrani bucks made the attempt to walk across every year, weighed down with large water bottles and joking to their friends about how once they had trekked the length of the arid wilderness under the boiling sun they would immediately turn around and run back. But they knew that the long walk across the barren waste was not really a joking matter. Those able to toe a straight line for two hundred miles mostly lived through the trial but about one in every five didn't survive it because they strayed to east or to west and the *çorak atık* was five hundred miles of death from side to side.

Almost all of the mob around the stocks wore the purple and the contempt that such men of proven worth felt for the mewling, self-effacing poltroons of Gathkarees was a tangible odour of violent disgust that hung in the air like the blade of a guillotine.

"These are not guests," murmured Ealdræd to himself, "When the landlord gives away his dwelling to the lodger, the guest has become the owner and the dispossessed is but a servant in what was once his own house."

Eiji gave the Aenglian a pained look as if to say can we please leave at once. She found it very hard to endure the burden of having to witness so intense a level of craven cowardice and self-abasement. She had fallen into the habit of referring to the wretched Gathkaree men as *dikebiri*, the castrated. Her opinion of them was, if anything, even lower than the derisive hatred that the Ahkrani felt for them. Under Eiji's code of conduct, any man who permitted others to

288

express scorn toward him and did nothing to revenge himself should commit suicide as soon as possible. Women, too. For any person to remain alive under the taunts of disdain and ridicule was a fate worse than death. Throughout her own long months of agony as the slave of the Khevnics she would have ended herself in an instant if she had ever had a single opportunity to do so. Life without dignity should not be lived. Eiji shook her head in wonder that there could be men anywhere upon the earth who would bear to tolerate the insolent mockery of others when it would be so much easier just to kill their enemies or to kill themselves. But then Eiji knew nothing of the religious policies that ruled in matriarchal Gathkar, nor would she have been able to make any sense of such an ideology if it had been explained to her.

The outlandish-looking couple on the enormous roan horse had moved some way off from the scene at the stocks and had reached the other side of the harbour square when a lively shout of delighted discovery told them that Eiji had been noticed. In a trice, four uniformed members of the group of Ahkrani soldiers were sauntering over towards the odd pair with the undoubted intention of accosting them. The Ahkrani soldiery felt themselves kings in this land of inferiors and why shouldn't they filch the sexily exotic oriental wench if they took a fancy to her?

For all their wine-soaked good humour Ealdræd did not mistake the very real danger they represented. It was a situation that called for delicate judgement. If he were to kill quickly and decisively those four who were even now approaching, would their comrades-in-arms by the stocks run to support them or hold back, dissuaded by the threat to their own life and limb? It was a gamble which he calculated had to be taken. If the four drunkards got close enough to lay hands upon the girl the fight would *not* be immediately decisive, and a skirmish *would* encourage their comrades-in-arms to take a hand in the matter, he felt sure. Only a devastating lethality would suffice; a shocking demonstration of human mortality that would stop them in their tracks.

Ealdræd slid down off Hengustir and demanded one of the Tehlitzim swords from Eiji. She placed it in his hand so instantaneously that she might have read his mind. He told her in Ehngleish to remain in the saddle and only her profound respect for him enabled her to comply. It was not her way to sit idle when her loved ones were in jeopardy. As he turned to confront the threat presented by the four soldiers he did not grip the sword in the normal way but drew it back as if it were a javelin. And in just that way he threw it.

The man who was his target had no more anticipated such a tactic that he had imagined that the big horse might sprout wings and fly away. Nor did he have the least idea of what a spearman of the Pæga, that clan of Aenglians into which Ealdræd had been born and the heritage of which flowed with the blood in his veins, could do with a thrown missile. Despite the curve in the sword it flew straight and true, the briefest of silver flashes over the distance between the spearman and his target, before burying itself almost to the hilt in the Ahkrani's stomach with a frighteningly disembowelling impact.

Consternation and outrage erupted amongst the other three and behind them a few heads turned to see what was happening on the other side of the square. The reaction of the remaining three was predictable; their indignation and desire for revenge would make them rush forward at a sprint. But Ealdræd already had the second sword poised at his shoulder and then it was loosed, blinding as a bowshot, and incredibly a second man lay dead with a sword delivered through his body from a range of forty feet.

The laughing, jeering mob over by the stocks were silenced as if all their vocal chords had been severed with a single cut of a knife. That an individual man could rally so terminal a defence sent its message loud and clear. To approach this man was death. How many more swords did he have in his armoury to kill his enemies before they could get within a dozen yards of him?

Disloyally leaving the two Ahkrani who had been slain lying where they had fallen, the other pair withdrew to their regimental compatriots, judging wisely that the admittedly very tempting erotic appeal of the slant-eyed young woman was none the less insufficient to take the risk of dying for. Ealdræd had won his wager. Eiji was sorry to lose her lovely new swords but Ealdræd was glad to be rid of them. The sword was not his weapon of choice. All the same, it had turned out to be a lucky thing that Eiji had kept them.

The chastened Ahkrani soldiers, very conscious of their dishonour in retreating from the affray, vented their spleen by giving the Gathkaree in the stocks a good beating with their fists, but they declined to pursue the murderous westerner and his siren temptress. For the second time in a week Ealdræd and Eiji had killed honoured guests, transgressing the law and storing up even

290

more cause to leave this defeated country as soon as possible. But in the middle of so much indolent anarchy and idle pandemonium, it seemed likely that their small contribution to the general turmoil would pass unnoticed.

They hurried on to the docks but there only disappointment awaited them. The sooner they sailed for Langelais the better they both would like it and a sail might have been had for the asking in other circumstances. But not today. There was a three-mast ship and a dozen fair-sized boats tied up at the quays, bobbing on the tide alongside a small flotilla of fishing sloops. All of them were burning fiercely. The ship and every last boat in the little fleet of the harbour of Phari had been torched for fun or devilment and they would blaze until they had sunk so far into the sea that the water doused the fire. A rabble of arsonists and their supporters were making merry on the dockside, toasting their own valour as the huge sails of the ship were enveloped in sheets of crackling flame and the smaller vessels burnt like tinder.

There was nothing else for it. Ealdræd and Eiji must take up the road again and travel further south, placing their hopes on Porta Aberta. If things were as bad there, the Aenglian would have no choice but to abandon his plan to sail to the Barony and reverse his horse's steps back to Piccoli and the chance of a mad dash across Bhourgbon. For the only other craft on these waters on which he might buy passage over the ditch were the tiny flat-hull rafts used by the rod-and-line fishermen and they would obviously not be large enough to accommodate Hengustir on board. A more substantial craft was needed and if he did not find it in Porta Aberta, he would find it nowhere. He cursed this surrendered nation of priestesses and madmen who laid themselves in humility at the feet of any foreigner who wished to spurn them like a cur with his heel.

*   *   *

Back in the days of the Gathkar Republic the great harbour on their western seaboard had been known as *Chave Na Porta*, which meant 'the key in the door', but after the revolution the rulers of the queendoms had renamed it *Porta Aberta*, which meant the 'open door' and it had lived up to its new name, exceedingly to its detriment. Once a major maritime city, it was now so totally overrun with presumptuous Ahkrani that it could more properly be considered a colony of imperial Ahkran; as a portion of the dominion of Sultan Asiz Faizul whose soldiers continued to move casually north up through the southern regions of the queendoms without a blow ever being struck in the defence of once proud Gathkar.

Ealdræd had bought two *andar capas*, cloaks for riding, during their progress down the coast, making sure not to buy them in the Gathkaree style but in the more popular Tehlitzim fashion. He did not want to be mistaken for a Gathkaree. Wrapped in these he and Eiji made their still less than inconspicuous way toward the harbour. Around them the city was awash with crimson and yellow-ochre due to the vast number of Ahkrani military who were in residence. So large a martial force had no legitimate business in Porta Aberta but who amongst the government officials would challenge their right to be there? Sultan Asiz Faizul, their liege lord, frequently sent regiments and even brigades of his troops on manoeuvres in Gathkar, treating the territory as already being little more than an extension to his own realm, ripe for usurpation.

Even the Gathkaree ruling caste in Porta Aberta had been unable to shield their hypocrites' eyes from the reality of the situation outside their temple walls. Unrest and disorder were everywhere in the streets as looting and pillaging went unpunished. The city tottered on the brink of riot. Accordingly, the high-priestesses had determined to take the firmest and most resolute measures to quell the growing anarchy; they had called a conclave of the entire coven of priestesses, all three hundred and thirty-three of them, to sing to the goddess for salvation. They would perform the enchantment of *livramento útero*, the womb deliverance, to beg Ertamis for a cessation of conflict, the end of masculine aggression, and a restoration of maternal harmony in hallowed feminine wisdom.

Presiding over this mystic hex-craft the high-priestesses of the temple sat enthroned in the enormous chamber called the Palace of Love and Adoration. At one side of this devotional hall the elders amongst the priestesses played flutes and struck drums and shook bells. Around the other three walls the sisters stood and chanted, singing their mantras and incantations in the charm of conjuring, whilst across the floor the young novices danced, skipping and leaping in a ballet that had been choreographed to emphasise the physicality of the female. They rolled their breasts and revolved their backsides and pumped their hips forward in appeal to the goddess to acknowledge their gender-kinship with her. They swooped and spun around, their pink gossamer veils trailing out behind them, as they fluttered their arms and perched on tip-toe and bowed before Ertamis, evoking the magic of the *livramento útero* so that the milky fruit of the sacred sorcery would come.

All day and all night and into the next day they played their music and sang their incantations and danced their adoration in the devout belief that no violence of the male temperament could possibly withstand the pure ascendancy of moral womanhood under the lunar divinity of the many-breasted and the unassailable rectitude of *Mwanamke-mkuu,* the Supreme Woman.

At the time when Ealdræd and Eiji arrived in the city, the temple coven of Porta Aberta had been praying and performing their rite of womb deliverance continuously for thirty-six hours. Every hour on the hour a humble male functionary appeared at the doorway of the outer temple to announce to an oblivious citizenry that the entreaties of the faithful were raised to the most holy on their behalf, whereupon he would appeal for public calm and beg for a restoration of the rule of law. This benign conjurement of the matriarchs was the only succour to which the citizens of the harbour city might look for their relief.

In the incident subsequently referred to by the Gathkarees as 'the tragedy of the denunciation and censure of souls' it was this lowly functionary making the announcement at the door of the outer temple who was the first to die.

The triangular edifice of the Temple of Ertamis was the tallest, broadest, and most impressive building in the city, as was only right and proper. This four-sided pyramid, square at its base, was built of slabs of stone that took four dozen men to haul into place with rope and tackle. Its architecture facilitated a series of chambers on different levels inside the building so that as a woman moved inward toward the centre she also climbed up from the lower to the higher levels. This reflected the hierarchy of *Mwanamke-mkuu.*

The top and most central level was the vast Palace of Love and Adoration where the goddess herself was reverenced in supplication. One level down was the softly echoing Chamber of Solicitude where all three hundred and thirty-three priestesses lived and loved in peaceful and obedient communion. A single long dormitory entirely surrounded the Chamber of Solicitude that was encircled within it, with numerous entrances on all four sides. These two levels combined constituted the Inner Temple, consecrated to the female and never to be despoiled by the presence of the male. Lower than that was the Outer Temple which was mostly given over to the Chamber of Preparations where the male acolytes worked at all the domestic services that were needful, not least keeping the fires of the boilers steaming in order to heat the stone chambers above where the priestesses performed their ceremonials effectively nude. The boilers provided an under-floor source of heating that kept the chambers of the Inner Temple overhead at a very comfortable temperature even for those who wore no garment but the priestess' veil, although the sweltering boiler-room itself was like the very living inferno of hell for the sweat-drenched and skeletal men who toiled there.

From the outside the gigantic geometric structure looked like it had descended from the skies from another more knowledgeable dimension of existence, which was exactly how it was supposed to look. The functionary at the main entrance was on duty with four guards, all male Gathkarees, who stood to attention without weapons. Each of the entrances on all sides of the pyramid had a similar affectation of four unarmed guards.

The functionary was a tall man in a pristine white gown, physically gaunt and full of gravitas, with a voice that boomed so resonantly that it put people in mind of some prophet of past ages. Thus far his hourly requests for civil harmony had fallen somewhat distressingly upon deaf ears but now the area around the temple seemed to be filling up very rapidly with a boisterous and undisciplined throng of Ahkrani soldiery. A surly and disquiet bunch, they had brought amphoras of wine and goatskins of beer with them, the strong stuff imported from the south, and they drained off the heady brew in quantity. They showed no decorum or concern for social etiquette despite being in the vicinity of the holy temple. In fact some few relieved themselves against it, quaffing their beer and pissing against the sacred stones.

A Gathkaree accused of desecrating the temple in this manner would most certainly be sent to the crab-pits, the form of capital punishment favoured in Gathkar because it was believed not to involve an executioner and would therefore not stain the soul of anyone but the guilty man. The accused who had been condemned to the crab-pits was staked out naked in a pit of giant crabs to be eaten alive, and it was commonly the case that as much as a third of his total body weight might be devoured by the crabs before the man in the pit finally stopped screaming and died. This usually took about four hours. As a capital sentence this also had the virtue of being ecologically sound. But, naturally, only men who were not honoured guests suffered this punishment.

Increasingly, the Ahkrani numbers around the temple grew until their congregation took on a feeling of menace. Unsupervised by their officers, the Ahkrani horde had the scent of hostility in its nostrils. The rowdy multitude was transforming into a brawling beast, and like all crowds it had a dynamic of its own. Some co-ordinated organisation was at work because the gathering of hundreds of men was swelled by hundreds more, until over a thousand had assembled, and before long their sheer weight of numbers became intimidating. Why were they here? the functionary wondered anxiously and the guards beside him palpitated in fear. Although they were commissioned to guard the temple, as mere Gathkarees these men would not have felt that they could presume to interfere with, or lay supercilious hands upon, honoured Ahkrani guests.

A shiver of anticipation swept through the mob. The regimental sergeants, the çavuş, came to the front of their surly comrades and this brought the whole motley crew into a sense of common purpose for, like a flock of birds changing direction in flight, they suddenly stalked up to the gate with the clear intention of entering. Their goal in doing so, whether plunder or whatever else, was irrelevant to the impiety inherent in the act; it would be a sacrilegious intrusion for them to enter the temple for any reason. The functionary stood frozen in shock, opened his mouth as if to speak but both he and the guards were brushed aside. Then they were knocked down and the soldiers began kicking them about for sport. Flesh was torn, blood was spilt, bones were broken, lives were taken. At all four gates the men on guard were beaten to death as the whole multitude poured into the temple like bees into a hive.

The political ascendancy of the priestesses of Ertamis had never been confronted with the reality of unbridled violence. Although their public pronouncements on the subject could have filled a library, indeed it had filled more than one, they had no real understanding of violence at all. The ideological compliance of their menfolk had occurred incrementally so that outright rebellion had been circumvented. But this slow incremental control of attitudes and beliefs had not taken place with their honoured guests. These foreigners brought a fresh and uncontaminated perspective to their evaluation of matriarchy.

The real butchery began as the first Ahkrani soldiers came together in the Chamber of Preparations with the Gathkaree male acolytes who fled in terror at the unspeakability, the unthinkability of what was happening but whose escape merely led them into the arms of more Ahkrani who were filling the Outer Temple from all sides and blocking all exits. Running futilely in blind panic, the Gathkarees were hewn down and cut to pieces.

A shrill feminine screaming erupted as the blood-splattered crowd of soldiers discharged itself through the various doorways into the Chamber of Solicitude of the Inner Temple. Most of the priestesses never left the temple and had no personal experience of men. They viewed males solely in terms of the received wisdom of the religious dogmas in their sacred texts. Consequently, to them men were sub-human brutes that instilled an extreme horror and repugnance in any priestess who permitted her thoughts to stray onto unholy things. The sight of moustached and bearded Ahkrani in their crimson and yellow-ochre, their *shafra* knives drawn and gleaming, running into this sanctum of female sublimity in direct violation of the consecrated and the sanctified was to these women a vision of the end of the world. This was Armageddon visited upon the earth. Fleeing inwards deeper into the temple, they retreated in squealing terror into the Palace of Love and Adoration, finding it inconceivable that the intruders would dare to follow them into this vessel of the Supreme Woman. Surely no creature, no matter how degenerate and decadent, could possibly be so vile as to break so imperishable a taboo?

The coven of priestesses already within the palace, after thirty-six hours of continual song in their pious petition to the almighty, were in a condition of total exhaustion. The dancing novices were near to fainting with fatigue. Initially they could make nothing of the noisy influx of their sisters wailing in such extreme distress and fear. Then, beyond the startled terrified women, they saw the defilement of their temple by the presence of those that the blessed lunar goddess had decreed were unworthy.

The Ahkrani had always heard that the priestesses of Ertamis worshipped naked except for a veil and now as they romped eagerly into one of the temples of this bizarre cult of matriarchy they discovered that it was true. More than three hundred fancies from the youthful novices not yet out of their teens to the haughty elders who had spent half a century within these walls, all were resplendently female as any with eyes could see.

296

The priestesses who had dashed in from the Chamber of Solicitude ran up the wide terraced steps to seek refuge amongst their sisters and all drew back on the Alter of the Womb of Ertamis, as far away as they could get from this unimaginable onslaught from the foulness of the world outside. The men prowled forward like a pack of wolves, the leering lechery on their hawk faces matched only by the muscular contractions in their hands and forearms as they seemed to rehearse what they about to do.

One of the high-priestesses took command of her frantic juniors, calming their unseemly comportment with the firm tone of one who was long accustomed to command. She was a woman of fifty, her grey hair turning to silver beneath the transparent pink gossamer veil, the slimness of her figure reflecting the ascetic life of the spiritually dedicated adept who lives on one bowl of rice each day and spends all of her time praying, dancing, and kneeling in worship in the temple. She felt no embarrassment at standing nude, looking down at the gang of libidinous men swarming around the lower tiers of the sacred steps, and she made no attempt to conceal her nudity. This was because, to her, it was much the same as being naked in the presence of a dog or a cat; some inferior species. These males were not fully human as the high-priestess understood the concept. One did not feel ashamed of being naked before the eyes of an animal. That mere men should see the breasts and vagina that in the high-priestess' virginal life no male had ever seen before was, of course, an immutable sin. Yet it was but the external show of the more serious sin of the transgression of soul that had been committed this day.

The high-priestess positioned herself on the topmost step that led to the alter and fixed her implacable gaze upon those who had profaned her faith by their crass intrusion. She lifted up her arms in a plea for silence and such was her air of authority that the raucous mob of soldiers became hushed for a moment. She reminded herself that these were honoured guests who perhaps had failed to comprehend the sacrilege of their own actions. This catastrophe was surely the fault of the Gathkaree males who had been placed on guard at the temple doors and who had been unforgivably derelict in their duty; yes, they were the ones to blame and they would answer for it by being put to death in the crab-pits. The high-priestess was strong in her faith. With all the nurturant majesty at her command she proclaimed:

"Honoured guests, we have always respected and celebrated your culture and welcomed you to share in the rich benefits of our society. Always we have esteemed you most highly. Why do you desecrate our most sacred beliefs and values by this violation of our consecrated ground? Will you not withdraw and commit no further profanity against us?"

A lean vulture of a man with a nose like a pelican's beak and a moustache that hung down almost to his chest stood truculently to the fore of his fellows. There was a smear of gore over the embroidered sleeve of his kaftan. He it was who answered. With a cackling laugh he said:

"Woman, you have mistaken us for your cockless dregs of Gathkarees, but we," and he punched the air with his fist as he declared it, ". . . we are the Ahkrani!"

At this there was a cataclysmic boastful roar from the thousand or more men at his back and they rushed up the steps to the alter to take possession of the prayer-weakened and foolishly self-deceiving women like the invading marauders that they had always been. The trapped priestesses were surrounded by a force that outnumbered them three times over, and the odds were about to get worse. The *shafra* knives flashed and blood spurted as the Ahkrani dispensed with the elderly and the unattractive women, scorning to profane the sanctity of their cocks on females that were undeserving of fucking.

The Palace of Love and Adoration became an abattoir, a charnel house of death. The forlorn begging of the priestesses as they were stabbed and ripped from abdomen to ribcage by the razor-sharp *shafra* blades mixed with the euphoric baritone laughter of the Sultan's elite in a cacophony of human monstrosity. Many of those devoted to Ertamis flung themselves across the alter only to be dragged back under the knives. Fully half of the sisters were deemed to be unworthy of the status of rape-slaves and were hacked apart, all three high-priestesses among them.

The murders accomplished, the ravishments began. The cult of *Mwanamke-mkuu* had always insisted that rape was a fate worse than death. The Ahkrani, who were not of this opinion, none the less seemed determined to prove the maxim true. That night one hundred and fifty priestesses of the coven of the city of Porta Aberta were slaughtered under the *shafra* knives and equally as many were brutally and repeatedly raped by over one thousand mostly drunken

Ahkrani soldiers from the Sultan's own personal brigade. All the priestesses were virgins but as the Ahkrani were notorious sodomites, their victims were ravished anally as frequently as vaginally. Some of the priestesses were torn open by the savagery and depth of the sodomy they suffered. There were nine or ten men to each woman and the females were subjected to the roughest of handling, as they were made to serve over and over again the carnal desires of those who did not adhere to a belief in the Superior Woman.

The broken and wretched priestesses were then whipped out of their temple, now a sepulchre of matriarchy and a tomb for its clergy, to be thrown upon the tender mercies of around four hundred Murgl, Tehlitzim, and Buntuu bandits who had heard of what was afoot at the Temple of Ertamis and had hurried along there themselves, keen to join in with a mass rape of the priestesses of the lunar goddess who were heartily loathed by their honoured guests for the unforgivable insult to manhood that was the essence of their doctrine. The screeching, weeping, bawling women stumbled out under the lashing from their despoilers into the arms of others of a similar bent.

A few Gathkaree men were so aghast at the horror that they actually sought to rally their courage and protest against this treatment of the holy sisters. They pleaded for mercy and reminded their honoured guests that the female is superior to the male and that a male's honour consists in his humble recognition of . . . . But they had been pummelled to the ground almost before these words had been uttered. And before the absurd protesters were stomped to death under the heels of their guests, those stout-hearted Buntuu and Murgl and Tehlitzim fellows decided to strip the Gathkaree men to see just what they had between their legs.

*   *   *

The sun was shining, the wind was brisk, and the morning had a sharp, clean feel to it that gave a man the optimistic impression that life was worth living and that much of value could be achieved with a little necessary effort. The weather was ideal for sailing and the mercenary spearman, Ealdræd of the Pæga was refusing to permit the contrariness of the Gathkaree boatman to spoil his good mood. The veteran had found his boat, a forty foot fishing sloop with a reinforced hull, oddly named *Refúgio*, that was sturdy enough to let Hengustir stand in its centre without capsizing the craft. They might have herded three or four horses of ordinary size into the sloop and Ealdræd was confident that the warhorse would be safe aboard.

The boatman would take them no further than the port of Citadelle in the Barony of Langelais but that was all that Ealdræd would ask of him; just to be rid of Gathkar, even if it meant being in Geulten and therefore enemy territory. Along with Forteresse, Citadelle was one of two heavily fortified buccaneer strongholds that sent ships forth to raid and plunder for the 'sea-barons' of Langelais, a fiefdom that relied heavily on lawfully-sanctioned piracy for its wealth. The Barony had its own ways of doing things which had ensured that they had taken no part in the recent Battle of Proctors Wæl against the Ehngle. The Aenglian was not worried that the sailors of Langelais would refuse him passage on a ship sailing west, not when he had gold in his purse.

No, the only problem was that this Gathkaree boatman had no official permission to take to sea. There had been gross disorder during the night, some crime of terrible enormity had taken place, and the political administration of Porta Aberta was suffering a form of paralysis. Very few administrators had shown up for work this morning and their offices were closed. The Aenglian had heard something of what had happened from the gossip in the streets about an attack upon the temple of Ertamis. He'd overheard two Bhourgbon wool merchants giggling over the news that all the priestesses had been murdered or raped, and the temple burned to the ground. Now all the Buntuu and the Murgl and the Tehlitzim in the city were bragging that they would do as much to every temple in Gathkar and the Ahkrani military were mobilising to formally annex the country into their empire. But Ealdræd cared nothing for any of that. What he cared about was getting under sail while the wind was high. The boatman, however, could do nothing without the correct bureaucrat's wax-seal on the correct piece of parchment.

Rather than argue the point, Ealdræd cuffed and buffeted the boatman around the head to drive him back into the fishing sloop, the Gathkaree all the while apologising but explaining that it was strictly forbidden to sail without his being authorised to do so. Ealdræd kicked the toady on board and demanded that he get underway at once. The meaty fist that the mercenary waved under the boatman's nose was a sufficiently convincing argument. The flustered, whining creature began untying the quay ropes and raising the main mast sail aft. With the big mercenary standing over him, he quickly got the sloop moving. But still he sought to remonstrate that they must go back for authorisation. He was not upset at being manhandled, nor at the commandeering of his boat; but he was distraught that they were sailing without official sanction.

Eiji, whose nerves were a little frayed at having to undertake her first ever sea-voyage in her nineteen years of life, a daunting prospect, found the boatman's feebleness to be the final straw. She was no longer able to restrain her outrage and temper. She had held her tongue as her Effendi had commanded all through this country of lunatics, and she had continued to keep her peace even despite the fact that her silence in the camp of the Tehlitzim merchants had not prevented their being attacked by those traders at the cost of her beautiful black horse whom she missed as she would miss a brother. Even though this attack proved that holding her tongue did not stop thieves and rogues and other vermin from attempting to rape a poor Menghis girl and kill her master, none the less her tongue had been held because her Effendi had wished that it be so.

But this wheedling coward of a fisherman was more than a daughter of the steppes could stand. Eiji was incandescent with frustrated wrath. She poured the vitriol of her foulest language down upon the bowed head of the penitent Gathkaree in a ceaseless torrent of indignant ferocity that was unusually obscene even by her own high standards of abusive swearing. Hardly stopping to breathe she lashed him with a tirade of insulting invective that she had been bursting to release since they had ridden though Phari. The remorseful fisherman could understand not a word of this string of ripe and fruity Menghali name-calling but, knowing himself to be inferior in both sex and ethnicity to a woman who was so obviously foreign, his religious beliefs meant that he was in a position to do nothing but accept her scolding admonitions as justified and righteous.

When the teenage Menghis, red in the face and shaking her little fists at him and at the whole of his cursed country, finally ran out of her extensive catalogue of rebukes, recriminations, reprimands and reproaches she threw her head back and shouted to the heavens to sweep these blasphemous female-worshipping Gathkarees from the face of the earth. Then she spat juicily onto the top of the man's bowed head, and stared at him with murderous intent as the fishing boat slowly pulled out to sea.

Chapter 8

A Scattering Upon the Sea

Guy Hélon had never seen oriental eyelids before today and at first impression he had found them intriguingly attractive and beguiling. But now as they glared malevolently down upon him from a range of twenty inches, he had occasion to revise his earlier opinion, repent his having acted upon it, and think that perhaps he had been over hasty in both his opinion and in his attempt to discover more about the personality that lay behind those eyes. Guy was, at second thought, inclined to believe that her disposition was as hostile and vicious as her hand was swift and sure in planting the point of a dagger at his throat. Finding himself forced back against the stones of the tavern wall by the pressure of the sharp iron against his windpipe he held very still. As he tried to focus his vision upon the disconcertingly lethal weapon he noticed, with something more than academic interest, that it had a nastily serrated edge to its blade and a falcon-head pommel on its hilt.

It was common enough for a man's life to be threatened in the waterfront quarter of Citadelle with its labyrinth of ramshackle low-level slums, dumps and dens, yet still Guy had allowed himself to be taken unprepared, as a man will when he makes assumptions about people. He had expected to meet only intoxicating eroticism from those bewitchingly feline eyes, not sudden razor-sharp hazard, and his disoriented mind feverishly wondered how he had gotten himself into this potentially deadly situation.

Guy had spent his youth in Poitil, the capital city of Bhourgbon, until an unfortunate encounter with the city guard during the hours of darkness on the premises of a pawnshop where Guy's presence could claim no legal entitlement had caused his exodus from the capital dressed as a washerwoman. Fleeing to the relatively independent adjacent state of Langelais, he had eventually ended up in the huge bustling port of Citadelle where he had passed the last five years working as a stevedore on the docks. The harbour city was a messy, sprawling place that prospered by trade both legal and illegal, which offered opportunity to a well set-up lad like Guy Hélon. The maritime merchants of Langelais would take a profit wherever they could find it and their peacock pride at being the feared and notorious pirates of the Geulten nations did not mean that they would sniff and turn up their long noses at an honest and legal commission. They boasted of their outlaw exploits of brigandage but they would happily take the money from a lawful job of work, too.

Guy liked to spend his evenings in the various public houses of that part of the waterfront known locally as *bordel quais*, the brothel quays, where a working man might fill his belly with a passable meal in accordance with his purse, wash it down with a heady beverage or two that might dull the pain of the day and ease his night-time's slumbers, and even rent a trollop for twenty minutes if his coin would stretch to it.

Tonight the Bhourgbon stevedore's patronage had been bestowed upon an inn called the *Côtelette de Mouton*, the Mutton Chop tavern, and it was here that he had noticed the woman with the uniquely exotic countenance. Amid the assembled motley of sailors, harlots, artisans, derelicts and drunks that comprised the usual clientele of the Mutton Chop there were always a parcel of strangers, for this was a seaport town and many folk were in transit. But none like her. Alien languages and foreign attire were things any citizen of Citadelle was accustomed to and about which they were nonchalantly blasé, but not quite as alien as this little miss. For several minutes he had sat contemplating her and her companion, a gruff soldierly looking type with a weatherbeaten face under a hooded mantle of soft leather that had been pulled back off his head to disclose a simple four-plate iron pot basin helmet. It fitted so comfortably that it looked like he had been born wearing it. All around the couple was the loud, raucous hubbub of the alehouse but they seemed strangely separate from it all in their own intangible cocoon of intimacy. They displayed no interest in anyone else in the tavern and, remarkably in the circumstances, no one else appeared to show any interest in them.

She was covered from neck to foot by a long riding cloak that Guy thought was probably Tehlitzim or possibly Piccolian. But the woman herself most certainly was not a native of either of those countries; she was from much further east. Her hair was entirely covered by her coif over which she wore a torse tied under the chin by a barbette in the Langelais fashion. The old man she was ensconced with, the pair of them curled up close together on the corner bench, was similarly cloaked and whilst he was big in the shoulders and upright in carriage he did not, in Guy's ill-judged estimation, present too great a threat to a much younger man of good Bhourgbon stock who honed his muscles daily as a stevedore. There was grey in the old fellow's hair and beard, which he wore loose and unbarbered. He was no more Tehlitzim or Piccolian than was the girl, although in his case he was a westerner. Guy wondered how far west. Ehngleish perchance?

This idea brought a slow lazy smile to the Bhourgbon's slyly handsome features. If the grandpa was a man of the Ehngle, he would find no friends in Langelais or any of the Geulten territories. The defeat the previous summer of the Oénjil army and their Geulten allies under the Duke Etienne en Dieu by the coalition Ehngle army under the Eorls of Wehnbria had starkly heightened the perennial antagonism between the two races. Citadelle itself was in ferment over the preparations for the Geulten riposte later this year when the weather improved, so if the fellow was a Heurtslin, Sæxyn, Aenglian or of any other Ehngle nation he would likely be taken for a spy if any undue public attention were drawn toward him here in the Barony. And how could it not be? It would be difficult to avoid being noticed when he was accompanied by an oriental from the spice-scented semi-mythical lands of talking monkeys, and goat-headed men.

It was long past the bell for the second dog-watch and the seafaring community was partaking of its meal before bed. The close proximity of so many unwashed bodies, many of them achingly at rest after a long day's labour, meant that it was hot and steamy in the Mutton Chop and once or twice the girl opened her cloak a little at the front to let the heat out and to fan herself with the edges of the garment. When she did so Guy Hélon had a momentary glimpse of the firm swell of her breasts as they pushed out under the thin linen of a bright green Tehlitz smock that reached no further than halfway down her naked thighs. So scanty was her clothing that it was completely at odds with her wearing of the demure coif and torse. With the cloak fastened she looked perfectly respectable but with the outer layer flapping open she was exposed as a flighty little strumpet. Guy had laid his carnal gaze with appetising pleasure upon the somewhat waif-like yet sturdily built creature whose only other attire was a tight girdle from which hung a dagger in a cheap ornamented scabbard and a pair of ewe-leather boots that she wore without strapping so that the leather drooped slack and baggy around her ankles. The Bhourgbon swore softly to himself that she was worth half a dozen of the ordinary whores of the *bordel quais* and his imagination caught fire with an improbable hotchpotch of speculations and conjectures as to the catalogue of debauched sexual techniques, unknown to western women, in which she had doubtless been trained from an early age.

After his fourth flagon of *sang de bœuf*, a local concoction of rum and ale which was popularly believed to be strengthening and had therefore been given the heroic name of 'ox-blood', the self-assurance of the bold Guy Hélon had reached the point where thought gave way to action. Elbowing his way over to where the slant-eyed minx and her elderly escort were sat, the two of them still paying no heed to anyone but each other, the Bhourgbon plumped his backside down on the bench next to the woman. As he did so he clumsily jostled aside the whiskery tallow chandler who was already sitting there surreptitiously eating his dinner of warmed-up pottage. A splash of pea and potato hit the filthy wooden floor but the tallow chandler was half the size of the stevedore and he knew better than to provoke a confrontation in which his poor tired bones might be broken, so if he damned the man at all it was only in silence under his breath. He twisted away slightly on the bench to turn his back upon Guy Hélon.

Naturally, the tallow chandler wasn't the only person to have taken note of the Bhourgbon's arrival. The man who may or may not have been Ehngleish was staring at him levelly, not in anger but merely in readiness. The astonishingly foreign girl was looking at him also, but with a hint of a sneer to the set of her jaw. Guy returned the man's stare but realised, now that he was so much closer, that although the fellow was surely over forty years of age he still exuded an air of physical dynamism from which the wise would avoid any rash entanglement. But Guy felt that it was too late for a change of heart and that to abandon his manoeuvring for possession of the girl would cause him to feel the shame of an ignominious retreat. He was still young enough to consider this a reason to proceed.

Looking squarely at the man but speaking to the woman, he said: "Wench, when I have dispensed with this inconvenient greybeard I shall expect you to show a proper and fitting submission toward . . ."

He spoke no word further. Anticipating a move from the man he was taken entirely by surprise when from beneath her cloak the oriental virago whipped out her knife and brought it up under his chin before he had so much as drawn a breath. His head thudded painfully against the stone wall behind him as he snapped back away from the weapon, but in vain. She had her point poised for a death thrust that he was helpless to prevent. No one in the crowded hostelry had observed the minor incident taking place behind the tallow chandler's back. A small trickle of blood ran down Guy Hélon's neck. She was many inches shorter than he but from his cowering position half-lying on the bench she seemed now to loom over him. It was then that Guy Hélon saw the ferocious menace in those alien eyes and had second thoughts as to his plans for an evening's entertainment. The tiny ogre hissed into his face:

"I am Eiji of the Kajhin, of the community of Alijah, the most prestigious of all the Menghis nations dwelling upon the limitless grasslands of the Great Steppes under the gods of the pony-riders. This man is my Effendi. You dishonour us both. Get you gone or I shall fillet you!"

She said it in a combination of Menghali, her own language, and Ehngleish, the language of her Effendi. The mixture was less than entirely coherent. But as Guy Hélon understood neither tongue, it made little difference. The serrated edge of her dagger and its point pricking at the skin of his throat made her meaning plain. The honest belief, frail but clear, chimed in his mind that he might die; here and now.

Had he known more about her, he would not have been reassured. Despite her recent exposure to other societies and other cultures, Eiji remained typically Menghis in every way. There was no word in Menghali for mercy, nor any word for mitigation. The habits and customs of the people of the steppes had never given rise to such concepts. They were an unequivocal race. Therefore, to Eiji, the preservation of her dignity and that of her master unquestionably took precedence over the value, if any, of this Bhourgbon's life. He had been gratuitously abusive and the justice of executing him was beyond dispute.

Added to which Eiji had not long ago suffered the larger part of a year as a beast of burden and involuntary comfort woman in abject enslavement to a band of Khevnic abductors who had carried her off from her home on the grasslands. This horrific and loathsome defilement had then been followed by a worse one during the months that she had endured a nightmare existence as the rape-slave of a Czechu caravan to whom the Khevnics had sold her. Her incessant and continual degradation at the hands of the bestial Czechu were as monstrously obscene as they were agonising, and would certainly have proven fatal had the man whom she now addressed by the title of Effendi not taken her away from the caravan at the cost of the lives of three Czechu brigands.

A prolonged ordeal of relentless torment is not something that the victim is ever able to shed entirely. Certain features of her character, which had always tended toward the impulsively aggressive, had been hardened and conditioned by her experience into an explosive reflex over which she had very little control. And yet she could control it, at least in part, for she had a countervailing influence: her respectful obedience to her Effendi.

Ealdræd had cautioned his volatile paramour to be very discreet whilst they were in Langelais because they were, in effect, slap bang in the centre of an enemy camp. They might bide there safely, he calculated, but only if they were circumspect. He had unplaited his normally braided hair and beard for that was a style which would identify him as an Aenglian. In the present state of politics his ethnicity alone would be sufficient to get him killed. But his command of the Geulten language was good so that he might disguise his nationality, and he even had a Bhourgbon accent which helped, this being the same part of the world as where he had first learned the mellifluous speech of his enemies many long dark years before.

In spite of Eiji's conspicuous appearance, they might move about the city seeking their passage on a ship, but best to do so at night and by approaching ships' captains personally and in private. The coif and torse he had bought for her made her appear somewhat more like a Langelais mademoiselle, at least when she was cloaked. He had hoped to find some form of mesh veil that might attach to the torse to cover the evident foreignness of her face but the street vendors had let him down, having no such thing in stock. In the light of this, Ealdræd had gone to some lengths to ensure that she understood that during their stay in the Barony discretion would most definitely be the better part of valour.

Fortunately, her natural intelligence had overcome her engrained ethnic resistance to this sort of idea. She had understood. This was the reason why, in the Mutton Chop tavern, Eiji had been so restrained with the Bhourgbon pig despite his insults to her and her Effendi; it was why she had stopped short of instantly carving open his sweating flesh as he deserved. But now, with her dagger unsheathed and at Guy Hélon's jugular vein, she was at a loss as to what to do next. For Eiji, a drawn blade had only one purpose and having decided not to use it for that purpose she was momentarily perplexed.

But the big Aenglian alongside her was already on his feet and, taking Eiji's prisoner by the arm with his right hand, he made it apparent that his own twenty-inch broad-bladed knife was drawn and in his left fist beneath his riding cloak. Eiji, always swift to follow his lead, concealed her own naked dagger under her cloak. There was a sickly smile on the stevedore's face as he got to his feet. The two comrades then proceeded to calmly walk the Bhourgbon out of the hostelry between them.

Reluctant to embarrass himself on his home turf of the *bordel quais* by calling for help, Guy was ready to break free and bolt for it as soon as they were outside but, once in the street, he found that the old man's grip upon his arm was like an iron manacle. Who could have imagined that the grandpa would be so strong? Lacking the wits to conjure up an alternative, Guy Hélon permitted himself to be marched down the deserted alley toward the rear of the Mutton Chop tavern, out of sight of any passing pedestrian, where he was sure a bruising beating awaited either himself or the fellow with the iron fingers. Well, then, let it be so. Guy was not so daunted that he did not still fancy his chances against the greybeard in a fair fight. Just let these two put aside their weapons and Guy would show them how a Bhourgbon can crack a head.

As they stepped deeper into the dark shadows of the alley the foreigner released Guy's arm but, before the Geulten could rub some life back into the numbed limb, without warning those iron fingers had smothered his mouth from behind and a lancing pain tore up through his spine. The Aenglian's knife was embedded ten inches into the stevedore's back. The dead man, having uttered no sound, dropped to his knees and then pitched forward onto his face in the dirt. His killer used Guy's own clothes to wipe the blood from the blade. Then the tall greybeard spun on his heel and strolled casually back out of the alleyway and down the street, his diminutive slant-eyed devil sauntering along beside him. There was a faint smirk on her dainty lips.

As they walked leisurely back to their temporary quarters in a room behind a bakery, taking the less frequented streets for discretion's sake, Eiji mused upon the incident with satisfaction. It was not the first time she had learned a valuable lesson from her companion. The propriety of her obedience to him was confirmed repeatedly by such episodes. Not only was it right to be guided by him, for he was her master, it was also advisable and good sense, for he was wise in the ways of these western barbarians. To have killed the Bhourgbon in the alehouse would have brought trouble upon them but to have let the swine live would have been folly because he would certainly have informed upon them to the authorities for spite. Her Effendi had settled the dilemma quietly and without fuss. As ever, she found him a man worthy of her respect.

*   *   *

Not long since, the Aenglian mercenary soldier Ealdræd of the Pæga and the Menghis female Eiji, who was to him a concubine, a comrade-in-arms and a devoted companion, had travelled through the violent social unrest erupting in the Gathkar Queendoms. Much to their shared relief they had escaped the political perversities of that deviant and benighted land by sailing to the comparative sanity of this buccaneer port of Citadelle in the Barony of Langelais. They had rented themselves a dwelling whilst they sought passage on a ship that would take them further west to the Ehngle peninsula. Their time in the city had been circumspect and peaceful, notwithstanding their brief skirmish with Guy Hélon.

Citadelle was one of the great privateer strongholds ruled by the famous Talebot family of 'sea-barons'. For generations the Talebot had made their fortunes from the theft of other people's property upon the ocean wave and all along the coastline on which they occupied so strategic a position for the interception of sea-borne goods and chattels. The Talebot family were the rulers of what was nominally a fiefdom of the Geulten kingdom of Bhourgbon, but the Barony was as defiantly independent-minded as it was rapacious and venal, both in its Baron and in its people. The current Baron was the insatiably avaricious Baron Talebot du Pillard, the latter honorific meaning 'the plunderer'. He was a credit to his predecessors. Like each sea-baron before him the larger portion of what he had in the way of wealth was derived primarily from the piratical loot of privateers in his officially unofficial service.

His fortunes continued on the rise, for the news sweeping the country was that King Henri of Bhourgbon was filling the coffers of the Baron Talebot du Pillard to the very bursting point in his attempt to hire as many ships as could be had from the Langelais fleet for use as supply vessels to provision the Geulten army during the forthcoming resumption of hostilities against the Ehngle. Not that it was really any doing of the actual King of Bhourgbon, for Henri was a ten-year old boy, who was as spoilt and irresponsible a pre-pubescent cherub as could be found for a thousand leagues. It was the young monarch's numerous and competing advisers amongst the aristocracy who were making the decisions, especially the royal favourite the charismatic Comte Gerard D'Ancel for whom the regal tyke exercised a distinct preference that betimes united the rest of the nobility in loyal opposition to the throne. But upon one thing they were agreed: if a coalition Geulten army were again to attempt to penetrate the Ehngle peninsula, then it must have sea support, both as supply lines and, if possible, as fighting ships to harass the coastal towns of Wehnbria.

For this reason the ports of Forteresse and Citadelle, and a dozen other smaller landing places besides, were bristling with ships at present, all kept unoccupied at anchor whilst the high and mighty made the whole Barony wastefully idle with waiting for the outcome of the diplomatic and financial bargaining. Consequently, with so many vessels being held in reserve for military duties, it was no easy thing for a wandering Aenglian and his Menghis consort to secure a voyage westward on a Geulten ship at such a time as this. In fact, it was next to impossible.

That they were finally given a captain's name to ask for was more by luck than good management. Ealdræd overheard a discussion amongst a gaggle of seamen who were arguing the toss over a skipper that some thought a fine example of Langelais independence and others thought a wretched traitor to the three crowns of the Geulten Alliance. He was a buccaneer in the classic tradition, taking commissions from the Baron Talebot as they were offered but not relying solely upon them and seeking any other paying commissions that might come his way as readily as those that were sealed with his lordship's sanction. The name of this privateer's ship, with a less than subtle punning wit, was the *Espadon*, 'the swordfish'. The captain under discussion was a sadistically malicious adventurer called Faramond. Whatever his other virtues and vices, no one on any side of the discussion doubted his sadism or his malice.

Captain Faramond was said to be the son of an itinerant Piccolian street vendor and an Eildressian younger daughter of a minor lordling who had unaccountably married and, being subject to a great deal of social abuse in conservative Eildres, had in the end migrated to the Barony of Langelais, having been attracted thither by its reputation for liberal independence. Whether this biography was true or not only Faramond himself might know, but one thing that the crowd of disputants came to consensus over was his utter lack of fidelity to his adopted homeland. Not only did he not feel any allegiance to Langelais, he felt none toward the entire Geulten people. It was typical therefore that he, of all those captains whose ships were in harbour, would defy the official edict and be provisioning his craft to set sail west.

The *Espadon* was said to be headed for Ville de Murs, the 'city of walls', a port on the south coast of the Duchy of Oénjil. The *Espadon* was supposedly heavy laden with armaments for the intended hostilities in the summer but what the actual cargo was, who could say? Anyway, a bill of armaments would serve as the ship's manifest as well as anything else. Maybe it was even true.

Ealdræd had caught up with Faramond in the tapsters room of the 'Swan and Feathers', a seedy back parlour that served as a chamber of marine commerce for the black market trade. The good captain was not averse to the prospect of two additional passengers for he had upwards of ten who had bought passage already. The two men appraised each other warily as they spoke as to berths and prices, for both were souls who had seen the world and so were disinclined toward trust or tolerance. The mercenary gave no reason for his wanting to travel, nor was any reason required or enquired after. He guaranteed to place silver in the captain's hand on the day of sailing and that was what mattered.

Ealdræd had brought Eiji with him for the negotiations because he needed to gauge the mariner's reaction to her unique presence. An oriental would make for an expensive slave because such a rarity would enjoy scarcity value. The veteran soldier need to assess whether Faramond might take it into his head to set a squad of his bully-boys on to the lone Aenglian to steal the girl for himself. There was no other way to try to evaluate this than by letting him see the girl and scrutinising him for any tell-tale signs or reactions.

Faramond's conduct was exactly what Ealdræd had hoped it would be. He had gawped openly at the little foreigner, obviously registering a measure of astonishment that one of her folk had found her way this far west, then he had wiped her from his thoughts as he turned back to the person that counted; the person who was paying.

311

Ealdræd marked him down as a basically honest rogue; one that would still bear watching but who might keep his word if there was no particular motivation to break it. The captain offered the big outlander and his queer-eyed doxy two yards of deck on the sheltered leeward side of the ship under the overhang of the forecastle toward the bow. They would also each receive per day from ship's stores one round loaf of black bread, five inches of cheese, one tankard of water, and one pint of Guillain wine. The Aenglian's horse would be stabled with the other animals below decks and would be fed and watered twice a day. The cost in total was nine silver pieces. It was daylight robbery, of course, for such a short trip but it was, to say the least of it, a buyers market and the price wasn't open to haggling. Ealdræd's decisive nod sealed the contract and Faramond made that small circular motion of the fingers that all southern Geulten make to confirm a bargain made.

Had Faramond been aware of just how much gold and silver the wily veteran was actually carrying in his saddlebags, larceny would undoubtedly have followed. But Ealdræd showed no sign of clandestine wealth. His leather doublet and breeks were plain and the stitching was badly split at the shoulders and upper arms. His boots were good but had seen wear. All that could be seen of Eiji's apparel was of the simplest; a cloak, a coif, and torse. Only Ealdræd's horse, the colossal blue-roan Hengustir, a powerhouse of a warhorse standing seventeen hands tall, constituted a distinct financial asset and it was not so very extraordinary that a professional fighting man should be well-mounted.

The *Espadon* was due to sail on the early morning tide of the day after tomorrow. Ealdræd and Eiji decided to spend the intervening time in their rented room behind the bakery wallowing in comfort and large meals in order to rest up fully before their sea voyage. Living closely adjacent to a baker's oven had the advantage of being warm day and night and the Aenglian spent a little more of his secret store of coin on such culinary pleasures as could be purchased from the local vendors. Some of this they consumed for their satisfaction now and some was put aside for when they resumed their journey, to supplement the meagre provisions they would receive from the ship's stores.

Hengustir was tethered just outside in a fenced off area at the rear. Ealdræd had been able to get him good quality hay and a sizeable quantity of vegetables and the superb beast was contented for the time being. Ealdræd never resented the amount of time and attention he paid to the animal's well-being on a daily basis for the stallion was a gracious monument to horseflesh, its muscular weight and high intelligence marking it out in Ealdræd's expert experience as an exemplar of its species. He was fond and proud of his equine friend.

*   *   *

There is a well-known saying amongst the Murgl nomads who live in the barren territories north of the Mountains of God, that the prudent man should "never kick a pregnant camel for they seldom see the funny side". This phrase, which loses something in translation, was entirely unknown amongst the buccaneers of Langelais, perhaps because none of them had ever seen a camel. This was unfortunate for Captain Faramond because the sage wisdom of the Murgl maxim might have afforded him a timely warning and spared him a deal of trouble and wounds.

Ealdræd and Eiji were at the quayside soon after the dawn rose, for the ship would be setting sail on the early tide. The loading of the vessel had been done unannounced the previous night and that had set many-a-tongue wagging because no ship would take on her cargo in the dark unless there was something to conceal, but the manifest was signed in the approved manner by the harbour master and no one else had any say in the matter.

Ealdræd led Hengustir up the gang-plank, its boards creaking under the animal's 2,000lbs of muscle and bone. Ealdræd paid over the passage money into the calloused hand of the captain and a seaman showed Eiji to the yardage of deck that was to be their berth whilst the Aenglian mercenary led Hengustir down into the hold below decks where a permanent stables had been erected, for horseflesh was a routine part of the freight on a merchant craft. Being familiar with the hungry impoverishment of ordinary sailors, Ealdræd bribed the farrier to take good care of his horse. A judicious bribe made all the difference The Aenglian had known farriers who starved their equine charges simply in order to sell the surplus grain to find the coin to feed their children. It meant nothing to Ealdræd if the farrier's children starved or died from a surfeit of lampreys, but Hengustir must be well-fed. The small gratuity would ensure this for it was understood that if the man took the remuneration but failed to faithfully preserve the horse, then his life would be forfeit to the mercenary's blade.

Ealdræd joined Eiji on deck and they kept out of the way whilst the crew of a dozen or so able seamen bustled about in the business of making the ship secure for sailing. The Rigging Boatswain was busy shouting pornographically derisive comments at his inferiors as they hauled anchor and heaved on ropes through wooden pulleys to haul canvas. There were a dozen other passengers, and a mixed lot by the looks of them.

Captain Faramond had brought his latest doxy along on the voyage with him; a salaciously flaunted peppery-tempered Latinate beauty called Clothilde; the type to take the description of brazen hussy as high praise and revel in it. Her figure was a minor miracle and she dressed to make this phenomenon known to the widest possible audience. Every curvaceous inch of Clothilde suggested that she could take on any ten men in a marathon of lovemaking and wear them all down to a shadow. She was a conceited woman with a lot to be conceited about which, naturally, made it worse.

Captain Faramond had brought something else on board with him too: the curse of Elysande. This vengeful harridan was making her strident vocal presence felt in no small measure just a few yards from the *Espadon*. She was to the fore of a gaggle of her friends and supporters all of whom had come down to the quays to spit upon Faramond's departure and damn his infidelity. Elysande had been the captain's Citadelle concubine before the recent arrival of Clothilde who had usurped her position and stolen the eligible Faramond from the red-haired and garrulous Elysande. The thrown-over whore was in a prideful fury, laying down a witch's curse upon the unfaithful Faramond and promising all who sailed on the *Espadon* no return from their blighted voyage.

It was not an idle threat. Elysande was known to have dark powers and many there were who would never dare to cross her for fear of supernatural retribution. Cedric, the publican of the Ducks and Drakes public house, had thrown Elysande out of his premises one night when she was much taken in drink and the sorcerous baggage had invoked a hex of shrivelling upon his cock and balls. It was popularly accepted that Cedric had been impotent ever since. Of course there were sceptics who claimed that Cedric had always been impotent even before the charm of withering, but then there are always those who refuse to believe what others see plainly.

Sporting a mass of curly ringlets, a painted façade in the place of an ordinary visage, and a voluptuous figure undeniably designed by nature for the begetting of a multitudinous progeny, the trollop Elysande was in a high old temper at her desertion by Faramond and her substitution by Clothilde. The harpy's voice called down justice from the dead and the unborn in her defence at such piercing volume that Captain Faramond commanded his Master of Arms to have a couple of men stand to with bows to discourage any advance by the concubine's party should they attempt to board the ship.

As the gangplank was withdrawn and the hull of the craft kissed goodbye to its harbouring, Elysande lifted her loose dress high up to her ribs to expose the fertile swollen bulge of her pregnancy. She was truly bountiful with child; so heavily expectant, in fact, that she looked close to dropping the brat right there on the dockside. Whether the child was begotten of the captain was, given Elysande's profession, naturally somewhat uncertain and debatable, but *she* was not in any two minds over its parentage.

She hoisted her left foot high on to a dock post and brought her forearm through her legs and up under her hairy cunny to shake her fist at the departing *Espadon* in lewd mimicry of an erect phallus. Her braying entourage cackled with laughter but Faramond had already closeted himself in his cabin and Elysande gesticulated obscenely only for the benefit of the crew who paused in their duties to gape and leer. But their expressions dropped like Cedric's limp dick when they heard the seething shrew lay an invocation of barren desolation upon the ship. They knew what that meant. The witch had damned the captain and all who sailed with him to the fate most feared by the men of the sea, that of being lost in the immeasurable wastes of the world of water. They stared aghast at this malediction and shivered at its portent. The clamorous bitch's ranting and cursing rang in their ears all the way out of port.

*   *   *

Halfway through their second day out they passed the point of land known as *Adieu Marin* or the sailor's farewell, and it was here that every captain had to answer the same question: to hug the coastline into the *Baie de Serments*, the Bay of Oaths, so as to minimise risk, or to sail directly north west for Oénjil, so as to maximise speed.

Most experienced hands took the later course for there was little serious jeopardy so long as the shore was visible on the horizon. Faramond invariably steered for Oénjil and this time, if anything, he took a rather wider berth of the Bay of Oaths than was usual. The old hands amongst the crew took note of it but then dismissed it as typical of Faramond's devil-may-care attitude.

Thus far Eiji was largely content with her second experience of life aboard ship. They had settled down on their berth of two yards of deck, using Ealdræd's saddle as something to lay back upon. It smelled of leather and horse-sweat, a comfortingly familiar aroma in contrast to the brisk tang of brine in her nostrils. On the leeward side, their small allotment of personal deck space was more or less out of the prevailing wind and with a blanket beneath them and Ealdræd's spare clothes buttressing the saddle, they made themselves tolerably at home. The Aenglian placed his spear and javelin flat on the deck between the saddle and the upright planks of the fore-castle wall so that they would not roll. He nestled their small supply of additional food there also. Theirs was one of the more sheltered places on board and the mercenary was well-pleased with their allocation. It was open to the skies but noticeably less windswept than those whose lighter purses had paid for space in the middle of the main deck. Even so, it was little enough for nine pieces of silver.

Eiji had not been looking forward to their forthcoming sea-voyage with any pleasurable anticipation. It was only her second experience of the sea and it promised to be even more intimidating than the first. In her childhood on the steppes she had learned, to the benign amusement of her father, to swim in the river and she had felt a strong sense of achievement when finally she had been able to swim the whole sixty yards from one bank to the other. With this as her only prior knowledge of the subject, the nineteen year old had found that their trip across the water from the Gathkar Queendoms to the Barony of Langelais had quite literally opened her eyes in the matter of just how big is the ocean.

She had been quietly impressed when they had sailed down the inlet from the sea called *La Fossé* and had actually been enjoying the new experience until she cupped a handful of water from a bucket drawn from the sea and swallowed a mouthful only to be shocked at the totally unexpected salt content. Having spluttered and coughed for long enough to bring up phlegm and then rinsed her mouth with three mugs of thin ale, the first of which she spat out, the second and third of which she drank, she had enquired of Ealdræd if all the water of the sea was befouled. Not knowing quite what to make of this description he had merely answered that none of it was fit to drink. Ships must take their drinking water with them in barrels when travelling overseas. Eiji's expletive-laden judgement upon oceans in general and this one in particular at having so much water and none of it fit to drink was colourful in the extreme.

But on that earlier trip she underwent another new sensation as they had rounded the finger of land so suitably named *Le Doigt* and she had seen over the low rail of the boat the jaw-dropping, panoramic, incomprehensible void of the great western ocean laid out before her in all its immensity. This gave rise to no derisive aspersions. She had scarcely believed what she was seeing. Such a width of blue on an unimaginable scale. It went further than vision could reach. As any sane person would expect, their fishing sloop had kept very close to the Bhourgbon and Langelais coastlines throughout the entire journey, never more than a mile off-shore, but Eiji had been unable to keep her dark eyes from repeatedly straying southward to gaze askance with wonder at all that infinite water. If such a thing were not unthinkable, she might almost believe it to be more immeasurable than the Menghis Steppes themselves.

Her relief at stepping foot on dry land at Citadelle had been considerable although she had naturally been careful not to reveal her fear of the ocean to her Effendi for that would have been shaming. Moreover, it was increasingly important to her to ensure that she guard against any misconduct on her part in front of those around her. This was not merely because her dignity would not permit her to be condescended to by others, nor even that her behaviour reflected upon her master and lover, although both of these things were true. It was that the realisation had slowly borne in upon her as she travelled through these various foreign countries with their different types of foreigner that she was almost certainly the first and only Menghis that any of these poor backward peoples had ever seen. For this reason she was, so to speak, an ambassadress for Menghis culture. She had determined to make it plain to these westerners just how a properly civilized woman behaved for they were, after all, nothing but ignorant savages who knew no better. In the Menghali language they were *ghazboutyr* meaning 'those who cannot speak properly'. She must conduct herself in such a way as to demonstrate to them the pre-eminence of the ethnic culture in which she had been raised.

317

So now that they were afloat a second time, their ship not hugging the coast as before but sailing out into the ocean proper, taking them into that everlasting and desolate absence of land which before she had only gazed upon in wonder, Eiji firmly resolved that she must hold her head high and stare down the threat of apparently certain death that it presented to her.

During her first sea-born expedition in the Gathkaree fishing boat she had at least felt the reassurance of the nearby coast, close enough to distinguish the detailed features of sandy beaches and rocky promontories. Not so with the *Espadon*. As they passed the *Adieu Marin* the shoreline rapidly fell away to starboard and, standing in the bow to observe these strange marine operations, Eiji found herself with an ever widening stretch of water opening up on her right and an eternity of ocean on her left. It made her heart rise into her throat. She even took hold of the rail in a white-knuckled fist for support. The wind snatched at her hair and the sense of speed was terrific. They were hurtling over the vast empty nothing of the ocean. As the land receded behind them and the dim shape of the Bhourgbon coast ahead lay impossibly out of reach, it was as if they had leapt from the peak of one mountain summit with the intention of landing on the peak of the next mountain summit. They were poised in the air like a balletic Murgl gypsy dancer. It was a leap into the jaws of death.

All at once the thrill of it eclipsed the fear of it. Eiji was hurtling through the air. Eiji was a bird. One of the beautiful predators of the steppes. Eiji was a red-tailed eagle, a goshawk, or a black kite with its wings widespread and just hovering in the sky, sailing on the high air currents. Eiji was in flight, gliding, soaring in the heavens. Eiji was . . . . Ealdræd, who had been reclining against his saddle dozing, looked across at her from the fore-castle and wondered what on earth she was grinning at so widely. Her grin was all over her face.

But before long Eiji had need to recall her resolution to show fortitude before the ghazboutyr. Toward the end of the second day the Master Navigator, Sewal, the most knowledgeable man on board and a pilot who could tell his course home merely by sniffing the breeze, collapsed to the deck clutching his stomach. Something was wrong with his innards, a terrible pain that made him writhe continually and scream of devils in his belly. Something had ruptured in his organs and he was passing blood from his bowels. He was consigned to his bed with dark looks of foreboding from the

318

crew. There was a good deal of low muttering amongst those who knew their trade that this was a circumstance foreshadowing consequences that all might come to rue. There was much talk of curses and of augury in tones of grim acknowledgement of an anxiety justified. The name of Elysande was mentioned often, though never kindly.

Sewal was the man most relied upon where the safety of the *Espadon* was concerned. A ship's captain may be king of his maritime castle but his primary function was discipline and good order; it was the navigator who knew the currents and tides that were so crucial to safe sailing. Although the standard practice of all mariner's apart from those of the Canbrai Isles was to stay within sight of shore, there was always the danger of ill-winds and treacherous currents dragging a ship outside of coastal waters into the open sea. Consequently, whilst the navigator was not needed to plot a course for a journey such as this one, where they were tracking the familiar coastline of Langelais and Bhourgbon, should some mischance befall them such as an undertow, an underwater current flowing strongly away from the shore, or perchance a persistent northerly gale which would drive them seaward, then Sewal would be the only man on board who would have a chance in a hundred of plotting a course back again. Indeed, the Master Navigator's primary duty was to keep a watchful observance to ensure that no such calamity befell them in the first place.

The morning saw this tragic misfortune confirmed. Sewal the navigator died, following a night of continual shrieking agony that was woefully harrowing for everyone on board who merely had to listen to it, let alone for the poor seaman who had to suffer it before the merciful release of death. And it was barely an hour after they had put his body into the water that the aft-castle lookout hollered over to Captain Faramond that he espied a Canbrai ship to port. The mere fact that the craft was so far away from the coast told him what manner of crew must be aboard. All upon the *Espadon* strained their eyes to the south and the sharper sighted amongst them could indeed spy a Canbrai raider out hunting and within another hour it was as plain as day that the Canbrai pirate was heading directly for the Geulten ship.

Faramond decided not to try his freight vessel against so severely testing an opponent. By luck nightfall came down whilst the Canbrai was still a good distance off to port. To avoid it the captain did what no one would expect of any Geulten cargo tub, he sailed further out to sea. As near as he could judge he set his bow straight west so that by morning the Canbrai could search every cove on the Bhourgbon shoreline and not find the rich prize of the *Espadon* for his ship would be where no one would think to look for it, on the south-western horizon.

To give the man due credit, it was an audaciously intrepid plan and it damn nearly worked. By dawn the Canbrai pirate was alone off-shore with its cut-throats scratching their pates as to what had become of their prize. They cruised along as close inland as they dared to take their deep-keeled vessel but not a sniff of the heavy-laden trader fat with portable plunder could they find.

With good reason. The crew of the *Espadon* watched the sun rise from a point just over the horizon in a sea haze, free from all detection. But there wasn't a man on board who wouldn't have wished himself in shallow water and at grips with Canbrai pirates rather than to find himself where he, in fact, now was; disappeared off the edge of the world, below the horizon, and beyond the sight of land. No one would find them there, right enough, but how were they to find themselves?

Captain Faramond had an answer for them: they would steer by the sun. It rose in the east and set in the west, so they had simply to keep the sun to starboard in the morning and to port in the afternoon to be heading north, on their way to the Barony of Oénjil and a safe harbour at Ville de Murs. It sounded almost reasonable such was the confident self-assurance with which he said it. But no sooner was his back turned than other opinions were voiced; in whispers but in earnest. Any captain who deliberately set sail for open water had a suicidal disregard for the safety of the men who served under him, they said. It was more than suicide, it was bloody murder, they said. He had as good as placed a noose round all their necks, they said. The ill-omens of sailor's lore had foretokened just such a catastrophe. Had Elysande not cursed the ship? The pregnant slattern's hexcraft was manifesting itself before them. Many amongst the passengers had picked up from the crew their superstitious premonitions and were quickly convinced.

Irrationally, Clothilde came in for a share of the blame also. She was a sprightly and good looking woman, which set the female passengers against her, and she was a sexy bitch who enjoyed exercising her power over men, which set the male passengers against her, and it was known to be unlucky to have a woman on board who was anything but cargo, which set the sailors against her. Such is the burden of successful harlotry. Her habit of parading about the deck as if she owned it had ruffled a few feathers, since when it came right down to it she was only the captain's latest fancy piece, and nothing puts respectable people in a bad humour with greater alacrity than a low whore affecting superior airs and graces. General opinion appeared to be that contrary-minded and disputatious women of Clothilde's stamp will pluck a man from his comfortable berth in dry dock and start trouble with their sisters in prostitution just for the fuss, excitement and drama of it, when such things ought better to be left alone.

Only Faramond's reputation, frequently demonstrated for any who required evidence, as a man with an insatiable capacity for savage violence kept the mutinous disposition of the crew in check. He began carrying a long bullwhip with him when he left his cabin to prowl the deck, scowling at the wind. Faramond with a whip in his hand was a prospect few cared to tackle. But no man's reputation can hold out indefinitely against the ill-favour of the gods or black witchery. After all, fear of a flogging was a commonplace terror on board ship for a working seaman. What was that compared to their mortal dread of the curse of Elysande?

Within coastal waters where the shoreline was still visible, a steady gaze in that direction could bolster a poor sailor-man's courage. But once out into the open sea it was a very different matter. Anyone, however salty an old seadog they might be, who found themselves no longer able to view the land that was life, inevitably felt the cold chill of horror. No one was exempt, for this fear was inescapably human and therefore universal. The alarmed expression that was fixed upon Eiji's anxious face said it all: whatever had become of the ground? Had the very earth itself vanished? The blue green void that had so fascinated her had now swallowed her up. It was all around on every side as far as the eye could see.

Ealdræd could recognise the rigid fear in the face of the Menghis girl at his side, mixed with an encroaching panic, and no wonder. She came from a people for whom the great grasslands of the steppes are thought to be limitless; no culture on earth is more land-locked than that of the Menghis. Yet here she was with her Effendi surrounded by the vista of a world made only of salt water in which one might drown, sinking down and down forever, with not so much as a single rock or pebble of land to set her feet upon.

Eiji, a daughter of folk who were almost born riding on their spirited ponies, had told him before setting sail that when a child she had learned how to swim, as if to say that he need have no worry on her behalf. But Ealdræd had not told her that which barely needed saying in the situation they were in now, that swimming would help no one should the ship fail for they were too far from shore for anyone on board to swim the distance to the nearest landfall. Ealdræd made the sign of the sevenfold preservation of Buldr.

A strong east wind was running against them and held both its strength and its direction all day, forcing them further off-course to the west. With the restricted ability of a ship like the *Espadon* for tacking and jibbing, the mariner's science being still little more than in its infancy, there was no option but to lower all sails to reduce their pace, and run before the easterly chewing their nails. Captain Faramond attempted to calculate how far they had been blown yet further out to sea and compensate, but the next day the damnable wind grew fiercer. Faramond raged that all his luck was bad. It was as if the very elements themselves conspired against him. Others knew that it was not nature but the unnatural arts that vexed his every effort.

On the fifth day, with none but the captain having faith in his calculations to navigate them north to the coast of Oénjil, the small community of able seaman under his command refused to take orders. The reality was that, with no sails rigged and drifting before the wind, there was precious small work for them to do in any case but it was the principle that counted with Faramond. Was he master here or not? He laid into those closest with his cracking bullwhip and carved deep cuts into the first three men in as many seconds. The ragged group of sailors retreated before its lacerating force and Faramond demanded their obedience. Grumbling and cursing the men abandoned their half-hearted rebellion and consented to once again be governed by him. But there was nothing sincere in their recantation.

The next day Clothilde was found murdered. She had left her lover's cabin for a moonlit walk after he had drunk himself into a belligerent, self-pitying stupor by bedtime. Her narcissistic belief that she was untouchable had proven to be quite unfounded. Her murderers had not cast her corpse overboard to hide their crime. They had hung her dead body from the mast to declare it overtly. The beautiful woman had been stripped naked and strung up by the wrists with a ship's rope. Her throat had been cut and she had bled to death like

322

a pig in a butcher's yard. The blackish red of the dried blood covered her like a dress from her chest to her toes and had congealed in a pool on the deck below her gently swinging feet.

When Faramond saw this sight in the cold light of the new day, half blind with the roaring of his hangover and half mad with fury that any aboard should do violence to his woman, he had lost all control of himself. His bullwhip was nowhere to be found; stolen whilst he snored drunkenly no doubt and flung over the side to the devils of the sea. But in his temper he sprinted bare-handed into the thick press of crewmen nearby throwing punches to the left and right, expecting them to yield to his charge. However, with the murder of Clothilde a line had been crossed and this time the sailors stood their ground. Smothering him with their weight of numbers, they cudgelled him with their gnarled fists, pounding on him eight to one, and the captain it was who was beaten bloody and sent hurtling back to land on his arse on the bare boards of his own deck to his great chagrin. The remainder of the crew withdrew from the incident, uncertain as to whether this was open mutiny or not. Faramond returned to his cabin, blustering mightily. Slowly, all those of the crew who were still faithful to him, which amounted to six men, joined him in his cabin in the stern of the vessel while the rebels occupied the bow.

The *Espadon* was now divided into two hostile camps of roughly equal number, with the helpless passengers taking no side. The captain held a council of war with the faithful, swearing fearful oaths of retribution, but command was slipping through his fingers. Wisely, Faramond kept the ship's store of armaments inside his cabin and so he was able to arm those still loyal to him with as much iron as they could carry. At the other end of the ship, the mutineers had only belaying pins and marlin spikes with which to defend themselves. Even so, the imminent battle would likely kill half the sailors on board which would greatly hinder the sailing the ship when this deplorable gale finally dropped and they could haul canvas and head north again. If the crew were too badly undermanned to sail the ship it would seal the fate of the *Espadon* and they would suffer the death of all.

It was at this stage that Ealdræd, exasperated beyond endurance by such rank stupidity, took a hand in events. He approached the captain's party aft to borrow a longbow and a quiver of arrows from their hurriedly assembled arsenal. None of the seamen had any skill with the Ehngle weapon, and only the skilled could shoot a 90lb longbow, so it was no real loss to them to hand it over. Besides, they had no objection to the big mercenary joining their meagre force when combat commenced. But the soldier had his own idea as to how to bring about an end to this absurdity. With the longbow and quiver stowed over a brawny shoulder, he ran swiftly to the boom where it was connected to the mainsail at the gooseneck and began climbing up the rigging of the main mast. There was no sail to impede his progress but the wind did its best to pluck him from the rigging and hurl him bodily into the deep. It was no easy climb for a man who wasn't a sailor but up and up he went until eventually he was sitting atop the crossbeam, bolstering his back against the upright mast and perched fairly firmly in his eyrie, his long hair and beard fluttering like pennants in the cold east wind.

It was proof of the lack of military understanding amongst the crew that no one else had thought to take possession of this position of decisive strategic advantage. But the wily and knowledgeable veteran was not one to miss a trick like this. Both camps had watched him, open-mouthed with incredulity, as he had scaled the mast. Now his obvious yet fatal tactic was put into operation. The powerful six-foot longbow was not ideally suited to his seated position amongst the rigging but in his experienced hands it would serve his purpose. He nocked an arrow and calmly proceeded to draw a target on one of the mutineers in the bow. The flexible yew of the longbow bent deeply and the animal sinew of the string creaked as he pulled the goose-feathered shaft to his ear. Then he let fly. With the force of a thunderbolt seventeen inches of cedarwood arrow sprouted as if by magic from the cook's chest. The other thirteen inches were buried inside him, as the iron bodkin of the arrowhead burst out through his back.

Only as late as this did it apparently occur to the mutineers that they had small chance of concealing themselves from this assault because from his vantage point he was high enough to look down upon them. They scurried for cover as a second shaft impacted to deadly effect between the shoulder blades of the carpenter as he tried to wedge himself behind the anchor pulley. The archer's accuracy was devastating. One fellow had lain flat behind the wrapped role of spare canvas for the foresail but he had left a leg astray from his hiding place and Ealdræd bent the yew again to put another of his long cedar arrows through the thigh. The bodkin arrowhead struck deep into the wooden deck and nailed the man to it. The fellow's scream was echoed in the lusty battle cry of Captain Faramond and his followers as they ran pell-mell down the deck to storm the opposing camp, their weapons raised high in their hands. There was no need for a further demonstration of longbow technique. Faramond's men swept over the rebels in the bow cutting slices out of all and sundry. Faramond knew only one method to quell mutiny, that of slaying everyone involved, and the slaughter of the rebels was comprehensive. Ealdræd had hoped to avoid this, for it would leave the captain with a crew of only six men, but there was nothing he could do about it from his position aloft.

In the cheerful celebrations afterwards Faramond flamboyantly awarded the longbow and quiver to the Aenglian as a prize of arms. Ealdræd's wry cynicism at this over-generous outpouring of largesse was something that he shrewdly kept to himself.

That evening the wind finally shifted to a southerly and before the spit had dried on his thumb Captain Faramond was ordering all sails hoisted and getting the ship underway in the right direction at last. Sailing continued through the night and all the next day and they were making good progress although their drinking water was getting very low. They'd had no sight of land for over five days. It was the curse of Elysande. Everybody knew it. None but the captain even pretended otherwise.

By the time the ship had, by Faramond's reckoning, pushed its way northward once again to a point where, in his opinion, given with a prayer to the heavens, they were three hundred and fifty leagues westward of their intended destination, the water had run dry and Faramond had a barrel of wine brought up from the cargo hold. When they cracked it open it contained Guillain claret and mugs of the rich fruit of the vine were handed out to everyone, mariners and passengers alike. It made a welcome change to the stale scrapings of the water butt. Of course, it would also mean that the crew would be in a continual state of drunkenness from this point on.

If Faramond was right in his navigation, they were located approximately eighty leagues south of Aenglia, or as it may be Merthya if he had overestimated the strength of the wind. They would be south of the Canbrai Islands if he had underestimated. Any of these three outcomes was a wretched disappointment for the commercial backers of the *Espadon* whose consignment of freight goods were intended for sale to the Geulten, unless the captain overcame what few scruples he might have and traded his cargo with the enemies of his kin. But all that really mattered for the time being was to find land; any land.

Ealdræd didn't know whether to be pleased by this turn of events or not. Their situation was a desperate one, yet should they survive it, and he believed they might well do so, then it seemed that his journey west had been greatly accelerated by the curse that had been laid upon this unhappy ship. On the other hand, perhaps he was placing too great a faith in Faramond's seamanship.

The barrel of Guillain non-vintage was half empty when there was a cry of anguish from the starboard rail and all heads turned in that direction to discover that the Canbrai carrack had reappeared on the skyline. Or perhaps it was another ship of the same design, they had never had close sight of the previous one. Either way it made no difference. It was like a punch in the stomach for those aboard the *Espadon*. All that they had been through was for nothing. They may as well have fought the pirate when they were off the Bhourgbon coast when they'd had a full crew and the distance to shore had been a fraction of what it was now. Faramond had lost his wager and lost it badly. The enemy's intentions were unmistakable and this time the slower, wide-waisted *Espadon* had no hope of evasion or escape. By god and all his tortures, it *was* the curse of Elysande! Even Faramond was convinced and he bellowed his own curses in return at the diabolical demon-fucking baggage of a brothel slut and sent his wishes up to heaven that the pregnant whore's baby be born with horns and a tail.

What was approaching them under the midday sun was more than any ordinary ship, it was an ocean-going carrack. This confirmed that it hailed from the Canbrai islands. The Langelais cargo ship was by this stage in its misfortunes almost so far west as to be in Canbrai home waters. Ealdræd knew of them from the days of his youth, for they were occasionally hostile neighbours to the Pæga. There was a long-standing peace between them, sporadically broken by raids on Aenglian seaside fishing villages. But it did not pay to make feudal enemies of the Aenglians and for the most part the men of Canbrai took their swift carracks further east to trouble the fat freighters of every country between Merthya and Ahkran. The regular success of these raiding parties was reflected in the hatred that other men who earned their living upon the ocean had for all things Canbrai.

Some claimed that the Canbrai were mermen with webbed hands and feet; others that the Canbrai never anchored in harbour but sailed without ceasing upon the waves. The tales were plentiful, for the folk of the Isles had been seafarers since the peoples of the world were first born in the Well of Mægen and only they, thus far, had mastered the construction of the carrack with its three separate masts, each carrying a sail to bestow upon the carrack a speed unknown to the older patterns of shipbuilding. Cargo captains would stare hollow-eyed with fear and covetous wonder at the high-castled fan-tail sterns of the Canbrai carracks and the sheer weight of wind caught in their square rigged foremast and their lateen rigged mizzenmast. They had been called the kings of the sea and were, truth to tell, the only ship yet built purposely designed for ocean-voyaging outside of coastal waters. When rigged with full sail and hurtling forrard in the attack, as this one was, the hull of a carrack would hum like a cat purring. In an astonishingly short space of time it traversed the distance to the *Espadon* and within two hours those on the Geulten ship who watched its progress could make out the predatory faces of the Canbrai pirates as they shook their grappling irons at their prey.

In contrast to the sleek velocity and responsiveness of the carrack, the *Espadon* failed to live up to its name; it was less 'the swordfish' and more like a whale. It was both bigger and heavier that its assailant but neither of these qualities were in its favour. The carrack skimmed over the water like one of Ealdræd's bodkin-pointed arrows descending to pierce the clumsy armour of its bulky foe. Its crew, three dozen warriors or more, were hanging their arms over the side of their vessel and banging their swords and shields against the wood in a repetitive rhythm. As they pounded the hull they called out "Widewe Wōp! Widewe Wōp! Widewe Wōp!" It was the name of their ship: the 'Widow Weeping'.

Eiji was astonished to discover that she understood what they were saying. It was her Effendi's language; it was Ehngleish. Bewildered, she asked him how this could be and he explained that although these were not strictly his people, the Aenglians, they were close neighbours and were a part of the nations known as the Ehngle. Whereupon, in perturbation over a question of honour, she wanted to know if she and her Effendi were to fight against these Ehngle on behalf of a Geulten ship and crew?

Ealdræd was forced to admit that there was no good outcome for them from this conflict. He had no great love for the Canbrai since the Pæga had often fought against them in his boyhood and if the Widewe Wōp was victorious, he and his companion might be taken as slaves. If the *Espadon* were to triumph, it would be a success for his enemies; a Geulten conquest of those toward whom, however little love he might bear them, he at least felt a closer allegiance than to the men of Langelais. But the reality was yet more pitiless because Ealdræd and Eiji's participation in the sea-battle could hardly affect the outcome in any case. The Widewe Wōp so greatly outnumbered the remains of the Geulten that they were certain victors. The killing of the mutineers, in which Ealdræd had played a significant part, had depleted their numbers too severely for them to stand any chance against the enemy that was swooping down upon them. The Canbrai would demand the surrender of the Langelais privateer and the latter would have to comply. Captain Faramond had not even bothered to issue weapons, so futile would be any attempt to fight hand-to-hand.

But it transpired that these diverse speculations were superfluous for the battle was to be forestalled in a manner that none had foreseen. Captain Faramond, his crew reduced by the suppression of mutiny to a mere handful, his vessel very much slower, more sluggish and less manoeuvrable than that of his adversary, knew that his ship was lost, his cargo was lost, and with them his life. His doxy Clothilde was dead and his own decease had been arcanely engineered by the vengeful blasphemies of that cow Elysande, rot her womb. It was all up with the good captain and, as anyone could have affirmed, Faramond was not a man to accept his own imminent death without doing everything in his power to take as many others with him as he could.

And he had the means. The wind was driving the *Espadon* straight toward the oncoming Canbrai which was on an intercept course. The Master Rudder was pressing his full weight on the wheel in an attempt to turn his low-laden vessel aside from the attack but Faramond snatched up a hatchet from a nearby bag of carpenter's tools, charged the Master Rudder where he stood at his wheel, and struck him down viciously. Standing astride the dying Master Rudder, the incensed Faramond held the wheel steady and true, getting the full wind into the straining canvas of the sail, and letting his ship run head on at the Canbrai.

At first the crews of neither vessel understood his purpose. Only when it became apparent that they were in danger of cataclysmic collision did they begin appealing to their respective captains to sheer off. The Canbrai captain had determined to do precisely that, for he did not wish to risk his carrack, but the madman at the helm of the *Espadon* was of quite another mind altogether.

328

Finally grasping his lunatic intention, the remaining members of the crew rushed to the stern to seize the wheel. A mortal struggle ensued and Faramond dealt fatal blows to three of them with his hatchet before the remaining two bludgeoned him down to his knees. The Boatswain snatched the axe from his captain and hacked Faramond's neck through in half a dozen crude slashes.

But Captain Faramond had achieved his aim. In the final act of his life he had chosen to show the true malignity of his character in its full measure and he had succeeded unconditionally. For all the efforts of the Canbrai to twist their carrack onto a line away from the looming menace of the solid Langelais craft, they could not turn in time. They barely managed to lean their carrack sufficient to miss the reinforced keel-head of the oncoming *Espadon* before the latter rammed the half-turned Canbrai amidships. The two wooden craft met in a hideous splintering collision that buckled braces and sheared clean through the clinker-planking, and in mutual destruction ripped open the twain with catastrophic results. Both hulls were breached and the futtocks of the carrack, the huge curved timbers that formed the ribs of the ship, were split. Both craft were so badly ruptured that they began to sink instantly, locked together in a deadly embrace.

In place of the skirmish at sword-point that the Canbrai had been expecting, the dead privateer captain had given them the sailors' despair: shipwreck at sea with the loss of all hands. As the men of the Widewe Wōp clambered over the side of their own vessel, flourishing their weapons, to leap across on to the deck of the *Espadon* they discovered that there were almost no enemies left alive and no one left to fight except a dozen or so passengers on the quarterdeck who clearly made no pretence of resistance. Even as this realisation came upon them they became horrifyingly aware of how badly holed their own vessel was and with stark comprehension of what this meant a great despondent wail went up, for now the ocean would claim them all.

Mindless panic ran riot. A women amongst the passengers fell to her knees and started praying penitently to her gods for salvation. A Canbrai sailor kicked her in the stomach and damned her to hell. The pirates who had boarded the *Espadon* were so incensed at the irreparable calamity the Geulten had caused that they began laying about them with their cutlasses, hacking down the screeching passengers in revenge. As the ocean poured into the bilges of the

Widewe Wōp it rolled violently against the *Espadon* and wrenched the crushed fragments of its bow below the surface of the waves. The cargo vessel lurched violently, knocking everyone off their feet. The pair of ships continued sinking with appalling rapidity, enmeshed in one another in a reciprocal demise.

Men started jumping into the sea to swim for it but the Aenglian had sense enough to know that if they were too far from land to see it, they were too far to swim to it. Those taking to the water and trusting to the power of their limbs were dead men. The old mercenary racked his brains for what to do. One benefit the experience of his years had bestowed was that it had taught him the lesson of the importance of considered judgement. More times than his memory could reliably inform him he had been in a position of close peril and just as many times he had witnessed folk destroy themselves through precipitant action. He thought that even in this dire condition a ship of such size must take several minutes before disappearing entirely. He must pause to reflect and deliberate. In the past he had lived when others had died because intelligence had guided his deeds. It was not impossible that they might somehow survive this, even though it was dreadfully improbable, if he could but find some way to shorten the odds against him. Then he remembered Hengustir! His horse was below decks and much of that level was already flooded. What could be done for Hengustir?

The veteran hustled Eiji up the tilting deck to the high point at the aft-castle and told her he must seek to see if Hengustir was still alive below but that he would return immediately and that she must not leave the ship ahead of him. The girl was looking at him as if hoping that somehow he could find a solution to their predicament, if perhaps he might grow wings and fly them to safety, or disclose some secret knowledge that would somehow overcome the terminal jeopardy of shipwreck. As she watched him lower himself through the hatchway and descend the ladder into the cargo hold, Eiji was wearing a mask of frozen apprehension.

Ealdræd left the deathly pale girl by the aft-castle and went looking for his horse before deserting the ship. He had no idea as to what he might do for the loyal and noble animal but he went looking. The noise in the hold was deafening with so immense a quantity of unbridled alarm and frenzied hysteria in so confined a space. The stable where Hengustir had been kept was a collapsed ruin. He must be somewhere amongst the other horses and animals but in the screaming confusion Ealdræd wasn't able to find him. Yet he could not depart without making some attempt to rescue so fine a mount, a horse he admired above any other he had known. The ship had listed starboard and many of the horses had been thrown down, some breaking their legs in the fall. One or two of the beasts had been ripped open against the torn timbers of the hull.

There was a dark strain of some other fluid mixing with the seawater that was pouring in through the great cleavage in the side of the ship. This other fluid was a burgundy red. At first Ealdræd took it to be blood but then realised that, no, it was wine. There were hundreds of barrels lying scattered and smashed from which issued forth enough wine for a man to drown in, and who's to say that one or two lost souls hadn't literally done so on this accursed day? This was evidence of Captain Faramond's true purpose on this voyage, anyway. The *Espadon* had not been bound for Ville de Murs in the Duchy of Oénjil at all. It had been headed for the nest of little smugglers quays called *pȳrel cȳse*, the 'hole in the cheese', in Wehnbria just an hour's night-passage across from the west coast of Oénjil and a regular spot for smuggling Geulten goods into the Ehngle peninsula.

The broken wine barrels only added to the dismal carnage below decks. The Aenglian dashed through the melee, knocking against the writhing bodies of screaming animals in his haste to find his Hengustir. In his heart he knew that even were he to find the stallion there would have been precious little that he could do to help the splendid creature. There was no chance of survival for the blue-roan. The best that Ealdræd could offer would be a quick death from the knife rather than the black gasping horror of drowning. But the chaos was overpowering. There was no sign of his beautiful stallion's ghostly grey hide anywhere. Perchance the sea had taken him already. Realising the utter futility of what he was doing, the heartsick soldier emitted a long mournful groan and turned away to return to Eiji. He must seek some means to succour his own life and hers; to save those that it might yet be possible to save.

She was waiting for him on the exact spot that he had left her. She seemed as motionless as a statue in petrified rock, as if incapable of thought in the teeth of the scale of the events that had overtaken them. This young woman who had not surrendered hope even when she was a yoked rape-slave under the lash in a Czechu caravan of Khevnic nomads, now found herself rendered incapable. If there had been an enemy to kill or to escape or to deceive, she would have been alive with action. But how can a person kill the ocean, escape an infinity of water, deceive the very sea?

Ealdræd came back to her from the direction of the captain's cabin and strode up to her quickly. He was carrying a goatskin bag of brandywine and a sizeable cabin door that he had ripped from its hinges. It was wide enough for two and thick enough to float under their combined weight. Or, at least, he hoped it was. She looked up at him and he saw that all the colour had drained from her face.

He almost choked when he told her: "Hengustir is drowned. If not yet, then very soon and inevitably." The dismal cast overshadowing his battered soldier's face would have told her more than his words just what this loss meant to him. His superb Hengustir. To suffocate in the brackish water of the western ocean, dragged down into the abyss. How could the gods tolerate the injustice? For such a beast to die anywhere but upon the field of combat was indecent; an aberration. But both ships would be submerged in mere moments and there was nothing on board which might carry an animal the size and weight of the magnificent stallion. It was a bitter blow but there was simply nothing to be done.

All this was etched deep into his expression of dire dejection but her vacuous empty stare saw none of it. Overwhelmed by circumstances, she had all but lost her wits. Ealdræd thrust his grief from his thoughts and focused upon the urgent necessities under the immediate and calamitous peril that confronted them. He started to remove his boots and bid her copy his example. Eiji was very slow to respond. He ripped off her torse and coif, then slapped her once, smartly across her pallid cheek. As a red imprint of his hand bloomed upon the ashen skin, some animation came back into her eyes and she began to tug off her boots. There was still a vacancy about her, as if all understanding had departed, but she was at least in motion again. But he would need her more lively than this when they leapt overboard or her own fear would kill her.

He explained that they must discard anything that would be heavy when sodden. It would mean that they would have nothing to cover themselves with for warmth but they must just suffer that. He was already in only his doublet and breeks, having dispensed with the bundle that contained his gambeson tunic and mail shirt. Ealdræd took his knife and cut a slit in the stitching of his doublet and then slipped his small bag of coin inside the lining. It was as secure as he could make it in the circumstances. Many months and a thousand leagues ago he had received twenty pieces of silver from his friend, the General Eádgar Aeðlric, to match the gold he had received from the Eorl Atheldun in Wehnbria. These monies had paid his way ever since and there were still five pieces of silver and ten of gold left. He would need them to re-provision himself if, by any extraordinary fluke of luck, he were to live beyond the next few days.

He almost forgot his old pot basin helmet. How long had he worn that? He'd had it from a Sæxyn blacksmith all of a dozen years ago. That smithy had done good work; it had seen plenty of hard service since and never failed him. But it too must be cast aside. He could not afford to carry any metal but his fifteen pieces of coin in the water. Eiji's cloak was thrown upon the growing pile of discarded belongings and her girdle after it. It was necessary, too, that they abandon all their weapons. His spear and javelin, his knife, all must be left behind along with his newly acquired longbow. It was a sure sign of Eiji's extreme mental distraction that she let her dearly cherished falcon-headed dagger be tossed away without a word. Ordinarily she valued it slightly above the value of breathing.

When she was stripped to her linen Tehlitz smock he hustled her over to the rail, bidding her take hold of the goatskin of brandywine. The sea around them was full of struggling bodies as various fools sought to find salvation in swimming. Others were clutching at the ship as if they expected that it would remain afloat. Some of those whose faculties were still intact had sought out whatever bits of broken hull and wreckage they could find to grab on to as life preservers and were fighting over possession of them.

Just as Ealdræd noticed this he saw in his peripheral vision a burly figure with a flourishing moustache striding up purposefully. It was the Boatswain and although he was no longer carrying the captain's hatchet he did have the captain's head in his hand, holding it by the hair. Perhaps the fellow had it in mind to steal the cabin door that Ealdræd was carrying. Not waiting to enquire the man's business, the Aenglian thrust the bottom edge of the door as hard as he could into the fellow's teeth. He heard them shatter loose from the gums as man and moustache both hurtled backwards under the tremendous impact. Not concerning himself with the outcome of the matter, in a second Ealdræd was guiding Eiji over the rail. He looked down and saw that directly under the rail the first two yards of water were a wildly flailing pandemonium of human and animal bodies, all thrashing about in a frenzy to survive and yet, by this very action, ensuring the deaths of all concerned.

Eiji's obedience to Ealdræd had, over their time together, become second nature to her and it was this that saved her life. When he urged her to leap from the deck as far as she could, her obedience proved stronger than her terror. She propelled herself clean over the struggling mass of drowning folk and her feet hit the waves in clear water, alongside the dogged veteran who crashed into the sea still holding tightly to the cabin door. He pushed the improvised life-raft ahead of him as he swam over to where Eiji was treading water and he blessed her when he saw the goatskin of brandywine still in her grasp. Even half insensible she was resolute and tenacious.

A few moments later they were both laying their torsos across the sturdy oaken door and with their legs trailing in the water they were kicking steadily to drive themselves away from the rapidly sinking ship, splashing their way through the flotsam and jetsam that was spreading out in a great rippling circle around the two submerging vessels. Everything on board that would float proceeded to do so, creating a wide scattering of the small objects of human artefact bobbing and riding the waves.

Ealdræd had no idea of navigation so, with the assumption that the captain had been sailing the *Espadon* in roughly the right direction for landfall before the collision, and taking his bearings from the position of the sun, he made a fair guess at the captain's heading and kicked at the water. He might place no hope in swimming but neither was he of a character to simply cling to the wreckage and pray that time and tide were with them so that they might be swept to landfall by the prevailing currents. He and Eiji were strong enough to give the current some help by nudging their raft forward with their methodically thrashing legs and, the veteran of a thousand encounters with death, he knew the value of giving bare chance a little help.

Amid the frightful turmoil of distress and disorder, they and the few other survivors who had come up with the same idea, paddled their pieces of wreckage off into the uncharted emptiness. They all seemed inclined to go in the same direction and it was almost like an unruly flotilla of toy craft that splashed its way northwards. Behind them the listing wrecks began to plunge downwards with greater speed to an accompaniment of the shrieking of timbers and the forlorn wailing of the doomed. The distorted human howling was mixed with the terrified neighing of the few remaining horses and Ealdræd's head dropped in sudden weakness at the unbidden thought of Hengustir, but he shook the image out of his head and set his feet to smashing their way relentlessly through the implacable and uncaring nature that had killed his horse.

They were still ploughing their wake when night fell. The tough old mercenary's legs felt like lead and his lower back was on fire with pain. He knew Eiji must be feeling it too, though she was still kicking hard. If they persisted, sooner or later the weight of their own fatigue would drag them under. They must have a spell of rest. He hauled himself up to sit astride the cabin door, gripping it with his calves, and the girl climbed up to likewise sit astride in front of him, her back pressed against his chest and his big arms wrapped around her. Their balance was surprisingly easy. The main danger was sliding off in the wet. The sturdy door skipped along the waves and they clung on to it and to one another. Now that he had the leisure to look, he realised that he could spy none of the other survivors. They had all drifted apart during the hours since the wreck.

Chilling cold descended from the brightly mocking stars overhead. The stiff breeze developed an icy edge to it. They could no longer feel their feet. There was no opportunity to sleep, the ocean was too rough. Eiji had not said a word to Ealdræd since darkness overtook them but as the eternity of night went on she half twisted round to bury her head under his chin and spent several hours clinging to him in that position and softly mumbling some manner of song in Menghali. It was a gentle, lilting tune and the melody seemed to take her thoughts to some other time and place. Ealdræd was glad of it, for there was little enough that he could say to her by way of comfort. The sea would have its way with them now. Each rise and fall of the swell beneath them told of the limitless power of the enormity that carried them so carelessly along on their blind journey.

The music of the Menghis people who dwelt upon the grasslands of the steppes over three thousand miles away, an inconceivable distance by any normal person's measure of the world, mixed with the lapping and splashing of the foam in an ocean that no living Menghis, save one, had ever heard of. The Aenglian listened to Eiji's rather off-key rendition. The song had a verse and chorus structure that seemed to go around and around in an endless circle. It had the see-saw rhythm of a child's nursery song and her salt-cracked voice breathed the words huskily. Her mind was in her memories, as far away as any star. He shut his eyes to let her lullaby carry him away with her.

Ealdræd awoke with a start to an awareness that a dim grey glint was turning into daylight. At first he found his body unresponsive. He had set rigid in his seated position but, praise be to Buldr, neither of them had slipped from their place; Eiji was still asleep in his arms. Waðsige, god of chance, had so favoured the two soaked and shipwrecked remnants of the *Espadon* that they had been graciously permitted to live another day. The veteran tried to ease some movement into his stiff back and gasped audibly as a latticework of rending aches shot through him. He moved his arms about in the attempt to get his blood circulation going. His inflexible fingers were lumps of sausage and his thighs had cramped agonisingly. Only a lifetime in the saddle enabled his wracked muscles to recover to the point where he was able to move his limbs like a puppet responding to tugs upon the strings. Slowly some warmth of life re-entered his flesh.

This movement woke the girl snuggled down half inside his doublet. She cried aloud, a high-pitched yip! of stinging pain, as her first conscious awareness was of a sensation of sharp needles piercing her tortured thighs. She tried to rub the awful discomfort from her knotted leg muscles with her hands. Ealdræd told her to move her arms and legs about to wake them up and the two puppets performed their weird dance, a speck upon the sea.

They each had a good long drink of brandywine from their goatskin. When they strained their bloodshot eyeballs in what they supposed was their general direction of travel they thought that it may be, just perhaps, that they could see a steady shadow sitting on the horizon in the far distance ahead. That shadow could mean land. But they could not be sure because their sore eyes were so encrusted with salt that nothing they might think they saw was as clear or as certain as it might normally be. Fatigue, too, had taken its terrible toll on them both and even Eiji's youthful vigour could not keep her mind from clouding. Having endured most of the night in freezing wakefulness, she now found herself beset by an overwhelming desire for sleep that kept lowering a veil of foggy lethargy over her disordered senses.

Still, a mere shadow of land was sufficient as a tantalising possibility to get them trailing their legs in the water again and kicking to impel the cabin door forward toward that faint hope. All the two puny humans had left from now on was their strength of character. Both had characters of stubborn intransigence. Somehow the pair, by an effort of intractable will, got their unfeeling legs, numbed with cold, moving mechanically up and down, up and down, under the dogged, indomitable, obstinate, mule-headed, bloody-minded insistence of their refusal to die; kicking, kicking, kicking.

*   *   *

Nob of the Oswaldmǣgþ, the shunned tribe of the accursed, was harvesting cockles on the beach which, along with shrimp and various other small seafood, were a staple of the diet of all the tribal groups of the islands. He squatted low on the sandy flats of the wide-curving cove, disturbing the sand with his hand-rake to encourage the cockles to come to the surface, then scooping them into his cockle bag. It was low-tide, the best time for the harvest. The little sea-creatures fed in the shallow water then burrowed just below the sand when the tide receded. Nob knew well how to entice them up and collect them for he was fifteen years of age and the Oswaldmǣgþ teach these tasks to their children as soon as they can walk.

The thin adolescent worked his way systematically along the stretch of coastline that, it was understood, belonged to his family. He barely looked up from his work since he knew every inch of this beach in its unvarying, changeless permanency. Each morning of his young life Nob had done what he was doing now. He almost didn't think about it, his body moved without his needing to pay attention to his actions.

Nob like to think instead about the man he would become, a Canbrai buccaneer and the toast of the ten thousand waves. Such dreams were the best of life. As he shuffled along, head down for cockles, his thoughts were full of the adult Nob defeating enemies in single combat and ravishing tavern wenches who turned out to be changeling princesses who had been switched at birth by evil witches. He was a little repetitious in his fantasies but he never tired of them. So lost in that better other world was he that he had all but drawn level with the two prostrate bodies when he found them. A big man and a small woman. Both lay on their backs with their eyes shut. The boy halted in his tracks with but one thought: were they dead or unconscious? It was not the first time he had discovered a body on his beach but it naturally took him aback all the same. The last corpse had displayed many mutilating wounds, so on that occasion mortality had not been in question.

Nob noticed that there was something wrong with the woman's eyes. They weren't as round as they were supposed to be; sort of narrow and slanted. Her smock was half torn off and her bare breasts were exposed. Her skin seemed not quite the usual colour. A shiver ran down his spine. Could she be a minch-maiden or a brine-sprite; one of those uncanny spirits who lived in the depths of the ocean? Yet her shapely body was profoundly female. Nob lingered over her, sexually aroused, and when he reached out to touch her he discovered that her flesh was warm. He withdrew sharply. Alive then.

Losing his nerve, he shuffled hastily over to the man. Leaning over him Nob saw that he was old, almost as old as uncle Siward, and had many scars. He had a long beard and his doublet and breeches were badly torn especially around the arms and shoulders. He was a powerful looking man and Nob took a few steps back to be out of harm's way. The lad was on the verge of running home with the news as fast as his legs would carry him when the woman stirred. He spun round to see water trickling out of her mouth. Then he turned back and was jolted by fright.

The man's eyes opened.

Chapter 9

The Canbrai Accursed

The thin beggarly boy burst into the crofter's cottage, his undernourished face brightly animated with alarm and news. "Fæder! Fæder!" he shouted as he rushed in, then came to an abrupt halt at finding his father absent. Only the hollow expressions of the women stared back at him from the cramped single-room dwelling, their faces set in stone from a lifetime of patient enduring stoicism. Before the stone could crack into an enquiry about his obvious excitement, the boy skipped briskly back outside and with the energy of the wild hare ran for the flock of scraggy sheep on the leeward side of the hill where he knew he would find his uncle Siward.

It was from this straggling flock that came the rough woollen tunic that was the lad's only garb, covering his thin frame from shoulders to knees with a woven fabric so coarse that it was abrasive to the skin, raising red rashes on his pale flesh from the constant friction. Woven on his mother's loom, it was typical of the *isen wull*, the 'iron wool' produced from the wiry coats of the half-starved sheep of the Canbrai Islands; animals with as much goat in them as lamb. Though it was scarcely adequate for the chilling ocean winds that constantly buffeted the outcrop of land upon which the boy had spent his life, this rude tunic was his entire wardrobe in all weathers. Wool was not so plentiful that he might expect a replacement garment whilst there was still wear to be had out of this one. The boy was also barefoot, his feet blackened with encrusted dirt, clogs being reserved for only the adults of their tiny community. His name was Nob and he was of the Oswaldmægþ, the tribe of the accursed.

Siward sat amongst the ewes and rams, as much a part of the landscape as the animals he was shepherding, slowly carving on a bone that would in the course of several weeks be transformed into a whistle-flute for one of the children. He reacted slowly at first to the sudden arrival of his nephew in a frantic flurry of scrawny knees and elbows. The pace of Siward's life rarely exceeded a placid ramble. In contrast to this, Nob's excited and largely incoherent jabbering about deformed outlanders washed ashore on the beach of cockle-cove was bewildering, yet it caused Siward to stir from his indolence and catch the contagion of panic from his nephew for at least it managed to convey to the shepherd that something of major importance had occurred of which his brother Ulfbert, as head of the household, should be made aware.

With Siward now awoken from his habitual lethargy, man and boy ran like billy-goats down the hillside to the fishing river. Ulfbert and his younger sibling Waulud were perched at the river's edge either side of a narrow point in the fast-flowing waterway where a fallen tree against the embankment narrowed it still further. Between them they held a net which they repeatedly lowered into the river, scooping it back out whenever they thought they had caught a fish. Their pickings for the day so far were not overly impressive, consisting of three rather smallish tench and one emaciated carp. Including the women and children they had a family of nine to feed.

In the presence of his father and two uncles Nob was required to tell his tale more slowly and in greater detail so that all might understand. The lad swallowed his fretful anxiety and described in something like calmer tones how he had been harvesting cockles on the sandy flats of the cove at low-tide when he had stumbled across the prostrate bodies of a big old man and a small young woman apparently dead to the world. But, he said with an air of pride at his own boldness, when he had approached them to look closer he had discovered that they were both alive. In fact, as he had been standing over them the woman had stirred and the man had opened his eyes. At that, Nob had instantly fled for the support of his kindred and to give the alarm.

The men were much taken aback at this story, clustering together but saying little, none being of a mind to know quite what to say. They did not doubt the boy's word for he had not the wit to invent a lie, and whilst the occasional corpse was thrown up by the sea from time to time, the three brothers could none of them ever remember living souls being cast ashore. The menfolk of the family Lameleg, named for their ancestor Wallace of the Lame Leg who had founded the croft here four generations earlier, looked askance at each other and shook their heads slowly from side to side in disapproval and misgiving. Foreigners come to the island? It could bode nothing but ill. Such unnatural advents could only foreshadow things most ominous and threatening. With his next comment the boy made these dark presentiments more certain.

Nob, warming to his role in all this and feeling a gratifying sense of his own importance, made a special point of mentioning that although the old man on the beach appeared human enough, t'were not so with the young woman. He had noticed how there was something wrong with the girl's eyes. They were narrow and slanted; sort of squinted. They weren't as round as eyes were supposed to be. In other respects she was formed in the manner of normal females except that her skin seemed not quite the usual colour. Surely, he suggested, she must be a brine-sprite or a minch-maiden sent from the kingdom below the waves into the world of men to lure them to their doom. This was the only possible explanation of the sinisterly alien abnormality that revealed itself in those reptilian eyelids. Her elderly male counterpart was, no doubt, her servant and champion.

Nob confessed nothing about how this other-worldly temptress had lain on the sand with her loose linen smock half torn off of her comely body by the sea to expose her magnificent breasts. Any implication that he had been sexually aroused by the sight of her was something that it would not be politic to admit to his censorious family. His mother would flog him over the barrel if she suspected that he had felt an erotic arousal toward a foreigner from outside the clan. Family married family; that had always been their way and must always be so.

Ulfbert agreed that Nob's conjecture was surely the most probable reason for the creatures on the cockle-beach. They might be grindilows, selkies, or mermen of any kind; like as not a sprite or a minch as the boy had said. Be whatsoever they may, all that mattered was to get rid of them. But three men and a boy were far less than was needed for so daunting an undertaking. Mermaids and sirens might steal a man's soul as quick as blinking. A stronger war party would be necessary. They must fetch the men of the family Reave from the next croft, named for an ancestor called Meduw the Reaver who was much given to abduction and rape. The two families were less than friendly but, even so, they were cousins with a shared ancestry and would help in a crisis.

It took the best part of an hour to find and then convince the Reave men that Nob's tale was a true one. The twins Finian and Firgul were for thumping the boy bloody to teach him not to come spreading lies to the Reave's but their elder brother Énnae, in keeping with his character, declared that he was in favour of seeing

341

things for himself. At this, the united cousins set off for cockle-cove to deal with these intruders, should there prove to be any.

Nob had found the bodies not long after dawn that morning but the sun was climbing toward noon by the time he returned to the same stretch of shoreline in company with his father, uncles and the Reave men. The beach was entirely deserted. An expanse of empty brown sand mocked the incredulous Nob, as if to damn him for a liar. The twins swore they found no humour in the boy's joke at their expense but the lad gave his oath that it was no joke, on his honour it wasn't, and Ulfbert Lameleg took the boy's part in the quarrel and matters were rapidly coming to blows when Énnae's wiser head once again prevailed. He offered the opinion that if the minch-maiden and her selkie had awoken so many hours since, they would not have remained where they were, but would instead be off about their mischief. Consequently, the war party should search inland for the sprites.

With common sense thus restored they soon happened across two pairs of very tangible footprints that traversed the sand and disappeared into the interior of the island. Following in the same direction, they had hiked no more than a mile from the cove when they came upon the two sea-creatures who had been thrust unwanted into the lives of the family Lameleg and the family Reave like jetsam. Topping a small rise in the ground they almost walked smack into their quarry and had to swiftly take cover behind the scrub bushes and nettle hedges that skirted a grove of stunted apple trees. The minch-maiden and her servant were barely twenty yards away and were just as Nob had described them; the man being old enough to have grey in his hair and the woman being comely and half the age of her companion. The Lamelegs and Reaves watched attentively and could definitely make out the slight yellowness of the woman's skin but could not confirm the deformity of her eyes as she had her back to them. Even so, they no longer questioned the veracity of their slandered informant. Strangers the boy had said and, sure enough, strangers these were. Anyone not of the people of the Oswaldmægþ had no business to be on the island at all. The war party waited silently in their position of concealment.

Within the grove Ealdræd of the Pæga and Eiji of the Kajhin were taking their ease. They had need of it. Having found themselves miraculously alive and ashore after their shipwreck at sea, they were making some attempt at recovering their befuddled and exhausted senses. Those who have been convinced that death was about to claim them are apt to be confused by the curious sensation, against all the odds, of breath in their lungs and blood flowing in their veins.

They had no way to know exactly where they were and both were far too overcome by the extremes of fatigue to care. In fact, they had beached on what was the last known piece of land in the world; the westernmost landfall of the Canbrai Isles. Had the ocean's current carried them west at any greater speed, or had they kicked their floating cabin door along any less vigorously or given up their kicking at any point, then they would have slipped passed the last of the islands and been swept out into the lost unknown; the limitless nothing of the endless waves. Even in ignorance of this fact, Ealdræd breathed a silent prayer to Buldr and blessed his good fortune in having Eiji to lend the strength of her legs to that of his. He could guess well enough that if either of them had been alone on that cabin door, then his or her death would have been inevitable. As it was, their combined strength had been, by the skin of their teeth, just barely sufficient for survival.

With the initial return of consciousness they had merely lain on the beach where the tide had tossed them and panted like overheated dogs, marvelling at the joy of feeling the ground beneath them. But neither was a character much given to ascetic reflection on the philosophical vagaries of existence when their fleshly appetites demanded attention, and as the morning sun rose higher they recovered sufficiently to become aware of the painful holes where their stomachs ought to be. Without further delay, therefore, they had clambered to their feet and moved off inland to seek sustenance, for they were utterly famished.

Fortunately food had not been long in the seeking. Their ordeal by sea had drained all the vitality from their limbs but with the renewed chance of life provided by the firm sod underfoot their respective physical constitutions had been resilient enough to limp and shuffle the mile it had taken to come across the trickle of a stream from which to drink adjacent to a natural orchard of paltry apple trees. After quenching their thirst in the crystal clear brook they had gathered armfuls of tiny green apples and wolfed them down one after another to fill their aching emptiness within. The fruit was still on the trees because it was not yet ripe but hungry bellies could not wait on summer's ripeness or the owner's permission. They ate voraciously, being so ravenous that they might cheerfully have eaten a plate of Buntuu lice-worms which, although considered a great delicacy amongst the Buntuu, have earned that nation the nickname amongst their Ahkrani neighbours of *suka mangkok*, meaning the 'people of the puke-bowl'. Happily Buntuu cuisine was not on the menu and the sharp, bitter flavour of the apples tasted like the ambrosia of the gods to the starving pair of storm-tossed travellers. They consumed with relish, savouring every mouthful.

The orchard had not been planted, for the trees were distributed higgledy-piggledy without design by the random chance of nature, but it would none-the-less be a valuable resource of natural sustenance for the local population, if there were any inhabitants in wherever this place was. The apples were of the type called 'pips' in Aenglia, reminding Ealdræd of just how near he now must be to his homeland. Could this perhaps even be the coast of Aenglia that they had been washed up upon?

Eiji sat down on the ground with her back propped against a tree, a picture of drowsy relaxation, and Ealdræd followed her excellent example. The drinking water and the fruit had done wonders in restoring some vigour to his over-expended muscles but he was still desperately tired. There was a rigidity throughout his lower back and thighs that would take some days to ease. He and the girl had perforce slept on the beach but a little doze to aid their digestion would be very welcome. He would concern himself with questions of where they were and what to do about it when they were both better rested.

No sooner had his backside hit the grass and his head leaned back against the bark of a shady tree than he was sound asleep. Thirty yards away the twins, Finian and Firgul Reave, emerged from behind the scrub bushes and nettle hedges from where they had been watching. Their patience had been rewarded and the tantalizing scent of self-affirming violence was in their nostrils. Énnae Reave waved a hand at them to linger, to wait until the sprites were more deeply asleep, but the twins were having none of that. As Énnae rose to go along with them, for when the assault was made all must attack together, Ulfbert and Waulud Lameleg appeared at his side. But Siward and Nob Lameleg hung back some yards behind.

Eiji was feeling very much better, her belly full to swollen with the delicious apples, but she thought that she would feel even more replete if she could relax her aching body up against that of her Effendi and lay her sleepy head upon his chest. There were few

344

things in life she took greater pleasure in than being curled up in cloister with her master. So she started to crawl over on her hands and knees toward him to satisfy her inclination. That was when she noticed the ugly men rushing in at them from amongst the trees.

The look of shock upon her exotic countenance was as nothing to the expressions of terror that forthwith swept over the faces of the Reaves and the Lamelegs. Nob had been right; she was some unnatural monster from the ocean. None of these men of the Oswaldmægþ had ever heard of an oriental or had one described to them, let alone seen one for themselves. The eastern cast of Eiji's eyes stopped them in their tracks. The Menghis girl was from a land so far distant from the Canbrai Isles that the denizens of these crags of rock in the western ocean would not have believed that any such place as Menghis could possibly exist. For a moment they simply stood frozen and gaped in awe.

Eiji shrieked "Effendi!" and Ealdræd's lean body uncoiled like a bullwhip. He was on his feet before he was actually awake. At the sight of five men close by, two of them armed, he took in and comprehended the danger of the situation at a glance. He had abandoned all his weapons when the ship went down, being concerned only to attempt to survive the ocean, so he and his Menghis companion had nothing but the few rags of clothes that they stood up in. But sleep and fatigue were shaken off in a second as he prepared himself to receive the enemy bare-handed.

Recovering from their stupefaction at the sight of the minch-maiden, and with an advantage in numbers sufficient to bolster courage in the faint-hearted, the five Canbrai men leaped forward to fall upon the sea-devils. The twins, several paces in the lead, charged at Ealdræd, Finian swinging a huge, misshapen lump of wood that had been crudely fashioned into a bludgeon, Firgul wielding a small bodkin, a sharply pointed knife in an arrowhead design. Énnae ran wide, trying to circle around behind the tall foreigner to attack from the blind side.

Ulfbert and Waulud, neither of whom carried any weapon, ran pell-mell at the diminutive Eiji, their hearts in their throats with fear of the unholy, praying that she would not conjure them off to a thousand fathoms below the ocean depths by dint of some magic charm. The woman crouched to meet their onslaught and snarled a string of unintelligible foreign words that sounded to the islanders exactly how they imagined a supernatural hex would sound. But Ulfbert and

Waulud were not without courage and continued their headlong rush at her.

From the periphery, Siward and Nob danced around excitedly shouting encouragement but displayed no signs of wishing to engage in the battle personally. They were content to roar and shake their fists.

Ealdræd sidestepped a clumsy blow from Finian, smashed a fist into the fellow's temple that stunned him, and in that second grabbed the bludgeon from his hands. Firgul hurtled in behind his twin but Ealdræd, with the tactical mind of a veteran, jumped sideways so that he kept Finian's body between himself and Firgul. As the latter tried to swerve in his course to aim his charge at Ealdræd he crashed straight into Finian from behind and they both went sprawling on the ground. The Aenglian struck down with the bludgeon and cracked Firgul over the back of the head so hard that he lost consciousness, dropping his bodkin.

Eiji surprised her first assailant, Ulfbert, by leaping straight at his chest as he came in close and then clinging on to him, her legs around his waist, her fingers seeking to rip his eyeballs from their sockets. It was so unexpected that he was momentarily nonplussed, shutting his eyes against her fingernails and trying unsuccessfully to dislodge her but doing no more than tearing her linen smock down the back. Then Eiji grabbed his head in her hands and sank her strong young teeth into his nose, biting deep to draw blood. Waulud had arrived by this time but when he found that pounding on her naked back with his fist achieved no effect whatever, he began trying to prise her off his brother by hauling with all his strength on her shoulders. But the girl was holding on like a limpet, still biting Ulfbert's nose as more and more blood poured down his chin and chest. In the struggle all three crashed to the ground together and Ulfbert screamed hysterically as her teeth cut clean through the tough flesh and she bit an inch off the end of his nose. She spat it out with a sneer.

Énnae's strategy to assail his opponent from the rear had failed because in defeating the twins Ealdræd had reversed direction. As Énnae threw himself forward, bending low in hopes of snatching up the bodkin, the Aenglian mercenary thrust with the bludgeon, an unconventional use of the weapon, and struck his man on the crown of the head. Half-stunned, Énnae was defenceless when the Aenglian stepped in and used the bludgeon after the intended manner of its design and hammered it into the man's skull, which cracked and bled under the terrible impact. The man of Canbrai lay very still at the mercenary's feet.

Waulud shifted his grip from Eiji's shoulders and managed to get one arm flexed tight around her throat to drag her sideways half up on to her feet to pull her off the profusely bleeding wretch underneath her. Simultaneously, with his free hand he punched her repeatedly in the breasts to quell her raging ferocity. Finding herself unable to break free from his grasp despite the violence of her struggles, she seized the wrist of his punching fist in both her hands and continued to fight by stamping down on Ulfbert who was still flat on his back on the ground clutching at his face. The barefoot girl got her heel into his ribs and genitals three of four times before Waulud was able to wrestle her away.

At this point Finian called out beseechingly for a halt. Events had not transpired as he had anticipated. Both Firgul and Énnae were unconscious and perhaps dead, the stranger from the sea now brandished both the bludgeon and the bodkin, and Waulud could do nothing with the minch-maiden except hang on like grim death with his arms wrapped around her in a bear-hug for fear of what would happen if her released her. At best he might crush her enough to crack her ribs.

"Truce! Truce!" implored Finian forlornly, and Waulud joined in with the cry, "Truce! Truce!"

"Let her go!" commanded Ealdræd to Waulud, and the latter was so astonished that the demon spoke his own language, the language of the Ehngleish, that he opened his arms almost without thinking about it.

Eiji, free at last, spun around upon the instant and kicked the unsuspecting islander as hard as she could in the testicles. Waulud went down in a crumpled heap, choking for breath, darkness and nausea consuming him. Ealdræd had to bellow like a bull "Eiji, desist!" to stop her from pursuing the matter further. Once her savage bloodlust was raised, only the stern authority of her Effendi stood any chance of controlling her. Waulud rolled over weeping to slither away.

"What do you on Gehorgie and how do you speak our language?" asked Finian, not quite keeping the tremble out of his voice.

"I am Ealdræd of the Pæga, a spearman of Aenglia. I speak my own language. Where is this place; be these the Isles of Canbrai?"

"Aye, Canbrai, aye," nodded Finian, as if not quite making sense of the answer. "This place is called Gehorgie. But if you are of the Aenglian Pæga, why do you comport yourself with a selkie?"

"She is no marine-spirit," replied Ealdræd with a dismissive grin, "she is as human as you or I. She hails from a country further from here than any Canbrai carrack has ever sailed, a land so distant that its name would mean nothing to any man within a thousand miles of where we stand. She is a woman of the Menghis, a nation of the steppes that lie to the east of Tehlitz and the wastelands of the Khevnics."

"It is you who lie," said Finian warily, "for there are no such places in the world as those you name. She is a grindilow, a mermaid siren of the deep, and you are her champion."

"She is not," asserted Ealdræd firmly, "and as that fellow can tell you," he gestured toward Ulfbert, still groaning on the grass miserably failing to staunch the flow of blood from his amputated nose, "she is her own champion."

Eiji raised her chin with pride. The dialect in which the islanders spoke Ehngleish, her Effendi's native tongue, was not so very dissimilar to Ealdræd's own. Consequently Eiji, whose lessons in the language had been continuing apace during the preceding months journeying with her master, could follow the discussion without too much difficulty except for the references to such things as grindilow's which were new to her. The words of respect she had received from the mouth of her Effendi did her honour and she felt that this was no more than justice for had she not earned them? Had she not fought two of these *ghazboutyr* bare-handed and emerged victorious? She said, more or less in Ehngleish, to the poor inferior specimen of a man who had sued for peace:

"I am Eiji of the Kajhin, the purest tribe of the Menghis, the peoples of the empire of the steppes, and I pity you poor *ghazboutyr* in your craven cowardice."

Ghazboutyr was the Menghali word for foreigner. To Eiji, everyone born west of the steppes was *ghazboutyr* and therefore somewhat less than civilized. Finian, Siward and Nob shuddered as they heard the alien creature speak in words that they could understand and the outlandish barbarism of her accent merely confirmed for them that she was not of this world.

Ealdræd gave an abbreviated explanation of how he and the Menghis had been brought to Canbrai. There was little point in wasting words on these peasants who lacked the necessary knowledge and awareness of the world to understand that his tale was true. The arrival of himself and Eiji in so far-flung a location in the condition they were in, he wearing nothing but the sorry remains of a leather doublet and breeks, she in nothing but the torn remnants of a green linen smock, might have testified on their behalf as to the veracity of his story. But such subtleties made no impression upon the minds of mere bog-trotters. They could not see passed the oddity of the girl's oriental eyes.

However, a distrustful and vigilant peace was finally agreed when Ealdræd fished inside the lining of his ragged doublet, being careful not to reveal how much coin he was carrying, and offered a gold piece to the Canbrai to purchase new clothes and a spear. He held out the golden penny for all to see.

The Oswaldmægþ did not trade commercially with anyone, not even the Canbrai of the other islands, for the descendants of Oswald were the accursed and were shunned. This meant that they had no use for coin as such and had very little chance to acquire any valuable metals. But their smiths did have the knowledge of smelting metal and they could melt down gold into something which they did value like rings, or bracelets, or an ornament for the hilt of a sword. The paucity of opportunities to lay hands on such treasures made these scarce objects all the more desirable. So the remains of the menfolk of the Reaves and Lamelegs were not averse to getting this precious metal precisely because it so seldom came their way.

Grudgingly, they agreed to discuss an exchange. Despite the evidence of the fight, they seemed not to realise that Ealdræd and Eiji were in a position to kill them all. The fact that they were on their home ground caused the Canbrai men to view their consent to trade to be some kind of concession; some form of indulgence or special dispensation to the outlanders. But Ealdræd had lived too long to permit himself to be perturbed by such arrant nonsense and Eiji took her lead from her Effendi so the whole parcel of them trod the road back to the croft of the Lameleg family for parley, the unconscious

Énnae and Firgul being carried over the shoulders of Finian and Siward. Waulud limped awkwardly in the rear, leaning his weight upon young Nob. Ulfbert shuffled along holding his shirt to the bleeding ruin of his face.

*   *   *

It was to be two days before Ealdræd and Eiji were in a position to buy new clothes to replace their rags. The Lamelegs and Reaves had nothing in the way of clothing and weapons to sell even if they had wanted to. Their idea was to trade *isen wull* blankets for Ealdræd's coin. The Aenglian, of course, refused. But then it was discovered that Énnae had died from his injuries and so the twins ran off back to their own croft swearing to have nothing more to do with the bringers of misfortune. They were not alone in this attitude. The appearance of the Menghis girl at the home of the Lamelegs caused the women of the household to set up a dreary and doleful wailing that threatened to become maniacal, so Ealdræd put it to Waulud that if he would act as guide taking Ealdræd and Eiji to whoever was the leader of this scattered community, someone who might have goods for sale, then Waulud should receive half a coin in payment. Despite this remuneration being about fifty times what the job was actually worth, the crofter was at first very reluctant to consent to the suggestion, for he feared to be alone with the two weird outlanders. But he eventually agreed because it was the quickest way to be rid of them, so that the Lamelegs would not have to feed them and the womenfolk could cease their constant mournful howling.

It meant leaving the isle of Gehorgie and paddling their cautious way in Waulud's log boat between two adjacent isles and then over a narrow strip of sea to Wearg, the largest of the islands occupied by the people of the Oswaldmægþ. Eiji was not best pleased about trusting her fate to the sea again after their recent experiences but she understood that they could hardly remain on Gehorgie for the rest of their lives. Waulud's meagre vessel was about fifteen feet long and was constructed of whole logs nailed together and sealed with tar made from wood resin. It could hold no more than four passengers in safety and it had no sail, only an oar in the stern. Ealdræd was surprised that a Cambrain could own so poor a craft when the Canbrai Islanders were world-famous as the greatest mariners upon the sea. It was puzzling. Waulud was careful to stay close to the shore of each little island they passed and whenever they came to an open stretch of water he rowed with such energy that he must have believed that all the sea-sprites in the ocean were chasing his little boat.

To call anywhere 'Wearg' was also peculiar for it meant 'one who is a cursed outlaw'. Again, Ealdræd's curiosity was piqued. During the journey he asked Waulud to tell him the origin of this odd name and what was the history of his people. The Aenglian knew something of the Canbrai already, having been raised so nearby on the mainland, but he had no knowledge of the internal politics of the islands.

Waulud was not an especially garrulous person, being of a taciturn disposition by nature, but in these unprecedented and highly nervous circumstances he was grateful to have a familiar subject to occupy his mind and take his thoughts away from the siren female who was sitting in the bow of his tiny craft. Not only was she a most unnatural creature but moreover he could still feel the abiding and nauseating ache in his genitals where she had planted her foot during the fight. He hoped silently to himself that she was suffering a similar throbbing hurt in her breasts where he had dealt her several hefty thumps. Telling the tale of his tribe, Waulud kept his quietly murmured discourse directed at the tall Aenglian, for he at least was no sprite. With the waves lapping against his log boat, Waulud related the history that formed the entire background to his conception of the world.

There were three mægþ; three family clans of the Canbrai. Two made up the populations of the majority of the chain of islands but the third and much smaller clan made their home only at the southernmost tip of the archipelago. Although the two larger clans were eminent seafarers who ranged far and wide across of the western ocean, in stark contrast, the third clan never left their isolated abode.

Once they had been *bróþor*, brother tribes, each with a chief born of the same father. Back in the unknowable times long past it had always been the Canbrai way; three brothers to lead the three mægþ. The sons of one of these three would thereafter become the next generation of clan chiefs so that the blood-tie of all three clans was continually replenished. But the old ways were broken in the days of Osgar, Oswin and Oswald.

Oswald had attempted to make himself the sole ruler of all the isles but he was defeated by his brothers in battle and his family were declared *awierged*, the accursed; excommunicate from all others of their kind. This undying curse had been laid upon the seed of Oswald for his affront to Osgar and Oswin. And for the two centuries since that time of woe his progeny had been shunned by the other Canbrai clans, leaving the Oswaldmægþ as the outcasts of the islands.

In this way the mægþ of the Canbrai became separated in their bloodlines and thereafter each was named for, and descended from, only one founding brother. They were the Osgarmægþ, the Oswinmægþ, and the Oswaldmægþ. The clans descended from Osgar and Oswin occupied all but the isles that were the most distant from the mainland. These last few rocky outcrops were left as the prison of the clan of Oswald, rejected by the other two tribes of their *bróþor* kindred for the last two hundred years.

Theirs was the last piece of solid ground before the emptiness of the great western ocean. They had been left with nowhere to live but the very end of the world, a spit of land clinging to the outermost edge of human habitation. Perhaps this was why Waulud's home isle was called Gehorgie, meaning spit. But the word might also take the meaning of being spat upon, and this was the more likely origin of the name, just as Wearg was a name to describe its inhabitants, the ones who are accursed as outlaw. Spat upon as the *awierged*, the Oswaldmægþ bided in the last place on earth.

But it would not forever be so. Waulud's voice took on fresh heart as he turned his tale to the future. His was the generation of the Oswaldmægþ for whom vengeance and retribution would come. For it was in this generation that the Mædencild had been born. Long had they awaited her coming to free them from the tyranny of excommunication. More than once in the past their ancestors had believed her to have come to bring them salvation but on each of those occasions their belief had been proven false and they had been defeated again by their more powerful cousin tribes. But this time, in this generation, there could be no doubt.

The Mædencild, the virgin redemptor, the child of wonders, the maiden redeemer, was the repository of all the hopes of the Oswaldmægþ because she was a *Scinnlæce*, a sorceress of the craft, a practitioner of wicca. The Mædencild was said to have command over the power of *wælcyrige*, the hex known as 'the chooser of the slain' by which she could lay the hand of death upon any.

Waulud's grimy and maudlin countenance had become suffused with a beatific light as he spoke of this miracle that would release his folk from their long degradation, and the radiance of it continued to illuminate his grubby features as he rowed them into harbour at Wearg.

Ealdræd's first impression of the place did nothing to justify this glow of optimism for the future. It was clearly a much more substantial community than that which resided on Gehorgie, with numerous cottages clustered together into an extensive village. There were urchin children everywhere wrapped in their filthy shawls, all being nagged incessantly by scarecrow women in their kirtles, long gowns of linen and cambric, and the wimples that were still worn in these parts rather than the coif. The presence of the wimple prompted Ealdræd to realise how far behind the times were the people of this shunned race. The coif had largely replaced that item of feminine attire at least a century ago on the mainland, yet here, only a few hours sailing from Aenglia, it had yet to be introduced. This was not so with the other tribes of Canbrai. They, as great seafarers, knew of all the latest developments in the modern world. The Oswaldmægþ had truly been set apart.

Socially they were ceorls; peasants who held their own lands as freehold, owing no allegiance to any lord and performing no boon work on lands held in fief, because the political structure amongst the isles was based upon clan allegiance, as it was across the water in Aenglia. Theirs were lives spent in the cutting of the peat for fuel, the spinning of the *isen wull* for their crude habiliment, and living off a diet of salt herring and fish eels supplemented by whatever else could be reaped from nature. Ealdræd noticed signs that scurvy was common, a distemper caused by eating too much salted fish.

There was a blacksmith's in the village, though he had little enough smithying to occupy his time and was for the most part a fisherman like the majority. It was from him that Ealdræd bought himself a seven foot spear made in ash and topped with an iron-leaf blade fifteen inches long. The iron was of poor quality but it did his heart good to have a spear in his hands again. The money was well-spent as much for his morale as for the weapon itself. He bought the spear and a reasonably new tunic in plain wool weave for himself, as well as a linen kirtle and a bodkin for Eiji, along with clogs for them both, for one gold penny. He was overpaying considerably at this price but he was exasperated at living in rags and, anyway, such largesse would impress the natives. For half of a second coin he paid for lodgings and meals for the two of them in the blacksmith's workshop for as long as accommodation would be needed. The remaining half coin went as payment to Waulud.

Eiji turned her nose up at the kirtle for the gown covered her right down to her toes, a style which wasn't to her taste as she associated it with elderly women and, anyway, it didn't suit combat. But there was nothing else and at least it felt comfortingly warm after spending two days wearing only the remains of her smock, so in that respect it was welcome. Ealdræd used the linen of her discarded smock as an undershirt beneath his new tunic because the thing was damnably itchy. They settled down in the workshop which was probably the cosiest place in the whole village due to the warmth of the smithy's forge. They ate with the blacksmith and his wife; herring fishcakes and potatoes being the usual fare.

Their arrival, naturally, caused a sensation. Emissaries were despatched to carry word to the Mædencild and there was a good deal of speculation about what she would have to say on the subject. Ealdræd kept his distance from the locals, with the exception of Hesryk the blacksmith, because initially a degree of social friction had been caused by the way that the children kept blatantly staring at Eiji. The adults did their share of gawping also, but out of the corner of their eye so as not to be too conspicuous about it. But the guttersnipes knew nothing of subtlety and would simply stand and gape intently. Not one to tolerate anything that she considered an insult, Eiji had slapped a couple of the children hard across their impertinent little faces to teach them a lesson, and then she had done the same to one of the mothers who had complained about what the woman claimed was the mistreatment of her offspring. There might have been trouble but for Ealdræd's imposing presence nearby with a spear in his hands. Thereafter the children were ushered away from the smithy and the staring was conducted more surreptitiously so that Eiji could maintain her dignity by affecting not to notice.

On the second day there was a great hubbub in the centre of the settlement, with almost the whole community gathering around a figure in their midst. Ealdræd and Eiji were called upon to present themselves and, playing along for safety's sake, they did so. The person to whom they were presented was a gawky fifteen year old girl in a dirty but decorated kirtle and wimple, with lank blonde hair hanging to her waist and a pastily unhealthy complexion. She was so undernourished, like all of the Oswaldmægþ, that she looked even younger than her age. In comparison with Eiji, who was only four years her senior, the skinny Canbrai virgin looked very much the child. But then that was a part of her exalted status, for this was the Mædencild; the saviour of her people, a natural-born sorceress, and frequently given to fits.

She had an impressive convulsion upon meeting the foreigners, erupting into spasms and contortions of theatrical magnificence, undergoing a full paroxysm of writhing and shrieking before finally calming down to announce that the appearance of outlanders at this propitious moment was a sign from the gods that the day had come for the Oswaldmægþ to rejoin the world of foreigners beyond the waters. No longer would they live apart from others.

Great cheers went up as all hailed the glorious news. They had all been waiting in anticipation of this for months. At last the Mædencild had declared the advent of their redemption and their revenge, therefore it must be so and would be so. Men rushed to get their weapons as if they thought they would set to sea at this very minute.

Seeing a chance to get off this island and thereby take a step closer to the mainland, Ealdræd offered his and Eiji's martial support in any forthcoming war against the enemies of the Oswaldmægþ. There was more cheering at this and a positive ovation of applause. The mercenary swore grandly that he would lay a dozen decapitated heads at the Mædencild's feet. The skinny adolescent babbled some mystic gibberish at this, which everyone took to represent her pleasure and acceptance of this offer, provoking further acclamation and adulation. Total confusion reigned until wiser heads started to organise matters in a more deliberate and orderly fashion.

The next day they began collecting their boats together, all of which were about the same size as Waulud's log dinghy. Stores of food and drink were amassed and weaponry was sharpened. They were a fishing community who wished to transform themselves overnight into an army. It wasn't like any army that Ealdræd had ever been a part of before. The Aenglian mercenary couldn't remember ever having seen any military preparations that quite resembled this rag-tag-and-bobtail militia. He wasn't sure who they were intending to fight but he was quite sure that they would never live to sing any songs of victory. He would have to keep an eye peeled for the first available possibility for himself and Eiji to sneak off before this sorry lot ever reached a battlefield.

In the meantime Ealdræd and Eiji, having been sanctified by the child of wonders as a good omen, had become much favoured in the eyes of the community and were treated as privileged guests. The mother who had argued with Eiji over the slapping of the children was publicly flogged for her disrespect to those who had found approval with the Mædencild. They hung the beseechingly penitent mother naked from a horizontal tree branch and she was given thirty strokes of a long leather whip. Eiji enjoyed every one of them, watching the bloody spectacle with a huge grin of gratification on her prettily malicious face. When the badly beaten mother was made to kneel in contrition at the feet of the Menghis, Eiji magnanimously forgave her with ostentatious ceremony to the great satisfaction of the assembled villagers.

But that night on some clean straw in the blacksmith's workshop it was Eiji who was on the receiving end as Ealdræd interlaced their enthusiastic fucking with repeated spankings, welting her proffered backside with the strap that Hesryk used to strop his knives. He was her Effendi and she expected no less of him. The strapping had the effect that it always had on the lewdly submissive Menghis; she rutted like a stoat and purred like a cat. It had been a while since they had been in a position to enjoy their carnal pleasures and they made up for their recent enforced abstinence by making absolute pigs of themselves in the comfortable, forge-heated smithy. He trimmed her up smartly with smacks from the strap and she milked him till his balls ached. Ealdræd greeted the dawn feeling in dire need of a good night's sleep, and Eiji saluted the rising sun with a healthy appetite for her breakfast.

And then, with the morning no more than two hours old and seemingly before the people of Wearg quite knew what they were actually doing, the preparations for war had been completed, everyone was equipped, and they were all out on the water. The Oswaldmægþ took to the oars in a flotilla of their small boats lashed together by strong ropes so that they could better withstand the open sea. Northward they paddled, the righteous army of the Mædencild, passed the empty barren rock of the Geæmetigan, so named because no one had ever lived there, and onward to Pithkin, the most populated atoll of the southern isles in the Osgarmægþ archipelago, the closest enemy landfall.

The bracing freshness of the breeze wasn't sharp enough to keep Ealdræd from dozing gently through much of the voyage but Eiji wasn't about to join him in sleep because she could never again feel safe on the ocean, especially with the boats being seriously overcrowded in order to bring along as many fighters as possible. Fortunately, the wind was behind them and, although there wasn't a single sail amongst them, they fairly sped over the dull grey white-crested waves in a flourish of skilful rowing.

The coast of Pithkin was a mass of pebbles under low cliffs. The flotilla came in on the tide and hauled their boats up beyond the high water mark, shown by the change in the colour of the stones bleached by the sun. There were pathways aplenty up through the cliffs and soon the army of sixty, fifteen of them women, plus two less than committed foreigners, was striding along like a gaggle of geese through the unsheltered and inhospitable terrain of coarse grass and hillocks. There could be no formal declaration of war, neither side having any government to speak of, nor any means to communicate with the enemy, and so the first the Osgarmægþ would know of the invasion was when someone amongst their number noticed the column of Oswaldmægþ marching upon them.

Happening upon a hamlet of five cottages the vengeful inheritors of Oswald struck without mercy. They put all the buildings to the torch and as the residents rushed outside to flee the flames these panic-crazed yokels were hacked down by the iron-inlaid wooden maces of their besiegers and then cut to pieces by the arrow-shaped bodkins of the rejoicing Oswaldmægþ. Led by the all-prevailing power of the Mædencild, what blood-revenge would suffice for her folk to take upon those cousins who had so cruelly set them apart?

The next habitation was slightly larger and whilst the hamlet was again burned to the ground and all of the tribe of Osgar that were found were put to death, some few of the locals were able to run for the cover of their modest but high-grown wheat-field and successfully escape. They would head at speed for their brethren and disseminate the news of the military campaign that had been unleashed.

Events continued in this way throughout that first afternoon and all of the next morning, after a night of rapacious celebration and conceited clairvoyance of the triumphs to come. The larders and storerooms of the dwellings they destroyed were naturally looted and the army grew bolder on a full stomach liberally saturated with wine. The Oswaldmægþ were not used to alcohol, having only barley beer at home and that poorly fermented, so the guzzling of rich and fruity wines, previously plundered by the Osgar in their pirate raids on the southern kingdoms, gave the Oswald the warlike courage of giants and their procession swaggered along merrily.

The women amongst the Oswald took particular delight in butchering the Osgar women who had been raped during the sack and pillage. They accepted that rapine was the right of every man-under-arms on active service as spoils of war, but witnessing their own husbands violating the Osgar wenches induced a distinct sense of grievance in them for which, in a spirit somewhat lacking in justice, they blamed the Osgar trollops who had been raped. For this reason they carved up their ravished rivals amid all manner of hellish screaming, using more malice than expertise with the knife. But their enthusiasm for the work more than made up for any deficiency of technique.

In mid-afternoon, as the mob of the Oswaldmægþ walked in their martial glory through a thick cluster of trees and out into an open field, they found themselves confronted by the accumulated forces of the Osgar on Pithkin. Word had reached the various hamlets and villages hereabouts and all who heard it had congregated in the field of the henge stones of the summer solstice, which was the central location of the whole island. They were assembled to repel the invaders.

The two tribes drew themselves out into ragged lines facing each other, a mere thirty yards apart. The Osgarmægþ outnumbered the trespassers slightly and were by no means intimidated by the half-drunken howling rabble. Their contempt for the accursed, the despised *awierged*, was a habit of mind that they had been raised with from childhood and people do not fear those whom they genuinely believe to be inferior. There was much boastful abuse thrown back and forth from both sides.

Ealdræd and Eiji had played no part in the campaign thus far, merely keeping well out of the way of the blood feud. When a horde of ignorant people with a sense of grievance went on a rampage, they recognised no rules of engagement or military code of war; hence the atrocities which had already been committed. The most prudent course of action in such circumstances was to stand well back and say nothing. But now it seemed likely that the Aenglian and the Menghis would get drawn into the forthcoming battle and it was as plain as could be to the experienced eye of the knowledgeable mercenary that the Osgar were both the physically stronger and the better armed. Coming from so legendary a seafaring culture, they were provisioned with armaments from around the world. Most of them had sturdy cutlasses that would make short work of the bodkins, maces, cudgels and bludgeons that proliferated amongst the Oswald. Covertly, the veteran soldier started to manoeuvre Eiji inconspicuously toward the far end of the battle-line so that they might be in the best position for a swift desertion from the field. This, after all, was a fight that was nothing whatsoever to do with either of them.

Eiji's attitude could not have been further removed from that of her master. Although she had experienced fights to the death before, this was to be her first pitched battle between armies. She did not see it, as Ealdræd did, as an inconsequential brawl between bumpkins. She would do battle alongside her Effendi and her heart was beating fast at the prospect of what was to come. She was armed only with her bodkin and a cudgel that had been loaned to her but she was undaunted by this because she had a plan. She would hang back off the edge of the skirmish until she could take someone from behind with her cudgel or bodkin and get hold of the defeated enemy's sword or axe or whatever it might be to properly arm herself. Then let them beware the fighting spirit of a daughter of the Menghis. She fidgeted in her eagerness.

Then something happened to lift Ealdræd's spirits greatly; the best thing that could possibly have happened from his point of view. The Osgar send forth their champion to fight in single combat. This might mean a pitched battle could be avoided altogether. It required only a champion to represent the Oswald. No doubt there would be some over-confident young buck alight with the honour of his ancestors but with as much knowledge of combat technique as the man in the moon, who would step forward to fight and be speedily bested by the colossal thug who stood forth as the champion of the Osgar. This monster was of Ealdræd's height but heavier by fifty pounds. Muscularly stout, he had a complexion so ruddy that his face was almost crimson. This was before he had even performed any physical exertion. It was due to this blood-engorged countenance that he was known as Blodréad for his red-face.

The alarming thought struck Ealdræd like a arrow from the sky that some fool amongst the Oswald might suggest that he, the outsider whose arrival had been so auspicious a portent for their tribe, would make a suitable and worthy champion. Perhaps they would expect him to feel honoured at the prospect of laying down his life for their sake. But Ealdræd had no intention of dying for this pack of worthless Canbrai fishermen. He was a professional whose place was in a proper army, fighting with and against men who were worthy of combat. This riot of civilians was beneath him. Ealdræd was racking his brains for a convincing excuse to shirk the dubious privilege, should it be offered to him, when the unfolding of events made manifest that he would not be called upon to participate in a clash of arms with the mighty Blodréad. But he could scarcely credit who it was that would do so.

In accepting the challenge of single combat the Oswaldmægþ sent forth the one person amongst them that they knew could not be defeated by any mortal opponent. They sent forth the Mædencild. The thin fifteen year old girl tramped out with a bombastic grandeur which in no way befitted her bodily stature whilst the ranks of her enemies goggled, then hooted with derisive laughter and cackled with disbelieving scorn. There was widespread spitting, the Osgar sign of sarcastic contempt. Blodréad, who at first was disposed to be insulted, instead saw the funny side and began chuckling so hard that it looked like he was going to burst a blood vessel. He laughed till he was coughing and gasping for air. Someone behind him bellowed "Send out her baby sister, send out the swaddling infant!" and Blodréad redoubled his scarlet chortling until he was bent double from his uncontrollable mirth.

The child of wonders carried no weapon and had removed her wimple so that her long blonde hair flew like a banner in the wind. Behind her the hushed Oswaldmægþ, paying no heed to the mockery of their combatants, set up a low devout chanting of "Scinnlæce O Wælcyrige, Scinnlæce O Wælcyrige, Scinnlæce O Wælcyrige . . . ." at which the willowy body of the Mædencild bent back like a longbow, her arms shot aloft, and a single high-pitched note sounded shrill from her throat.

In that very moment the laughter stopped. All the abusive hilarity ceased and the gleeful condescension fell from the faces of the Osgar. The riotous sound of ribald amusement dropped out of the air like a candle being snuffed out. It was replaced by the single piercing tone of the Mædencild. She held that note for an eternity, on and on it went, beyond all understanding, on and on until the minds of those who heard it wanted to claw out their own ears for relief from its terrifying oppression.

And then the convulsions started. The twig-like body shook and shuddered, the mouth foamed and the tiny muscles tensed in appalling seizures of awesome demonic possession. The girl thrashed about like a puppet being shaken by the very gods themselves. Blodréad was rooted to the spot only a few feet away and as he stared in chilling apprehension it seemed as if his ruddy face became mottled, with parts of it turning pale and other patches growing darker into a livid burgundy. Mesmerised, his lips hung slack and his powerful body was rendered immobile.

The conjuring held all who beheld it spellbound and all the while the Oswaldmægþ maintained their pious chanting "Scinnlæce O Wælcyrige, Scinnlæce O Wælcyrige . . . ." In the midst of the violence of her tumult the Mædencild erupted into speech. Her inchoate raving and ranting, the frenzied writhing of her arms in appeal to the spirits of the sky and of the bowels of the earth, her other-worldly wailing and cries of mystic incantation sent ice into the soul of Blodréad and set the pulse pounding like horses hooves in his temples. He was a true believer in the arcane power of the hex, like everyone else. Staggered by the freakishness of her jabbering and babbling he grew cold inside as the apprehension stole over him that this child was indeed a *wælcyrie*. Suddenly her hands extended forward in his direction, the fingers outstretched, the nails like claws. Staring deep into the eyes of the massive warrior before her, she smote the champion of the Osgarmægþ with his own deep-rooted and lifelong faith in the occult. The veins were raised on his bull-like neck and his arms were full of the prickling of needles. Pain seized his pounding heart. His knees began to buckle and he dropped his cutlass.

An immense groan rose up from the Osgar as they saw the power of the Mædencild. Her eyeballs rolled back in their sockets to show pure white with the lids open. Blodréad cringed, visibly struggled to breathe and clutched at his chest as if his vitals were collapsing inside him. Then, just as the girl's tremors began slowly to subside, a crippling agony lanced through his heart, a numbness spread through him, mist dimmed his vision and he fell face down on the ground, jerked once, and lay still. He was stone dead.

All the warriors on both sides were struck mute by this absolute proof of the enchantment of a *wælcyrie*. They had all born witness to the truth, that the Mædencild commanded the hex of 'the chooser of the slain'. Let all swear by their own eyes that she could lay the hand of death upon any. The witchery of the shunned folk had brought the curse of Oswald back amongst the Canbrai to visit retribution upon them.

Then a roar of unrestrained triumph trumpeted from the mass of the Oswaldmægþ and they charged. It took only seconds to cross the short space between the two armies but the Osgarmægþ scarcely raised their weapons in their own defence. They had no fight left in them. They were opposed by a power that no man could defy. Unable even to run away, they were doomed souls. The onslaught of the vengeful progeny of Oswald crashed into them like a stampede of howling wraiths and the Osgar were hewn down like wheat under the scythe. The carnage was grotesque as the Osgar were quite literally ripped apart. It took less than five minutes for all of the soldiers of Osgar to be put to death but the mutilation of the corpses lasted the best part of an hour.

Ealdræd and Eiji, the latter somewhat truculent and reproachful toward Ealdræd at his having held her back from the fighting so that she'd had no real opportunity to participate in the killing, went trudging around the piles of bodies plundering for weapons and clothing before it was all ruined by the gore-drenched desecration of the dead being indulged in by the euphoric Oswaldmægþ. The field of battle had much to offer, for the Osgar had been well-equipped and most of the Oswald, bloody to the elbows, were more of a mind to rend flesh than to steal armaments.

Ealdræd did come across two young men squabbling over an ornamented broadsword for which both had a covetous desire. It was splendidly showy because it was so enormous. When he paused by them they offered him the broadsword, being rapturously overtaken with a sense of gratitude to this human prophecy of Oswaldmægþ resurrection. But to their total amazement Ealdræd declined the offer of the sword. With the blade being so long it required a heavy pommel on the hilt to counter-balance the weight of the blade, making the whole thing cumbersome and clumsy. As a practical professional soldier he preferred more useful, serviceable weaponry.

He found it a moment later in a beautifully crafted oaken spear, about six feet long, the top third of which was a sheath of iron, polished till it gleamed, with a long-bladed hewing spearhead which could be used to slash as well as thrust. He threw away the cheap spear he had bought on Wearg and took up the beautiful oak. He also managed to collect a scale-mail shirt that would fit him and a rather fine dirk constructed wholly of iron but with riveted leather strapping for its handle. It was an elegantly slender stiletto dagger and would serve as able support to his spear. In addition, he claimed a chainmail coif. When he rejoined Eiji she was wearing a cutlass on her right hip and a poniard alongside her bodkin on her left hip, all attached to a man's wide leather belt which on her smaller frame she had wrapped twice around her waist. She had found a pair of boy's boots that were more or less her size and she carried a pot-basin helmet which was not dissimilar to the one that Ealdræd had lost when they were shipwrecked. When he tried it on it didn't fit as snugly as his former helmet but it would serve to do the job and he gave the Menghis a saucy kiss in return, along with the chainmail coif which she may as well have since he now had a helmet again. Eiji, of course, took intense pleasure in the ownership of killing tools and she was so pleased with her darling new cutlass that she was in transports of delight swishing it about in her diminutive fist and uttering several of the more obscene Menghali battle-cries and war-curses.

Over the next two days the Oswaldmægþ ran amok across the whole of Pithkin, berserk in their religious fervour after the vindication of the Mædencild, and slaughtered every living human they could find there; children, men, women, old and young, indiscriminately. Their capacity for the infliction of suffering showed no limit and they appeared to have no other concern for as long as the massacre and butchery lasted.

Ealdræd and Eiji spent this time searching through the many vacant dwellings on the island to improve their store of equipment. They struck gold in a sizeable manor house which had a concealed chest buried under a trap-door in which they found a number of items that were not of Canbrai manufacture. More loot brought back from pirate forays. This included a very expensive brown leather sleeveless gambeson tunic cut in the Bhourgbon style with extended shoulder-pieces. It went well with the scalemail shirt Ealdræd had retrieved from the battlefield, making the latter much more comfortable to wear, and it meant that he could cast aside the itchy tunic that was scratching him pink. The treasure chest also provided him with a pair of Wehnbrian ankle boots. He would have preferred something that covered the shins but any leather boots were better than the wooden clogs he had been wearing. For her part, Eiji was able to improve vastly upon her linen kirtle in the form of a fabulous blue and green heavy silk chemise and high-waisted doublet in what was surely the Gathkaree fashion, which gave evidence of just how far south the Canbrai privateers raided. It wasn't exactly a Menghis sartorial design but the silk reminded her of home and it left her bare legs free; she disliked the constraint of the long *ghazboutyr* gowns that smothered the legs with material. The doublet should help to keep the ensemble sufficiently warm, at least for the summer.

Ealdræd's desire was, as before, to move closer to the Aenglian mainland. Consequently, when the Oswaldmægþ announced their intention to row east to the island of Withern in the territory of the Oswinmægþ this was good news. Withern was nothing but a hop, skip, and a jump from the peninsula of Aenglian land owned by the Pæga. He had not set foot in his own clan territory for twenty years but it was apparent that fate was pushing his destiny inexorably in that direction. Well, if it must be so, then so be it.

They took to their boats again, supplemented by several larger craft that had previously belonged to the Osgar and which actually sported a sail. The row boats were lashed alongside these to be dragged along by ropes, so that all might benefit from the technology of sail power. Eiji was quick to claim a place in one of these larger vessels, keen to have as sturdy a conveyance as was available when travelling on her least favourite element. She and Ealdræd stood in the bow in their new apparel and armour looking quite the most impressive members of the fleet, although they were not alone in having looted successfully. A stolen smattering of fancy tunics and gowns were on display in all the boats, and the Mædencild herself was now attired in the glossy drapery of a full length cobalt blue dress in Guillain silk that transformed her and made her look considerably more suitable for her role as a visionary ecstatic. In the rapture of a faith proven justified, the jubilant and exultant Oswaldmægþ discussed continually the way they had laid waste to Pithkin. The thought of it held all their spirits high. Someone struck up a rousing song, was joined by several other voices, and soon all were chorusing together. They sang as they sailed. They were to be the future masters of the Canbrai Isles. The accursed had become the blessed and the long-awaited day of redemption had been delivered unto them in a holy child.

*   *   *

Three dreadful days later, on the island of Withern, in one of the very many lodge cottages left empty by the dead of the Oswinmægþ, Ealdræd plied such knowledge as he had of the healing arts. He claimed scant lore of doctoring but he had acquired wisdom in the treating of wounds from his lifetime of soldiering. Such expertise was often required. The dwelling was six yards square and secure against the elements, providing shelter and warmth from the hearth fire that he had kept constantly smouldering since the day of the second conflict of the Oswald campaign; the battle upon the ridge. He had slept little during these ministrations, dozing sporadically over his fire and over his fallen comrade, tending both patiently.

The Menghis lay on a bed of loose furs under a sheepskin blanket sweating and mumbling in Menghali as the shadows of the fire danced around the walls of wattle and daub. Her fever had broken but there was still danger for the bleeding had been profuse and terrible. If she survived, which he believed she would for she was strong, then there would yet be the horror of the discovery of the loss that she had suffered to be endured. Her right arm was swathed in copious bandaging, all of it saturated in her lifeblood. The wound to Eiji's hand and wrist had been very serious, haemorrhaging blood from an artery. The enemy's axe had almost cut the hand off completely. It may as well have done so, there had been no possibility of saving it.

The one saving grace was that it was not her weapon hand, for Eiji favoured the left hand and it was the other that she had lost; or rather, the remains of which had perforce been cut from her while unconscious. The Aenglian had used a serrated dagger taken from a foe's corpse. He had sat in the hellish firelight, gritting his teeth, sawing through the bone of her wrist and, with each hideously audible rasping of the blade, swearing his hate upon the spiteful windings of Waðsige, God of Wars and Lord of Chance.

The veteran mercenary had, in the perils of his long life, had much occasion to both exalt and revile old Waðsige and today was for the latter. This divinity did not propagate wars, that could be left to his human playthings. Waðsige was a god to revel in the mixed fortunes of warfare, and in the credo of Ealdræd's folk it was to Waðsige that a man prayed for the good luck that caused the arrow to strike the soldier standing next to him in the ranks instead of hitting the prayerful disciple. Waðsige presided over the warrior's gamble in wagering his life in the lottery of war. But the god had offered meagre salvation to Ealdræd's young companion this time. True, she lived, but with only one hand. Her right arm now ended at the wrist.

She had also suffered a deep stab in the thigh but that had severed nothing, it was but a slice into the meat of her leg and it was already healing. It would be stiff and sore for a while but offered no other threat. The same could be said for Ealdræd's own wounds from the recent combat; a slash across the neck, a nick from a spear where it had penetrated the links of his scale-mail and pierced his belly, and a massive bruise to the area of the kidneys that had damaged him inside so much that he had been pissing blood ever since. This last would be the kind of wound that would return to trouble him on cold winter days in his old age. If he had one. He was still inside enemy territory with a badly crippled comrade and nowhere to escape to except the country across the narrow straits between Canbrai and the mainland, and that was the country of the Pæga from which he was forever exiled upon pain of death.

But there seemed to be no immediate jeopardy, for which he was grateful. They needed time to recover from their injuries. So many of the local population had died that those remaining were keeping well out of sight in case there were still soldiers afoot, which at least permitted the Aenglian a brief interim in which to begin to heal.

When Eiji awoke on the morning of the fourth day, before she was even properly aware of her surroundings, her left hand moved instinctively to the awful agony in her right hand. It felt as if her hand were holding hot coals. She groped for it. The moment of confusion which followed, the mystification over the arm that was too short, the puzzlement at the limb which ended where it should not have ended, the baffling shape of the heavily bandaged stub where she should have felt her other hand, all this was almost more appalling for the Aenglian to witness than what came next; the stricken comprehension, the queasy realisation that crawled with grotesque slowness over her sweat-laden face. The keening wail of desolation that emerged from her throat to articulate her shock and grief was the cry of the wild animal caught in a poacher's trap that must gnaw off its own leg to escape; nature irreparably transgressed.

Eiji was too honest in her emotions to pretend a stoicism that she did not feel. The woeful loss was so irrevocable a tragedy that it set her to bawling and whimpering like a Merthyan banshee. Then a sustained black gloom settled over her that the Aenglian knew better than to try to break or placate. He did not insult her with words of comfort. There were some strange cultures he had known, mawkish cloying cultures of sickly sentimentality, that insisted upon parading their compassion by forcing the ailing to listen to empty bland platitudes and insipid banalities intended to alleviate their pain. But such speech only made matters worse by usurping the place of a candid declaration of the sufferer's true feelings, thereby repressing what was better expressed than suppressed. Ealdræd knew this because, like the Menghis, the Aenglians also gave vent to their misery openly, giving tongue to all the frustration, rage, resentment, and impotent fury by which the sick are afflicted, attempting no lying disguise; primal in their wretchedness and misery. Eiji's embittered sorrow was real. There were no words that could compensate her for the hand she had lost. Words of comfort would have been an act of disrespect. Instead Ealdræd gave her a quart clay bottle of Canbrai mead that had been left in the cottage by its deceased owner and kept out of her way to let her drink herself into oblivion. She sipped angrily from the bottle every few seconds amid her indignant and aggrieved tears. She drank in dismal despondency until she wept tears of mead.

Then, while she slept, the Aenglian went hunting for a smithy or for someone skilled in the working of metal and leather. There was a piece of equipment that he wished to have made for which the skills of a blacksmith would be needed. It took him over a day to lay one by the heels in a country that had become remarkably depopulated by the war of the Canbrai mægþ, and even then it was only a blacksmith's apprentice that he found. But the lad must do for lack of anyone else. The boy's fear of the outlander rendered him incapable of movement and it was necessary to buffet him along to inveigle his co-operation in returning with Ealdræd to the cottage in which Eiji lay. During his search for this fellow the mercenary had acquired from diverse other deserted Oswinmægþ cottages the materials required for the plan he had in mind. He issued precise instructions to the apprentice who, once he had grasped the foreigner's purpose and understood that he was here to work, not to be killed or raped, set about the task with a will.

Ealdræd spent the interlude laying beside the sulkily silent Menghis girl, sharing another quart with her, sharing her despair, sleeping in fits and starts, listening to the apprentice at his hammering, and thinking back over the events of the battle upon the ridge on the island of Withern.

Nothing about of the second conflict of the campaign of the Oswaldmægþ was the same as the glorious victory on Pithkin. The Oswin on Withern had received advance knowledge of the Oswald ahead of their arrival. Doubtless an Osgar refugee from the massacre on Pithkin had sailed to Withern while the delirious Oswald had been throwing away their advantage of surprise by wasting time prowling through every nook and cranny on Pithkin searching for anyone still alive. This adjournment had meant that when the Oswald's flotilla of boats finally did make what they hoped would be a secret landing on the opposite side of Withern from its main harbour, lookouts were on hand to spy them and to light warning beacons. The invaders had got no further than to make their ascent up the wet shale of the northern cliffs and gather themselves together atop the crags when they saw on the horizon the massed Oswinmægþ troops en route to intercept them.

The Oswald had been at sea for hours, rowing through the channels between the smaller isles in the west of Oswin waters, much of it against the prevailing wind. Having hauled their boats ashore they had then made the climb to the crags. They were in need of rest and food. But they would have the leisure for neither. Even they knew enough of battle strategy to realise that they must not be assaulted by the enemy with their backs to the cliff's edge. Forming their straggling battle-line and staunchly girded with their improved armoury, they hurried to find a piece of ground upon which to make a stand. They found a ridge some half a league south that would give them the slight advantage of higher ground.

Only a mile across the broken ground and forage grass of the heath the Oswinmægþ marched on stalwartly, their resolve to defend their homeland written in every stride and sinew. As they closed the distance it became clear that the Oswin outnumbered the Oswald nearly two-to-one. But the children of the accursed were not downhearted for they were led by the child of wonders and, inspired by their belief in the Mædencild, surely the numbers of the Oswin counted for nothing. Already they whispered their chant softly to themselves, "Scinnlæce O Wælcyrige, Scinnlæce O Wælcyrige, Scinnlæce O Wælcyrige . . . ."

Close enough now to discern the features of the opposition, the Oswinmægþ picked up the speed of their approach. Within one hundred yards they were running, within fifty they were sprinting, and the clamour of iron rattled thunderously as they ran. Massed together, they were a sprawling, multi-headed beast bristling with blades of all shapes and sizes, hurtling toward the fearless and immovable Oswaldmægþ.

The Mædencild stepped forth several paces into the rapidly disappearing gap between the two armies and raised her hands aloft. The slim figure in the shimmering cobalt blue silk dress uttered a shrill demonic shriek to summon the faeries of her hexcraft, her body arching, her arms outstretched, and half a dozen of the warriors in the front row of the Oswin, now a mere twenty-five yards from her, hurled their javelins in unison at the target in front of them. Three of the missiles went wide. One landed on the girl's foot, nailing it to the earth. The other two ripped murderously through her torso and throat, passing several inches of iron and wood right through her puny flesh. The impaled child went down under this hail of death in a splatter of blood and entrails. She lay in the mud, a pale blonde doll in a blue rag.

When a man sees his god torn down from its pedestal right in front of his eyes, when the idol is shown false, the extremity of his compulsion to be revenged against this god is exceeded only by his desire for vengeance against those responsible for revealing the falsity of his belief. All the faith he had invested in his religion is made mock of, and the one he hates and blames the most is the messenger who delivered this unsought for truth. The men of Oswald had come to this place to be avenged for generations of exclusion. For that they would have torn the men of Oswin from their souls. But now they had a fresh wound crying out for justice, and for this they would rend and cleave and rip and shred every living thing that stood in front of them. With the front rank of the Oswin just a few yards from contact, dementia released an unearthly hatred in the Oswald and with the uncaring fatalism of men already dead they stormed forward to crash against the oncoming bodies.

From that first impact, the carnage was unspeakable. In a pitched battle the two armies were evenly matched. Despite the fact that the Oswaldmægþ had acquired cutlasses, armour and more besides from their raid on Pithkin, the Oswinmægþ were still the better armed, they had the weight of far greater numbers, and they were motivated by one of the strongest of all motivations in war, that of defending their homeland. But the Oswaldmægþ were driven by the inhuman ferocity of religion and a faith betrayed. Those that had not been driven stark mad by the death of the *wælcyrie* were fanatically convinced that the Mædencild would rise again. Death could not claim the chooser of the slain. At any moment she would float back to her feet and the haunting music of her song would be heard to the destruction of the enemy. The incendiary fervour of the psychotic Oswaldmægþ offset the military advantage of the Oswin. As a result of this equality neither side gained any supremacy and they fought on and on, unable to do ought but butcher one another until there was nobody left. It was the very worst of all the many different forms of battle; a war of attrition; a fight to a standstill.

Ealdræd and Eiji fought, having no option but to fight. With events overtaking them and the Aenglian veteran fully aware of how the strategic superiority lay firmly with the Oswin, Ealdræd had hustled Eiji along the Oswald battle-line to where a naturally occurring motte, a raised mound of earth, rose up with a sizeable boulder behind it. This position was very much the best on the field and Ealdræd took possession of it for himself and the Menghis by barging his way in among the mob to take up his post directly in front of the substantial slab of rock. This had several benefits. The motte increased further the height advantage of the ridge in forcing their antagonists to fight slightly uphill, and in enabling Ealdræd to see over the head of the protagonist he was currently engaged with so as to be alert to who else was following on behind. On top of which, the boulder would prevent any wily opponent from sneaking up from the rear. He placed Eiji on his left, for he was right-handed and she was left-handed so that way their weapon arms would not get entangled. They were not quite at the far end of the Oswaldmægþ battle-line but, thankfully, they were nowhere near the centre.

It was not a meeting of national armies that might last the whole day. This was combat between family tribes; fifty of the Oswald against near a hundred of the Oswin. From the death of the Mædencild to the final crawling away of the few maimed and mutilated who yet lived took no longer than twenty minutes. Neither side engaged in anything approximating tactics, It was simple savagery, warrior against warrior, and the Oswald were insanely inspired. Heedless of their own mortality they lunged into the fray without thought of defensive strokes, willing to take a wound to give a wound and bearing up to fight on under such disabling injuries that only the divinely enthused could have borne them. The Oswin smote stoically and well but the Oswald would take a sabre thrust in the guts and then hack down the man who had delivered it before slashing wide to decapitate the man next to him, the sabre still protruding from the killer's midriff. Oswaldmægþ who had lost legs fought on in blind fury although prostrate on the ground, hewing their weapons into the foe from below. Those who'd had their bellies ripped open still swung murderously with their swords and axes even though their innards were hanging through their tunics. There were Oswald laying ferociously about them despite having had an arm cut off or their jaw torn away. They were a tempest of deranged wrath breaking upon the line of the determined Oswinmægþ, who themselves fought heroically but who fought as men not as demons.

The centre of the conflict quickly became a mountain of corpses as the two armies bore in toward the middle, concentrating the thick of the press at that point. In her bloodlust passion for the fray Eiji was moving with the press of bodies in that direction, her cutlass in her left hand and her poniard in the other, scything away lethally with the cutlass and keeping the poniard for the death stroke of any who got inside her sword. The closeness of the melee of struggling, brawling warriors meant that her disadvantage in height was largely circumvented. Men were crashing against one another, their weapon strokes entangling, some blows striking those who were already dead. As the tide of battle carried those on the flanks to crush into the lethal maelstrom of the centre ground, Eiji drifted with it, hacking and slashing.

Ealdræd roared at her to hold her ground. They must not throw away their advantageous position upon the motte. But it was impossible to hear anything above the tremendous din of battle cries and iron smiting iron and dying men screaming. The Aenglian hurriedly despatched the Oswin in front of him, a sturdy fellow in a helmet and breastplate, by driving his spearpoint up under the chin and into the brain. The helmet offered no protection to the head for an attack from below. Then the veteran went after Eiji.

Already the woman had been enveloped by the heaving, wrestling mass. He had lost sight of her. Then there she was, being driven back by a tall Oswin deploying two swords. Eiji could not defend adequately against them with her cutlass alone, the poniard being too small to parry a sword, and was giving ground to escape the deadly pair of blades. There was also a stream of blood pouring down her leg. A dying opponent, his neck half hacked through by her cutlass, had flung out an arm as he went down and Eiji had felt his bodkin stab deep into the muscle of her thigh. So now, as she retreated from the dual swordsman, her bleeding leg was already beginning to respond more slowly, almost limping.

And then a snarling Oswaldmægþ with a iron-plated bludgeon smashed into the right arm of the swordsman, crushing the bone in his upper arm, and leapt upon him, dragging him down. As the swordsman turned his remaining blade upon the Oswald, Eiji cut into his shoulder with her cutlass and then she was stabbing her poniard repeatedly into the swordsman's back even as the Oswald was hammering the bludgeon over and over into his shattered head.

Ealdræd placed his mouth up against Eiji's ear and bellowed "Eiji of the Kajhin!"

The veteran knew the peril of approaching a soldier in the midst of the charnel house of the battlefield. Overcome by aggression and fear they lash out at anything. But the formality of this address by name and the familiarity of the voice was, as he had wagered, enough for her to react without striking out unthinkingly with her gore-dripping poniard. The small oriental face looked up at him like some feral creature interrupted whilst eating its prey.

Pulling on her arm and shouting about maintaining a defensive position with their backs to the boulder, he urged her back to the motte. She followed in a slight daze, the usual disorientation that attends upon immersion in combat, as he half-dragged her along. In doing so he was paying less attention than he should have been to the tumult all around. Pain exploded in his lower back as a wiry little weasel of a fellow smote hard into his kidneys with a mace and the Aenglian had to let go of Eiji to turn and face this new assailant. The impact had knocked the spear from the Aenglian's hand but the weasel was within arm's reach, drawing his mace back for a second strike. Acting from pure reflex, Ealdræd threw an arm around the man's neck to secure the head and then plucked out an eyeball with his thumb. This distracted the screeching wretch for the two seconds it took for Ealdræd to recover his spear and disembowel the mace-man, who wore no armour.

A great bear of a fellow with a red beard wielding a Wehnbrian double-headed axe, each blade a flat razor sharp fan of iron, came at Ealdræd before he could disengage his spearhead from the little man's spine. The swing of the Oswin's axe would have taken the Aenglian's head off had it been accurate but his skill was lacking and the mercenary just managed to evade it, angling his head out of the way but feeling the blade slice through the skin of his neck just above the scale-mail shirt he was wearing. The momentum of the blow took the attacker off his balance. His weapon was badly

372

chosen. None but the Wehnbrians are masters of the double-headed axe. The Oswin manipulated it poorly. Eiji's cutlass came round in a wide circle and caught the man behind the knee. It didn't quite hack through the leg but it brought him down on his knees and Ealdræd instantly snatched his dirk from its sheath at his waist and drove the blade under the Oswin's armpit aiming for the heart, as Eiji's poniard sunk deep into the man's neck, its point emerging to split the bear right through the gullet.

Ealdræd recovered his spear and no sooner had they got the boulder behind them again than they had to confront the final charge of the Oswinmægþ. So swiftly had the mass murder been accomplished that the battle was almost over. There were relatively few left on the battlefield now who were still fighting, and only a handful where Ealdræd and Eiji took their stand. A halberdier confronted the Aenglian, his long-handled axe with its spiked end clashing with Ealdræd's spear in an intricate fencing match. The halberdier knew how to deploy his weapon and Ealdræd had to concentrate with focus to parry and deflect the leaping, dancing halberd, awaiting his chance. He knew it would come.

Two yards away Eiji, spitting Menghis war-curses, came to blows with a pallid teenage boy carrying a short sword. The petrified lad was desperately tired and little skilled, yet Eiji was feeling the effects of the wound in her thigh and was similarly untrained in the cutlass, so they smashed away crudely at each other, their blades ringing sparks at every collision of iron. The boy lunged, the woman turned it aside with her own blade and his point drove straight into the hard rock behind her. He was overextended, his head leaning forward. With a cry of elation Eiji saw the opening and thrust the point of her poniard into the enemy's throat, then she twisted it to open the gaping wound wider. As the boy choked and looked up in horror, Eiji reversed her grip upon the knife-hilt, pulled her blade free in a spray of blood, and raised her poniard high to strike again. An Oswinmægþ warrior armed with a Vespaan hatchet was close behind the dying boy and saw the target. Lashing sideways he brought the hatchet across laterally and the axe-head cut into the poniard hand, all but severing it. Eiji reeled away, not yet knowing what had happened, instinct impelling her to escape.

The hatchet-man strode purposefully forward to pursue his opponent and stepped straight into the razor-sharp point of Ealdræd's spear which struck him full in the face and gored an inches-deep crevice where his bulbous nose had been. The man dropped his axe and clutched at his face as Ealdræd skewered his blade back out again, carving off half of the chewed up features. The Oswin pitched over. The devastating damage to his torn flesh would not itself have proved fatal. It was the shock that had killed him.

The halberdier came in again from the side. Ealdræd had presumed him dead when the Aenglian's spear had shattered his pelvis and, with the man writhing on the ground, perforated his chainmail to stab him in the abdomen. But the fellow now showed his mettle by getting back up on his feet to make one last attack upon the tall mercenary. Ealdræd blocked the weak halberd strike and thrust repeatedly into the man's chest once, twice, thrice, bursting a hole through the chainmail and getting in a lethal blow.

Eiji was propped up against the boulder resisting with all her remaining strength the overwhelming need to faint. She looked down at the ghastly ruin of her hand. It was cut through just below the wrist, the thumb and fingers hanging in bloody tatters, and more blood was pumping forth with every beat of her heart. Eiji's vision blurred. Something loomed up at her from out of the mist.

A fair-haired Canbrai pirate armed with nothing but a Langelais parrying dagger, his other weapons having been lost in the melee, bore down upon Eiji. Half-blind as her senses succumbed to the pain, she swung her cutlass around and down at the indistinct shape but her drained condition made the movement very slow. He caught her cutlass on his parrying dagger, the crossbar of its hilt designed to curl out and back inwards to form an open circle which would catch an adversary's blade. With a strong twist of the wrist he wrenched the cutlass out of her grasp and then punched his fist into her skull to club her unconscious to the ground. The balefully grinning pirate was bending to pick up the cutlass with which to finish her off when the Aenglian's spear struck him between the shoulder blades from behind and cut clean through his heart.

Ealdræd kicked the pirate's body out of the way and placed his feet either side of Eiji on the ground. Standing over the fallen body of his comrade, he swung his spear around into the on-guard position. His breath hissing through his teeth, his chest heaving, he scanned the slaughter before him looking for life. There was none. The fair-haired pirate had been the last of them on this part of the field. He waited to be certain, for many of the dying were still moving, and when he was convinced he sank wearily down upon one knee to examine Eiji's hand. He knew at first glance that she had lost it.

Ealdræd himself had been wounded by a sword thrust to the side that had pierced his scale-mail and he could feel his leather gambeson sticking to his flesh with fresh blood. He had received the knock much earlier in the conflict but had thought at the time that his mail had turned the sword-point. He had been wrong. But he was in no immediate danger, it was Eiji who would soon die from loss of blood. The veteran tore a shirt from a nearby corpse and ripped the linen into strips, applying a tourniquet to the girl's lower forearm and binding the wrist very tight. It would have to serve as a temporary measure until he could cauterize the wound with fire.

He carried her in his arms across the field in search of some shelter where he could attend to her properly. He walked through the mortal remains of the two armies. Of the one hundred and fifty souls who had scorned death just half an hour earlier, all but five or six were now dead. Already the carrion crows were descending to feast. He saw a figure limping away to the south, another crawling in his trail and like to die, and two more holding each other up as they headed slowly for the trees to the east. Besides those, there was himself and Eiji. Ealdræd's oak spear and dirk had proved mortal to the foe eleven times that day. The toll from Eiji's cutlass and poniard was perhaps four or five, it was impossible to be sure in the confusion. He had soldiered like the experienced professional he was, and she had battled like the Menghis tiger she was, and both had come through alive. But not whole.

Those events were now four days past. Eiji, drunk on mead and melancholy, lay in her sick bed in the lodge cottage. She would live, but her spirit was as wounded as her body. Ealdræd went outside to see how the blacksmith's apprentice was doing at his commission. It transpired that the clever lad had done a fine job of work and kept closely to Ealdræd's specifications as to the construction of the piece of equipment he was crafting. The mercenary was so pleased that he made a mistake; he let the boy leave.

Returning inside the cottage Ealdræd carried the smithy's work before him like a gift, which is precisely what it was. He laid it on her belly for her to examine. It was a black sheath of stiff leather studded with highly polished iron plates. The sheath was tailored to fit over Eiji's forearm. At the end of the sheath was a ten inch double-sided iron blade with a small hook on either side of the flat of the blade. It was a formidable weapon and with the iron-plated stiff leather of the sheath to act as a form of shield, it gave her the means of both attack and defence in close combat. It would not guard her against a heavier weapon like a sword or an axe, but against an opponent with a knife or smaller scale weapon she would be armoured effectively.

Eiji could not attempt to put it on because the flesh of her cauterized wrist was far too raw. But she comprehended what it was and that it was hers. Ordinarily Eiji liked nothing better than the acquisition of weaponry and even in her despair she recognised and appreciated the peculiar beauty of the thing. But it was still too soon for the gift to cheer her spirits. She managed a small unconvincing smile that lasted about half a second. Yet the Aenglian thought that perchance he saw her eyes recover something of their former glitter in that vanishing moment.

Later that night three men tried to creep up to the cottage to murder the foreigners while they were sleeping, but Ealdræd was in a mood to brood and his wakefulness confounded their intentions. Not willing to engage so dangerous a soldier, the three disappeared into the night, but the mercenary knew they would be back and that from now on it would be hazardous to sleep. Doubtless the blacksmith's apprentice had been relating his tale to whatever neighbours he still had left and some of those had come calling. Ealdræd should had slit the apprentice's throat but it was too late to regret the error.

There was nothing to hold Ealdræd amongst the Canbrai Islands when he could all but smell the sweet green meadows and forests of his beloved Aenglia in the wind. The cottage he had taken up residence in was at the eastern end of Withern so that he could even see the mainland when the sun was up, just beyond the last island in this group.

Next morning Ealdræd carried Eiji down to the quays used by the local fishermen, the girl still wrapped in her bed of loose furs and sheepskin blanket. He appropriated one of the several little fishing boats abandoned by their dead owners, laying her in it carefully along with their store of food and weapons. He would row across to Aenglia. He was no sailor but the trip was not far and he would be able to see his destination all the way. It meant landing in the territory of the Pæga, but there was no other choice unless he were to attempt to navigate the dinghy around Cape Weald, which extended out into the sea until it almost touched the isles of the

Oswinmægþ and which would take a day or more to paddle around in order to reach the territory of the Glæd clan.

Eiji wasn't fit to undergo twenty four hours in an open boat, and he didn't want to take unnecessary chances on the water. No, he resolved to seek a haven in the country of his birth, the ancestral home of the Pæga clan, the land from which he had been forever exiled so long ago.

Chapter 10

The Exiled Youth

In the discreet seclusion of a copse surrounded by new growth saplings a tall man with a battered face adorned with a braided beard and similarly plaited hair which hung like thin rope to his shoulders squatted over a dead hare caught in a snare. His knife skinned the small beast expertly until, having peeled enough of the furry hide to get purchase with his fingers, he took a firm hold on the loose skin and with a single sharp pull he ripped the outer layer off the raw meat of the body in one efficient motion, turning the skin inside out; a useful piece of rustic lore engrained in him from early boyhood.

The flourishing of diverse nature in these hills and dales made the countryside around him an appetising larder of bountiful provision. Every coppice was a possible source of pigeon or wild partridge to be speared and cooked over a low fire; each bank of hillside likely to contain a colony of rabbits to be lured from their holes; every thicket might conceal a freshwater pond laced with carp or some such, flickering temptingly through the placid pool below a patient kingfisher perched on an overhanging branch, where a man might lay a net for his own supper alongside the blue and orange king of fishermen.

As the braided fellow re-set his snare and stood up, his tiny kill in his hand, he paused a moment to stretch his aching legs and lower back. The stiffness took him these days when he spent more than a few minutes on his haunches. It didn't seem so long ago that he could crouch as low as a roosting crow for hours on end, but age was sapping his vigour and whilst he was still both fast and strong it was his stamina that wasn't all that it once had been. He was over forty years of age and the many scars on his body spoke of innumerable wounds, large and small, accumulated in a lifetime of travails; wounds which had always healed but which had never healed entirely. Past hurts, like past loves, had a habit of involuntary reminiscence from time to time and this old soldier had experienced an over-generous share of both in his portion of life. It wasn't so surprising that his muscles complained when he expected them to perform like those of a man of twenty. Not that a feline stretch couldn't set him to rights again in a few luxuriant seconds, and there was no noticeable diminution in the suppleness of his body as he strolled silently back toward his concealed encampment, his dinner still bleeding in his fist.

He was in the midst of the westernmost stretch of the immense tract of forest of the Cape Weald, the peninsula of heavily wooded land in northern Aenglia that stuck out into the ocean like a hedgehog with a back full of bristles. It was a deciduous forest of seemingly limitless oak trees, still in full bloom as the summer lingered on, their sunshade of broad leaves like an awning overhead sheltering a carpet of acorns. The majestic giants were reverenced by the tribes of the Aenglia and some of the oldest of these gnarled behemoths had reared up their limbs on this spot for more than 300 years. So close was the tie that bound the community of men to the icons of their woodland home that it was said of the Aenglians that they were stout-hearted because the sturdy wood of the oak was their heart.

The only thing that seemed to outnumber the oaks were the teeming squirrels, their chestnut red bodies scrambling up, down, and around the tree-trunks and leaping with comical yet acrobatic abandon from one branch to another. The multitude of mighty broadleaf oaks were interspersed with copper beech. Set amongst the prolific oak the smooth straight trunks of the tall beech trees had been forced to grow beyond their usual height, topping 100 feet or more in order for their close knit oval leaves to reach above the canopy of the oak and find the nourishing sunlight. With the predictable unfairness of nature, this had produced a ring of bare ground at the base of each tree where the plant life had been deprived of daylight by the Beech's own enshrouding cover of leaves in the constant competition for life. But with nature's abhorrence of waste this bare ground often erupted in mole-hills as some form of life made use of whatever there was to utilize to its own advantage.

The man walked steadily through the rough undergrowth as if he were on an established trail but there was not so much as a track; his confidence derived simply from his familiarity with his environment. Ealdræd had been born and raised in the woodlands of Aenglia although until a fortnight before he had not set foot in the clan country of the Pæga, his own folk, for two decades. This hiatus notwithstanding he was as much at home here as the wren or the thrush that would occasionally dart by overhead then settle to feed on the grubs to be found amongst the windfall fruits that were rotting on the ground as late summer slipped imperceptibly toward early autumn.

He was dressed in a durable brown leather sleeveless gambeson tunic, long enough to reach his mid-thigh, cut in the Bhourgbon style with small unornamented epaulette extensions at the shoulder and worn underneath a shirt of scale-mail. His boots were strong leather to the ankle and at his belt was a scabbard containing an elegantly slender and unusually long dirk forged from a single piece of iron with riveted leather strapping for its handle. In one hand he held the skinned hare by its feet, in the other he carried a beautifully crafted oaken spear, about six feet long, the top third of which was a gleaming sheath of polished iron honed to a razor sharp point. Yet 'carried' was not an apt description. An observer, had there been one, could not have helped but gain the impression that the weapon was a part of his body; an extension of the muscular arm, a long deadly finger that grew from his fist. The spear did not move clumsily like mere baggage, its movements were sinuous and organic like a human limb under the control of a human mind. The relationship of the Aenglian fighting man with his spear was said, without humour, to be spiritual in character.

The wild bluebell and anemone quivered in the light breeze of the warm day to scent the air aromatically in the man's nostrils and he passed a beaver's lodge on a trickling stream which he knew had not been there yesterday. In the last few weeks he had learned every inch of the terrain around his camp for half a mile in all directions. A long-necked Pine Marten showed a rare sighting of its weasel face and bushy tail before snarling away up a tree and Ealdræd wondered to himself what had brought the irascible night-prowler abroad during the hours of daylight. At the approach of the Pine Marten a squirrel disappeared into its den inside a tree hollow obligingly made by some long-departed woodpecker. Ealdræd tramped along, not bothering to step quietly as he drew closer to his temporary dwelling.

Awaiting him there in a sunlit glade was a short, compact, lithely athletic woman of oriental mien. Her jet black hair was cut in a straight line at the neck. Draped over her head was a chainmail coif. She was wearing a blue and green heavy silk high-waisted doublet and chemise in the Gathkaree fashion that exposed a portion of her bosom and left her bare legs free and unencumbered. The material had once been exquisite but was now somewhat dirtied and bedraggled. She wore a cutlass on her right hip, with a poniard and bodkin on her left hip, all attached to a man's leather belt wrapped twice around her waist. On her feet were a pair of boy's boots. Eiji sat upon a dead log tugging a peculiar looking leather and iron sheath on to her right forearm. Both sheath and arm ended at the wrist for she had no right hand.

It was less than a month since they had landed on the shore of Aenglia after the battle upon the ridge. In the intervening time they had done nothing but rest. With one of them an exile and the other a Menghis foreigner, they were both intruders in the territory of the Pæga and they had wisely kept themselves carefully hidden while Eiji's arm had recovered from its terrible wound. Ealdræd had chosen this woodland vale for their encampment because it was in a part of the country not much frequented by the Pæga. This was not merely because it was so far to the west, for there were numerous fishing villages along the coastline. No, these one hundred acres were the Beaducwealm, the vale of the war dead, and a place of cultural reverence. A century past the celebrated Pæga chief Uldwald had been defeated in battle here and buried with all his fallen men in an unmarked communal grave on the site of his downfall. The Beaducwealm was not taboo but it was considered to be in rather bad taste for anyone to loiter overlong on this ground. Ealdræd wished the old chief's ghost no disrespect but it was the best place for the Menghis and himself to remain hidden whilst she healed. The plentiful wildlife in the forest ensured that they would not starve and a stream, a tributary of the River Flod, ran nearby for water. He had found a natural trench from a dried up river course that might help mask the light of his campfire, and the small plunder which he had brought away with him from the Canbrai Islands included a number of heavy furs that served admirably as a bed. Erecting a structure of interweaved branches above and around the cushions of fur, he had constructed a reasonably waterproof hut for himself and the invalid.

Physically Eiji had healed with remarkable speed. It was her soul that was heartsick. She put on a brave face for her dignity's sake, but the black shadow of her maiming cast a gloom over her that would not quickly lift. She was barely twenty years old. In the maturity of his experience, her male companion, her Effendi, did not seek to hurry her. He understood the loss; had he not been a soldier all his life? Physical and emotional loss were his stock in trade; the giving and receiving of injury. He merely bestowed himself in patience and made no complaint at her brooding.

It was the idleness that was the greatest danger for him. Ealdræd was a man accustomed to constant travel and this enforced inactivity was fretful to him. He hunted daily to keep himself occupied. Two days previously he had killed a roe deer whilst it was peacefully chewing the cud, its short antlers so incongruously warlike on the placid beast, and there was meat enough for a week left uneaten, but he went off to check his traps and snares regardless as a way of passing the time.

The young woman sitting on the log completed the tentative operation of sliding the strange arm-sheath of stiff black leather up her right forearm until it covered her flesh to the elbow. The skin of her stump had been too raw to attempt to wear it until a few days ago. Her dark eyes examined the rows of polished iron plates which studded the leather like scale-mail and the ten inch double-sided knife-blade with its two small hooks on either side that was built into the end of the sheath. It had been designed to provide her with the weapon her missing right hand could no longer hold. It was a very inventive way for her to be armoured, given her disability.

Fortunately she was left-handed so she was still able to wield her cutlass and knives in her favoured hand. It might well be that she was better provisioned for combat now than when she'd had two hands, but it did not compensate her for the maiming; nothing could. Still, the Menghis folk were not the kind to weep their lives away. Hers were a pragmatic people and what could not be cured must be endured. In a world ruled by the exercise of martial power amputation was as commonplace as childbirth.

The girl looked up at the approach of her man and for the first time since the battle on Withern her mysteriously alluring epicanthic eyes held something of the bold insolence that came naturally to her. She raised the blade that extended from her wrist and smiled defiance at misfortune. Ealdræd felt the weight of the last few weeks lift from his shoulders. His woman was becoming herself again. She had always been one to delight in the beauty of a weapon.

"Handsome," she affirmed, flourishing the sheath-blade, and Ealdræd barked a short laugh at her pun. That she could joke at her calamity strengthened his heart.

Her command of the Ehngleish language was now more than sufficient for conversation, though her accent was redolent of the infinite grasslands of the far eastern steppes rather than the meadows and pastures of the Ehngle nations. During the course of their journey together she had improved her ability in this strange vocabulary and grammar by incessant enquiry of her Effendi, seeking to make sense of his alien western culture through an understanding of the language that expressed it. He would have seemed every bit as foreign as his speech as far as any other Menghis was concerned but to Eiji he was her master and her husband and they were family because they shared what he called the *beaduferhð*, the war soul, the warlike spirit. Besides, what any other Menghis might have thought hardly mattered since there was not another of her people within three thousand miles of where she sat thoughtfully admiring her glittering, armoured arm-sheath.

"What is its name, Effendi?" she asked.

"It is called a *wæpen-scæþ*," Ealdræd replied. "One such was worn by Gaderian, of sacred memory, who in the days of our grandfathers turned the tide of the war against Aldfrith of the Wódnis by stealth and courage when he entered the picket of the enemy's raiding party at night and slit the throat of the sleeping Aldfrith before escaping on the chief's own horse. I heard that tale told many-a-time when I was a boy."

"Wæ-pen-sc-æf," repeated Eiji slowly to herself, pronouncing each syllable separately. "Wæpen-scæf." Then she looked back up at him and said: "There were men while you were hunting. They rode by on the ridge of the hill." She gestured through the trees and up toward the skyline with her good hand. "Their heads were in the clouds and they saw nothing."

Since making their camp here Ealdræd and Eiji had witnessed the local inhabitants passing by quite frequently despite the reverence due to the *Beaducwealm* and the respect owed to Uldwald and his fallen comrades. The old customs, it seemed, were not as honoured as had once been the case. Ealdræd supposed that social habits might alter somewhat in twenty years; that might explain it. But what was much more shocking to him was the fact that none of these random travellers had so much as suspected the presence of two trespassers in the wood. It seemed inconceivable to him that his own people, the Pæga, could be so poor in their forest lore and so slack in their security. In his young days the constant state of defensive readiness among the Pæga would have sniffed out two interlopers with alacrity. If this display of inattention were anything to go by, the present generation of Pæga were not all that he expected of them. Although it was fortunate for himself and his silk-clad companion that they had not been discovered, it besmirched his clan pride that his kith and kin could walk by blind and deaf to the existence of two outsiders in their midst.

This vaguely unsettling thought, and the fact that Eiji was so improved as to be wearing her *wæpen-scæp*, encouraged him in the belief that it was time to move on. When he declared his intention to leave this encampment tomorrow morning Eiji looked pleased. She had spent time enough at her rest. Her normal temperament chaffed at inaction and with the alleviation of the worst of her despondency her regular disposition was beginning to reassert itself. She was a woman of character, not a mewling babe at her mother's teat.

There was a question as to whether the two could pass unmolested if they set forth upon the public road. Ealdræd's authentic Pæga dialect was an advantage, as was his braided hair and choice of weapons. Although his clothes were not of local manufacture he might yet travel the roads of Aenglia and be acknowledged as a true-born Aenglian. The danger was the possibility of meeting someone who might recognise him from his younger days as an exile under lifelong banishment. He could not doubt that such recognition must surely come eventually but in the meantime he should be safe enough. It was the Menghis that would draw comment and gossip. But then that had been the way of it ever since the two of them had first met and ridden together into faraway Piccoli. In the Barony of Langelais, unable to disguise her oriental features, he had explained at length the need for politic discretion and she had plainly understood the need and had acted upon it, even though she was ordinarily the most indiscreet of personalities. But there was little point in trying to exercise discretion when the children gawped and squealed and pointed at the unnatural slant-eyed foreigner as they had in the Canbrai Isles. Doubtless they would do so here as well. The Aenglians would not have ever seen, been told of, or even imagined a Menghis, any more than had the Canbrai. His plunder from the isles included a cloak which had a hood and that might shade her face to some extent but they would still have to give an accounting of themselves to anyone who saw those eyes and cheekbones.

There was a road of many miles that snaked its way northward through the Cape Weald more or less parallel to the coast but six leagues inland. In this part of the country it was known as Patch Lane and was generally little travelled, although once beyond the forest it turned into Slow-acre Lane, which had been a significant thoroughfare for centuries. Ealdræd determined to follow Patch Lane north at least as far as the River Merc before deciding whether or not he might chance taking a road east.

The mercenary's purse contained five coins of silver and eight of gold, as well as the two golden rings that he had stolen from the castle of the Visconte Lasinni in Piccoli. He could also sell their furs, given an opportunity, or perhaps he might barter them in trade. What he needed was a horse or, better still, a brace of horses. He and Eiji would make slow going on the road stomping along on foot and the attendant fatigue would increase their danger. Tired fighters make for easier killing. Trudging a score of miles a day would take the edge off their vigilance. A surprise ambush would find them a moment delayed in their response, a second late in their parry, an inch short in their counter, and so their lives would be lost. Ealdræd was an Aenglian and they lived on horseback. Eiji was a Menghis and they were pony-riders before they could walk. They must have a least one animal to ride, and they must have it with all despatch. What Ealdræd would not have given to have his superb Hengustir returned to him. But that was a sad thought and best left for a time when he had a tankard of ale or a jug of wine in his hand.

Patch Lane was a highway that varied from being a furlong in width to little more than a few hands-breath wide depending upon the ubiquity and density of the trees that crowded in upon the road from either side. Ealdræd had expected it to be playing host to only very occasional traffic this far west in the Weald and he was surprised at the number of people, all of them on horseback, who passed by the pair on foot. As often as hourly they shared the road briefly with some fellow traveller. Even so they had no trouble. Eiji kept her head lowered and Ealdræd's Pægan salutation meant that they went their way without interference. But it caused Ealdræd to wonder on this increased population in the Weald. Perchance some new town had been established in the region since last he had passed this way, or it may be that there was a village nearby of which he did not know.

Yet they happened across no such civic settlement as the day wore on, and it was on a long empty stretch where Patch Lane had narrowed to a few yards in breadth and they had the road entirely to themselves that violence struck from quite another source. The forest wildlife would seldom if ever attack a mounted rider, daunted by the combination of man and horse, but a pedestrian was at greater risk.

Three wild boar, each of them the size of a large dog apart from their short legs but more than twice the weight, broke suddenly from cover and came hurtling toward the Aenglian and the Menghis. The bulky pigs, their deadly curved tusks thrust out foremost from their bristling snouts, came rushing in at the legs of their human prey. Their snarling and squealing was a sound to chill the blood and their speed was blinding. The solid 200lb of their stout ash-grey bodies made a perfect battering ram. They dashed in, savage and bull-like, and as the first one reached him Ealdræd was forced to leap high to clear the path of the oncoming brute. The second boar was closing upon him, too, and the moment his feet returned to earth to give his throw the support necessary to generate real power, he hurled the two yards of ash and iron at the centre of the beast's thick-skinned chest. The spear carved through solid meat and transfixed the animal like a skewer. He had missed the heart but the wound was certainly fatal. The squeals became even more hysterically shrill as the boar thrashed about in its death-agony. Ealdræd, confident that no further danger would come from that quarter, looked around to see what had become of Eiji.

The third of the brutes had, through the sheer force of its bulk, knocked the girl to the ground for she was 70lb lighter than the animal and the beast had the momentum of its charge behind it. As she landed with a crash upon the ground, flat on her back, it came in ferociously with its sharp upward-rearing tusks aimed at her face, vulnerably exposed even in her chainmail coif. Her cutlass was pinned under her thigh and in the half-second that it took the boar to launch itself forward to rend and gouge at her face there was no time to snatch either poniard or bodkin from her belt. But no matter, as the pig's hideous snout loomed over her for the kill she brought her right arm across like a boxer throwing a hook punch and stabbed the monster in the side of its bone-thick head with the ten-inch blade of her *wæpen-scæp*. Had she not timed it perfectly the blade would probably have broken on the animal's solid cranium but the punch was as sweet as could be and the beast, its brain sheared through, was dead pork in less than a heartbeat.

The other boar had run straight on after Ealdræd had jumped over it, and had disappeared into a dense mass of brambles and nettles. Battering rams are not built to turn and fight, they move in one direction only. Good riddance to it. Ealdræd's senses were fully alert as he scanned the trees on either side for any further threat. But all that remained of the disturbance was the sound of birds in flight.

Lying on the ground with a dead pig on top of her an exuberant Eiji looked up at her Effendi with a huge grin of pleasure all over her young face, proud and elated at her kill. This was her first happiness in a month and it did her more good than all the medicines any potion-peddler ever concocted. The new addition to her armoury, the *wæpen-scæþ*, had proven its value beyond all doubt. Though the weapon was still unfamiliar to her, in the heat of the moment her natural fighting instincts had found the tool she needed and she had deployed the *wæpen-scæþ* to strike the death-blow as if she had been using it all her life.

It took the combined efforts of both Ealdræd and Eiji to roll the weight of the dead pig off her and by the time they took to the road again they were encumbered with a considerable store of square-cut slabs of fresh meat wrapped up in pigskin; enough to keep them fed for several days journey. The remaining one and a half carcases of pork they cheerfully left behind for other carnivorous forest dwellers to devour. By dawn the bones would have been picked clean and anyone riding along this road in the morning would find his horse's hooves kicking over fresh skeletons.

*   *   *

On the late afternoon of their third day on the road Ealdræd and Eiji walked into the village of Wiht, a ramshackle collection of huts and cottages with no village wall but encircled by a defensive ditch and embankment. The ditch was two yards wide and two yards deep. The earth that had been removed had been used to create the embankment on the inside of the ditch, rising two yards high and thereby combining with the excavation to confront any attacking force with an obstacle taller than the height of a man. It was referred to as 'the yardage' and it was a barrier that none but the most exceptional horses could leap. The only passage for entry was a gap in the yardage wide enough to navigate a wagon or cart.

There were no villagers immediately outside this protective barrier so the new arrivals strolled through the entrance to be met by the sullen and distrustful gaze of several children who instantly scrambled away to warn their parents. Ealdræd went over to a rusty old bell hanging from a rope that had been nailed to the crossbar of an upright post in the ground, rather like a tiny gallows. He rang the bell forcefully to announce his and the girl's presence. The bell was a device called 'the stranger's gate'. It was the custom in the north of the Ehngle peninsula for any stranger who arrived without having been seen by the inhabitants to give formal warning with the bell in order to declare that their intent was not hostile. Those who placed value in etiquette would ring the strangers gate for formality's sake even when their coming had been witnessed.

The durable cottages were typical Aenglian dwellings; split-log, single story buildings with an angled roof of thatch and a narrow slit-window in every wall, each window covered by an exterior wooden shutter. Also characteristic was the stable annexe attached; a thatch overhang at roof height, extending seven or eight feet, supported by two simple upright beams at the far end. This offered shelter to the cottager's horse or horses and, in some cases, their cows. Eiji noticed that several off these stables had a log wall at one side but one side only. Her forehead creased in puzzlement until she realised that the wall invariably faced the not very distant sea, the direction from which the prevailing winds would come, and deduced that the more prudential owners of livestock had built windbreaks for their animals.

From one such cottage a tall man in a russet tunic and leggings emerged, carrying an ash spear with a barbed point. With his braided hair and beard, he might have been Ealdræd's brother but a decade or so younger. Eiji's curiosity was piqued by this for she was unused to seeing anyone but Ealdræd with a beard plaited in this style. Her Effendi whispered to her that this must be the head man of the village. They would parley with him. The broad-shouldered fellow strode without hesitation up to the strangers gate and, when at two spear-lengths from the unknown visitor with the strange-eyed attendant, he set the butt of his own spear on the ground at his feet, and leaned upon it casually. He had the self-possession to pause and glance wryly over the unusual travellers before he spoke.

"This be the village of Wiht," he declared. "I am Caelwun, Thegn and Holder of the Manor."

Eiji was further intrigued to find that the man's voice and bearing was a mirror reflection of her master's. She appreciated fully for the first time that her Effendi truly had come home.

"I am Ealdræd, mercenary soldier returned from wars abroad. This is my companion, a Menghis woman from far eastern lands."

Caelwun had never heard of Menghis and cared nothing about wars abroad, having troubles enough on his own soil. But since Ealdræd was obviously a man of the Pæga and he evidently vouched for the outlandish creature at his side, the Holder of the Manor made no hostile move against them, merely nodding slowly as if in acknowledgement of what had been said.

Ealdræd had not expected that someone in so remote a place would recognise him, just as he had gone unregarded on the road, and his expectation proved correct. He might have passed by Wiht without stopping for he had food aplenty but there were two things he lacked that Wiht might supply: a horse and information. He needed a mount if he was to travel in greater speed and safety, but he also wanted to learn whatever news he could about what had occurred amongst his people whilst he had been so long away. To judge from the timbers of its construction this village was apparently newly founded, so it was natural enough that he should ask why they were settling the ground this far west. In a friendly tone of jovial sympathy he observed:

"With so few inhabitants it must have been hard labour to fell the trees of the forest and clear the ground for your village. What brought you to settle in Cape Weald?"

A certain cast of suspicion crossed Caelwun's face, as if he were wondering what the stranger's motivation might be for speaking as he had. The Thegn took his weight off the spear and drew himself more erect before he answered:

"Mayhap we are more numerous than first appears. Besides, with the Glæd and the Wódnis so prolific in our old hunting grounds, where is a man to go if he wants to maintain his dignity unsullied as a son of the Pæga?"

Talk of incursions into Pæga territory by the southerly clans was a shock to Ealdræd for although he had heard rumours of such things from elsewhere in Aenglia over the years he had not on those occasions believed that it could actually be as he had heard it described. Even when such comments had led to blows between himself and the speaker he had dismissed as nonsense the stories they had related. As recently as last summer, shortly before the war

389

in Wehnbria, he had heard a whisper that all was not well in Pæga lands from a master armourer of the Wódnis from whom he had bought a spear and two javelins but, for all that he respected the man's craftsmanship, he had discounted his speech as mere gossip and idle chatter. Yet here was a Thegn of the Pæga admitting as much himself. Ealdræd pressed the man for details but the fellow now seemed reluctant to speak, as if he had said too much already. Thereafter he was so resolutely uncommunicative as to be mute in anything like unnecessary conversation. But Caelwun did manage to grunt out the few monosyllables required to sell these itinerant wayfarers a horse; a brown and white piebald mare. He had not especially wished to sell one of his horses, and seeing that the footsore travellers were in dire need of transport, Caelwun was in a strong position to haggle and would not sell for less than three pieces of silver or two of gold. It was an exorbitant price but needs must as circumstances demand, and Ealdræd agreed that if the head man would include two skins of cask beer and a round of cheese to make the travelling easier, then he would meet the price. The bargain was struck.

Caelwun showed no interest in their furs and Ealdræd judged it inopportune to pursue trade or barter with any other resident of Wiht. The hard-bargaining Thegn had hinted at no invitation to enter beyond the outer wall and the strangers gate. This meant that they were not welcome. It was hardly a surprise when Eiji was of such alien appearance. No matter. It suited Ealdræd well enough to gain a few miles on horseback before dark. The village was too small to offer much beyond a skin or two of beer and he had already arranged that. With their purchase of a horse they could get on at a livelier pace and if they were to leave at once, well then, so much the better.

*   *   *

At dusk the following day they came to a halt in the long shadows of the oaks. Ahead was a small but sprightly river the name of which Ealdræd could not remember but beyond it, he knew, was a town called Brunan in the Burgh of Bruanon. He had resolved that he would enter the town and see what befell. He needed to know if he might move freely through his native land. He would spend the night in Brunan and use his own name. When he rode on in the morning he would have a better measure of the level of risk. If the good people of Brunan did not kill him first as an exile returned without permission.

Since leaving Wiht he had made enquiry of such persons as he had passed upon the road as to the incursions into Pæga territory by other clans of the Aenglians to which the Thegn Caelwun had so cagily alluded. All were disinclined to speak and some refused to say more than a non-committal confirmation of what Ealdræd had already been told, but where they did expand upon this knowledge their news was all bad. So the old soldier desired to speak of it in greater depth with the burghers of Bruanon.

The pair on the piebald horse skirted round the river and made toward the town gate. Their approach was in full view of several townsfolk but it caused no disturbance for travellers were not so uncommon as to engender a fuss. Inside the yardage the routine with the bell called the strangers gate was repeated as before although this time merely as a formality since there was considerable bustle in the town near the gate. When they noticed Eiji there was consternation. This was no commonplace itinerant but a wanderer of abnormal peculiarity. Who was this veteran fighting man that rode with so disconcerting a female perched on the horse's haunches behind him? And who or what was she? Within a minute a sizeable gathering of the populace of both sexes and all ages had come to see the entertainment of so unfamiliar a migrant.

As he had in Wiht, Ealdræd explained himself to the Holder of the Manor as a mercenary recently returned from service in the armies of foreign kings. The senior Thegn in Brunan was Aethelfrith, a man of Ealdræd's maturity with three strapping sons. Bald as a coot and beaky as a crow, it seemed likely that Aethelfrith maintained his position as the head man partly through the wisdom of his experience and partly through the strength of his sons' spear arms. A natural and workable method of government. The 'aethel' prefix to his name meant that he was of very noble birth and this was reflected in the assurance with which he spoke:

"I shall wish to hear of thcoo waro abroad you speak of," he said, in a rather declamatory manner as if he were talking as much to the crowd of eager watchers around them as to Ealdræd and Eiji themselves. "I bid you welcome, mercenary, and your exotic servant-concubine also. You may dwell the night and tell us tales of the weird and faraway peoples that you have seen and other such freaks of nature."

Ealdræd was wont to correct those who assumed that because Eiji was so obviously a foreigner she must therefore be his slave or his domestic chattel, for although she shared his bed he preferred the term 'companion' in recognition of her status as a worthy and valiant comrade-in-arms. But on this occasion he thought discretion to be the better part of valour and let the error pass uncorrected. It was seldom a sagacious tactic to censure a Thegn in earshot of his admiring subordinates, not to mention his loyal sons, especially on so brief an acquaintance. Eiji knew quite enough of the Ehngleish language to understand talk of harlotry but she displayed no visible discontent at the description Aethelfrith had employed. Impulsive she may have been but she was no fool. If the townsfolk took against them she and her man would have no chance in battle against so many and, when she kept her dangerously volatile temper in check, she had the intelligence to discern the most sensible strategy appropriate to a situation and abide by it.

The pair were taken to Aethelfrith's hearth in company with the most important dignitaries of the town, where they were treated to a splendid meal of venison with barley-bread and strong Ehngleish ale. Ealdræd spent the hours until darkness regaling the whole company with several long and bloodthirsty stories from his adventurous past, extravagantly laced with a few outrageous lies about shape-shifting female sirens in the Gathkar Queendoms, Bhelenese mariners with gills in their necks, and giant warriors nine feet tall in the Fiefdom of Vespaan. Aethelfrith and his court enjoyed it all immensely, especially the lies. After that, the mercenary and his woman were entirely at liberty to move about the town as they pleased and they took the opportunity to barter their furs for a small canvas tent-pavilion just large enough for the two of them to stand up in and lay down in to sleep. It was not in the best of repair but it was still functional and Ealdræd was pleased to get it in exchange for the furs.

Throughout the next day the locals' bewildered inquisitiveness about Eiji had them all buzzing like bees around the tree under which the visitors had pitched their tent and the travellers did not go short of friendly offers of food and drink from the citizenry as an excuse for conversation. Knowing that it would be impossible to defer all this enthusiastic curiosity, Ealdræd determined to make use of it as a chance to discover more about the recent history of the Pæga. And so questions were traded back and forth and in-between explanations of who or what a Menghis was and where so distant a country might be located, he received news as to who the most prominent war-chiefs were these days and what events of note had taken place in recent years.

Brunan was a substantial town, with a population of perhaps two hundred all told, most of whom took the time at some point to stroll by the tent where the odd-looking strumpet was staying with the old mercenary in order to take a gander at the weirdling. Many loitered long enough to hear the talk and to join in. Despite this, there were none who recognised in the scarred visage of the returned warrior any distant echo of the boyish Ealdræd who had been exiled twenty years past. But, then, why should they? Ealdræd's home town was some distance from the Burgh of Bruanon. He had travelled to Brunan and other settlements in the west in his youth but merely as an adolescent of no importance riding in the train of his father. Although the town included a fair number of people old enough to have been alive then, the probability was that he had never met any of them before. And whilst his name was amongst those publicly proclaimed amongst the outcast at the time of the banishment of the *ealdmægþ*, it had been a long list and his had not been a prominent name. It would likely mean nothing to anyone this far west so long after the event. With growing confidence in his own security, he turned the discussion to the consequences of the political revolution which, unbeknown to the talkative townsfolk, had cast him and others like him out of the society of the Pæga.

It was the Aenglian way to refer to the dates of things in terms of where they stood in relation to an event of great significance. They might speak of something which happened four years after the 'winter of the floods'; the date of something else might be identified as being a year and a half before 'the victory at Penrith', and so forth. It was therefore perfectly normal for Ealdræd to ask about what had occurred in the years following the time of the banishment of the *ealdmægþ*, and when he did so a nightmare was revealed to him.

The story of the banishment itself was one that had lived within him every day of his adult life. It had all started when a charismatic new leader had arisen amongst the Pæga. He was Raedwald, known to many as Raedwald Mildgyð, the latter word meaning 'battles gently'. Although formerly a celebrated man of the spear he was also a public speaker of intense and persuasive rhetorical power, and it was through his skill at oratory in the medium of diplomacy that he sought to pursue his revolutionary prophecy for a cultural renaissance of the Ehngle. The scope of his vision had been breathtaking; this man had attempted nothing less than to unite the diverse clans of the Aenglians together and, moreover, to make alliances with the neighbouring Ehngle nations of the Heurtslin and the Merthyans, in order to forge a massive federation. The two latter nations had been too disordered and disruptive for there to be any reliable authority to represent them with whom to make treaty, so that part of his design had come to nothing almost immediately, and not even Raedwald had ever suggested an alliance with sorcery-shrouded Bvanwey. Instead he had concentrated his political energies upon merging the clans of the Aenglians into one kingdom; a realm of mutual clan respect and an equality of clan honour. To do so he had determined that the Pæga must lead by example and surrender their distinctive clan identity to embrace a collective understanding of themselves as Aenglians of the *Geinnian Gehwelc*, the cultural policy to 'include everyone'.

Ealdræd's father had been a fierce opponent of Raedwald and Ealdræd had followed his father both from duty and from preference. They were of the party of the *ealdmægþ*, those who wished to preserve the ancient ways of the Pæga and hold fast to their own unique ethnic identity. The son had been blessed with a close relationship with his father, Ealdian, whose wife had died as a result of her still-born fifth child and whose other three children had all died in infancy. Ealdræd, the one remaining son whom chance had favoured over his four dead siblings and who had survived to manhood, was Ealdian's pride and the validation of his life. Son and father were united in loving respect. They had been everything to each other. They had both opposed and despised this new politics of Raedwald, a man who had put away the spear and who fancied himself ready to redefine the unique character of the clans of Aenglia in order to merge them and augur a new age of glory for the wider nation. His speeches stirred up the belief that all the Ehngle nations, Wehnbria, Sæxyny and the rest, might be fused into one all-inclusive multicultural amalgamation.

That such a thing went against all the evidence of ten centuries of history meant nothing to his enthused disciples and the contagion of faith spread like a plague. The political power of Raedwald and his followers had grown by leaps and bounds until it had enabled them to force the *ealdmægþ* into a dilemma from which they could not extricate themselves; to preserve their customs and identity they must declare war upon the new order, but they could not take up arms against their own kith and kin, their brother Pæga, without destroying the very thing that they wished to preserve. In the ensuing confusion power was conceded to the revolutionaries whose first act was to banish all those who would not conform to the new society. All the supporters of the *ealdmægþ* were exiled in the year of *Acennan Geinnian Gehwelc*, the year 'to give birth to the inclusion of everyone'. Several of the ringleaders of the *ealdmægþ* had been executed, Ealdian amongst them. And so the movement to include everyone began its rule by excluding those who had to be swept aside to make room for the new regime.

Ealdræd, being still young enough to be thought a lad acting as a dutiful son rather than a full adult member of the dissenting party, was amongst those sentenced to permanent exile. Still in his teens he took to horse and rode south. In subsequent years he had met some of the other exiles, usually by chance, in various countries of the world but gradually over time he had lost touch with all of them, and it was very likely that they had all died from one cause or another.

Now, at the other end of his life, so long after the agony of that time when he had wept tears of blood, Ealdræd sat in conversation with the good burghers of Bruanon and heard what had been the consequences of all this social upheaval for the clan that the young man had so loved but had been forced to leave behind him, as it seemed, forever.

The *Geinnian Gehwelc* had not led to a peaceful co-existence of mutually respectful cultures as had been envisioned and promised. Instead it had produced constant quarrelling amongst the speakers at the *Micla Gemot*, the Great Council, and after a year or two of incessant dispute, it had fostered frequent outbreaks of internecine war. All the other clans argued only for themselves and it was the Pæga under Raedwald who made the concessions. He made concessions in Pæga territory and in Pæga pride and in Pæga dignity. He was ready to sacrifice everything for the sacred unity of the *Geinnian Gehwelc*.

The clans of southern Aenglia, the Wreocan and the Wotton, were far less politically expansionist in character than the land-hungry clans of the Glæd and the Wódnis and were in any case much further from the Pæga hearthland. But it was a different matter with the nearest neighbours. Ownership of the northern isles and fjords of the Aenglian coastline had once been honourably divided between the Pæga and the Wódnis, each having those isles

395

adjacent to their territory on the mainland. Now all the isles were in the hands of the Wódnis including the largest, *Ganot ieg*, the island of sea-birds. There had even been Wódnis encroachments from the east upon Pæga mainland territory between *Ganot ieg* and the traditional Wódnis lands.

The geographical landmarks that had formerly defended the borders of the Pæga had seemingly succumbed to the new politics. Servile allegiance to the new ideology had left the frontiers with too few men willing to defend them. The *Hege Meras*, the 'hedge lakes' that previously had formed a barrier strong enough to preserve all lands to the north of the lakes as Pæga territory, were now proving to be easily passable by the Glæd clan from the south. In the days of honour the *Hege Meras* had all but made the Pæga territory into a massive island, a broad sweep of heavily wooded terrain between the Canbrai Isles and the rest of Aenglia, for with the lakes in the south and the sea to the west and north the Pæga were almost encircled by water. Where the lateral string of lakes ended, there began the western bay known from the old tales as 'The Cut' where Yrre the ill-tempered god of the sea had sought to cleave Aenglia in twain from Cape Weald to the estuary of *Nædl éage*, the 'needle's eye', to separate the Pæga from the other clans. Old Yrre had almost succeeded but now the *Hege Meras* were not a hedge of lakes to dissuade a foe, they seemed little more than a picturesque spot to pause and bathe during the journey north.

Moreover, the distinctive pair of small peninsulas called the *Twa Tungan*, the 'two tongues' that protruded into the turbulent waters of The Cut, had long been thought of as the key in the lock of the door that opened the road into the ancient homelands of the Pæga, and consequently they had been guarded vigilantly from time immemorial. But the *Twa Tungan* now had many settlers from the south and were rapidly developing into permanent Glæd colonies. Many of the village communities of the Pæga had retreated north-west before this allegedly peaceful but determinedly persistent northward crawl by the Glæd, just as elsewhere they were falling back under a westward advance by the Wódnis.

It was often said by prominent persons amongst the *Geinnian Gehwelc* that none need worry about this encroachment because, after all, did the Pæga not also emigrate south? And it was true that some of the Pæga who had embraced the surrender of their clan identity in favour of the *Geinnian Gehwelc* had left the soil of their ancestry to live amongst the Glæd and the Wódnis, although they were not well-esteemed there. The Pæga had earned no respect from their neighbours for their unilateral sacrifice of clan fidelity. On the contrary, their cousins to the south took advantage of it but despised them for it. There was certainly no abandonment of their own clan identities by the Wódnis and the Glæd for all that these Pæga of the *Geinnian Gehwelc* had thrown away theirs.

Having been in banishment and a wanderer in the world throughout this time of indignity for his kith and kin, Ealdræd had witnessed nothing of this grotesque cowardice at first hand. Whenever he had heard whispers of these dark days for the Pæga during his journeying through other regions of Aenglia he had always shunned the very thought that such wickedness could possibly be true. He had disregarded the rumours as being nothing more than the abusive gossip of traditional clan-rivalry. It was unthinkable that this shamefully craven feebleness could ever have been committed by his beloved Pæga. Yet now that he had heard it from his clan brothers and sisters, heard it from their own lips, he had no choice but to believe it. He must accept the appalling and obscene truth about the *Geinnian Gehwelc*.

*   *   *

The following morning the travellers continued upon their way, the woman sitting close behind the braided warrior on their piebald mare, her breasts resting warmly against his back, her thighs overlapping his hips. They rode slowly, with an air of despondency. Ealdræd's gaze remained fixed upon the road ahead, but Eiji's beguilingly elusive countenance was lost in abstraction. There was a lot on her mind.

She worried about her Effendi all the way north as they left Cape Weald and the long winding of Patch Lane slowly turned into the broader, straighter highway of Slow-acre Lane. Ordinarily silence would not have bothered her for they were neither of them overly given to trivial chatter, each predisposed to the inscrutable in their different moods, but in the fifteen days that it took them to reach the River Merc he had spoken barely six dozen words. She knew that they were heading for the place of Ealdræd's birth and childhood, a major Pæga habitation called Rede and that this was three days ride east of the Merc. But aside from that they had no plan and he had become so deeply sunk in thought, brooding gloomily upon the full

397

horror of what had become of his folk that she grew increasingly concerned for him. It seemed to her that where she had lost a hand, he had lost the future of his lineage; his posterity. All that he had heard in Brunan had broken his heart. His people seemed destined for oblivion, for erasure from history. Everything that his father had feared had come true and worse. Even in exile Ealdræd had been afforded the comfort of his ethnic identity, for this he took with him wherever he ventured, just as Eiji did hers. But if the ethnicity itself should expire . . . ?

The girl pondered at length during the silent journey northward on her own beloved Kajhin tribe three thousand miles over the horizon. When she had been taken from her home by Khevnic raiders who had sold her into slavery the Golden Kingdom was already in the process of dying under the ethnic revenge of its former dominions. The Khevnics had been mere serfs to the great Imperial Khans of the Menghis Empire at its zenith, but now it was the former serfs who were the force to be reckoned with. So, too, was it with the Bera tribes of the wastelands that had once bent the knee to any Menghis on horseback but who now raided the Golden Kingdom with impunity. Were there any Menghis pony-riders left alive to keep the flame of their former greatness burning, to thunder across the grasslands and bring death to their enemies? She did not know what had become of the Kajhin. Was she the last of her kind, as her Effendi feared he was the last of his? Her eyes glistened with the tears that welled up from the infinite pool within. Not for the first time, she felt as if she had fallen out of the world. She leaned in closer to nestle her head against the broad back of the man in the saddle and held him round the waist with the hand she had left to her. Were they not two bodies with one soul?

It was when they came upon a trading post on the banks of the River Merc that an incident occurred to prove all of Eiji's melancholy conjectures justified. Like any other river the Merc served as a mercantile waterway with merchants making use of the river as a means to transport their goods. The hamlet of Wrixl had grown up at a spot where the traders commonly gathered in a clearing within the forest at the southernmost point of the large horseshoe curve in the river. As Ealdræd and Eiji approached the small settlement on their piebald mare a parcel of disparate rogues were busily engaged in haggling over prices at a row of stalls upon which numerous wares were laid out.

The closest table had an assemblage of various bows, arrows, quivers and accessories for sale. These were being perused by three Aenglians who had tiny bronze beads woven into their braids announcing their clan as the Glæd, meaning 'bright'. Their tribal ethnicity was named for their gaudy hair decorations. The Glæd had been the habitual enemies of Ealdræd's own clan for generations until the policy of *Geinnian Gehwelc* had afforded them free access to Pæga territory. On the other side of the table a Heurtslin trader, his face and neck decorated with tattoos in the manner typical of his people, was regaling the trio with the splendour of the craftsmanship of his merchandise.

Not so long ago it would have been almost as rare to find a Heurtslin this far west as it would be to find a Menghis. But over the last two decades the seagoing ships of the men from the land of lochs and mountains had plied their business along the northern fiords of Aenglia and had eventually found their way down its western coast where their shallow draft vessels had ventured inland along its many rivers. Times were not as they once had been.

At a distance of ten yards the sound of the mare's hooves caused the three men of the Glæd clan to turn their heads in the direction of the horse and when their eyes rested upon Eiji their mouths dropped open, then their faces broke into malicious smiles. They were all dressed in thick woollen doublets of simple design with breeches and drawstring slippers but beyond that they were very different physical types. One was extremely stout and of medium height, one was tall and thin, and the third fairly short but stockily strong. The tall one took a few steps away from the merchant's stall, chuckling to himself and Ealdræd reined the mare to a halt. He sat utterly immobile in the saddle and Eiji grew tense at the awareness of imminent danger, her left hand taking a grip on her cutlass.

"Well, my lads, look at this," said the tall Glæd bombastically. "I knew the Pæga favoured foreigners over their own kind but take a gander at the freakish concubine this one has in tow!"

Laughing, he ambled over toward the couple on horseback. He couldn't help but notice the smooth expanse of firm flesh revealed by the shortness of Eiji's chemise as she sat astride the mare and he raised his eyebrows in lewd approval. His fellows remained standing at the merchant's stall and he enquired over his shoulder of his comrades:

"But the barbarous baggage may be worth a tumble. Do you think he has brought her forth to sell her to a prime specimen of honourable Glæd manhood?"

The Menghis felt a vibration surge through Ealdræd's muscular frame but it was not the trembling of fear, it was an overflow of rage that erupted from the marrow of his bones. All the bitter melancholy and black fury of his days of brooding surged up from within his afflicted soul and sparked alight in passionate wrath. As the tremor swept through him his skilled fingers plucked the riveted leather hilt of the long dirk at his belt and, bringing his arm over backhanded in one continuous sensuously circular movement he released the razor-edged iron blade like a dart that flew unerringly to bite deep into the throat of the loud-mouthed Glæd while he was still mid-chuckle. The man was knocked backwards by the impact and fell struggling to the ground, clutching at his windpipe as he began drowning in his own blood.

Eiji would expect her man to kill anyone who so deliberately insulted him and would not have respected him had he done anything less, yet she could tell that this Glæd who had so impetuously volunteered himself for death would have died just the same had he remained mute. Ealdræd had been burning with the urge to kill for the last fortnight and no better object for his desire could have been found than a Glæd or three. He had executed the fool with the grim finality of the headsman's axe. But one death could not sate his appetite. No more could a thousand.

A subdued hush struck the congregation of traders and customers in the tiny hamlet of Wrixl as all attention was suddenly fixed upon the gore-drenched man wriggling and choking his life out upon the soft wet earth. For a long moment nobody else moved as Ealdræd slid down from the horse followed by Eiji. Not a flicker of emotion had passed over the mercenary's stone face as he had butchered his man. Nor had he uttered a word. The veteran in the sleeveless gambeson and scale-mail shirt drew from his saddle-sheath a beautifully crafted oaken spear, its polished iron head sharpened to an immaculate point that gleamed in the pale sunlight. Eiji slid her cutlass from its scabbard and held it out in front of her, eloquently menacing alongside the blade of her *wæpen-scæþ*.

The stallholders and their patrons seemed to shrink back physically at this unexpected turn of events. Some of them were already beating a hasty retreat for the cover of the nearby trees. This was no business of theirs. They wanted no part of it. But the two men of the Glæd who had just witnessed the demise of their friend could hardly do likewise. They were not, after all, cowards. Their only choice was to fight. Being Aenglians, each carried a six-foot spear and knew how to use it. Grasping their weapons with a resolve born of the absolute certainties of their culture, they strode forward to meet their enemies, then broke into a roaring charge.

The stocky Glæd bore in fast at Ealdræd but the latter turned the fellow's thrust with an artful twist of his own spear and jabbed the point into his opponent's left shoulder. He could easily have made the blow a fatal one to the heart but the man's death was insufficient to satisfy the cold frenzy of the Pæga's revenge. He intended to cut his enemy to pieces. The two men spun apart, the shorter man spraying blood from the deep gash in his body, to confront each other at spear-length. The Glæd launched himself forward again and felt pain tear into his belly.

The stout man rushed at Eiji more ponderously for he was fat and lacked the mobility of his friend. Believing his small adversary no match for him the stout man sought to despatch her with a single powerful thrust of his spear. The Menghis crouched in a defensive posture then slashed his spearhead aside with a swipe of her cutlass. The ten-inch knife blade of her *wæpen-scæþ* sliced the air just an inch from his chubby face as he reeled sideways to evade its lethal threat. Moving at twice his speed she was on him in a second. Recovering his balance he parried her cutlass strikes as best he could, realising now what a predicament he was in. Adopting a protective stance he rooted himself to the ground and employed all the subtleties of his knowledge of the spear to deftly smother her assault in a flurry of abrupt deflections. Eiji's attack, though far less expert, was overwhelming in its ferocity. She snarled and hissed aloud with every swipe and thrust of her cutlass, such was her fighting blood, although she herself was entirely unaware of the noise she was making. This vocalisation of her warrior spirit was as natural as her implacable intent to cleave him asunder.

Ealdræd's evasion of a desperate stab at his groin allowed him the fraction of a second required to pierce his opponent's upper arm, ripping a gruesome trench into the meat of the muscle. After four clashes of arms the stocky Glæd knew how badly outmatched he was. Despite the grey in the Pæga's beard there seemed to be no way to get passed the old man's guard, whilst the Glæd could find no defence against the veteran's brutal counter strikes. Bleeding copiously from penetrating cuts in the shoulder, belly, thigh and arm, the shorter man had acquired a disabling wound each time they had come to blows. This last injury robbed him of the ability to wield his own weapon with efficiency. Confronted with the inevitability of his own death the Glæd recklessly hurled his spear at the Pæga and immediately threw himself bodily at the man, hands outstretched to grapple. The unexpected attack of the thrown spear very nearly succeeded, glancing off Ealdræd's mail shirt as he rapidly sidestepped in surprise. The stocky fellow's body lurched passed, unable to stop, and before he could turn the Pæga's spearhead buried itself six inches into his back, severing the spine and felling the man. The mercenary tore his spear free as the Glæd dropped dead on his face.

Eiji's cutlass was everywhere and her stout adversary began to wilt under the pressure of the sheer relentlessness with which she assailed his defences. The slightest hesitation on his part brought the iron edge of one of her two blades within a hair's breadth of his heavily sweating skin. He attempted to keep her at a distance with a technique by which, in one motion, he would parry and then revolve the spear in his hands to jab the butt of the weapon at her stomach. But Eiji ignored this and even took a thump in the gut in order to get in closer to her opponent. She lashed out savagely and the cutlass cut the spear clean in half, leaving him with a yard-long shaft of wood which he flailed wildly. With a scything sweep of her sword she connected with the hand that held the shaft and sliced through his fingers, sending the remainder of his weapon flying. In a panic he stuck out his other hand to fend her off and the knife of her *wæpen-scæþ* pierced right through the palm. Staggered he collapsed to one knee and even before he saw it coming her cutlass descended like a guillotine to embed itself in the top of his head. Life had already left him as his obese body crumpled at her feet, both her blades stuck fast inside his flesh.

Ealdræd stood glaring about him as if to challenge anyone else who might be willing to try their luck. There were no takers. Aside from himself and his Menghis companion the hamlet of Wrixl was suddenly deserted, all parties having made themselves scarce when the bloodletting had started. Eiji was hauling on her cutlass in the effort to wrench it loose from her enemy's skull. She finally had to put a foot against his shoulder to get enough purchase to pull her weapon free. Panting from the exertion of the combat she sheathed her sword and, rubbing her stomach where she taken a solid thump from the spear butt, she rejoined her Effendi.

Before moving on Ealdræd decided to purchase a longbow and two quivers of arrows from the Heurtslin trader, for their quality was excellent, but the merchant was nowhere to be found. The moneygrubbers, it seemed, valued their hides more than their stock. Ealdræd damned the poltroon, then took the longbow and three quivers without payment as a trophy of war. It would make his hunting of game much easier during the remainder of the journey.

Despite the glory of their victory, which had cheered Eiji considerably, it did not alleviate the pitch dark mood into which Ealdræd had sunk. As they headed east toward Rede his disposition returned to its former pessimism and he was as morose as ever. But whatever his distraction and depression, it did not affect his navigation. Three days ride from the River Merc the piebald mare carrying Ealdræd and Eiji clip-clopped steadily into Rede, which had once been the home of Ealdræd's boyhood. It was a major town by Aenglian standards, a community of over five hundred souls, and so too big for a strangers gate. The yardage encircled the entire municipality but appeared to be in poor repair.

They erected their tent-pavilion on the outskirts of the community without seeking the permission of the Thegns or any municipal leaders. The new arrivals would be approached and asked to account for themselves soon enough. The senior man in Rede was the Thegn Caedwalla, as had been his father before him, but he ruled as the chief of a council of elders, not as head man. It had long been this way in the larger towns for there could be no single person with the power to exercise political control over five hundred unruly Aenglians. Or, at least, that was how it used to be.

Whatever the situation now, Ealdræd seemed not to care. He took no precautions. He used his own name openly with everyone as if there were no reason for judicious concealment. His explanations of Eiji's presence in Aenglia were brusque and pre-emptory. Eiji could feel the rage smouldering inside him, though what it betokened she could not conceive. She had not seen him like this before. For the first time since they had met on the far away Tundra of the Torvig Steppes she found herself acting as diplomatic understudy for her surly and truculent Effendi, playing the role of mediator and conciliator with those people who took an interest in the strange couple. She attracted unremitting attention as usual and tried hard to keep her patience as she answered the same questions repeatedly, over and over again in her imperfect but comprehensible Ehngleish.

Ealdræd met no single person whom he had known when he was young. There were some folk present of his age who had been living in Rede back then; Gwendl the seamstress, Bhede the cooper, and Hild the brewer were all of an age to be contemporaries of Ealdræd but none of them remembered him at all, nor he them. They confessed themselves to have known of more than one man by the name of Ealdræd but they could summon no recollection to match the grizzled veteran who stood before them. He went so far as to speak to them of the expulsion of the *ealdmægþ*, the followers of the old ways, but although they did have some memory of those tumultuous events, all they could tell him was that the revolutionary Raedwald had died not eighteen months after the eviction. Stabbed in his sleep by an unidentified assassin. None the less the work he had started continued, carried forward by hundreds who had taken hold of his vision.

Ealdræd began to make direct enquiries about old acquaintances but no one seemed to know the names. When he did find someone who had known the people of whom he spoke he was invariably told that they had died years ago; the names he mentioned were a litany of the dead. So he found, with a certain grim irony, that he was accepted back into the Pæga peacefully and without the least trouble from anyone because there were none who remembered the violent passions and aggressive belligerence of the political rivalries and internal clan hostilities which had brought about his exile in the first place. The issue on which his life had turned, the conflict which had occupied his thoughts for almost a quarter of a century, was to the citizenry of Rede nothing but an inconsequential piece of unregarded history. It made him wonder how much sooner he might have returned. He had assumed that the cause of his banishment would be as fresh in everyone else's mind as it had always remained fresh in his, but that had proven to be foolishness. Whilst to the freebooting mercenary his fall from grace and his casting out was an ache that burned as painfully as if it had happened only yesterday, to the rest of his clan all these things were dead and gone; the irrelevant undertakings of the previous generation.

And so the veteran soldier and the Menghis took up their residence in Rede. They kept to themselves. In Eiji's case it was the only way to avoid her cutting someone's throat when she was asked what was wrong with her eyes for the fifteenth time in a day! It seemed to her that she had told about three hundred people the answer to that question and surely those three hundred could tell everybody else!?

In Ealdræd's case he could not shake his disappointment and embarrassment at the deplorable lack of disciplined and bellicose martial spirit amongst his people; their humble docility and their unassuming meekness. They were not his people any more. No wonder a man of resolute character like Caelwun had removed himself to the Cape Weald and founded the village of Wiht. This was why Caelwun had spoken of a man having to move west to maintain his dignity unsullied as a son of the Pæga. It may be that Ealdræd should do the same. He spent hours thinking gloomily upon the betrayal of the Pæga. This new society of the *Geinnian Gehwelc* had in the years of Ealdræd's absence robbed his people of their sense of their own worth. Consequently the prestige and abilities of his clan had greatly diminished. The Pæga were now much weaker than once they were. Why, there were men here who handled a spear no better than a Geulten.

The enfeebled and degraded condition of the present day Pæga was the surest evidence of the wisdom of his father's allegiance to the *ealdmægþ*. Moreover, Ealdræd's deep experience of the world had reinforced his father's insight in clinging steadfastly to the old ethnicity. The son's journeys through many and diverse lands had demonstrated to him time and time again that people need to be embedded in their own culture and not obliged against their will to be accommodating of customs alien to themselves. That was the mistake made by Raedwald and all those who had followed him. They sought to take away one tribal loyalty to make room for another. But tribal loyalties cannot be discarded without complete social disorder. Let the Pæga be the Pæga, and then they can be Aenglians and Ehngleish too. But deprive them of their Pæga identity, and the rest must fail in their turn because the eradication of their own heredity will undermine all. People must understand their own place on the earth and that is defined in contrast to those who do not belong there. Raedwald's vision was all on the future and not in the least upon the past. He would not understand that if folk are required to abandon their old sense of who they are to become something new, they end up with no real sense of themselves at all. They do not know who they are.

One afternoon a group of a dozen or so of the young men and adolescents came to the tent of Ealdræd and Eiji to ask him to speak to them of the wider world that was such an unknown quantity to them. He had seen so much and they had seen nothing. No one they knew had travelled further afield than the Aenglian border with Merthya. Would he not regale them with tales of his travels? Several of the lads were highly vocal in their requests but others hung back on the edge of the crowd, keenly interested but bashful. Amongst the shy ones was a lean juvenile called Wacian, meaning 'the watchful', a quiet sombre lad of seventeen years. He never took his eyes off the two inscrutable wanderers who had so ruffled the habitual passivity of their provincial town.

For the first time in a long while Eiji saw animation return to the weather-beaten countenance of her Effendi. She could almost swear that she could see the expression on his face resuming the strength of will that was its normal aspect but which had been so sadly absent these past weeks. Ealdræd gazed for some moments at the boys and then smiled. It was a smile without reservation, full and honest. The lads took this as acquiescence and a ripple of excitement went through them.

The mercenary strode over to his camp fire and sat down comfortably. They scurried hastily to find places for themselves around the fire and Eiji joined them, carrying a jug of mead which she cradled in her arms as she curled up in Ealdræd's lap. Her sexual allure was not lost upon the boys, nor was it diminished by the oddity of her oriental features and the knife she had in place of a right hand. These simply made her more exotically intriguing. The provocative prominence of her breasts, the youthful jut of her backside, the slender athleticism of her legs, and the affectionate yet respectful deference with which she treated her Effendi stimulated several prompt erections amongst the company. Whilst the old man had their ears it was the seductive girl who held their eyes. Ealdræd waited for everyone to settle before he began.

"As you men should know, to the south of Aenglia, below the clan hearthlands of the Wreocan and the Wotton, is a broad strip of land commonly called the *Flitan Epel*, the disputed territory. For longer than the age of a grandfather's grandfather's grandfather this ground has been a part of Merthya. But these fifty years or so the Sæxyns have also claimed it as an extension of Sæxyny because in some areas its migrant population has assumed a Sæxyn majority. At the time of my tale, the Sæxyns had been establishing permanent colonies along the coast, including a deep water port, until the coastal region became known as 'the enclosure'. It was entirely

406

Sæxyn dominated because the Merthyans had fled the vicinity except for a few stray war bands fighting a rearguard action.

The Sæxyn presence there was considered a violation and a dishonour by the Merthyans, of course, as who wouldn't think it so when folk with foreign ways take up residence without permission or consent in places where your ancestors lay buried and where your duty to your posterity is undeniable. The Sæxyns said that they were bringing greater prosperity to the area because the port would bring in trade from abroad, but what was that to the men and women of Merthya whose sires and grandsires had held that land from time immemorial?"

Quizzical frowns flitted across the faces of the boys around the camp fire. This was strange talk to the ears of those raised under the *Geinnian Gehwelc*. Allegiance to the soil of one's fathers was not what the youth of Rede were accustomed to hearing advocated. Their elders routinely spoke of mutual conciliation amongst differing peoples but this veteran of foreign wars, who had come into their lives bearing proof of his experience of the world in the form of the Menghis woman, clearly understood things from quite another point of view. Yet something in them responded to it strongly. The name Ealdræd meant 'wise counsellor', being comprised of two words, *eald,* which meant 'mature or wise', and, *ræd,* meaning 'counsel or adviser', and there was something about this greybeard that they found compelling. They were all rapt attention as he went on:

"At first the Sæxyn pioneers had been almost all young men in the original waves of immigration but by the time of which I speak they were importing wives from Sæxyny itself and in the wake of these came the inevitable children. The Merthyans, who initially had tried hard believe that the Sæxyn incursion could make no lasting alteration to a country that had stood essentially unchanged for longer than living memory could encompass, now awoke in shock and resentment to the reality of their situation. Colonisation was an established fact within the enclosure and was progressing steadily further inland with every passing day upon the calendar. With Sæxyns building their distinctive wattle cabins amongst the woods and in ever closer proximity to the widely dispersed ragtag of Merthyan communities that occupied those areas, the two nationalities met upon the road with increasing frequency. Blood was shed and hearts were hardened. The Sæxyns damned the Merthyans, claiming that there was room enough for all to live in peace if the Merthyans would but surrender some of their ground, and the Merthyans damned the Sæxyns, saying that the invader had come with a sword in his hand and conquest was no peace."

The dozen or so adolescent boys were alive with interest as Ealdræd recounted this history. Their hearts beat faster in their chests as they sat captivated and beguiled by these doings of long ago and far away. They hung upon his words. The Pæga mercenary had selected his story with care from the hundred tales he might had chosen. Every word of it was true and he told it just as it happened. But of all the little group around the fire, only Eiji understood precisely why it was *this* narrative that he thought it beneficial that they should hear.

"Well, it must be two decades past that I took pay in arms there. I was not so very much older than the eldest of you. I had little enough commitment to any Sæxyn cause or that of their enemies but I was a wild and free young lad back then with nothing to live for and nothing to lose. I had no home, you see, and so cared little for anything. I suppose my natural sympathy was toward the Merthyans whose country it was but I was of neither of their nations and would cheerfully have fought for whichever side had the silver in their purse to meet my price. The Merthyans, being farmers, had nothing but dirt. The Sæxyn settlers were similarly short of coin but their aristocratic liege lord was not and he would pay a pretty penny for severed Merthyan heads. What was a few decapitated Merthyans to me?

So I joined the mercenary company serving the noble Eorl Hengist who had sole charge of the military wing of the Sæxyn expansion, sent unofficially at the behest of old King Leof to bolster their armed forces because prior to that both sides had been made up largely of sod-breakers and seed-planters. A degree of soldierly organisation and strategy from an experienced commander in the field could make all the difference to the Sæxyn campaign. I happened to be in West Sæxyny and with such a hollow rumbling in my belly and no way to fill it that I accepted hire into the Eorl's army along with a motley of other mercenaries. We numbered a company of around ninety altogether under his Lordship's fluttering pennant, but these were split into three troops of thirty, the better to cover the country for the terrain of the *Flitan Eþel* was a combination of steep high hills and water-saturated vales little better than bogs, and the roads were not good.

In the troop in which I rode there was many a fine upstanding soldier, aye, and many a bastard rogue, too. A sundry bag of miscellaneous soldiery, as is generally the case in such circumstances where the campaign has no glory and the pay is one good feed a day and whatever you can steal. What were their names?"

The boys sat frozen in concentration, apparently willing the storyteller to conjure up the names, certain that every detail of the lives of such professional fighting men must be endlessly fascinating. In the effort of memory the veteran scratched his braided chin to raise a few ghosts. Forward came the spectres, apparitions, and wraiths of the long dead; all of them still as young as the day they had died. As they came to him Ealdræd named them for his audience. He did not disappoint, for fascinating they were indeed, each more exciting than the last.

"There was Bawdewyn, a Sæxyn deserter from Prince Godmir's army who, finding starvation and paid work a worse fate even than soldiering, had signed up in another of his country's armies, this time under the Eorl Hengist. He comes to mind right enough. It's difficult to forget a man whose nose had been eaten away by some malady of the pox so that he had nothing but a gaping hole to breath through. Good man with a throwing axe, though, as is often the way with Sæxyns, and never backward in taking his place in the line when a war-trump sounded.

There were two Aenglian brothers, Rheged and Noden, amongst our number and besides them an Ymbærnan, one of the travelling nation of the caravans who have no country of their own. I do not recall his name but it is likely that I never learned to pronounce it. The brothers were marvellous fellows, true Aenglians and sons of our own clan, the Pæga. Rheged was the older and a man deserving of the highest respect. He fought not for duty nor for pay nor for glory but because it was the one true expression of his spirit. He and his brother had taken themselves off out of Raedwald's new social order even before any were outcast for they knew that they could have no place in his society."

There was a gasp or two from amongst the lads at so disparaging a mention of their elders great hero, Raedwald, and more than one young man shifted uncomfortably. This was dangerous talk. A few of the boys glanced over their shoulders to see if they were being observed but no one wished to interrupt the tale and the momentary uneasiness passed. They fervently wanted to know more about the two Pæga brothers who had fought in the army of a Sæxyn Eorl.

"Rheged was devoted to his beadu-cræft, the true craft of skill and strength in war. For him none but the warrior was blessed with a soul; those who had never experienced the peak exaltation of battle had only the mewling lactation of mother's milk where their soul should be. Rheged found all human meaning and divine purpose in the death-struggle and pitied those who knew nothing of its frenzied rapture. Noden was cast in the same mould and lived for two things only: the spear and the begetting of babies. It was his life's goal and his fondest boast that he intended to sire one hundred sons before he died. He certainly lost no opportunity to add to his tally. Such mighty souls are larger and more splendid in spirit than the impoverished smallness of the world they inhabit, and they fight in the euphoria of self-realisation whether they stand in a regimental army of thousands or a straggling skirmish line of twenty.

There could be no starker contrast than to mention next a Cerdycite in our troop called Toland who, being a man of his people, was not to be trusted. The Cerdyc have won their reputation for treachery and duplicity through the hard labours of constant betrayal and perfidy at which they toil with great industry. This Toland was frequently at his religious prayers and, in kindly humility, he acted toward the world with the serenity of a universal benevolence, so it was as plain as day to anyone who knew his arse from his elbow that no reliance could be placed on this Cerdycite's honour. Though doubtless he had his usefulness in any matter of knavery. And you boys take heed of what I'm saying in case you should ever visit the city-state of Cerdyc yourself in your manhood.

We had an admirable female mercenary, too. Moiré her name was, now how could I have forgotten her? She favoured twin bludgeons, twenty inches of hardened teak with a spiked iron ball on the end. With a hammer in each hand she could do a deal of damage to a foe, particularly if they lacked a shield. She was a powerful woman. Her style was crude but often effective. She outweighed many of her male counterparts in muscular fortitude and, being of a sexually promiscuous persuasion, out-whored them all whenever she could get her thighs around the face of a pretty young doxy."

As Ealdræd said this there was a stirring of profound interest from the older lads in his audience and some signs of mystification among the younger boys. They would have liked to have been told more about Moiré's erotic proclivities. Eiji would also have enjoyed hearing more about this formidable lesbian in her Effendi's past, although in her case it was the woman's fighting abilities which caught her interest. A robust youngster in his late teens called Fraomar, bolder than the rest, opened his mouth to seek further enlightenment on this absorbing subject of Moiré and the doxies, but the veteran was in full flow and Fraomar missed his chance.

"I remember a Heurtslin fisherman whom we called Beþwyr, meaning wicked or depraved; an appellation not bestowed upon him at birth by a malicious parentage but won for himself by his own deeds and conferred with dishonour by his disgusted comrades and peers. He had been raised on the shores of Loch Mòr and was little better than a beast. I once saw him eat a live crab raw and the thing was still struggling for its life when half of it was already inside Beþwyr's stomach. His dining habits were always primitive at best, which perchance explains why he had the most evil-smelling farts of any man I ever met.

And there was Godric Dudley, a Wehnbrian cowherd who had turned his back upon cowshit and milk to pursue a life with the longbow. And couldn't the man shoot. The Wehnbrians are wise in their laws which make all adult men practice upon the bow for an hour a day come rain or shine. Godric was a paragon of the art of bending the bow, Buldr be praised. He was a good comrade to ride with, too, for he had a fund of stories to amaze and amuse; some of them true. We were a fine assortment of common humanity when I look back upon it now. All our troop of thirty were a mixed bag, with few of a like kind, and nothing to hold us together except the desire to avoid starvation.

Anyway, the first thing that the Eorl Hengist did to make his presence felt in the *Flitan Eþel* was to arrange a parley with a Merthyan faction under some gutless shite called Derian who was seeking a course of peaceful reconciliation between their folk and the Sæxyns by advocating their negotiated co-existence in the disputed territory as fellow Ehngle. Hengist met with Derian and his conspirators at the Henge stones of Covbury. The massive circle of stones stood atop a prominence that overlooked the sea. The imperishable Henge was the work of ancestors unremembered even in the campfire tales of the scattered communities of West Merthya but those stones could fairly be said to symbolize the very soul and certainty of the Merthyan's belief in the rights they had to the land; rights that were invested in the soil and embedded in the rock; the proof of their presence on this sod since ancient times. And it was here that Derian came to negotiate away his Merthyan heritage with the warlord of the invader.

The Eorl Hengist attended the parley with fifty of his men fully beweaponed and upon a prearranged signal Derian and his pack of infantile peacemakers were all slaughtered to a man and to a woman. And a good day's work, all things considered. But this was no more than a prelude to the real campaigning. The massacre of the peacemakers was mere expediency. The Eorl wasn't about to waste his time on half-baked dreamers. Reconciliation would require compromise on both sides and he knew full well that each side would hold fast to the honourable course of justice to their bloodlines, though it required outcomes that were the exact contrary of each other. Appeasement was an affront to the dignity of both Merthyans and Sæxyns and found love in no man's heart. I swear that if we hadn't slain Derian's poltroons then the Merthyans would have done so for shame that their own people could grovel and call it goodness. Those who followed Derian did so from a fear that if they did not lose some they must surely lose all, but they concealed their cowardice from themselves by the fraudulent charade of pretending that they acted from an upright and righteous moral rectitude. The Eorl Hengist knew sufficient of the world to see through such blatant deceit and foolery.

Not all the Merthyans were dross of that sort, however There were folk of mettle amongst them. During the summer of my service to the Eorl we sought a Merthyan war-band who had been terrorising the Sæxyn settlements along the coast, and doing so with much success, striking without warning and then disappearing back into their hills. These were the stalwart men of their nation whose swords and axes claimed ownership of all the land to the sea and exercised the right to bestow harsh penalty upon the upstarts who had usurped this acreage from their Merthyan kindred. They were men, I confess, after my own heart and I would have ridden with them proudly. This gang of daring rascals was led by the notorious Hwít, a man who had clearly got his name from the pale shine of his blond hair that was almost white, the name Hwít meaning 'glistening white'. This was unusual in a Merthyan for they are a dark people on the whole with hair as black as the curls of an Ahkrani.

We came to blows with them in the very midst of the River Coerflód, a waterway that was eighty yards wide but no deeper in its centre than a man's chest, its banks heavily draped with the weeping willow, its current indolent and slow. The valley which had been cut by this river in its more fretful younger days contained the market town of Dráfcombe, sitting either side of the river and the site of the battle was upriver from the town. How the rivulets of red must have tainted the water of Dráfcombe that mortal day when our two hordes of death-dealers met thigh-deep in the sluggish and unhurried Coerflód.

There were thirty of us and perhaps forty of them, so there was no very decisive advantage in numbers. At least, not so much that good soldiers couldn't overturn the advantage. And they had maybe a dozen archers to our half dozen, so that wasn't decisive either. We came upon one another from opposite sides of the Coerflód and our approach through the half-felled forest that the townsfolk had yet to entirely clear was cautious. Being few in number, there was no occasion for the subtleties of generalship; each band took cover behind the trees on their bank of the river and every man kept a good solid tree trunk between himself and the speculative pot-shots of the enemy archers."

The boys sitting around the fire outside Ealdræd's tent-pavilion were as motionless as statues, utterly enthralled by the thrilling enchantment of his narrative. A slight nip had entered the air as afternoon became evening and the front half of each lad was being toasted by the fire while his rear half was slowly chilled by the passing of the day. But they felt neither, nor the numbness in their arses. The charm of the tale held them in its grip for they knew what was coming next.

"But there were those amongst us who had more courage than patience. Rheged and Noden emerged all at once from cover and went screaming into the river at full charge and began wading as fast as the clinging water would permit. Their feet threw up huge plumes of spray as they battered their way forward. When I saw this I dashed out in their wake without even thinking, for we were all Pæga. But the three of us were not alone. The river was suddenly full of wildly flailing mercenaries stomping like mad things through the churned up Coerflód.

There was eighty yards to traverse with the river hampering our every step. A gift for their archers. Our Ymbærnan went down in the first volley along with three or four more of our fellows. He was running alongside me screaming his battle-cry when an arrow took him through his open mouth, ripping through the back of his throat

413

and out of his neck. Whether it proved to be a mortal wound or not I could not tell for, having committed ourselves to this foolhardy assault, we dare not pause in our onward rush. To turn in retreat would be certain death. I was armed with spear and buckler, with a knife sheathed at my belt. The buckler of course offered no protection as a shield against arrows and in the selection of the dead it had been, as so often, simply a matter of luck who survived the volley and who did not.

Their archers came forward the better to target their shafts at us and we might have been cut down badly except for the fact that our own bowmen, bless 'em, had a mercenary's good sense not to join in the charge with us but to stay on our bank of the river where they could ply their bows. Three of our six were Wehnbrians who knew their business and they concentrated their fire upon the enemy archers and spoilt their aim. Even so, the repeated flights of arrows had stripped more of our number from our ranks before we reached the far side of the river and were splashing through the shallows for our very lives. Then we were at their throats.

Rheged and Noden broke upon them with the fury of men who had just charged through a rain of arrowshot. Armed like myself in the Aenglian manner, they used their spears with devastating effect upon the foe. Farmers could not stand before Pæga warriors. The brothers ripped bloody ruin in the midst of the defiant but unskilled defenders of Merthya. The enemy were amateur soldiers, mere bog-trotters really, and they lacked the knowledge and proficiency of the trained warrior. We slaughtered their archers first, striking deep into groins and torsos with spearpoints that were too swift for the dying men to see. Then we turned upon their axe and swordsmen. My own attack upon the line of Merthyans did me no injustice for I sent many souls to Lord Wihvir in Hálsian. You see, boys, to find yourself still alive after a naked charge under fire from arrows lends a certain madness to a man that manifests itself in butchery. This is why battle is so often followed by massacre. When a soldier has lived through the fear and horror of breaching the enemy's defences he is so roused to a pitch of bloodlust that he can become crazed with killing. Those of us who crossed the Coerflód felt it that day.

Moiré, an arrow protruding from her left thigh, set about her on all sides with her twin bludgeons, scattering brains and gore in all directions, fighting like the very devil. Bawdewyn the Sæxyn drove his halberd into bellies and hacked at heads in a dementia of unquenchable wrath. Even Beþwyr, the Heurtslin fisherman, had been with us in the charge and made bloody sport of our adversaries with his long, double-edged poniard in the fleeting but fatal skirmish. The farmers were harvested like their own wheat. I saw nothing of Toland, the Cerdycite. Doubtless he ran and hid somewhere, as like as not."

His youthful audience giggled in derision at the poltroon weakness of the coward Toland. They were sure that they would not have behaved so shamefully had they been in his place. They would have been to the fore with the Pæga heroes Rheged and Noden, hacking and thrusting with their Aenglian spears and winning immortal glory. The boys could see it all glittering brightly in their minds as the veteran continued:

"I had momentarily disarmed myself, having got my spear trapped inside some fellow's innards and being unwilling to lose the weapon I was struggling to pull it out when a cudgeller emerged from behind a willow's drapery and got behind me. I knew nothing of this until the arrow hit him. The sound was like that of a cider barrel being split. Turning, I saw his arm raised with the deadly iron-weighted cudgel in his fist ready to cave in my skull, for I had lost my helmet in the melee, and the shaft of an arrow sticking out of his chest. He hung in the air for a moment as if not quite able to believe what had happened, then he crashed headfirst into the shallows of the river.

I shall say now what I have said many times before, Buldr bless the bones of sweet Godric Dudley, cowherd and longbowman, who saved my life that day with an arrow shot of eighty yards at a moving target that no other man who rode under Eorl Hengist's banner could have achieved if his own soul had been at stake, not just another man's life. If he be remembered by no one else this side of the frozen mists of Hálsian, he will live on in the heart of Ealdræd of the Pæga, who in a lifetime of military encounters never once came closer to death than when Godric Dudley proved his infinite worth with the longbow. I have lived many and many a day since then that I would never have seen but for Godric Dudley."

Eiji shifted slightly in his lap and drowsily murmured something in Menghali that Ealdræd supposed must be a blessing on Master Dudley. As far as Ealdræd was concerned Godric could have the blessings of all the gods in heaven in every tongue of the world. When the boys heard the softly husky intonation of the Menghali language the hair stood up on the napes of their necks.

"That Merthyan cudgeller was the last of them," said Ealdræd. "The victory was ours, and in the eerie quiet that always trails after a battle we survivors sat on the river bank and recovered our breath, happy to have our breath. On rolled the leisurely Coerflód floating the corpses away from our killing ground, on to the west until it connected with the Fléot, the estuary to the sea. We sat slumped with the fatigue of carnage, watching the lazy river current take with it the gaily spinning cadavers of many a defeated fighting man, face down in the water, whisked off to his final rest in amongst the hanging willow and the river reeds. The citizens of Dráfcombe would have to fish out the bodies or their drinking water would be spoiled. All but those who had the foresight and the providence to have dug themselves a well."

The mercenary looked down at his companion whose sleepy head was resting lightly on his chest and he added softly: "Such was my life before you were born, little one. Perchance it will be your life after I am gone."

"Aye, Effendi" replied the Menghis, "and perhaps while you still live. For, as I have seen for myself since being torn from the steppes by those bastard dogs of Khevnics, the *ghazboutyr* are many in their nations and there is too little land."

Ealdræd explained to the boys that *ghazboutyr* was the Menghali word for foreigner and meant 'those who cannot speak properly'. They chuckled at this strangely exotic word from a language of which none of them had ever heard before today. But then their laughter faded with the realisation that from Eiji's point of view they themselves were *ghazboutyr*. Disgruntled expressions appeared on a few faces as if to say, who is this foreigner to come into our homeland and call us names? And surely it is she who cannot speak properly, with that breathy guttural accent with which she mutilates the Ehngleish tongue?

Ealdræd waved away their temporary discontent, saying: "Everywhere I have ever been the local peoples have needed to set foreigners apart from themselves for without that they could not define themselves. It is natural. We understand ourselves not only by what we are but also by what we are not. Eiji will tell you, as I do, that peaceful co-existence is possible but not in the same territory. Each must have their own."

Unseen behind Ealdræd's tent-pavilion, the Thegn Caedwalla, chief of the council of elders, had been standing listening to the mercenary's yarn. It was all lies, no doubt; the type of boastful nonsense with which reprobates misled the impressionable young. But the vexed Thegn bristled to hear such a deliberate corruption of the sons of the *Geinnian Gehwelc*. He and his fellow council members should have examined this stranger more closely before permitting him to reside in Rede. He suspected the man of being one of the cast-off *ealdmægþ* who were exiled at the time of 'the great leap forward'. Caedwalla saw how right his father's generation had been to banish those who would keep the Pæga insular; an inward-looking, backward-looking parochial culture at odds with the wider world outside. Caedwalla was sorely tempted to step out from behind the tent to speak in defence of his faith and to denounce this Ealdræd as a false prophet.

And yet Caedwalla remained in his hiding place. Now was not the propitious moment. He could hardly accuse Ealdræd of insularity. Had the man not seen more of the outside world than any man in the community? Curled up at his feet at this very moment was a creature so foreign as to be inhuman. Eiji was the living confirmation of just how far Ealdræd's travels had taken him and how much he knew of far flung places that were a closed book to Caedwalla. Yet the arrival of this troublesome relic of the past might stir up discontent amongst the young with his recounting of rebellious stories which reflected the old way of the Pæga with its cult of the spear and its martial honour. As the Thegn crept away unnoticed by those seated around the fire, he promised himself that he would keep a close watch on this worrisome greybeard.

His story at an end, Ealdræd stretched out his legs to ease the stiffness from them, sighing gratefully at this relief. He had sat too long. Night had fallen. He planted his feet beneath him and rose to find his bed. Eiji's warm snuggling had stirred his loins to amorous appetite and he was of a mind to enjoy the wench in their accustomed manner.

The boys, reluctant to see him go, quickly asked him to tell them all that he had heard about the forthcoming war, far to the south in Wehnbria, against the Geulten. They had received some small word about last summer's Ehngle victory at Proctor's Wæl on the Wehnbrian border with the Duchy of Oénjil and wished most earnestly to know what had happened, whether Ealdræd had been involved in it, and what it betokened for this summer's hostilities.

417

The mercenary's assurance that he had seen the triumph at Proctor's Wæl with his own eyes from the hillside overlooking the battlefield, and a fine sight it had been to see the Geulten break and rout, had the youngsters panting for details but the old man was yawning and guiding his woman in the direction of his tent. His reasons for having been on that hillside at Proctor's Wæl were complicated and he had no desire to embark upon so convoluted a tale when his bed was calling to him.

"If you must be told," said Ealdræd over his shoulder, "then betimes I shall pass on the rumours and gossip that Eiji and I heard tell of when we were in Langelais earlier in the summer. If half of what was said there was true, then the war must have recommenced by now, for the summer is well-advanced. Aye, and it may be I'll relate another yarn or two, if you've the taste for it, about some of the many other brave souls I've met in my wanderings who stood high in Buldr's honour for their beadu-róf, their boldness and renown in warfare."

And with that he retreated into the growing darkness with his impossible slant-eyed foreign mistress and his air of impenetrable mystery, his broad back like a ship sailing through the fog of late twilight, his muscular arm wrapped comfortably around the shoulders of his Eiji.

The gaggle of boys broke up in whispers and soft swearing to find their own beds, but one silent lad sat on next to the glowing embers of the fire long after the rest had gone and thrilled to the thought of voyaging himself, just like this ancient Ealdræd, to fight abroad amongst strange creatures of magic and fancy, to ravish the women of exotic countries whose names he as yet had never heard of, and to win victories in wars whose chronicles he would relate to the envious young men of the next generation. Wacian, the watchful, sat long in the deepening darkness, the glint of the dying fire still illuminating his thin countenance, and his eyes sparkled.

THE END

Other publications by JP Tate

http://jptate.jimdo.com

Eiji of the Kajhin: Warriors of the Iron Blade, Volume 2

Continuing JP Tate's radical reinvention of the Epic Fantasy saga. No flying dragons, no elves, and no magic pixie dust.

The second volume of this allegorical tale begins twenty years after the end of the first volume and two years after the death of the veteran warrior, Ealdræd of the Pæga.

His son, Hereweorc, is one of the leaders of the Pæga resistance. Informed and inspired by the campfire tales told to him by his soldier-for-hire father, the young man is a serious threat to the ruling caste. But to Clænnis, the girl who is Hereweorc's apprentice in the study of beadu-cræft (the craft of skill and strength in war), he is a strict taskmaster and the object of her erotic desire.

At the same time the story of Ealdræd's wife, the formidable Menghis warrior woman Eiji, continues as she departs from Aenglia with three companions. Eiji has resolved to return to the distant steppes of her homeland. The many dangers of the road will make the journey more than perilous; many would consider it impossible to achieve. Eiji will have to fight her way across two continents in the quest to reach her native soil, facing hazards both natural and apparently supernatural.

As their two stories unfold, Hereweorc and his comrades in the resistance must find a way to free the Pæga clan from the political oppression they suffer, and Eiji must find a way to survive as she travels across the known world.

5509983R00248

Printed in Germany
by Amazon Distribution
GmbH, Leipzig